In the Shadow of the Judas Tree

Norman Morrow.

We must never forget.

In the Shadow of the Judas Tree.
Copyright © 2016 Norman Morrow

Author: Norman Morrow
Publisher: Norman Morrow
Cover Design: DJ Meyers

Copyright.

Norman Morrow asserts the moral right to be identified as the author of this work. This book is a work of fiction. Characters, names, places and incidents either, are products of the author's imagination, or they are used fictitiously.

This book is sold and subject to the condition that it shall not by way of trade or otherwise, be lent, resold, hired out, or otherwise circulated without the publishers prior consent in any form of binding or cover other than that in which it is published and without a similar condition including this condition being imposed on the subsequent purchaser.

All rights reserved.

ISBN: 1533248249
ISBN-13: 978-1533248244

Acknowledgements:

My grateful thanks for their help and encouragement to:

S. Sanders
C. McDonald
DJ Meyers
D. Stransky
AJ Monroe
The Inca Project
Maynooth Writers Group

To my family.

Chapter 1

1982 Castlebridge, Co. Kildare.

Stage fright consumed twenty-five year old James Brennan as he trudged down the path toward the front gate. In his line of vision, two girls, a little younger than he, stood on the lane alongside the church, partially hidden behind a parked van. Spotting his approach, one of the girls nudged her friend as she passed her a lit cigarette. They eyed him and giggled.

James strode by them, staring resolutely at the cobbles, wishing he could burrow beneath the stone to escape female scrutiny. Hunching his shoulders, he hurried into the protective shadows of the church, toward the sanctuary offered by the Sacristy door. His natural desires trailed guilt in their wake. Like a drowning man, he could only go under so many times.

Their teasing laughter still ringing in his ears, James entered the Sacristy and slammed the door shut. He tensed at the unexpected sound of muffled footsteps and muted conversations coming from inside the church and would have taken flight but for the girls outside. On the floor, a pair of muddy football boots sat beneath a picture of the sacred heart of Jesus. They'd been left on top of a pair of shorts and a rumpled jersey.

Resisting the urge to reach beneath his robes to scratch an itch, James looked up into a pair of cool, white marble eyes. The statue of Our Blessed Lady, serenity itself, gazed down on him. Itch or no itch, James had a job to do. Taking a deep breath, he approached the door leading to the main church. With head bowed and sweaty hands clasped in an attitude of prayer, he entered and promptly stumbled on the steps, to the amusement of the spotty altar boys. He scowled at them. Luke Ahern reddened, but Sean Lavelle continued grinning. All three genuflected before the altar then turned and faced the congregation.

Afraid to make eye contact with the parishioners, James focused on the large oil painting of Padre Pio hung in the centre of the back wall. After a deep breath, he opened his mouth and enunciated the ritualised words. As he spoke, everything else faded. All that remained was James, the saintly Padre in the distance ... and James' itch.

Memory directed his speech, but the itch soon became the centre of his universe. His eyes watered. Demented by the discomfort, his imagination ran amok. Padre Pio removed his outer garments, reached down his torso, and scratched. Blood gushed from the stigmata, and from his eyes, filling the canvas with a crimson river.

A child's laughter jerked James back to reality. He rubbed his eyes to regain focus. The child crawled on hands and knees, pushing a toy car up the aisle, his mass of blond curls bouncing as he moved. James expected the boy's parents would grab him at any moment and tried to ignore him. When he made it as far as the altar steps, James' expectations changed to prayers. *Ignore all such interruptions. Carry on regardless*, seasoned priests had advised. James tried. He really did. But when the little urchin ran the car up his shin, James' attempts to step backwards were blocked by the lectern.

'Vroom,' the boy said, grinning innocently up at him.

The wheels of the car rolled onwards, upward, above James' knee. He looked imploringly over the faces in the crowded church but saw only smirks from some of the congregation and disgust from others. Infants crawling around the aisle could be expected, but this lad was at least six. Unsure of what to do, he reached down and patted the curly head.

In response, the child's deep blue eyes danced with joy, and his arms wrapped around James' legs. When James was offered the little car, a chance to join in the fun, the bewildered priest glanced at the beams running the length of the church then settled his gaze on Padre Pio. The seminary hadn't prepared him for this. Nor had it ever suggested if he had visions of Padre Pio winking at him, he should wink back. Making a decision, James accepted the offered toy, dropped to his knees, and pushed the car along the carpet. 'Vroom vroom.'

The child laughed.

All heads turned toward the young woman approaching. Surrounded by the halo of light that streamed in from the window above the altar, barefoot, she appeared to float toward James. Long golden hair, falling over her shoulders, danced to the rise and fall of her breasts. Her hips swayed beneath a flimsy summer dress, her smile could light the gloomiest corner, but not the darkest heart it seemed for disdain and rebuke on many faces followed her path.

Still clutching the toy, James smiled at her, returned the car to the child and stood as she drew close. Bewitched by her heady scent, he gasped as she stood on her toes, reached up and feathered his cheek with a gentle kiss. So sensual was her touch, he struggled against the desire to meet her lips with his. A ripple of murmurs ran the length of the church. Horrified, heads shook. Muffled titters from a few men, were rewarded with an elbow to their ribs from respective wives.

The vision knelt, whispered to her child and took him by the hand. Head held high, defiant to the cold-hearted stares, she led him down the aisle to their seats. In a daze, James' wide-open eyes followed the gentle curve of her buttocks, visible under her light dress.

A cough from a kind soul returned James to the present. Padre Pio offered no advice, no solace.

'Suffer little children, and forbid them not, to come unto me … Those are the words of our Lord. Let us never forget them,' he said, gazing over the faces, watching disbelief fade and God's wisdom prevail.

As he prepared the Eucharist, her scent still clinging to him, he prayed she would not partake. James shuddered at the thought of her outstretched tongue. Within reach, yet beyond reach.

As usual, Agnes Murphy headed the queue for communion. Not for the first time, he ignored her pious stare, and looking over her head, his eyes met those of the child's mother. She winked and stood. Hand in hand with her child, they skipped down the aisle to the door. The church seemed darker after she'd left. Its cold stone walls closed in on him, on his thoughts, on his turmoil.

When Mass ended, he raced after the two altar boys as they made to escape, and cornered them in the Sacristy. Luke tried to hide behind Sean, an impossible feat as Sean barely reached Luke's shoulder.

'Luke, Sean, I'll forgive your tittering in God's house. Even a bishop could stumble. Do not do it again. Right?'

Luke nodded, 'Okay, sorry, Father.'

Sean stared at the floor, moving his weight from one scuffed shoe to the other, giving no indication he had heard a word.

'Be off home with you, Luke,' James said.

Luke glanced at Sean, removed his cassock and cotter, and scarpered.

'Sean, look at me.'

Sean broke into a grin as he lifted his head. About to lose his temper, James looked closer. The grin masked fear, a nervous reaction that could so easily be mistaken for cheekiness. When he took a step forward, the lad retreated to the corner and cowered, his arms raised and his fists clenched as though to defend himself.

'Relax, Sean. I'll not hurt you. I'll sit on that chair, and we'll talk.'

Sean returned his gaze to the floor.

'Do you play football?'

Sean nodded, ran a finger through his fair hair.

'What position?' James said.

Sean looked up, muttered and then spoke loud and clear. 'I'm a forward, the best on the team. I scored in every match this year.'

'Fair play to ya, Sean. I've got two left feet and couldn't kick snow off a rope. Is that your football gear on the floor?'

'Yes, Father.'

'Is there any need to bring it in here? It stinks up the room.'

'Father Sweeney told me to leave it there.'

'I see. I'll have a word with him.'

'Don't tell. Please, he will only get mad. Don't make things worse.'

'I'll tell ya what. In future, bring a bag for your kit and I'll not say anything to Father Sweeney. Now, off with you and don't be late for Mass tomorrow.'

Sean grabbed his football gear, raced to the door before turning. 'Thanks, Father.' In his rush to escape he dropped one of his boots.

The whole episode confused James. Why was Sean so afraid of Father Sweeney?

Today, aged twenty-five, he became a priest capable of saying Mass on his own. He should be celebrating this milestone. A single kiss had awoken desires he had striven to subdue. *May God forgive me. I'm not a priest, I'm a man.*

Chapter 2

Sleep eluded James. He had to see the child's mother again, had to find out her name. He pictured her, as the first shafts of sunlight pierced the lace curtains, running carefree through a meadow of wild flowers. Sleep came. In his dreams, he held her hand.

† † †

James pulled the duvet cover over his head. Unable to ignore the alarm clock, he dragged himself from the bed, dressed, and made his way downstairs to the dining room.

Father Michael Sweeney sat at the table, teasing out the remaining clues of a crossword. Aged fifty-nine, thin strands of grey hair, combed over the centre of his head, could not hide the baldness. Sharper than a ferret, little escaped his attention. Eyebrows raised, he peered over the rim of his glasses when James entered; the curious look left the young priest wondering if he had spoken to anyone about his first Mass.

'Good morning, Mick,' James said.

'By the look of you, you haven't slept a wink.'

'It's like an oven in my bedroom.'

'Hot, are ya?'

What did he mean? James ignored the question and strolled to the kitchen. By the time, he returned with the coffees, Mick had lit his pipe and was reading the front page of the newspaper. James placed the mugs on the table, and waved away the pungent smoke, aware it was pointless to complain.

'Have mercy on their souls,' he said, showing James the headlines. *"Ten die in London IRA bombing."*

James blessed himself. 'More innocent lives lost to the bombers. What cause is worth a single drop of blood?'

Mick banged the table with a vehemence that startled James. 'Show me one Englishman whose hands are not soaked with generations of Irish blood. You walk a free man on Irish soil, wearing the vestments of a priest, unhindered. Not all Irishmen enjoy what you take for granted. Brits out!'

'But ... we are Christians. Forgiveness is the teaching of Christ, the rock on which he built our church. We cannot condone murder.'

'Of course I can't condone it, but I understand their motivations, support their cause. I pray for their souls and their success. My grandfather ... you'd not understand. I've said enough.'

'Your grandfather?'

'Tortured, humiliated and rumours he was an informer were spread by the Black and Tans. Those murdering bastards of the Crown signed his death warrant when their gossip reached the wrong ears. Just another Catholic life lost for the glory of their fuckin' empire.'

James shook his head. How could this priest preach love and hate with the same breath, the same conviction? He had a more important paradox to consider, one he could not discuss with a living soul, except with the girl who had awoken feelings he had vowed to ignore.

'Sorry about your grandfather. Best we leave politics outside the front door.'

Flicking back hair that had slipped over his forehead, Sweeney grunted an acknowledgement. He reached back, took an envelope from the mantelpiece and slid it across the table. 'Another letter from your mother, posted three days ago.'

'She'll be wondering what I had for breakfast, and will request prayers for half of those in the cemetery near home,' James said.

'It's likely she misses her only son.'

'If she removed her nose from everyone else's business, she might. Máire Brennan would control the tides if NASA sent her to the moon in their new Space Shuttle.' James gulped back the strong coffee. Needing to escape, he decided to take a walk along the river. 'Would you like a trout for supper tomorrow?' he said.

Mick rubbed his hands together, licked his thin lips and laughed. 'Ya found a good one?'

'No! Not yet. I'll take a walk and see can I spot one through the Polaroid glasses.' James snatched the letter, stood and sidled toward the door.

'By the way, I hear there was a commotion at Mass yesterday.'

James' grip on the envelope tightened and then relaxed as he turned to answer. 'I'd swear someone put the girl up to it, a test for this new priest. God knows, I felt like running for the door after she planted a kiss on my cheek. I've never seen her in the church before yesterday, and I bet she won't come back after such disgraceful behaviour.'

'Unusual as it may seem for this village, nobody knows much about the girl or her bastard child. Such behaviour from a whore is hardly surprising.' Father Mick smirked.

James laughed. 'That explains it.' *God forgive me. She is not a whore.*

'It does. Stay clear of the likes of her. Now, be off and find my supper.'

† † †

James slipped into jeans and a tee-shirt and put on sunglasses. Remembering Sean's football boot, he fetched it from the Sacristy and tied it to the handlebars of his bike. Since the shutters were closed in Lavelle's pub, he continued past and cycled toward the river. After chaining his bicycle to a fencepost, he crossed a gate. Most walkers followed the track downstream from the bridge. Today, he preferred solitude, so he chose the more difficult trek upstream, negotiating heavy scrub, drains and ditches. Heffernan's field was an oasis, a fertile meadow long ago reclaimed from the wildness by the riverside. A lone, ancient oak tree cast deep shadows beneath its canopy and onto the water.

Arms drawn behind his head, he sat with his back against the tree and contemplated life. 'What am I thinking?' he asked the wise old oak. 'She has a child. What does it matter? I am a priest, a celibate servant of God. I cannot, must not yield to carnal, lustful thoughts.' The affirmation of his vows settled his anxiety, and he drifted off to sleep.

A football struck his leg, wrenching him from slumber.

'What the hell!'

'Sssh,' a muffled giggle came from behind the tree. Puzzled, he leapt up and edged around the trunk. Standing there, hands in the pockets of his short trousers, a lad, *her son.*

'Boo,' the child said.

'Boo,' said the sweetest voice James ever heard, and soft hands reached from behind and covered his eyes.

'Guess who?' she sang.

He felt her breath against his neck, a strange sensation, new, exciting and irresistible.

'It's the Virgin Mary, come to torture me. Have I neglected my duties?'

His hands found hers and lingered, flesh touching flesh for an intimate moment. When he turned, she reached up and removed his glasses. A daisy chain hung round her neck beneath tangled blonde hair. A white Greenpeace tee-shirt accentuated her bronzed unblemished skin.

'Cool, I'm a virgin again,' she said, as she took his hand and dragged him towards her son. 'This is my world, my son. Callum, say hello to Father Jamie.'

'Play football with me, please.' Callum ran to the ball and kicked it to James.

'Okay, Callum. On one condition, you tell me your mam's name.'

'Summer,' he said, 'I'm Maradona and you're Sócrates, Argentina against Brazil.'

James nodded. 'Summer can be the referee.'

The World Cup Final was played in Heffernan's field. Had Brazil a manager, he'd have screamed at Sócrates to keep his eyes on the bouncing ball, and off the referees' breasts. Callum shouted the names of famous players as he outwitted James. At full time the score was 7-0 to Argentina, three from disputed penalties, and the Brazil team fell to the ground exhausted. Summer lay amongst the long grass beside James while Callum wandered to the river to skim stones.

'That was so cool. Callum likes you, Jamie. ' she said. Plucking a blade of grass, she held it between the thumbs of her cupped hands and blew. James laughed loud at her attempts, plucked his own blade and joined the chorus of huffs, puffs and ear-piercing blasts.

'By the way, my name is James'

For a moment, she seemed to ponder on this. 'No. James is your priest name. With me, you are Jamie.'

'Tell me about yourself, Summer. Where do you live? Have you other children? Are you married?'

Her eyes wandered down his body to his feet and back up again. 'Do you like girls?' she said. Before he could answer, she jumped up and shouted, 'Callum, we must go. Say goodbye to Father Jamie.'

'But ...,' Callum said.

She drew a finger to her lips, 'Sssh,' turned, and taking Callum by the hand they walked back through the field.

Crestfallen, James stared after them. On reaching the top of the hill, she turned and shouted, 'We live in the cottage over here. Call tomorrow afternoon and bring beer.'

Her personality matched her name. Summer, over and over, he whispered, returning to the bridge. James sprinted alongside the bicycle, letting it freewheel downhill, and then vaulted onto the saddle. He rode like the wind, the potholes holding no fear for him.

On his way back up the main street, he noticed his two tormentors outside Lavelle's pub. One turned her back, wiggled her bum beneath her revealing skirt. Her friend shouted as he passed. 'Did ya get an eyeful, Father Sexy?'

Father Sexy spun the wheel of his bike and stopped inches from the startled girls. 'Ladies, I have an hour to spare. What have ye in mind?' Their bravery withered before his eyes.

The brunette blushed. 'Only messing, Father.'

'I'll expect ye at confessions this evening, otherwise I'll have a talk with your parents.'

Stomping on the cigarette butt, one of the girls had dropped, he laughed as they raced away. He untied the boot from the bike and strode in the front door of Lavelle's.

Seanie Lavelle leaned on the counter, counting loose change, making little neat stacks of coins. Reckoned to be a tough man by many, he ran a good clean pub and had a reputation for being fair as long as you didn't upset him. Apart from seeing him occasionally at Mass or sweeping the path outside the pub, they had not spoken.

One stack of pennies towered over the others. Seanie grunted, plucked four coins from the top of it, and tossing them into the till, bagged the rest.

'Mr. Ryan was a shite maths teacher, and I was a poor student. So you must be the new young priest, Father Brennan.'

'Father James Brennan. I'm pleased to meet you, Mr. Lavelle.' He offered his hand.

'Mr. Lavelle was my father. When we carried his coffin outside, the old tradition of formality went with him. Anytime you darken my door, leave your uniform out on the street. I'm Seanie. James, what can I get you?'

'Your son left this in the Sacristy,' James said, tossing the football boot onto the counter.

'For feck's sake.' Seanie seized the boot, a cloth, and wiped away the muck. Leaning over the side, he roared, 'Sean Lavelle, get your arse downstairs, there's a priest here to see you.'

Upstairs, a door banged.

'Will you have a drink? As it's your first visit to the finest pub in Castlebridge, it's on the house.'

James sat on a stool. 'I'll have a Coke with ice if you have any.'

Seanie faced the till and sank to his knees. 'Another bloody teetotaller sent to deny me a living. Look at the till. When it opens it brings music to my ears. When it remains closed, my heart bleeds. Did they not teach you how to drink in Maynooth?'

'I took the pledge when I was sixteen, and my mother would have killed me if I broke it.'

'So did I,' Seanie said, rising to his feet. 'My father filled me with porter, and my mother didn't talk to him for a fortnight.' After scooping ice from the bucket, he dropped several cubes into a glass, poured in a Coke and placed the glass on the counter. 'That will be forty pence.'

'I've... I've no money. You said it was on the house.'

'I did. I said you could have a drink on the house and the offer still stands. That rubbish is forty pence. I'll throw in the ice for free.' Seanie folded his arms.

James nudged the glass back across the counter and hopped off the barstool. The door offered an easy escape from this standoff. He took a step, stopped, turned and climbed back on the barstool. Staring over the rim of the glass at Seanie, he sank half the coke and burped. 'Since you begrudge the twenty pence you drop in the basket on the rare occasion you go to Mass, consider the next two Masses on the house,' James said, as he crossed his arms.

'Has Sweeney been bad-mouthing me?'

'No. Call it intuition.'

Seanie grunted, spat on the palm of his hand and stuck it across the counter. 'Mother of Jesus, at last Castlebridge has a real priest. James Brennan, you and me will be good friends. Now where the feck is Sean? Back in a minute.'

James laughed as he listened to Seanie's roaring. 'Come here. If I have to go up ...' Silence. 'Sean, Father Brennan is here to see you.'

The sound of a door opening, Sean bounded down the stairs and into the lounge.

'You forgot one of your boots. I gave it to your father,' James said.

Sean wiped his nose on the sleeve of his jumper, and caught the boot which Seanie tossed to him. 'Thanks, Father Brennan. Will you be saying Mass in the morning?'

'I will,' James said.

Sean walked to the door separating the living quarters from the bar. He looked back over his shoulder. 'Good.'

Seanie beamed, clearly proud of his young lad, 'He's saving up every penny he gets from doing altar boy at weddings. I've got a new fly-fishing rod and waders ordered for him, and as soon as he earns them, they will be his.'

James checked his watch. 'Seanie, I've got to go. I expect to see you at Mass to collect what I owe you.'

'Don't bet on it,' shouted Seanie as James left.

Chapter 3

Morning Mass passing without hiccup, James raced back to the house to divest himself of priestly garb.

Black, the colour of his shoes and most of his clothes; not at all suitable for what he hoped would be his first date with Summer. He pulled on yesterday's jeans and tee-shirt, lifted a can of deodorant and sprayed himself from head to toe. Rubbing his eyes, he emerged from the chemical shower, opened the wardrobe door and reached down for his "Jesus Sandals." *Black.* Resigned to having no other option, he collapsed onto the bed and cursed Lady Luck. She heard his pleas and guided his gaze to his suitcase on top of the wardrobe. *Cotton-eyed Joe. I'd er been married long ergo.*

He'd forgotten he owned a pair of cowboy boots, worn only once to a charity barn dance. Eager hands dragged the case off the wardrobe, tore it open and pulled out the *brown* boots. Made from distressed leather, with a golden buffalo etched on each curled up toe, he ran his finger over the silver ring holding the removable harness. He slipped on the boots and stuffed the bottom of his jeans down inside them.

Where do I get beer?

Father Sweeney had a few bottles in a press in the dining room, but removing a few would be too risky. The saloon seemed an obvious answer. Left with no other choice, he galloped outside, hopped onto the saddle of his bicycle, and made for the only familiar watering hole in town.

God knows why he expected the pub would be empty. Three men sitting at the counter turned and looked him up and down as he closed the door.

They look mean.

The oldest, a bleary-eyed codger with an enormous beer belly and matching chins, laughed. 'Lads, it's the Marshall.'

Their raucous response enticed Seanie from the backroom. 'Did I miss something funny from the brothers Kelly?'

'We were welcoming this cowboy to Castlebridge. He's looking for whiskey, a bale of hay for his horse and a girl for the night,' one of the brothers said.

Seanie grinned. 'In that case I can oblige with the whiskey. Seeing as the whole parish knows your wives are still virgins, I'd say they would jump at the chance of a roll in the hay with him.'

Fists flew across the counter, but met their match in Seanie. 'Settle down, lads. We don't want to upset the new priest. Come around the back, Father. This front bar is for the loungers and layabouts, the back for men of intellect and good manners.'

Hunched over the counter, the Kelly brothers drowned their embarrassment with porter.

'Confessions are after Mass this evening. Be there!' James ordered as he strode past them.

Seanie fiddled with the knob on a small television and twisted the coat hanger in every direction without success. 'Blast. I'll miss the racing. Do you ever have a flutter?'

'Flutter?'

Seanie gave up on the television, and returned behind the counter. 'God, you are greener than the grass on the football pitch. A flutter is a bet, a few quid on the nags.'

'Gambling is a sinful waste,' James countered.

Seanie grunted. 'It might be in the rest of the country, might be in whatever bog hole you crawled out from, but here in County Kildare it's a way of life. I'm not one to tell tales or partake in idle gossip, but I could name a dozen priests who couldn't pass a horse without placing a bet on it.'

'You're having me on.'

'You don't drink, smoke or gamble. Apart from praying and telling everyone else they are sinners, what do you do for fun?'

James thought about this for a moment. 'Fly fishing and tying flies. What do you do apart from gambling?' James said.

'Does Your Holiness mean, what do I do when I'm not taking the mickey out of young priests and running this pub?' James proffered a nod and the barman continued. 'I catch fine brown trout with professionally tied flies I purchased in a shop.'

Eager to prove to Seanie there was more to James Brennan than a collar, he seized this opening. 'I'll do a deal with you. I'm in need of two bottles of beer for a friend, and you certainly are in need of decent flies. Are you willing to trade for the finest flies your beady eyes ever saw?'

'How do I know they're any good?'

'How do I know you don't water down your beer?'

'Two dozen flies. Deal?'

'Deal!' Sealing the agreement, James wiped the spittle from his hand.

Seanie fetched two bottles of beer, two Guinness and two lagers, and placed them in front of James. 'Well, Mr. Teetotaller, which of those does your friend drink?'

'Beer is beer, isn't it?' James hadn't a clue, no more a clue than Seanie had of saying Mass.

'Is it for a he or a she?'

Ouch! The very question James feared most had been asked. Adding to the list of lies he told this week, he stammered. 'He, it's for a he.'

'I thought it would be.' Seanie smirked and leaned across the counter. 'Take the beer and if *he* prefers lager, tell *him* I said it's a girlie drink. Tell *him* to bring the two bottles back in here and I'll swap them for lager. Also, tell *him* I said, I will give *her* a drink on the house for *her* trouble.'

Knowing he'd be damned if he answered and damned if he didn't, James kept his mouth shut.

'Okay, let me make this easy for you,' Sean said, removing the two bottles of Guinness. 'Lager or Beer, which would she prefer?'

'Lager,' muttered James, unable to look at Seanie.

Seanie reached across the counter and patted James on the head. 'Look at me.'

James settled his eyes on Sean's shoulder.

'My young friend, do you think your God would lock a stallion in a stable on his own? Your dirty little secret is safe with me and will never be mentioned again. I suppose you want a bag as well?'

'We are only friends. A bag would be great.' James tried to smile.

'One thing before you leave,' Seanie said, wiping down the counter.

'What?'

'It's a bit premature to have the zip on your jeans open.'

† † †

Leaving the village behind, exhilarated by freedom and buoyed by his infatuation, James pedalled so fast the beer bottles risked being smashed against the bike. Pulling off the main road, he continued up a bumpy, pothole-riddled boreen. Occasionally, he stood on the pedals and peered over the bushes, trying to see the river and judge his position. He realised he needn't have bothered as there was no mistaking Heffernan's meadow. Its lush grass reached a gate along the roadside, and a little further, an ivy-clad cottage stood behind a jungle of unkempt greenery.

Pausing at the gate, he ran licked fingers through his tight-cropped fair hair, flattening any miscreants and calming his nerves. One cowboy boot following the other, he pushed the bike the last few yards onto the narrow path to the cottage. Callum's toy car, parked upside down at the side door, confirmed he had found the right place. *Are you sure about this? No. Yes. I don't know.*

Too late to change his mind, the door opened and Callum raced out to meet him.

'Father Jamie, Father Jamie,' he squealed.

James righted the car and pushed it along. 'Vroom. Hi, Callum.'

'Summer, Mam, Father Jamie's here.' Little hands nabbed James and dragged him inside the neglected cottage.

Summer looked so different in dungarees, more modern than the hippy who danced in the meadow in his dreams. Standing beside the single window, in front of an easel, her coy smile put him at ease.

'Jamie, you came. Cool, our first visitor. I'm putting the finishing touches to this. Grab a seat and don't peep.'

James sat on the rattan backed chair beside the open fireplace. Crunched up paper, crisp packets and other rubbish spilled over the hearth onto the threadbare rug and stone floor. Light flickered from two lavender scented candles on the wooden shelf above, casting eerie shadows. Numerous watercolours and sketches placed haphazardly on the walls, covered most of the faded wallpaper beneath. Many were of Callum, some of Heffernan's meadow and the river, others of people he did not recognise.

A single mug with the handle of a teaspoon peeping from the rim, sat on a short countertop alongside a rusty gas cooker. Above the sink, a cupboard whose door seemed to hang on a single hinge had yellowed from age and neglect. *Exactly what my place would look like if I had a choice.* So sickened by the sterile seminary and the priest's house – he yearned for the freedom offered by such a home. Callum sat at his mother's feet, glancing from the painting to James, and at times grinned. Engrossed in her work, Summer's gaze flicked between the easel and James. After an age, she stepped back, Callum nodded, and both of them smiled.

'Father Jamie, close your eyes,' Summer said.

Not knowing what to expect, he did as bid. Callum clambered over the back of his char. His small hands, smelling of crisps, reached forward and covered James' eyes. Hearing only Callum's excited breathing and something being dragged along the floor, his excitement grew.

'Jamie, you can look now,' whispered Summer.'

Callum's hands falling away from James' face, he opened his eyes. Every detail captured as though he gazed into a mirror, his deep blue eyes, square chin and crooked teeth, all painted from memory. Twice they had met, yet she had brought to life a painting that accentuated not just his image, but also his character. The slant of his shoulders beneath a white tee shirt, a certain boyish innocence and the way he clasped his hands when nervous. She'd written an inscription on the bottom corner. "Father Jamie. Summer & Callum 1982". Overcome by emotion, he stared at his boots.

Summer held a hand under his chin and gently raised his head. 'Sssh, hang it somewhere in your house. I think he likes it, Callum. Cool.' She sat cross-legged on the rug in front of James. Callum lay down beside her and placed his head on her lap. She stroked his hair.

'Summer, the painting is so beautiful. I'll treasure it forever, though I don't know where I can hang it. Between the Popes on my dining room wall would be a good place, but I expect Father Sweeney would choke if he had to look at two of me when eating his dinner. Thanks. Oh, I forgot, I brought some beer for you.'

Callum raced to the corner, returned with a bottle opener and handed it to James. Summer took the offered bottle and brought it to her lips, sipped a little and finding a gap between the rubbish in the hearth, sat the bottle there.

'Callum, it's time for your nap. Father Jamie will be gone when you wake.'

'Agh, Mam.'

'Son, please say goodbye. Show Father Jamie how brave you are.'

The boy kissed his mother and then wrapped his little arms around James. 'Goodbye, Father Jamie. Will you play football tomorrow?'

Staring at Summer, he answered. 'I can't tomorrow, but if your mother wishes it, I can come the following day.'

Callum insisted they shake hands before he disappeared into another room, leaving them alone. Summer sipped her beer, then took a rolled cigarette from behind her ear and lit it. After inhaling deeply, she offered it to James. Unlike most cigarette smoke, he found the sweetness of it enticing. Wanting to take it to please her, yet knowing he must surely splutter like the exhaust of an old car if he did, he shook his head.

'I don't smoke.'

'I don't either,' she said, giggling as she inhaled again. 'I've never talked to a priest before, never knew they could be young, handsome ... and kind. Can we be friends?'

Not knowing quite what she meant, he nodded, before blurting out the one question that had preyed on his mind. 'Where is Callum's father?'

'Don't know where he is, or even know his name. I sketched a picture of him after we made love in a tent at a music festival. Months later, I tore it up. It's strange I call it making love and weird to be telling a priest. I haven't been with another man since. It gets lonely here, only Callum and me living in this place. We moved in three months ago. You are the second person to show us any kindness.' She tossed the cigarette into the fireplace and finished her beer.

No father, no boyfriend. So easily could I slide down onto the floor beside her, to feel the warmth of her body against mine. Fearful of succumbing to desire, he stood.

'I'm only here two months and have been lonely for many years. Let's be friends, the best of friends; you, me and Callum. God knows what people will say or think. I best be off. If it's okay, I will call again in two days and play some more football.'

'Callum would like that. Must you leave so soon?'

God, I'd stay forever if I could. 'Yes. Duty does not allow me much freedom.'

Summer walked him to the door. He'd forgotten to take the portrait. She fetched it and handed it to him. 'Close your eyes,' she said.

Her hands slid around his waist, her breasts brushing his chest. He gasped as her lips touched his. Involuntarily he shook. Excited tremors, feelings only previously dreamt of, shook him. As though he had done it a thousand times before, he brought a hand to the back of her head and ruffled her silky hair. Giggling, she slid down and away from him.

'Close friends, that's so cool,' she said, opening the door and, winked as she shut the door.

Chapter 4

Torrential rain lashed across the churchyard, pelting against the stained glass windows and the slated roof. About to take their wedding vows, forty-year-old Nora Hickey and Cyril O'Hagan, eleven years younger, knelt in front of Father Sweeney. James and the altar boy, Sean Lavelle, stood to one side.

When a flash of lightning illuminated the stained glass windows, James counted under his breath. *One thousand, two thousand* ... At fifteen thousand, a thunderclap reverberated around the church, startling many of those gathered. Father Sweeney looked towards the roof and stammered, forced to repeat his lines. Knowing the lightning was three miles away, James smirked and winked at Sean whose face was paler than his surplice.

'With this ring ...' said Cyril. About to slide the gold ring on Nora's finger, several lightning bolts followed each other in quick succession. Cyril panicked. The ring fell onto the marbled floor, clattering as it rolled away and disappeared under a pew.

Nora gasped. 'Idiot.'

James nudged the altar boy. Sean rushed forward and dived under the pew. Moments later, rising like Excalibur from the lake, the ring appeared, followed by the boy, grinning as though he had saved the world from doom. Much to everyone's amusement, he handed the ring to Cyril, turned and bowed before strutting back to stand beside James. A few lads at the back of the church clapped.

Noting the cold look Father Sweeney gave Sean, James knew he would have to come to Sean's rescue after Mass ended, by explaining he had urged him to retrieve the ring.

Making the sign of the cross, Father Sweeney blessed Nora and Cyril. 'I now pronounce you husband and wife. You may kiss the bride.' He took a step away from the couple and stood beside James.

Cyril pursed his lips, kissed his wife and whispered, loud enough for both priests to hear. 'I'm the boss now. Don't you ever feckin forget it, Mrs O'Hagan.'

Cleverly concealed by makeup, the wart at the end of her nose now glowed. Her eyes widening, she pushed her tongue against the gap in her front teeth. Cyril tugged at the sleeves of his tuxedo. Even with his rugged features, few could deny he was prettier than the bride. He grasped her hand and forced her to turn and face their family and friends. Cyril smiled for the first time since the ceremony began.

Father Sweeney leaned toward James. 'Nora wanted a husband. Cyril wanted more land. He's not the half-wit everyone thinks he is.'

At the end of Mass, the priests and Sean made for the Sacristy. Before they reached it, the best man raced over and handed Sean a ten pound note. 'Double pay for finding the ring,' he said.

Inside the Sacristy, sealed from the rest of the church, Father Sweeney exploded. 'Sean, this is a church, not a theatre or a circus. How dare you act like a clown during my Mass.'

'Sorry, Father.'

Father Sweeney raised his arm and struck the lad a savage blow across the face. Sean staggered. James seized Father Sweeney's wrist when he attempted to deliver a second blow.

'Don't you dare strike Sean or any youngster. We are priests, not savages.'

Father Sweeney wrenched his arm away and hissed. 'May I remind you, Father Brennan, I am the parish priest and you are the curate? Would you like a transfer elsewhere, Dublin perhaps?'

'No need to remind me. This is the house of God. Sean did not deserve a beating. He saved the day and should be thanked, not punished for being a child. I nudged him into action. If you have an issue, it should be with me.'

Blood oozing from his bruised lips, Sean cowered in the corner and stared at the floor. 'I'm sorry, I'm sorry,' he muttered over and over.

Father Sweeney grunted. 'Okay. Don't let it happen again or you know what the consequences will be. Tell your father you tripped and fell. Off with you, and don't be late for Mass this evening.'

Sean wiped his bloodied lip, tore off his surplice and hung it up. He glanced at Father Sweeney, darted around James and raced out the door.

Shocked by the outburst he'd witnessed and with no experience in handling such situations, James avoided any direct eye contact.

'Father Brennan, I'm appalled at you interrupting Sean's deserved punishment. My role is that of a shepherd, minding all the flock and ensuring the sanctity of our Church is protected. When I act, it's the will of God. If that seems wrong to you, perhaps you need to reconsider your vows. Do you understand?'

'Yes, Father,' James said. Concealing his overwhelming desire to punch Father Sweeney, he hung up his cassock.

'Good. I suggest you get your fishing rod. Perhaps the solitude of the river will allow you to reflect on this matter.' Father Sweeney moved closer to James. When James turned to face him, Father Sweeney poked him in the chest. 'I'll put this down to your inexperience. Never make the mistake of crossing me again.'

† † †

Seething with anger, James made his way home. Whilst the welts on his hands from many years earlier had healed, pain from the invisible scars left by a vicious schoolteacher seared his thoughts. Brother Peter, his teacher, understood the power of fear, and few children had escaped his cane. All that subdued dread, hidden, and mostly forgotten, welling to the surface, and like that schoolboy, once again to the river he would go to escape its suffocating grip. Taking two steps at a time, he raced upstairs to his room, and fetched his fishing gear. The hinges of the front door felt his venom when he opened it and slammed it shut behind him.

As living proof of Darwin's theory of evolution, the Murphys carried news with a natural talent. This hereditary gift followed the female side of the clan, passed from mother to daughter since the time of the Vikings. Not that the males felt left out, for the art of drinking demanded as much single-mindedness to perfect as the accumulation of gossip. No bellyful of porter ever made it home without its owner carrying a fountain of knowledge. Providing a good dinner and a whiskey to wash it down, ensured that fountain spilled upon eager female ears. Apart from the men's reluctance to attend Mass, a certain harmony existed in the Murphy's home.

Agnes Murphy, being the blossom in her mother's gossiping eye, spent most of her time walking around the village, grabbing tittle-tattle from every nook and corner. This afternoon, she nearly lost her life as she crossed the street. But for the grace of God and an almighty swerve, James' bike would have cut her in two. Always seeking favour from the priests, such were her devotions that piety required a greater word to describe her. Today, fortune bestowed an unexpected blessing from James. Though the bike had described a wide arc, his grandfather's fishing rod did not. Imbued with a mischievous bent, like its former owner, it struck her arse a blow that reddened her from cheek to cheek.

In any other circumstance, he would have grinned. A glance over his shoulder confirmed her capable of whispering the tale of her narrow escape from death into every willing ear in the parish. More important, his rod was undamaged. No matter how fast he pedalled, the breeze tearing at his eyes could not wipe away the image of Sean cowering in the Sacristy.

A hot, clammy afternoon, further thunderstorms were likely. He made his way downstream, past the graveyard, and continued past his favoured pools. Sweating profusely in his waders, he cared not. Nor did the difficulties in finding a path through the heavy undergrowth deter him. Each step driven by a fury, over which he had little control, his agitated mind raced. Accepting he must be servile to the older priest exasperated him, denying a solution and any hope of calming. Ditch after ditch crossed, gates vaulted, he continued onwards, and stopped when he reached a stream. After kneeling down, he gazed at his reflection and cursed his own ineptitude. Not caring the river ran turbid from the earlier rain, he cupped his hands, drew water and splashed his face.

Despite his confused state, his hunter's instincts were a powerful force. Trout love any pool with an inflow, particularly in the dog days of summer. This he knew. Wading down the shallow stream, he ducked under the abundant wild thorny bushes along its course. Within fifty paces, he reached the river.

Upstream, fast water curled around rocks, darker pots strewn here and there. Below him, deeper water on his side, where the stream had cut its own path into the main river, and on the far side, more shallows. *Perfect*. More than perfect, a willow tree standing a little upstream offered some shade, under which he could rest until the river came to life in the evening. A warm, gentle breeze caressed his face. He lay back and observed the surface for any sign of a feeding trout. Even the occasional splash from small fish could not keep him awake.

Just after six, a distant thunderclap woke him from slumber. Dark clouds loomed overhead and numerous flies buzzed around. There was no need to count. The beating of the heavenly drums grew ever louder as meagre sunlight making its way through the weeping branches yielded to the angry sky. Clambering up the bank, he leaned against the trunk of the great tree, folded his arms, closed his eyes and waited, listening to the quiet, the unearthly stillness that followed each rumble of thunder.

Straight down fell the rain, with such force it seemed the gods were angry and wreaking their vengeance. As suddenly as it started, it stopped, leaving only droplets falling from tree branches, from the ferns along the riverbank and from James' drenched face. Steam rose here and there, dissipating under the vigour of the sun. A gentle breeze blew. Flies emerged from the sanctuary of bushes. Birds burst into song. James cast his eyes toward the river, sensing the change, as did all creatures. Trout stirred. James grabbed his fishing rod. An unexpected opportunity could not be refused and all thoughts of Father Sweeney and Sean were put to one side.

With two nymphs attached to his leader, he stepped into the river and cast. As though a conductor directing an orchestra, he flicked out his flies into every likely place and trout after golden trout came to hand. Some he lifted, admiring their butter-flecked flanks, their perfect fins and glistening scales. The rest he released without touching. Tired from catching so many with ease, his casts became less frequent, choosing with care where he would place the flies.

A deep area, the size of a pool table, fed by several conjoining flows caught his eye. Standing as still as a heron, he focused on it. A shadow moved beneath the surface, the barest glimpse of a feeding trout. He flicked out the fly upstream and struck when the leader paused on its drift back to him. The rod tip almost buckled in two, fought the strain of a sizeable trout's efforts to escape. After two strong runs, the trout weakened. In response, James raised the rod, drawing the fish towards his feet. Loud clapping from beyond the bushes on the far side of the river startled James. After he released the trout, he scanned the far bank. The clapping ceased, replaced by giggling and then a loud 'Sssh.'

'Summer? Callum?' He shouted.

Twigs snapped, bushes rustled, and still giggling, Callum and Summer stepped out into the open. Happy to see them, hopeful his judgement of the depth of the river was accurate, he waded across.

'C'mon, Jamie,' Summer said. 'Christ walked on water. To earn a kiss, you must too.'

Embracing as friends would, neither broke away nor clapped the other's back.

'Blasphemy,' he whispered, stooping as his lips met hers.

This time she did not slip away in jest. Stepping closer, she pressed against him, encouraging the first voyage of discovery that ignites a lover's heart. Hands that daily clasped in prayer found their own way. Each finger tingling movement following the curve of her spine, one up to tangles of sodden hair, the other lingering, pressing against the sudden softness of her buttocks, urging her ever closer. Passion overcoming fear, fear overcoming passion, he tried to pull away, distressed and ashamed.

Summer smiled. 'Sssh,' she whispered, washing away the confusion that overwhelmed him. Whatever his conscience said would be lies. No more than he could deny the Son of God, could he deny his feelings for Summer. Love or lust? — he called it love.

James stepped back and turned his attention to Callum. 'Hello, Callum. What are you doing along the river?'

Panic overcame the child. He searched for something. Racing back through the bushes, he squealed. Moments later he reappeared carrying a small bucket and showed it to James. 'Picking blackberries, Father Jamie.'

'Call me Jamie or James, only Father when you are at Mass.'

Black would be the colour of the berries had Callum waited another month or so. Swirling around in the rain-filled bucket, ruddy-green un-ripened fruit bobbed between the leaves and stalks.

Being serious was difficult when stifling a laugh, nevertheless James did his best. 'Callum, they are the finest berries I've seen this year. I expect you would like me to bring some ice-cream when your mother makes blackberry pie.'

'Yes please,' Callum said as he placed the bucket on the ground, careful not to spill the water. Giving James a quizzical stare that only a child seeking words to sort out an enormous problem could give, he kicked a stone. 'Can we have two types of ice-cream? Chocolate and banana.'

Summer lifted the bucket and handed it to Callum. 'If I'm to make pie, we need more berries than this. Go pick some, while I convince Jamie to bring plenty of ice-cream.'

Lost in the curve of her breasts, her nipples revealed through the near see through damp dress that clung to her, James imagined touching them.

'Isn't that right, Jamie O'Leerie?' she said, as she brought a forearm across her bosom.

'What, err? Yes, beer and ice cream.'

An awkward silence ensued after Callum left. Summer's cheeky grin, her hands sliding provocatively down her hips, invited James to taste the fruit of the forbidden tree. He wanted to. God knows he wanted to, even though such a thought should have dampened his desires. Trembling hands toyed with the straps of his waders. He shuffled his feet on the gravel, and looked everywhere except at Summer.

'Sssh,' she said, approaching him.

As though an observer, he watched her hand take his, marvelled at the slowness with which she brought it over her breast and guided it in circling sensuousness. Mesmerised, he noticed her lips tremble and listened to her quiet humming; her eyes closed and opened, sightless and smiling. He felt his bulging manhood push against his waders, and still he dared not move. Closed were his eyes when she pressed against him. No longer conscious of the world, liberated, he rolled a finger over her firm nipple and their lips frantically met. Succumbing to the sweetest pleasure he had ever known, he guided her hands around his neck. On reaching down, his firm hands clasped her buttocks, rocking her against his thrusting pelvis. Open were his eyes when he saw stars in hers. Tender was his kiss before Summer snuggled against his chest.

'Oops,' she whispered, and then giggled.

'Sssh,' he replied.

Happiness can be a fleeting thing, a moment grasped from a world that would contain joy, and declare it a sin. Not registering at first, the peal of a distant church bell scuttled his pleasure. Still holding Summer, he twisted his wrist and glanced at his watch. Seven o'clock, Mass would be starting. Tentacles of guilt accompanying the thought ruined the magical feeling of first love.

Standing beside the river, within the flows of which he could lose all sense of time, place and obligation; holding Summer who dared to see him as a man and not a priest, today had been a perfect day. Reality, a cursed place where dreams fade beyond remembering, returned with the image of Sean cowering in the corner of the Sacristy. *Damn, what a mug I've been. Go to the river and reflect. Father Sweeney, you bastard.*

Summer cried as he pulled away from her. 'Jamie, I'm sorry. I never meant to hurt you. I never meant to fall in love with a priest.'

Up and down the riverbank, he strode, kicking stones out of his way, muttering, making little sense to either Summer or himself. Hearing her gasp, his focus returned. 'Sorry. I witnessed a great wrong this morning, and it's about to be repeated. I'll call tomorrow with the ice cream for Callum.'

Summer sobbed. 'Don't hate me?'

'How could I hate you?' he said, taking her in his arms once more. 'I love you.'

Her sobbing followed him out into the stream. Water dripped from his waders when he paused on reaching the far side. Turning to face Summer, he shouted, 'I do love you.'

† † †

Without a thought for his own safety or the rod's, he raced back to the bridge, crashing through every obstacle in his path.

Pedalling as fast as he could, at a quarter past eight he reached Main Street. Ahead, a lone figure limped along the pavement, head bowed. 'Christ. No, I'm too late,' he thought. On reaching Sean, he stopped, hopped off the bike and let it fall onto the pavement.

Red blotches framing his eyes, Sean whimpered. 'Hello, Father.'

'Father Sweeney?'

'Yes.'

'What did he do to you?'

'I can't say, Father. I have to get home. I hurt my leg playing football.'

Sean brushed his way past James, his sobs tearing apart everything the priest held dear, sundering the cornerstones of his faith and kindling a fire that would never die.

'Sean, you can always talk to me. I will deal with Father Sweeney.'

Sean turned, smiled awkwardly for a moment, and then shook his head before crossing the street to his home.

Numbed by his failure, overcome by a sadness that devoured any lucid thoughts, James made his way to the church. His hands shook as he unlocked the Sacristy door and entered. Closing the door, he roared, releasing all pent up anger, fear and guilt. Falling to his knees before the statue, he screamed at the Blessed Virgin. 'How can you let this happen to a child? How can I believe in a God who would allow this? I know I cannot have two masters, and Sean has suffered because my lust blinded me to the evil that defiled the sanctity of this church.'

For an hour, he knelt there, moaning, urging a response from Mary, begging for help. As his sobs died away, a distant voice buried deep within spoke. *Only a coward could be so brutal to a child, only a weakling would allow it happen. You know what you must do and I walk with you always.* For a moment, he imagined he saw a tear flow down Mary's marbled cheeks.

A boy had become a priest; a priest had become a lover. That priest emerged into a man who stood with his fists clenched. With a steely determination in his voice, he faced the statue. 'Tomorrow, I will confront Father Mick.'

Chapter 5

In the half-light, James rubbed his eyes. Lying amidst the chaos of twisted, sweaty sheets and scrunched up pillows, he stared at the alarm clock. Unable to sleep, having played so many scenarios over in his mind, he no longer trusted his ability to think straight. *What if he gets me transferred to another parish? Who will protect Sean?*

Resolve that moments earlier, seemed set in stone, crumbled. Throughout the night, he fought his way to the summit of a decision, only to slide into the abyss, and forced to seek a different path. The grunts and snores coming from Father Sweeney's room were daggers, deepening the festering wound, and feeding the hatred he now felt for the man.

No matter how hard he prayed, any thoughts of absolving Father Sweeney fuelled his anger. Defeated and deflated, he lay. Craving silence, he covered his ears to drown out the thunderous tick of the second hand continuing its journey to damnation.

The simple wooden cross, on the far wall, drew onto itself the first rays of sunlight, haloed, like the images of Christ in Renaissance paintings. Compelled to stare at it, the burden which had weighed him down through the darkest hours of the night diminished. Earlier thoughts, no more than muddled meanderings, flooded back with a clarity that surprised him. *Where better to do battle than the Sacristy?*

After dressing, he closed his bedroom door, and crossed the landing to the staircase. Keeping to the edge of each step, he ensured their creaky timbers remained silent and his departure secret. The stink of stale tobacco in the dining room unnerved him, as if some part of Father Sweeney lingered there. Spying an apple in the fruit bowl, he grabbed it, and left by the back door.

About to kick at an empty coke can lying in the lane, he laughed at his own stupidity. Instead, he lifted it and every other piece of rubbish strewn on his route to the church. Thinking he would make a better refuse collector than a priest, and just to prove the point, he gathered every piece of litter he could find on the church grounds. He crossed the street to the bin outside the corner shop.

The spluttering approach of the bread van caught him off guard. He did not wish to be seen wandering around the village at dawn. The van stopped.

'Good morning, Father.'

'Paddy Murphy, good morning to yerself.'

Paddy leaned out the window, removed his cap and flicked his flyover back into place. 'Tis early you are up.'

'I couldn't sleep from the heat and thought a little exercise might leave me so tired tonight, my eyes would shut as soon as my head hit the pillow.'

'Ye young fellas are half daft. Listen to me. Take a good nip of whiskey before bed and your snores won't be long in following.'

'I would if I hadn't taken the pledge.'

'Suit yerself, Father. I better deliver this bread or there will be hell to pay.'

James chuckled on the way to the Sacristy. *Agnes will be devouring this tale with her cornflakes.*

Inside, the whiteness of the surplices hanging on the wall hooks mocked any notion this room stood as witness to a bullying priest. Digging deeper than he had ever done, he found a well of resolve, which would allay all his fear and youthful inadequacy. With that determination, he built a buttress in which Father Sweeney would not find any chink to sunder.

This apple is as sour as Sweeney. He tossed the remnants in the bin and sat cross-legged on a chair beside the statue of Mary. Ignoring an itch that moved from one spot to another, he remained focused. Despite his efforts to stay awake, his weary eyes closed, and he rested his head against the Virgins hip. Nearly four hours later, the sound of keys rattling outside woke him, just in time to see Father Sweeney burst in through the doorway. *Mother, I need your help.*

Sweeney glared at James. 'Jesus, Mary and Joseph, I thought we had been burgled. What dragged you from bed so early? Was it the heat again?'

'No. I'll not ...' Feeling a stammer mince his words, James took a deep breath. 'I'll not lie. Sleep evaded me all right. Knowing I slept in the same house as a priest who takes pleasure in bullying a young boy, I couldn't.'

'You think me a bully, is that it?'

For the first time, James peered deep into Sweeney's steel grey eyes, seeing something unfathomable, which chilled him to the bone. 'I know you to be a bully, a cold-hearted, calculating one.'

Sweeney's eyes softened as his mouth curved into a warm grin, yet he remained tense.

'Oh dear. You make me laugh though I admire your honesty. Perhaps I'll make a priest of you yet. If I acted foolishly yesterday, I am sorry. I don't know what came over me. Maybe I was unnerved by the thunder and lightning, and I reacted out of character when I slapped Sean.'

'I don't believe you. That slap was no sudden impulse. You wanted to hurt him, hurt him bad.'

'Think what you will. As God is my witness, it was a stupid, misguided reaction, and it won't happen again.' Father Sweeney grasped his cassock and pulled it over his head.

James remained seated. To ensure Sweeney understood the gravity of the situation, he folded his arms. 'If that's the case, why did you send me to the river? Not for the solitude, like you suggested. You wanted to finish what you started. I'm certain you used your fists again on Sean after last night's Mass.'

Father Sweeney hovered over James with menace. 'I didn't hit Sean again. I didn't want you here. It was embarrassing enough to apologise to a child without having someone else witness it.'

'You apologised?' James said, incredulous.

'Yes. On my hands and knees, on this floor, I begged him for forgiveness.'

'Do you swear that's true?'

'By almighty God, I swear it. Ask Sean if you like.'

James stood, wobbled for a moment, and then reached for his cassock. 'You won't lose your temper again?'

'No.'

'Thank God. I'm sorry if I misunderstood. I'll have a word with Sean. Maybe I'll bring him fishing to make up for your mistake.'

'That's a great idea. Where is he? Mass starts in five minutes.'

No sooner had he said it, the door burst open and an out of breath Luke Ahern raced in. 'Sorry, Fathers. Sean is sick. I'm here to take his place.'

Chapter 6

About to cross the road to Mahon's corner shop to buy ice-cream, James spotted the church's caretaker heading his way. Billy Egan, a retired undertaker, had lived his entire life in Castlebridge. James enjoyed his company, and Billy's dual personality intrigued him. Either entirely jovial or as serious as a judge at a murder trial, not until Billy spoke would James know which one approached. After losing his right thumb when a coffin collapsed on his hand, everyone referred to him as Billy No Thumb. When he made a fist, you had to read his face to decipher his intent. Thump or thumbs up?

Billy stared at James' crotch. 'Father Brennan, your zip is open again,'

'And you need glasses.'

Bill's hearty laugh made everyone on the street turn and gawk.

'Are ya heading for the widows, Father?'

'The widows? Is it a pub or something?'

Billy clutched Father Brennan's arm. 'Did nobody warn you?'

'No. Warn me about what?'

Pulling James even closer to his potbelly, Billy whispered. 'Una Mahon's father died aged twenty-eight. The brakes failed on his car. Poor sod, he was speeding to get home for his birthday party. Her husband died two years ago when he fell down the stairs.'

Billy's aftershave smelled more like eau de corpse than Cologne. At the first opportunity, James edged his way downwind. 'Are you suggesting foul play?'

'Father, you know me better than that. Some rumour-mongers suggested Una had pushed him, while a couple of her former boyfriends were adamant he jumped. The coroner's verdict of accidental death quashed the whispering. Between you, me and the church clock, I reckon he tripped from bedroom exhaustion, if ya follow me. It's hard to ignore the similarity.'

'Similarity?' James wondered if Billy was leading him into another one of his comedy traps.

'God rest the poor Divil. Like her father, Una's husband died on his twenty-eighth birthday. That's a queer co-incidence, isn't it?'

'It is. Is Una's mother dead? I haven't met her.'

'Leading up to the coroner's court, Una dressed in nothing but black. Tears flowed at every opportunity. The day after the verdict, she won best dressed lady at the Curragh races. I reckon Castlebridge proved too small to support two Mahon widows. Within a month, her mother had packed her bags and moved to Dublin to live with her sister.'

'Una made her leave?'

Billy made a fist and punched James lightly on the shoulder. 'If you say so, Father. My nose stays in my business. If you want some advice, do the same. Good luck!'

James laughed as Billy high-tailed it up the street. *One couldn't heed one iota of tittle-tattle in Castlebridge.* Common-sense is fine, but as he pushed open the door of the shop, he couldn't shake off the image of Una's husband tumbling down the stairs.

Una's miniskirt rode high up her bare thighs as she stood on the tiny platform at the top of the high stepladder. Stretching to pack boxes of chocolates on the top shelf, she craned her neck when James entered. A box fell from her hands onto the floor.

A week earlier, the brevity of Una's skirt would have rattled James. Instead, his eyes lingered a moment longer than any gentleman's should. When she caught his stare, her eyebrows fluttered for a moment, before one hand covered her gasp and the other pulled down the skirt. Modesty resumed, she placed her hands on her hips and smiled.

'Thank God it's you, Father, and not some leering, good for nothing. My poor husband, God rest him, he used to do this job.'

'I'm sure he did anything you asked. Shall I hold the ladder steady while you stack the shelf?'

'Would you, Father?' she said. Before he could answer, she turned to face the shelves and presented him with her wiggling backside.

Faced with more than a dilemma, his eyes roved up her legs and halted at the hem of her suede skirt. James lifted the box. As he handed it to her, he locked his gaze on the rusted bottom step.

'Hold me, Father. I'll break me neck if I fall from this ladder.'

She giggled when he turned. Left with little choice, James placed a hand on the small of her back. Una reached up higher than necessary, her skirt following, he stared at more than the rose tattoo on a cheek of her bare buttocks. Now, with nothing left to his imagination, for the second time that week, the temptation of Eve tested his vows. This time, guilt stemmed from his fledgling relationship with Summer.

Una stumbled and squealed. He reached to catch her. She fell into his arms with the grace of a swooning ballerina. When her lips sought his, he staggered back, knocking cans of beans off the shelf behind. Una fell from grace, but landed on her plimsolls.

'Oh my God, Father, what must you think? For a moment I thought you were my dear departed. He was about the same age as you are now when he died, and nearly as handsome. I've been taking Valium, and I don't know day from night. I'm only thirty-one, too young to be left on a shelf with ...'

'It's okay, Una. Sure there's no harm done. Aren't you still a rose in full bloom? Many a lad would be happy to take you up the aisle.'

Once again, her eyes fluttered and her swaying hips invited. As sudden as her provocative display started, it stopped. She glared at James. 'A rose? Did you come in here to take advantage of a poor widow woman?'

She raced around behind the counter. All business, she placed her hands by her side and smiled as though he had just walked in the door. 'Good afternoon, Father Brennan. What can I get you?'

To buy some time, James picked the scattered cans off the floor and returned them to the shelf. Thinking her mad, all images of Una's naked bum were dispelled and replaced by her tied up in straitjacket. With that in mind, he sidled to the counter.

'It's a fine day. I'd like a block of vanilla ice-cream, a block of banana ice-cream and two packets of wafers.'

While waiting for Una, he perused the front page of a daily newspaper. A small headline near the bottom corner caught his attention. 'Corporal Punishment Abolished – 5 Months On.'

'Anything else, Father?' She dropped the blocks of ice-cream into a paper bag and winked.

'I'll take this as well,' James said pointing to the paper. 'And, that will be all.'

If her face had grown longer, angels would have wept at the sight of it. 'Are you sure?' she said.

James finally understood the predicament faced by a cornered rat. Afraid a single word spoken out of turn would have her ripping his clothes from his back, he pointed to the Curly Wurly bars. 'Three of those please.'

Una fetched them, folded the paper, leaned over the counter and placed her hand on his. Damned if he withdrew his hand and God alone knew the consequences of leaving it there. He erred on the side of caution and held his breath as she spoke. 'Now, you keep your money in your pocket. Sure, didn't you save me from a terrible fall? Speaking of which, I hear Agnes had a lucky escape yesterday.'

James eased his hand away and gave it sanctuary in his pocket. 'Did she? Where did you hear that?'

Una leaned a little closer. James stepped back. 'Seeing as it's yourself, and because I hate gossip, I'll be honest with you. Agnes told Mary O'Grady. Mary let it slip when she came in earlier to buy fags.'

'Oh, I know her husband,' James said.

'Jesus, don't tell him she smokes. He'd kill her. Last year she had an affair with the butcher's apprentice. The butcher nearly fired the randy young lad. A week after the relationship ended, someone spotted her at a dance over in Elmwood. I'm told she was wrapped around the butcher, like a rasher around a breast of chicken. If Father Sweeney hadn't sorted out the mess, they'd be divorced by now, and so would the butcher.'

'Agnes was lucky. If I hadn't swerved, I'd have run her over.'

Una, in her efforts to get closer, shoved a jar of lollipops to one side, and almost lost balance. 'Next time she crosses in front of you, don't swerve.'

James seized the paper bag. 'I'd best be going or the ice-cream will melt before I get home. Goodbye, Una.' Not quite sure which Una he was dealing with, not risking any further advances, James turned and raced from the shop. He sprinted till the width of the road separated them. Even then, he glanced over his shoulders as he sped home. It would be two years to his twenty-eight birthday and he'd not tempt fate.

After bounding in the door, he pulled it shut. Out of breath, he fumbled with the lock. At the sound of the latch clicking shut, he leaned his back against the door and laughed out loud.

Father Sweeney had gone to a meeting with the Bishop. Fearing the worst, he checked the ice-cream before placing it in the freezer. Soft but intact. None of the messages on the answering machine were for him. With an hour to kill before he visited Summer, he lay on the couch and read the article on corporal punishment. It confirmed his opinions were accurate. While outlawing such punishment in schools had come into force five months earlier, the process of eradicating the habits formed over a lifetime would take years to complete, if ever. James considered placing it on the dinner table where Father Sweeney usually sat. Fearful of the consequences, he folded the paper and placed it on the coffee table.

Happy that the ice-cream was frozen, he made his way outside and cycled up Main Street. A number of people waved at him as he passed. The two young girls shouted, 'Good afternoon, Father.' James smiled, waved and even stopped to pick up some rubbish which he tossed into a bin. *If only they knew where I'm going.*

Fifteen minutes later James cycled toward Summer's cottage. Halfway up the boreen, he heard Callum's excited chatter coming from somewhere ahead. Pedalling faster, as he rounded a bend he could see Summer and Callum a short distance away. Summer shifted her shopping bag from one hand to another, struggling. They turned as he neared, and Callum let out a holler which would have woken a corpse. 'Father Jamie. Father Jamie.'

When he caught up with them, he dismounted, took the bag from Summer and hung it from the handlebars. 'Hi, Summer.'

Unlike Una, Summer didn't need to flutter her eyelids to set his heart thumping. Just seeing the sparkle in her eyes, the unassuming way she tilted her head and the gentleness of her every movement, each one of these bound him to her like links on a chain.

Summer smiled coyly, 'Hello, Father.' She skipped to the far side of the bicycle and placed a hand on the handlebar. Intending to put his hand on hers, James let go of the bike. Summer took off, pushing the bike up the road, leaving James in her wake and listening to her giggles. Callum blocked any attempt to give chase.

'Father, Jamie, what's in the bag on the bike?'

'I'll give you two guesses.'

'Ice-cream?'

James nodded. Callum grinned, held Jamie's hand and dragged him in pursuit of Summer. She stopped outside the cottage and waited their arrival. Callum grabbed the ice-cream bag and raced through the rusty gateway.

James turned to Summer after he took hold of the free handlebar. 'We'd better catch Callum before he scoffs the lot.'

Summer flicked her hair away from her eyes, gave James a curious look, and without fuss, lifted her shopping off the bike, and moved to the gateway. 'Thanks for the ice-cream and thanks for helping me with this bag. Goodbye.'

James shuffled his feet, baffled by her unexpected, cool demeanour. With one hand on the bike, he thrust the other into his pocket and toyed with loose change. 'Are ... Callum is expecting me to share the ice-cream with him.'

'Is he?' she said, placing one hand on the gatepost, and with the other, she raised the shopping bag ever so slightly, leaving no gap for him to pass. Subtle though her method, the message was clear.

The woman he desired and thought he loved, without force, had punched him in the gut. Disappointment muddled his thoughts. Though he wished to hold her close, and tell her she occupied his thoughts from dawn until dusk, his shoulders sagged as he grasped the handlebars and turned the bike for home. He trudged away, hoping she would call, telling him to return. Gravel crunched beneath his feet and the bicycle's rusty chain squeaked. He could not look back. He neared the corner. At the sound of the cottage door shutting, he closed his eyes and wept.

On his journey back to the village, he wondered, why she had slighted him without explanation. *Is it because I'm a priest? Damn this collar. I'd leave the priesthood if I knew she would have me.* Twice he turned back, but went no further than a few yards before self-doubt stopped him.

Focused on agonising, he paid scant attention to the road in front and almost fell when the front wheel sunk into a pothole deep enough to conceal a dozen bibles. The rim should have buckled under the impact. On a different day, he would have considered himself fortunate to have a punctured tyre rather than a split head.

Lost in his own crumbling world, though he waved and muttered good morning to everyone he encountered on his trek back up the Main Street, his responses were automatic and meaningless. In a village of several hundred people, he felt alone, for his turmoil could not be shared. Sweat rolled down his brow as he halted outside the Sacristy door and parked the bicycle against the church wall. Once inside, he locked the door and fell to his knees before Mary.

Mother, help me. I'm not your Son who befriended Mary Magdalene. Did he suffer as I now do? Did he have feelings for her? I cannot make sense of why Summer has snubbed me. If this is a test, then I have failed; failed God, my Church, and myself... and Summer.

James stared at the statue, willing a response from closed marbled lips. He laid his head against the bosom of Mary, and closed his eyes.

'You love her?' *Yes.* 'You love God?' *Yes, I think I do.* 'Can you love both?' James stepped away and sat down. '*I can deny neither of them my love.*' He gazed up at Mary, '*I can love God and Summer, can't I?*' 'Yes, James, you can and you must.'

He repeated her words, his words, and paced around the room, allowing the positive thought to invigorate him. 'But you are a priest.' *What?* 'A priest cannot love a woman in the way you wish to love Summer.'

James fell against Mary, his fist hammering her bosom with such force that blood oozed from his knuckles. '*Damn these vows. I am going back to the cottage. If she loves me, then I shall find a new job.*'

James opened the door and gasped. Father Sweeney stood outside, his arms folded and his eyes narrowed.

'F... Father Sweeney, I didn't expect you back till later.'

'I can see that. You seem flustered. Are you hiding a girl in the Sacristy?' Father Sweeney peered over his junior's shoulder, and then locked his eyes on him.

'No! Why do you think that?' James stepped out of the way. 'Take a good look for yourself.'

'On the way back to the house I spotted your bike. As I neared the door, I thought I heard voices coming from inside the Sacristy. Mick, I said to myself, Father Brennan being a young fella, he must have a lady in there.'

James scratched his head and laughed. 'Why would you think such a thing?'

'Call it a hunch.' Father Sweeney brushed past James and entered the Sacristy. 'Never mind, I was mistaken, thank God. I told the Bishop you will make a fine, obedient priest. If you have any doubts about anything, talk to me. Many a priest has gone mad and ended up talking to statues.'

Ever since the brutality he witnessed in this room and his experiences with Summer, James had changed. Tempted to tell Father Sweeney to mind his own business, he decided now was not the time to do so. 'I mislaid my wallet. Perhaps I was talking out loud as I searched for it.'

'Oh, I see, well that explains it.' As though a fatherly gesture, Father Sweeney placed his hand on James' shoulder. 'Let's go home. You can assist me sorting out the mountain of paperwork. The Bishop rapped my knuckles for being tardy.'

Chapter 7

'What is wrong with you? Some baptismal certificates are mixed up with wedding certs, and . . . I'll do it myself.' Gathering the papers together, Father Sweeney sorted them in separate stacks. 'I've asked the Bishop, several times, to consider renting a small office for the paperwork.'

James held up his hands. 'Sorry. Perhaps a coffee will wake me up.'

'Two sugars in mine if it's not too much for you to remember.'

James wandered to the kitchen, filled the kettle and sat at the table waiting for it to boil. He gazed at the picture of The Sacred Heart, and his mind wandered to Summer's dilapidated kitchen. Her artwork covered the walls with wonder and warmth, a loving touch lacking in this cold, repressive house.

Close to tears, as he poured the boiled water into the mugs, he wondered what Summer was doing. Painting a picture or curled up in bed with Callum at her side? In his mind, he reached out to touch her, to hold her. Less real than the steam which had whistled its way from the kettle's spout, she vaporised and he clutched at nothing more than memories. He wondered, whether she even knew his real name. Did she reach out to the first man who showed her kindness? Find warmth in a kiss, pleasure in an embrace, but did she recoil at the realisation she could only have a part of his soul, his heart, his being? The rest belonged to God, Rome and the Catholic Church.

By the time he'd returned to the dining room, Father Sweeney had the documents placed in separate manila envelopes. James shrivelled at the sight of Sweeney's spit-ridden tongue licking the stamps. That tongue which delivered rebuke, called Summer a whore and Callum a bastard. Every movement he made, every word he spoke, everything about the man now annoyed him.

'Here's your coffee.'

Father Sweeney took one sip and spat. 'No sugar. You know I take two.'

Salivating at this unintentional bonus, James turned and sat at the table. 'God knows, Mick, you should go on a diet.'

Mick grunted and fetched the sugar bowl from the kitchen. Two heaped spoons of sugar fell into the coffee with a splash, sending rivulets down the side of the mug, onto the table. With each stir of the teaspoon, the spillage became a river. As if some miracle had cured James of blindness, he realised the man he had shared this house with, was more of a pig than the bacon they ate.

'The dishcloth is by the sink,' James said, while Mick took a second sip of coffee.

Temper momentarily etched Mick the ferret's face. He stirred his coffee vigorously, and rubbed his thumb through the resultant spillage. 'Be a good lad, fetch the cloth for me.'

A smile curled around Mick's lips as James stood and walked to the kitchen. When he returned, carrying a single biscuit instead of a cloth, silence descended. The coolness in the ferret's eyes suggested winter had come early to the presbytery.

James waited a few minutes before he spoke. 'Dishcloth. I really am all over the place today. I'll get it.' Upon reaching the door, he turned. 'Fancy a biscuit, Father Sweeney?'

'Bring in the packet. I might let you have another one.'

Sure, and I'll sit here watching you dip them in the coffee, slurping, dripping and sucking. I've made my point. You know I've made it. Sucking all the biscuits in the world can't reverse that.

James returned, placed the biscuits on the table and lifted his coffee cup. 'I'm going to watch some World Cup football on the TV.'

Father Sweeney hated football as much as he hated the English.

With the door closed and the volume on the TV raised, James sat on the settee, rocking to and fro.

West Germany was playing France in the semi-final. With the score at one-all, and a draw in the offing, the game approached full time. James wiped his face and settled back to watch extra time. At the end of the additional thirty minutes, both teams had scored three goals. A penalty shoot-out would decide which team would get to the final. He sat on the edge of his seat, willing France to win. Kaltz nodded at his German teammates before taking the long walk from the centre circle to the penalty spot. Between the posts, French keeper, Ettorri, jumped and smacked the crossbar, rubbed his gloved hands together, and stood on the line with arms outstretched. Kaltz looked at the referee, glanced at the goal and...

The door opened. Father Sweeney peered into the room. 'Father Brennan, I'm sorry to disturb your enjoyment of foreign sport. I've been speaking to the Bishop. He's due over in Elmwood tomorrow and is to call here in the afternoon. One or two parishioners have been making complaints about you.'

James leapt to his feet and switched off the TV. 'Complaints! About what?'

Father Sweeney grunted. 'God knows. Some people cannot mind their own business.' He placed an unwelcome hand on James' shoulder, 'Whatever it is, I'm certain, I can assure the Bishop you are a fine young priest. There's nothing I need to know, is there?'

'No, Father. Maybe they complained about the girl's behaviour at Mass.'

'Indeed, that must be the reason. I suppose people could read that the wrong way,' Father Sweeney clapped James on the back. 'You explain to him she is a harlot, with a bastard child. I'll back up your story.'

'Y... Yes, Father.'

'Good. There is nothing amiss in this parish, nothing you or the Bishop need to worry about.'

James slumped onto the couch after Father Sweeney closed the door, and stared at the picture of "The Last Supper", hanging on the wall above the television. *Before the cock crows three times... can Summer ever forgive me, like Christ forgave Peter?* His gaze settling on Judas, he wondered what future befits a priest who would deny his love for a woman. *She has finished our relationship... what does it matter?*

If it hadn't mattered, he would have slept easy that night. An image of Summer and Callum infiltrated his dreams. Beneath his dangling feet, they wept as he hung from the branch of an oak tree.

Chapter 8

James pulled Summer's painting from its hiding place behind his wardrobe, sat on the edge of his bed and held it. He had hoped to close his eyes and, by letting the lingering scent of patchouli from the canvas wash over him, to feel her presence. The pungent aroma of turpentine denied him this small pleasure. Gold or wooden frame? Where could he hang it? These questions, he'd considered during quiet moments. Now, he wondered if it should remain behind the wardrobe to gather dust, until the paint cured, and Summer faded from memory.

He traced the outline of her signature, following the curving S. "Father Jamie. Summer & Callum 1982." *Jamie, were you a butterfly for just one day? A Father who can never be a father.* Taking one final look at his image on the canvas, he wiped his eyes, and consigned his heart and the portrait to the shadows, where they would be safe.

James braced himself, forced a smile to a face wracked with anxiety and sorrow, and somehow, found a thread of courage to turn the handle of the dining room door.

'Good morning, Father Sweeney.'

The smile of a mother greeting her only son coming home from America, or that of a father at the birth of his first child, these were burlesque compared to the grin on Father Sweeney's face.

'James, have you ever woken up so happy to be alive, that your pillow still bore your grin after you smoothed it out?'

Surprised by this question, James reached for the packet of cornflakes. Shaking the cereal into a bowl, he wondered what trap Sweeney had laid. 'Not recently. Perhaps as a child I did, not that I can remember ever sleeping with my face in the pillow. Isn't it dangerous?'

'Not if you keep your nose pointing to one side.'

And yours is long enough and sharp enough to reach the window. James munched on a spoonful of breakfast.

The volume on the radio was set low. Only when the nine o'clock news started would Father Sweeney lean over and raise it. Though barely audible, James sang along to the song on the radio. 'And the jester sang...'

'What did you say?'

'Huh? Oh, sorry. I was just singing along to the radio.' *Am I that jester? Sweet Jesus, what have I done?*

Father Sweeney emptied his pipe into the ashtray and pulled a fresh plug of tobacco from his tin.

James' teeth grated as he suffered this ritual for the hundredth time. Light, suck, suck, and blow. Sweeney's spluttering coughs and wheezy breaths reminded him of his father's old car.

'Aren't you a little curious?' Sweeney took a gulp of coffee and wiped his lips.

'Curious?' James said, lifting a stray cornflake off the table, he dropped it into his bowl. 'Being inquisitive could be construed as impertinent. Very well, why are you so chirpy?'

'I've worked tirelessly to ensure this parish functions like a well-oiled machine. Some busybody has cast aspersions on you, and hence on me. We cannot have that, can we?'

'I guess not,' James said. *I'll cycle to Summer's cottage after Mass.*

'Bishop O'Rourke is a dictator. Nothing would give him greater pleasure than to write a letter to the hierarchy suggesting this parish is failing in its duty.'

I'll tell her I am no longer a priest. James buttered a slice of toast and poured a cup of tea from the pot on the table. 'He seems a kind man. Why would he do such a thing?'

'Money. It costs a small fortune to run this parish. Elmwood is only nine miles away. It has a population double that of Castlebridge. He wants to amalgamate the two parishes. One church, two priests, and half the cost.'

'How apt.' James pointed to the radio. 'The church bells are broken.' *I wonder what music Summer likes? Surely not the Blues.*

The music died when Sweeney switched off the radio. 'Listen to me, and listen carefully. The Bishop's spies are witless gossipmongers. He rang an hour ago and has arranged to come here for ten o'clock Mass. Whatever ammunition he thinks he has, I'll disarm him, and he will leave here wondering if he'd have more success in shutting down Elmwood.'

James wished the Pope would arrive and amalgamate the Irish Catholic Church with the Protestants. Then he could get married and still serve God. 'What if I have done something wrong?'

'What? My God, that would be a disaster. Have you?'

'Yes, Father.'

'The girl with the bastard child?' Father Sweeney leaned across the table, demanding an immediate response.

'Yes, Father. Forgive me my sins.'

'You've had carnal knowledge with that slut, haven't you? I thought as much.'

James stared at the silent radio. One word, a simple yes would solve all. He was back in the meadow, holding hands with Summer. One word and he would be free. As he rolled his tongue, ready to seal his fate and his faith, he turned towards Father Sweeney. Something in those grey eyes, something he could not fathom caused him to reconsider.

'No, Father... what must you think of me? I allowed you call her a slut, her child a bastard, and in doing so, I am guilty of your sin.'

'My sin!' Father Sweeney thumped the table. 'What do you mean?'

James clenched his fist under the table. 'As Christ forgave Mary Magdalene, so we must forgive this poor girl. Isn't that our solemn duty as Christians?'

Reaching for his pipe, Father Sweeney chuckled. 'Good lad. I'll repeat this to the Bishop. Now go and shave. I'll see you in the Sacristy in twenty minutes.'

James rubbed his stubbly chin on the way to the door. About to leave, he looked back over his shoulder. 'I think we should read from Luke's Gospel today. You know the verses where Mary Magdalene is forgiven of her sins. Perhaps the Bishop could recite the words, and we can pray for forgiveness.'

† † †

I didn't deny Summer a third time, did I? Buoyed by a sense of achievement, James strolled down the lane ten minutes after Father Sweeney had left. Hard lessons had been learned at the seminary. Often, he trusted his own instinct when he doubted the character or motivations of others. Maybe this time, his own confusion and guilt made Father Sweeney seem more of a conundrum than he actually was.

On reaching the wall alongside the church grounds, he noticed the older priest remonstrating with Agnes at the side of the church. James stepped sideways and peered through the fuchsia bush growing behind the wall. Several times, Sweeney grabbed Agnes' arm and raised his voice. While the words were incoherent, it seemed temper drove their delivery.

I wonder if she's Sweeney's spy.

James could see the fear portrayed on Agnes' face, before she scurried around the back of the church. Sweeney bent and retied his shoe laces, stood, then waved. Worried he had been spotted, James drifted up the lane toward the side entrance. Only then, did he realise that the wave was directed to the cleric striding up the path. While both priests paid scant regard to their attire, Bishop O'Rourke's official robes were tailored to perfection. With each step, sunlight danced off his pectoral cross and gold ring.

All three met outside the Sacristy door. Sweeney's furtive glances at James suggested he was not pleased.

'Bishop O'Rourke, you are most welcome,' Father Sweeney said, extending his tobacco-stained fingers, together with a smile that would scare the crows in a cornfield.

As though offended, the Bishop raised his eyebrows before offering his hand at a height that ensured Father Sweeney had no choice but stoop to kiss the ring. When Sweeney rose, the Bishop faced James with a kindly smile. 'Young Father Brennan, it seems we have much to discuss.'

'Do we, your Grace?' James kneeled before the ring was offered, kissed it, stood, and opened the Sacristy door. He beckoned the Bishop to enter. Father Sweeney jumped in front of James and followed his Excellency inside.

Bishop O'Rourke stood before the statue of The Blessed Lady, bowed his head in silent prayer, and then turned. 'His Holiness, John Paul, faces many challenges in this ever-changing world. Let us not be afraid to admit that all young priests, now more so than ever before, will be tested to breaking point. Faith alone is no longer enough, and it saddens the Holy Father that respect for the clergy is at a low-ebb.'

James trembled and coughed. 'I beg your pardon, your Grace?'

Reaching forward, the Bishop placed his hand on James' head. 'Be not afraid. Whatever is your indiscretion, the Lord forgives those who repent, and the Church will protect you.'

James nodded, 'I'm not afraid, your Grace. I am confused. Complaints of which I have no knowledge have been made by a parishioner.'

Father Sweeney scratched his temple and ran his fingers through his balding hair, as though the Bishop's own unnaturally black mop caused him to check the greying-thinness of his own.

'Father Sweeney,' the Bishop said, 'You have concerns that this young priest has been seen in the company of a woman of ill repute.'

'That's what I have been told by a parishioner.'

James swallowed hard. *Whom can I trust?*

'I see.' The Bishop reached beneath his robes for his diary and his reading glasses. 'Let me see what you said.'

As his Grace thumbed through the pages, Father Sweeney grinned, and shrugged his shoulders.

'I see James is a little shocked. Ah, yes, here we are. Father Brennan has had a sexual relationship with a whore. Worse, she has a bastard child. An alarming accusation if it is correct. Is this allegation true, Father Sweeney?'

'I find little joy in my reply.' If the old priest could have appeared any more solemn when he wrung his hands, the dead would have risen. 'Yes.'

'Father Brennan, are these scandalous allegations true?' said the Bishop, closing the diary.

My God, the Bishop hates Sweeney more than I do. Does he really want to close this church? I feel like a pawn in this game.

'Your Grace, I took my vows to serve Our Lord, our Church, and the Catholic faith. During my first Mass, a child came up the aisle with a toy car and offered it to me. I did not see a bastard, I saw a little boy. His mother approached and kissed me on the cheek. Unusual, embarrassing, but I assume she did it as her way of saying thank you for not rebuking her child. Who am I to judge what is in her heart?'

'Indeed, that is for God alone to judge,' the Bishop said.

'Others have obviously done so. Christ said, "Suffer the little children to come unto me." Yet, Father Sweeney calls the child a bastard. Jesus forgave Mary Magdalene, yet Father Sweeney without knowing this girl's heart, calls her a prostitute.'

'Liar!' Father Sweeney poked James in the chest. 'Explain why you were seen cycling toward the girl's house. If not to avail of her services, what business had you there?'

'I'm not an altar boy.' James pushed the offending hand away. 'You cannot bully me.' James stepped in front of the Bishop, his back turned to Sweeney. 'Your Grace, if following the teaching of Our Lord is a sin, I am guilty. If offering forgiveness is a sin, I am guilty. A priest should not take the word of idle gossipers as truth. Yes, I found out where the girl lived and cycled out to her cottage. Unfortunate for me it seems, she was not there. She came to Mass once. I'd like to believe that with encouragement she may come again with her son.' *Every day would be nice.*

Stepping back, Father Sweeney clapped. 'See how he plays the innocent. I can assure you he is not fit to be a priest.' As though the cruelty of his words were insufficient, his jagged laughter befitted a man who now proved himself bereft of honour.

His Grace raised a hand, commanding Sweeney to be silent. 'Enough!'

Not knowing what else to do, James fell to his knees before the statue. He took out his rosary beads and began a decade of the Rosary. When finished, he added, 'Lord, forgive Father Sweeney, even though he knows what he does. Amen.'

Now, Father Bully, do your evil best. You gamble that if I mention your violence toward Sean, the Bishop will see it as my attempt to save myself.

Bishop O'Rourke paced around the room, glancing from James to Father Sweeney who seemed rooted to the spot. He stopped in front of James and placed a hand on his shoulder. 'Father James, I'm grateful for your honesty. I shall pray your faith remains with you always. Others here would be well served to examine their own consciences. Please make your way to the altar and wait for us there.'

The court was adjourned . . .

† † †

Even as he closed the Sacristy door, he heard the whispering inside the church. *What do I care what they say or think?*

Agnes sat on the front pew, at the head of half the gossipers in the parish. He approached the altar, knowing they scrutinised his every move. He sat, arms folded, legs crossed and stared at the crossbeams running the length of the church. *Summer does not come to Mass, yet her heart is pure. If Christ walked amongst these pariahs, they would find flaws and report him to the Bishop. What am I doing here?*

Father Sweeney's forced smile could not hide the rage in his purpled face as he trailed behind the Bishop in their solemn procession to the altar. Neither Luke nor Sean had turned up this morning. No doubt, the Bishop would have noted the absence of an altar boy.

O'Rourke took up position alongside James and whispered, 'Please mark the section in St. Luke's gospel where Christ forgives Mary Magdalene.'

James nodded and approached the table where Father Sweeney prepared to commence the Mass. As he searched for the passage in the Holy Bible, Father Sweeney leaned toward him and hissed, 'You are a liar.'

After marking the passage, James turned to gaze on Padre Pio. *Now, would be a good time for you to wink, Padre.*

Forcing a smile, he stared at Agnes. When she stared back, he leaned closer to the other priest. Keeping his eyes locked on hers, he whispered loud enough for her to hear, 'Let he without sin, cast the first stone.' Agnes' shocked eyes reflected Father Sweeney's reaction. James sighed, turned, and stood close to the Bishop.

During the Liturgy, James' mind wandered to Heffernan's meadow. *Beneath his feet, daisies sway in the summer breeze. He kneels, plucks a few and makes a chain. On rising, his pulse quickens. Hand in hand, Summer and Callum stand at the brow of the hill, their sorrow eclipsing the sun. Hands stretched out, he races through a thickening mist, calling their names. Their sad eyes pierce him, pinning him to some distant place on the horizon. As he nears, they fade into the mist. He falls to his knees. No, come back, please come back...*

Bishop O'Rourke moved to the lectern.

'The Lord be with you,' he said.

The Congregation stood. 'And also with you.'

'A reading from the Holy Gospel according to St. Luke.'

'Glory to you, Lord.'

'One of the Pharisees asked Jesus to eat with him, and he went into the Pharisee's house and took his place at the table. And a woman in the city, who was a sinner, having learned he was eating in the Pharisee's house, brought an alabaster jar of ointment . . .'

'The Gospel of our Lord.'

'Praise to you, Lord, Jesus Christ.'

After the reading, the Bishop waited for everyone to be seated, then took a step forward.

'Who among us is perfect, without sin? ...'

Some muffled coughs, a shuffling on seats.

'Father Sweeney, is he without sin? No. Me, your Bishop, am I?'

Agnes nodded. Had she been in school, she would have raised her hand.

'Father Brennan. Is he a sinner?' The Bishop's voice filled with authority, and so loud, even those at the back sat upright.

James shuddered. A ripple of smiles passed along the faces of the gossipers. Agnes' nodded so much she surely risked a dizzy spell.

'None here are without sin,' O'Rourke shouted, gesturing at each person present.

Agnes gasped. Everyone turned and stared at her, some laughed.

'Christ forgave Mary Magdalene, cast out her demons and absolved her of her sins. I've asked Father Brennan to breathe new life into this sinful parish. For that, his good name has been besmirched. My authority and the authority of Christ, Our Lord, have been ridiculed by nasty rumour and cold-hearted gossip.'

Powerful words cast their spell, heads dropped. As a Mother would sing a gentle lullaby to soothe a child, O'Rourke softened his tone. 'Christ can, and will, through his servant Father Brennan, absolve your sins through penance. After you ALL receive the Eucharist, and Mass has ended, make your way to the confessional. Amen!'

But I'm going to Summer's cottage. I don't care about anything else.

James trudged to the confessional box. Already, a queue had formed. Those in a hurry jostled their way to the front. Genuine penitents clutched their rosary beads. A few of the few younger men, who kept their eyes on Father Sweeney and the Bishop marching toward the Sacristy, made good their escape. James closed the door, slumped onto the wooden seat inside, and confessed to himself.
Bless me, Father, for I have sinned.

Tell me about your sins.

I denied my love for Summer.

You mean, you lusted after a woman and in doing so, denied your love for God. Say two Our Fathers, a decade of the Rosary and have no more lustful thoughts.

Our Father, who art in... I cannot.

Chapter 9

Good and evil. These seemed so easy to label after all he'd been taught from biblical parables, and almost two millennia of writing from learned men of the church. His education failed to provide him with the insight to understand what motivated men like Sweeney, those who walked in the shadows of these polar opposites. One may catch a droplet of rain in the palm of a hand. Its form lost, its existence marked by a dampness, which in time will vanish.
Who can understand such things, such men?

Honour demanded he leave Holy Church, and in doing so, offend his mother, and dishonour his vows. The many voices in his head had grown louder with his indecision, some imploring action, others counselling patience. A new, decidedly sanguine one joined the fray when he sat at the dinner table. *It is my will that you follow your conscience, for I direct all it advises, everything you will ever do.* Over and over these words repeated, drowning out his other thoughts, rising above his feeble, exhausted efforts to focus on the repercussions of the Bishop's visit.

'Must you do that?' Father Sweeney said, clattering his pipe off the edge of a plate.

James shifted his gaze from the spider-web crack on the window pane to Sweeney. 'Do what?'

Sweeney reached across to grab the knife James absentmindedly spun on the table. As his fingers touched the blade, James pulled it away. Holding it up, he pointed it at him for a moment, then toward the pipe. 'Must you poison me with your foul pipe? There is a trail of tobacco and ash from one end of the house to the other.'

The ticking of the clock accentuated the silence that followed. James placed the knife back on to the table and set his hand alongside. Even without looking up, he knew Sweeney watched for any show of weakness and, at every opportunity would provoke James to re-establish his authority. Subtlety, fatherly warmth, and cold, sniping remarks, the calculated methods Sweeney's used to orchestrate and control.

'Does the girl smoke?' Sweeney said, as Mary Kavanagh, their housekeeper, shuffled into the dining room carrying a tray. 'What do you think, Mary?'

Both Mary and the tray wobbled as she elbowed a newspaper out of the way. James leaned over and made space on the table. He gasped when she placed in front of him, the largest plate of hairy bacon and cabbage he'd ever seen. Potatoes in their half-washed jackets peeped from between mounds of over-boiled greens. Enough food to feed both priests offered in a single serving.

'Never fear, my skinny Fathers. Mary is back. Soon I will have flesh back on your bones and colour to your cheeks.' She squeezed James arm. 'You must be Father Brennan. I hope you last longer than the previous young priest, Father ..., Jesus, what was his name?'

Digging into the cabbage, Sweeney muttered, 'Smith.'

'Father Smith. He'd be the same age as yerself. January, two years ago, he arrived here from the priest's school in Maynooth. Poor fecker, he ended up in the nut-house in Dublin.' She doubled with laughter, 'Father Sweeney, do ya remember the day he arrived for dinner wearing nothing but his collar?'

Seeing no humour in the image, James lifted his fork. 'I'm pleased to meet you. I hope you have recovered from your illness. That priest. By any chance was his first name Fergus, and did he hail from Tipperary?'

'Do you know what? That explains his madness. Fergus Smith, Ballyporeen, from the same parish as President Regan's ancestors. Eat up your dinner, and I'll fetch the milk.'

A smile curled Sweeney's lips. Clearly avoiding conversation, he sliced a potato in half, scooped a dollop of butter onto his knife and dropping it on top of the spud, worked it around with his blade. James cut a sliver of bacon. While he chewed, he remembered Fergus. Everyone had liked him, a kind, funny lad who spent most of his free time poring over ancient manuscripts in the library. More suited to an academic life than a parochial one, it did not surprise him he didn't fit in, especially here, with a manipulator like Sweeney. Mary returned with two glasses of milk and placed them on the table.

'I better take my medicine,' she said, opening the drinks cabinet and pulling out the bottle of sherry. She filled a glass to the brim, raised it to her lips and sank all but a mouthful. 'Awful stuff, but I best heed the doctor's advice and take the double dose as ordered.' She squeezed her large frame into an armchair, eased a packet of cigarettes from her apron pocket and lit up. 'What were you saying about a girl?'

Occupied with teasing a lump of grizzle from between his teeth, Sweeney didn't answer till she asked a second time.

'I was asking whether you knew if Father Brennan's girlfriend smokes or not?'

Mary looked James up and down. 'I'd guess she doesn't. Will I give him a kiss and see if the smell of fags puts him off?'

'Do.'

The housekeeper whipped out her false teeth, leaned across the table and pouted her rubbery lips.

James eyed Sweeney's jacket, hanging from the back of one of the free chairs. He grasped a matted sleeve, wiped his mouth with it, and rose to his feet Mary howled with laughter after he kissed her hand, but Sweeney snarled at him. 'Sit. You are a disgrace.'

'I've no girlfriend, Mary. But I'm open to suggestions. Would you have a daughter as pretty as yourself?'

Sweeney thumped the table. 'Mary! You should be in the kitchen, or cleaning the bedrooms. I pay your wages and fund your medicinal requirements. You stick to doing your job, or I'll find a younger, fitter housekeeper.'

Mary stubbed her cigarette in the ashtray. Her rosy cheeks paled with shock and fear. 'I'm sorry, Father Sweeney.'

No longer hungry, James waited until she left, then pushed his plate to the centre of the table and moved to the door. 'I'm going for a breath of fresh air. When I come back, either you treat me with respect, or I'm phoning the Bishop.'

Sweeney's response was lost in the slamming door.

† † †

James wheeled his bicycle out onto the main street and weaved between two cars to reach the far side. A traffic jam in Castlebridge was so infrequent it seemed the entire village had come out to gawk. Ahead, he could see groups huddled together. Una shouted at him from outside her shop. 'A minor collision between the bread van and a delivery truck outside Lavelle's, Father.' He nodded and continued toward the accident, smiling as each group of voyeurs greeted him.

Soon the cause of the fuss became clear. Paddy Murphy's bread van had collided with a wine delivery truck, both spilling their contents.

Billy commanded the centre of the road, holding back the drivers, intent on trading blows. 'Easy lads, accidents will happen. Nobody is hurt, and there's no need for that to change.'

Paddy grunted, shook hands with the other driver and set to lifting his side door off the road.

'Red, White and Brown. Paddy, when did you start baking French bread?'

Paddy swivelled. 'Who said that?'

Seanie Lavelle, propped against the wall by his front door, grinned. 'Afternoon, Father. You should arrange for the Protestant vicar to come here as soon as possible.'

'Why? I've never met the man.'

Seanie kicked a loaf off the pavement. 'There's enough communion on the road to keep them going for years. Where are you going?'

James hopped onto his bike. 'How is Sean?'

'Grand. A small limp, he will be as good as new in a few days. By the way, I believe you owe me a box of flies.'

'Sorry, I've been busy. I'll tie them this week.'

As James cycled away, Seanie gave chase and grabbed the saddle. He leaned toward the priest. 'Tell Summer I've got a bag of Sean's old clothes for her.'

What? How has he figured out I know Summer?

Incredulous, he watched Seanie walk away, before steering out onto the road.

After the garage, he crossed and cycled along the pavement past the school, avoiding the potholes in the road that could swallow both man and bike. Each time a car approached, he hopped off the bicycle, and faced away, and got back up once the vehicle had passed.

Near the turn for the boreen, he scanned the road, ditch and hedges for anyone eager to report to Sweeney. Satisfied he was alone he continued his journey and took the turn.

'Hi, Summer. I just called to say hello. No. No. No. That sounds daft.' He thumped the handlebars. 'Hi, Summer. Please can I come inside? No. Act natural, like in the TV movies.'

Coming to a stop before Heffernan's meadow, he leant the bike against the brambled ditch. A single ripe blackberry caught his attention. He elbowed some briars out of his way and plucked it. Something prompted him to examine the ditch further along on his side. Everywhere, blackberries in various shades of ripeness flourished. *Why did Summer and Callum go to the river to pick berries?*

After licking his lips, he paced back and forth. 'Can we make love under the stars? I like that idea. Lord, what do I say? Hi. Hello. Hey there? How's it going? Think, think ... keep it simple. Something poetic? Nah, she'd laugh at me. Maybe she will laugh at me no matter what I say. If she does, I'll say, I love you. Eureka! Summer, I love you.'

If a herd of elephants had chased him up the road, he could not have cycled any faster. *I love you. I love you.* He dropped the bike at the gate, raced to the back door and stood there, panting. *I love you.*

Twice he knocked and waited, listening to his own heavy breathing. *I should have brought flowers*. Getting no response, he rapped, and banged on the door again. Rushing to the window, he peered through the grime, but could see little of the interior. 'Callum, Summer,' he shouted, as he walked around the cottage.

They are not here. Never having considered such a possibility, he slumped onto the step outside the door, clutched his head and stared at the weedy path. 'Where could they be? Playing in the meadow, down at the river or somewhere else?'

Convinced they must be down at the river, he made his way to Heffernan's meadow and stood on the brow of the hill. Hearing only the drone of a distant tractor, he cupped his hands and called their names. Beyond the oak tree, a swan floated downstream, arched its neck and then disappeared from view. Of Summer and Callum there was no sign.

Slouched over the handlebars, once more, the squeaks from the rusty chain marked his slow, painful ride home.

While the crowds had dwindled, several of the business owners still worked to remove bread and other debris from the front of their premises. Seanie leant on his brush and waved as James approached.

He let the bike free-wheel toward Lavelle's and stopped in front of Seanie. 'How do you know Summer?'

'A good barman is a friend to everyone. Your young lady returned the empty beer bottles.'

Aha. That's one mystery solved. 'When?'

'Is this a bloody inquisition? Yesterday, before she caught the bus to Dublin.'

To Dublin. 'Thanks.' *Why would she have gone to Dublin?*

Seanie laughed when he started to cycle away. 'James, she is pretty.'

†††

Sweet Lavender air freshener greeted James when he returned home. The shine on the hall table and marbled floor made him wonder whether he had entered the wrong house. He poked his nose around the dining room door to find Father Sweeney sitting there, arms folded. On the table, a whiskey bottle and two glasses suggested something had been planned. The old priest gestured to the chair opposite him.

'Please sit. It's best we each know where we stand,' Sweeney said. Twisting the cap off the bottle, he poured a measure of whiskey into each glass. Neither anger nor warmth, nor joy, nor sadness could be read from his demeanour.

This day cannot get any worse. All belligerent thoughts had died at the empty cottage. Any hope that he had a future to be lived rather than endured had deserted him. As he sat, James felt weaker, more vulnerable than at any other time in his life. Without a word, he accepted the glass, raised it to his lips and inhaled the rich aroma of the malt. Without a sound, he placed it back on the table, and nudged it toward Father Sweeney. 'Whatever pain you wish to inflict, make it quick, whether it be rebuke, anger, whatever tortures you've dreamed up these past hours. I do not drink, nor am I in need of fortification.' *Get it over with, I'm weary.*

Sweeney poured James' whiskey into his own glass. 'I'd hoped we could start afresh. But your demeanour suggests it's impossible. You are the third priest sent here by O'Rourke to spy on me. Smith, O'Malley, and now I face a Brennan. I'm tired of being on my guard, wondering when O'Rourke will find just cause to retire me, and wipe this parish from the map.'

'Fergus Smith was my friend.'

'Of course, he was. The devious rat pretended to travel to the library in Carlow, when in fact, he went there to report to the Bishop. O'Rourke is an Armagh man. Never trust any from that Protestant county, not even a Catholic. I'd swear his grandmother or great grandmother were planters.'

'You're mad.'

'Perhaps I am, driven so, by the likes of you. It appears I misjudged you. My mistake. I'll not make a second.'

'You need to realise something. I don't care what you think.' James tilted his head towards the window. He stared at the crack.

'One question needs to be asked. If you are man enough to give me an honest answer, then we can come to an agreement.'

James locked his eyes onto Sweeney's. 'Ask it and be done.'

'Are you O'Rourke's man, sent here to spy on me.'

'No. I am a priest.'

'Swear it on your mother's Rosary Beads.'

James sighed. 'Let this be the end of your madness.' He unbuttoned his collar and lifted the wooden beads over his head. Holding them between his hands, he rolled his thumb over them. 'I swear by Almighty God that I'm not here to spy on you.'

Sweeney downed his whiskey. 'That's a strange place to keep your Rosary Beads. In time, we may even become friends.'

James pocketed the beads and stood. 'I'll be courteous. On occasion, maybe even laugh in your company. Friendship with you comes at a price I'm unwilling to pay. I'm going for a nap before saying Mass this evening.'

'Time heals. I'll do my best to guide without interfering. Seeing as you expect equality, you must earn it by sharing the workload. As of tomorrow, add house visits, paperwork and parish council meetings to your itinerary. Come September, you can teach religion classes at the school.'

Blah, blah, blah. James nodded, and raced upstairs to his bedroom.

Chapter 10

Another Mass said; the daily ritual of speaking other's words to people he did not really know. Participants through habit, they nodded and prayed, though he wondered how many ever questioned their blind faith. Shoulders slouched like an old man; he traipsed after Luke to the Sacristy, debating whether he would once again make that lonely trek to Summer's cottage. *No point. She's gone five days, and it's raining.*

Father Sweeney stood facing the Blessed Mother in the Sacristy when James and Luke entered. Luke edged to the chair in the far corner, and sat as though waiting. Hanging around for what? An argument or afraid to make a sound that would break the impenetrable wall of silence between the priests. On meeting James' puzzled stare, Luke's cheeks reddened. The boy looked at the floor and toyed with the hem of his surplice.

Unsure as to why Sweeney dishonoured them with his presence, James defrocked and hung his cassock on a peg. 'Thanks, Luke, I'll see you here tomorrow morning.' James opened the door, and hunched his shoulders to meet the driving rain.

'Wait a moment, Father Brennan,' Sweeney said.

'What?'

'I'm due to give communion to old Sarah Casey in her home this morning. I'm afraid I have more urgent matters to deal with, and need you to attend in my stead.'

James pointed to the rain splattering onto the cobblestones. 'I'd get soaked cycling to Casey's farm. Can't you do it tomorrow?'

See him, Luke. Afraid of a drop of rain, he is. No, she would have a panic attack. You must go. Now!'

In biting down hard, James withheld an expletive that would have given Father Sweeney more pleasure than the death of a dozen English soldiers. 'Okay,' he answered, pulling the door shut behind him.

† † †

Mary stifled a laugh, but her burly frame shook. 'Mother of God, see what the cat has dragged home.'

Had he fallen into the river, James would have been drier. The heavens drenched his upper body, while spray from the bicycle and capillary action soaked the rest of him. Droplets falling from his chin, he unzipped his coat and dropped it into the growing puddle on the marble floor.

'Mary, turn your back.'

'A small peep, Father,' she replied, pouting her pudgy lips.

'No.'

About to remove his sodden clothes, he spotted the grinning ferret at the top of the stairs. 'Why?' shouted James. 'Why did you send me on a wild goose chase?'

Sweeney moved down a few steps. 'A what?'

'Old Sarah Casey has been in a nursing home for the past two years,' snapped James.

'Of course she is. Didn't I visit her there last week? Don't tell me you cycled out to Casey's farm. Saoirse Casey lives behind the garage, a four-minute walk from here.' Cold calculating eyes belied his mirthful expression. 'Mary, put on the kettle and make James a hot whiskey. I'd recommend a nice warm bath first. I feel so refreshed after mine.'

'I don't drink, and you said Sarah Casey,' James said, incredulous.

'You should take the whiskey,' snapped Sweeney as he sauntered past James into the kitchen. 'Make mine a large one, Mary.'

James tore up the stairs two steps at a time, rammed the plug into the bath and switched on the tap. Cold water flowed from the hot one. *Blast this, blast everything and every bloody one.* Veins stood proud on his temple as he twisted the tap tight, hoping Sweeney would pull a muscle the next time he needed hot water. Crossing the landing to his bedroom, he paused. The ferret's bellowing laughter and rasped coughs ringing in his ears, he lunged for the handle and wrenched open the door.

Not bothering to remove his sodden clothes, James collapsed onto the bed, and stared at the raindrops sliding down the windowpane. *I need to talk to someone, anyone. I can't continue with this miserable masquerade.* Seanie Lavelle seemed trustworthy, fatherly, worth consideration. Of all the people whose names he listed, only Summer would understand, yet he barely knew her, and she had disappeared. Desperate to find an answer, that voice, the one telling him to follow his conscience, guided him to a solution so obvious, he smiled. *I'll write to Summer.*

He fetched his pen and paper. Sitting against the slatted backboard of the bed, he pulled up his knees, and using his bible for support he placed a sheet of paper against it.

Dear Summer,
Great ideas seldom lead to flowing ink. Pensive, he sucked on the pen and stared at the whiteness of the paper.
~~Every day I preach the love of God.~~
I miss you and Callum. A gnawing sense of loss torments me. I've always known I should not have become a priest. Never man enough to defy my mother's wishes. Because I am a priest, we met at Mass. I guess, because I am a priest, you saw no future in our relationship. How ironic is that? Fearful of further rejection, I may never post this. Should I? Do you think we could be together? Even as friends, like we pretended when we first met? Father Sweeney is a nasty, conniving piece of work. Hell bent on making my life miserable. I don't know how much longer I can resist, without you, Summer, my only friend. I'd leave here, but with nowhere to go... I don't feel like eating, but must, I guess. I'll finish this letter after dinner and post it tomorrow, Thursday.

Hi Summer, it's Friday. I met Sean, one of the altar boys, today. Sweeney has been bullying the poor lad and he refuses to come to Mass. Sean has a choice, I don't. At least not an easy choice, if I'm being honest. I wish I could get him to reveal more, but I sense he is afraid. Are you still in Dublin? Seanie hasn't seen you, so I guess you must be. I'm going to bed early. I can't bear the sound of Sweeney's snoring or the stink of his pipe.

Oh, God. He's been rummaging around my room, I caught him. Searching for matches, he claimed. He is a liar. I'm hiding this letter under my mattress, no, under the carpet will be safer. What do you think?

Where are you? It's Friday again, ~~nearly the middle of June, it's~~ the start of July.

Monday. I'm all over the place. I dropped the Eucharist at Mass this morning, right in front of Agnes Murphy. The body of Christ strewn all over the floor. I see their sneering faces at Mass, out on the street. I can't get their whispering out of my head. Too many voices...

Another boring week! Sweeney made me refile all the baptismal certificates, again. I'm useless. I can't even be bothered to go fishing. I hate Sundays.

Where are you? I took a bus to Elmwood and bought some Christmas presents for Callum. Not sure about Christmas. Do you like turkey?
Wait. The newspaper thinks it's still July.

Not sure about God. Not sure... I told Mary, she doesn't answer. Nothing matters anymore. The lowest branch on the Oak tree is very strong.

I've so much to tell you. So little time. Can't think straight. I'd love to be a pilot or an engineer. It rained today. I think it might snow soon.

We could...

I can see you under the Judas tree. Please don't weep

Promise.

I could have told you, James...

I...

Chapter 11

Uninvited, love had come and gone on a summer breeze. Believing his life had become a masquerade, James ensured none knew of his turmoil. He shredded the letter and wrote a note for Summer. "We could have been happy. Love James." Resigned to his destiny, he felt no emotion or regret.

There would be no goodbyes. Three weeks to the day after Summer shattered his dreams of a life without a dog collar, he woke at his usual time, shaved, showered and dressed. After making his bed, he tidied his bedroom, polished his shoes, and placed his watch and cross on the bedside locker. No matter which way he arranged them, he could not achieve the symmetry he desired. James sighed, considering this a final humiliation. Illogical though his actions, he fetched his gold pen from the dressing table and placed it across the face of his watch, forming a cross.

With nothing left to do, he pulled his rucksack from the wardrobe and the note from under the mattress. After one last look around the bedroom, he closed the door and trudged downstairs to the sitting room. Standing in front of the picture of *'The Last Supper,'* he made his peace with God.

Christ, you surrounded yourself with your friends. Forgive me.

Calmer than he'd been in ages, he strode into the dining room. He poured a cup of tea and sat in silence opposite Father Sweeney. Absorbed in watching the other priest munch through several slices of toast, he spilled his tea when the phone rang.

'Answer it,' snapped Father Sweeney.

James walked to the hall and lifted the headset. 'Hello.'

'Is that Father James?'

'Yes.'

'Father James, your mother calling.'

'Hello, Mam. It's me.'

'Father James, is it yourself? This is a bad line.'

'Mam, it's James.' He shook his head. 'Drop the Father bit.'

'Don't be daft. Sure didn't I travel to Maynooth to see you ordained, and proud I was too? You're, Father James. I'll not hear you called anything else.'

Word for word she repeated her opinion to his father, Michael. James visualised him sitting on the old armchair by the fire, pretending to be interested, nodding as she nattered on.

'Okay, Mam. I know you hate wasting money on phone calls. Why did you ring me?'

'It's sorrowful the news I have. Your Aunty Maggie has taken a turn for the worst. Last Thursday, the phone rang just as Delia Moroney, dressed like one of them whores in London, arrived at the backdoor. Sure, I knew it was bad news. The hens hadn't laid an egg for two days, and I had your father warned. He told me I was daft, but I knew.'

James could have banged his head against the wall. 'What news, Mam?'

'Like I was saying, I knew the signs. Moroney's prize heifer had a stillborn calf last week. As sure as I knew my only son was born to be a priest, I knew bad news would come up my path before the end of the full moon. Isn't that right, Michael?'

Father Sweeney emerged from the dining room and caught James' attention. 'Your mother?'

James nodded.

Father Sweeney grunted, shoved his way past and wrenched open the front door. 'Right, I'll say Mass on my own then,' he said.

'See, your father agrees with me now. If I had a pound for every time I was right, I could buy a nice house up in Castlebridge and watch my son say Mass every day.'

'Mam, is Aunty Maggie dead?'

'Well, she is, and she isn't. Father Galvin gave her the last rites an hour ago. When he made the sign of the cross on her forehead, saints preserved, if she didn't open her eyes and speak. "Get me Father James." She whispered, but we all heard it.'

'Be straight with me. She said, get me Father James?' James said.

'She would have if that stroke hadn't twisted her tongue. "Get James." That's what she would have said, but I know what she meant, isn't that right, Michael?'

'Is she still alive?' James brushed a spider off the hallstand, and then repeated the question.

'She is, she is. Lord save us, if you don't get down here soon, the nursing home will charge for an extra month, and I know well they don't do refunds.'

James glanced at his watch-less wrist. 'Mam, get Dad to collect me from the station. I'll be on the evening train.' He waited for a reply before shouting down the phone. 'Did you hear that, Mam?'

'I did, I did. Don't be shouting at me. Hold on a minute. Michael, you'll have to milk the cows early, Father James is coming to see his mother.'

'Goodbye, Mam. I'll see you all this evening.'

'Did you hear that, Michael? My son, Father James will give Maggie the last rites. If that doesn't send her on her way, nothing will. God rest her soul.'

'Goodbye, Mam.' James hung up the phone, snatched his rucksack from under the dining room table, and raced upstairs.

First, he had to get to Dublin, and the next bus left at half ten. On with his watch. He had twenty minutes to get ready. Fate's tentacles had reached out, wrapped round, and drawn him back from the brink. A cold sweat marked his opening of the rucksack and pulling out a rope. With the untying of its noose, a layer of sanity returned. James vowed never to walk this path again.

Guessing two changes of clothes would suffice, he packed these, a toothbrush, his stole and holy oil. As an afterthought, he placed his bible on top. Somehow, he needed to inform Father Sweeney, but with insufficient time to get to the church, he pulled Summer's envelope from his pocket, and opened it. *I do love you.* He scribbled a message for Father Sweeney on the bottom of the sheet, and tore it off. Moving to the bathroom, he shredded the envelope and what remained of Summer's note, tossed them in the toilet and flushed. 'Hang in there Aunt Maggie,' he said, his gaze fixed on the spinning fragments of paper until they disappeared.

After leaving the note for Father Sweeney on the hallstand, he dashed outside, and raced to the bus stop just past Lavelle's. Already there, with its indicator blinking, he ran alongside the front of the bus and waved. The door whooshed open. Out of breath, James climbed the steps and stopped.

'Lucky for you,' the driver said, pressing a button to shut the door. 'As I was saying, had I noticed your collar, I'd be gone without you.'

'Sorry, my watch is running slow.' James pulled out his wallet. 'Return ticket to Dublin, please.' Apart from a few elderly people near the front, the bus appeared to be empty.

'You are young for a priest. Day or weekly return?'

A one way ticket would be best. 'Weekly, please. I'd guess you are no more than thirty. A bit young for a bus driver?'

Several button clicks later, a ticket emerged from the machine, and the driver ripped it off. 'Five pounds fifty. Is Mick Sweeney still a priest here?'

James took out a ten pound note and handed it over. 'Yes, Father Sweeney runs the parish.'

'Does he indeed?' With a sudden movement which startled James, the driver grabbed his arm. 'Tell that shrivelled bastard you met Jack

O'Brien on the bus. Remind him of my oath before his fuckin God. Someday, when his back is turned, I'll shove a shotgun up his perverted arse.'

Stunned by the ferocity of the driver's remarks, their potential meaning was lost on him for a moment. James mouth opened and closed. When he spoke, his voice was thick with emotion. 'Were you an altar boy?'

Deep-rooted fear evident in his hazel eyes, Jack O'Brien stared at him. Through lips that trembled, his murmured response a pitiful moan. 'No. Concealed from the other passengers, he stood, pulled out his shirttail and raised it up his back. 'Sweeney's blessing, daily administered.' Crisscrossed scars ran from the base of his spine ran to below the shoulder blades.

James leaned toward the driver, their faces inches apart. *Use both barrels, and before you pull the trigger, tell him one barrel is from me. O' God, I can't condone that.* 'Jack, I swear before my God, not Sweeney's, he will pay for what he has done to you. Killing him is too soft a punishment.'

After yanking down his shirt, the driver reached for James' hand and held it firm. 'Swear it, Father.'

'I swear it.'

'Swear it for my friends, who endured more than mutilation. Damn you, swear it.'

'What do you mean?'

'If I say anymore the bloody nightmares will return. Swear!'

'I promise, Jack. I swear. I'll see him rot behind bars.'

Turning on his heel, James walked to the middle of the bus, slouched onto a seat, and hoped the elderly people at the front hadn't heard. He tore open his rucksack and clutched his Bible. That voice, deep within, spoke so clear he feared he succumbed to the same madness that had afflicted Fergus. *Follow your conscience, follow your heart. I guide all that you do.*

The beauty of rolling green fields and bushes in full bloom could not dispel the image of the driver's back. *Is that what Sean would have received? And Jack's friends? Oh, sweet Jesus.* With each passing mile, horrible scenes played out in his head. Some he blocked before they came into focus, some too painful to contemplate, beyond his comprehension. With each question came the same answer. *Follow your conscience, follow your heart. I guide all that you do.*

Exhausted, James lay against the window and drifted off into a troubled sleep. 'Sssh.' Summer's voice, the sweet gentleness eased his tortured mind. 'Jamie.' He walked through the long grass in the meadow, answering her call. Something shook him. 'Jamie.' No, come back, he begged, as the meadow faded. Waking with a grunt, he wiped his tired eyes, wishing he were back in the land of dreams, and not looking out on the fields alongside the road. He closed his eyes.

'Sssh.'

I'm hearing voices again.

'Jamie.'

Go away.

A warm breath caressed his cheek. Lips lingered on his earlobe, nibbling and teasing. A hand on his thigh, moving upwards, so real he moaned at the pleasure of it. Moist lips pressed upon his. Afraid to open his eyes in case the pleasure ceased, he drew his hand around the dreamy form that left him aroused. Running his fingers through tangled hair, he brought his other hand under a breast, and listened to the soft, breathless humming. He opened his eyes and realised he hadn't been dreaming.

'Sssh,' Summer said, smiling. A tender touch drew his face to hers for a passionate kiss that left them both breathless. 'I love you, Jamie Brennan.'

Chapter 12

Summer's presence subdued the melancholic thoughts, which had consumed his dreams and every waking moment these past weeks. James edged closer to her. Bewildered at the well of emotion muddling his mind, he could hardly believe she shared his feelings. *She really loves me.*

'I'm James Brennan, and you are?'

She lightly thumped his shoulder. 'Summer. Three weeks,' she lifted and twisted his left wrist, 'and eighteen minutes since you walked away from me, and already, you forget my name.'

'Summer who? You made it obvious you wanted me to leave. I called to the cottage the next morning, the day after and God knows how many other times.'

'You did?' she said, shifting on the uncomfortable bus seat. 'Cool. Okay, Mr. Father Brennan. I'm Summer McMahon and I forgive you. Say three Hail-Summers and kiss me so I'm sure you're not lying.'

'No. Kissing you nearly cost me my job, my li... No more kisses until we know each other better.'

'Just one little one.'

'No!'

Summer folded her arms. 'Okay. You go first, Mr. Meanie.'

The bus stopped in a village. Two passengers disembarked, and a group of chattering teenagers flashed their student cards at the driver, and swaggered to the rear seats.

How much do I tell her? James gazed out the window.

Everything! That voice again.

An old man stooped with age, leant on his walking stick, staring at James. He waved, and his lips moved as if speaking, but to whom?

Tell her everything!

James nodded, the old man nodded, and gears grinding, the bus lurched forward. Looking back, James gasped. The street was empty, and again that voice blocked out all thoughts. *I guide everything you do.*

'Hey there, have you fallen asleep?' Summer said, nudging him in the ribs.

'Oh, I'm just wondering where to start.'

Summer giggled. 'Three wise men in funny hats followed a star to a little stable in, where?'

'Bethlehem.'

'James Brennan, where were you born?'

'Sligo.'

'Cool, I like Sligo. And the not so virgin Mrs. Brennan turned to her husband . . .'

'Michael,' he replied, lost in her radiant smile.

'Clever boy,' she patted his head. 'Little James, ran around all of Sligo searching for his true love. He searched high and low, but he couldn't find her. Every Friday night he walked three miles to a disco, and sat in the corner drinking orange juice.'

'Coke. Get your facts right young lady.'

'James sat in the corner drinking from a bottle of milk his mammy had given him. On his eighteenth birthday, after drinking ten pints of unpasteurised from his daddy's cow, he stumbled home alone from the disco guided by the light of a full moon. God, in the guise of a Leprechaun, jumped out in front of him. "I can help you find your true love," he said, pulling a shamrock from his hat and handing it to a startled James. "But only if you become a priest will this come true. If you don't, you will never meet her." An enormous red-spotted mushroom sprouted up in the middle of the road, a pencil and paper sitting on top. "All you have to do is sign this." "Cool," James said, as he seized the pencil and scribbled his signature. Delighted, and not considering the implications, he shook hands with God and raced home to tell his mammy the good news.'

'Nearly true, except I've never met one of the little people.' His cheeks, sore from laughing, tingled as James explained. 'Apparently, a harvest moon shone the night I came into this world. Redder than your mushroom. My superstitious mother took it as a sign, an omen. Some of my earliest memories are of her calling me Father James and of the smell of cow muck from my father's wellingtons as he berated her for such nonsense.'

'Your brother died young. I hope you don't.'

'My bother?' replied James, perplexed. 'I'm an only child.'

Summer pointed a finger at him. 'Jesus.'

On some matters, intended humour cuts deeper than a blade. Rebuke for suggesting such blasphemy twisted his tongue, begging to be heard. His heart, softened by undeniable love, forced a forgiving smile. 'Funny idea. Suggest that to my mother, and she would weasel her way into sitting by the right hand of God for all eternity. I'm

James Brennan, only son of Michael and Sheila Brennan, conceived by natural means.'

Are you sure?

That annoying voice again.

Concern in the slight wrinkling of her eyes, in the tone of her voice, Summer clasped his hand in hers. 'Where is the James I fell in love with?'

'I'm here, and happier than I've ever been.' Glimpsing the houses thickening into an urban maze, he knew that beyond the approaching town of Naas, the better roads would whisk them to Dublin, where they would part.

'Cool, if it were true. Look at me!'

Startled by a tone he'd never heard escaping her lips, he turned.

'It's an artist's heart and mind that captures. My brush guided by an image only I could see, I painted the innocence of a man who bewitched me within his church. Please, tell me what happened to him. I want my Jamie back.'

James sighed, stared out onto the dual carriageway and gathered his thoughts. Summer held him with sympathetic hands. Leaving out no details, he told her of his guilt over falling in love, his anguish when she turned him away. She swore, when he detailed Sweeney's violence directed toward Sean, his manipulating ways, the meeting with the Bishop. Pausing for a moment, choosing words with care, he explained that twice he had denied her when Sweeney called her a whore, and Callum a bastard. He could feel her shake when he admitted that but for fate, he would now be hanging from the oak tree in Heffernan's meadow. Finally, he told her about the bus driver. Silence followed his harrowing story. Tears dribbled down his cheeks onto her tangled hair, hers dripped onto his lap.

'Sssh.' She wiped her eyes, and then his. 'What sort of beast could do such things to innocent children? You must report this.'

'I will.'

'Father Sweeney lied to me.'

James stiffened. 'Lied, to you?'

'I called to your house yesterday and asked him where you were. "Cork", he answered, after he called me a whore. "He's been sent far away from sluts like you." I cried on your doorstep when he slammed the door shut. Fearful, thinking I would never see you again, I decided to return to Dublin.'

'God, he is spiteful.' Violence, never beyond the nature of even the mildest of men, James slammed his fist into the seat in front.

Summer raised her hands. Making little fists, she shadowboxed. 'I'll punch Sweeney's nose. I'm sorry for making you suffer. I fell in love with you, with a priest who was bound to God. Seemed cool at first, but then common-sense kicked my ass, so, I kicked yours.'

'Ouch! What now? What is common-sense whispering into your ear?'

'Sorry. What? Did you say something? I'm deaf.'

Even though they were more strangers than lovers, desire strangled any barriers to what he wanted. For the first time in his life, a determination to follow his heart empowered his thoughts. Fearless of the consequences, he turned to her.

'Summer, will you marry me?'

Only someone who grasped life with open arms could giggle at such a serious moment. 'It's a miracle. I can hear. I've been cured.' She sought his lips, brushed them with a whisper of a kiss. 'Cool, Mrs. Jamie Brennan says yes . . . yes, yes, yes.'

'Can you wait until I've dealt with Sweeney,' James said, holding his breath.

'I need all of Jamie Brennan, not half the man.' Her breath caressing his overgrown locks, she said, 'When you are free, I'll be your virgin bride.'

Conscious of the teenagers in the back seats, they refrained from obvious intimacy, allowing their hands to couple in unity.

'Virgin bride? Where is my soon to be son, Callum?'

'He's with my parents in Dublin. My Dad forced me to return to Castlebridge. He said, "If I didn't return with you", he would disown me.'

Incredulous, James stared at Summer. 'He doesn't mind I'm a priest?'

'Mind! ' Summer slowly twisted a lock of her hair, absentmindedly curling it around her finger. 'My parents never left the sixties; existing still under a haze of cannabis and flower-power. "Cool", they said.'

'Heart attack, sudden, but not life-threatening. That will be my mother's reaction. Humiliation will haunt her. I expect a slap on the back from my father. Not immediately. Later when we are alone, he will creep up on the subject, as a mouse to cheese.'

'So different. Different is good,' she said, snuggling against his shoulder.

'We are nearing Dublin. I've to go home and give the last rites to a dying relative. Duty, confounded duty, I wish it were otherwise. At most, I'll be gone four days. Do you have a phone at your parent's home?'

'Yes.'

Taking his pen from his coat pocket, he wrote the number on the inside cover of his bible. Silence marked the rest of the journey. Cloaked in the loneliness of impending separation, they clutched each other's hands, only letting go when the bus stopped and the teenagers stirred, ready to disembark.

'Please, wait for me outside. I need to talk to the driver,' James said, releasing her hand.

One by one, passengers gathered their bags and left. James strolled to the front. Slumped over the steering wheel, Jack rested his head on his arms, staring straight ahead, as if his subconscious would announce the news all of the passengers had exited. Outside, Summer weaved through the crowds. In his eyes, she lit up the world, floating like a beacon in the sea of humanity.

'Jack!'

Pale from tiredness Jack lifted his head, straining to sit upright. 'Damn you, priest. Memories, forgotten bloody memories resurrected by you. All the way from fuckin' Castlebridge, mile after fuckin' mile they replayed in my head.'

'I'm sorry. Just one question, then I'll leave. In which parish did Sweeney abuse you?'

'Parish! From the age of six to when I ran away at nine, I lived in St. Patrick's Orphanage on the Northside. For three years, that bastard beat me because I refused to become one of his *special* boys. The more complaints I made, the worse the beatings. "Ungrateful liar," that was what they called me.'

Unsure of Jack's reaction, James placed a hand on his head. 'Lord, protect this child, give him peace, and me the strength to fight this injustice. Amen,'

Jack reached up. A spark of hope illuminated a face wracked with pain, he grasped James' arm. 'I've prayed every day since. I cursed a God I never believe existed. Maybe there is a God, maybe he heard my cries.'

'There is,' James said, adjusting the rucksack slung across his shoulder. 'Few priests are evil. Remember that. I can only promise, I'll not rest until Sweeney is punished.'

James removed his collar and shoved it inside his rucksack. He jumped from the bus and took his first steps toward freedom.

Chapter 13

They held hands, as any young lovers would, laughed and teased each other on their way to the train station. Being only a short distance from the city centre, afternoon shoppers thronged the streets. Summer pulled him toward a jewellery store window, and pointed to a velvet display of rings.

'Ooh,' she said.

'Agh' He'd spotted the price tags on the engagement rings, and feigned to walk away.

She pushed open the door and dragged him inside the narrow shop. Behind the counter, the grey-haired owner, sitting on a high stool, with a Loupe glass covering one eye, examined a watch. Without looking up, he muttered, 'Good afternoon.' He continued to work. Tightening a screw, the jeweller slid the cover onto the timepiece and pressed it into place. 'Won't keep you much longer,' he said. Twisting the winder, he set the time. 'What can I do for you young folks?'

Where could I possibly get so much money? Hands deep inside his pockets, James toyed with the three pennies. For the first time, he tasted economic reality.

After a moment's silence, Summer nudged him and giggled when he failed to respond. 'Jamie, wake up.'

'Oh, I'm sorry. Can we examine the diamond engagement rings from the window display?'

'Certainly.' The Jeweller reached under the counter, pressed a button. The lock on the door clicked shut.

Summer ran her finger along the rows of sparkling stones, while James stood in silence, reflecting on how surreal the moment seemed. Hovering over the most expensive ring, she plucked it out of the display case and slid it on her finger, easing it into position.

'Darling, I simply must have this one.' Lifting her hand, she thrust it under his nose for him to examine. 'I know you prefer the one for twice this price in the other shop, but I'm a simple girl. Really, I am.'

'Are you sure?'

'Yes, honey.' She stood upon her toes, reached round his neck and pressed her lips against his.

Promising to return the following week to purchase the ring, they shook hands with the owner before leaving.

Once outside, Summer laughed uncontrollably. 'When I get home, I'll paint your portrait, capturing your shock when I picked up that ring. Priceless.'

'Come, we must go.' James held her hand, and strode down the street, dragging his hapless, giggling fiancée along with him.

Crouched on the pavement at a street corner, a beggar clutched a crumpled brown paper bag, the neck of a bottle barely visible. By his side, a tin can invited loose change from passers-by. Most people passed without even glancing at the unfortunate man.

'So sad.' Summer squeezed James' arm. 'Can we help him?' she said, a slight tremor in her voice.

James pulled his wallet from his pocket, opened a zipped section he reserved for emergency funds, and pulled out a ten pound note. He kneeled, and looked into the vacant, sunken eyes of the drunk. 'Please, take this and buy some food.'

The old man gagged and spat on the pavement. 'Have ya a spare ciggy, Father?' He snatched the note and pushed the wine bottle toward James' lips. 'The blood of Christ.'

'How do you know I'm a priest?' James said, startled.

'Thief!' rasped the old man. He snatched back the bottle, rose and staggered away, leaving a trail of curses in his wake.

Shocked, Summer leaned closer to James and linked arms, 'So sad. That could be me or you.'

James shook his head and checked the time. 'I'm going to miss the train.'

They dashed the short distance to Connolly Station, purchased a ticket and sprinted to platform number two, getting there with minutes to spare. Wrapped in each other's arms, they kissed, enjoying a rare moment where the threat of scrutiny by others did not exist.

'Four days,' whispered James, pushing her hair back from glistening eyes.

'A lifetime. I may find another man to comfort me.'

They held hands and drifted in silence to the door of the train. Even as he mounted the steps, she clung to him. 'Ring me,' she begged, her fingers losing grip on his as he turned.

Outside, she followed his progress to the centre of the carriage. He slung his rucksack under the table, between two sets of facing seats, and sat at the window. She placed her hand against the glass and mouthed, 'I love you.' With his index finger, he drew several large X's on the grimy pane, then pouted his lips and blew a kiss. High into the air, she leapt, caught it, cupped it in her hands and slipped it into her jeans pocket. *God, I love this girl.* James reached into the rucksack, pulled out his collar and reattached it. Summer covered her eyes for a moment as if the collar blinded her. A number of passengers stopped at his seat. Each changed their mind and moved further up the carriage. One child sat, made a funny face, only to be dragged away by his mother.

Somewhere in the distance, a whistle blew. The carriage door closed, sealed him from the hubbub in the station. Outside, Summer was downcast, her arms folded, a shield against the knot in her stomach he knew would match his. Click-clack. The wheels turned and gathered momentum. She ran along the length of the platform waving. Then she was gone, leaving only her image captured in his mind.

James looked up as the door between the carriages slid open. Hung on square shoulders, a tweed jacket measured to within an inch of perfection announced its owner as a man of means. Beneath a dense mop of fair hair, a youthful face smiled as he stumbled up the swaying aisle. The man, drawing nearer, James realised the boyish looks were a facade, hiding a man of at least fifty. James nodded as the stranger slid onto the seat opposite.

'Drumcreevan,' he said, proffering his hand, and held James' in a firm handshake. 'Charles Drumcreevan. And you are?'

'James Brennan.'

'Father, I presume. Any relation to Brennan's Bread?'

'No relation. My family are farmers.' James would have preferred a solitary journey home, and time to reflect on unexpected happiness.

'That's a shame.' Lying back against the seat, Charles brushed grime from the knee of his slacks, a casual, practised flick of his hand. 'My baker declines any further custom from me. A trifling sum I assured him would be paid in due course. The short memory of people is a tad annoying. My grandfather funded his forebears business, and now, he insults me over a debt of three thousand.'

'Ungrateful.' James nodded, stifling a grin. *That is a lot of bread.*

'Quite. Tell me, James. May I call you, James?'

'Certainly, Charles,' James said, gobsmacked at his unintended aristocratic mimicry.

'Excellent. What is the main difference between Protestants and Catholics? Answer me, my learned priest.'

Reluctant to discuss religion, James replied as best he could without being rude. 'Apart from obvious religious differences, I suspect you have your own observations to share.'

'Quite perceptive. Money. Catholic people have a little. Protestants still pretend they have vaults full of the bloody stuff. Old money,

James, is long gone and with it, the alliances, inbreeding and civilised society.'

'Inbreeding?'

'Forgive my coarseness, but let me recount a tale from my youth. My mother insisted I marry my cousin, Winifred. "Family tradition," she said, standing beneath a portrait of *The Drumcreevan*, my great-great-great and a load more greats, grandfather. Bugger if I could argue, not with him glaring down at me. Six years old and I was engaged to a baby.'

'Six!' James laughed, and then held his hand over his mouth. 'Sorry, but that's funny. Getting engaged so young is unusual.'

'Not as strange as my wedding night,' he replied. His grin suggested he wished to tease James with subjects not usually discussed with priests. 'Just about to saddle up, I looked down at Wimpy's eager face, as she readied to *ooh* and *agh*. Protestant ladies of breeding practiced such things, you know.'

'I didn't know.' James reached up and opened the sliding window. The rush of cool air calmed his desire to kill any further conversation.

'I saw my grandfather Cecil's eyes staring up at me. The same mischievous glint, the same narrow, upturned nose, and the same-shaped lips that used to curl around the bugger's cigar. My shotgun was primed and ready to fire. Otherwise, I'd have leapt from the four-poster bed and hurled myself out the window. By God, she's a true Drumcreevan; kept me saddled up till the bloody cock crowed at dawn.'

James pulled the Bible from his rucksack and slid it across the table toward Charles. 'Protestants have a reputation for being honest. Swear on this Bible that your tale is true.'

Drumcreevan leaned forward. 'Ha!' His laugh turned heads at the far end of the carriage, and the thud with which his left hand landed on the good book drew a gasp from the ladies in the adjacent seats. 'I swear it all to be true, so help me God, Jesus, the Saints and all that malarkey.' He pushed the Bible back to James and folded his arms.

'Are you sure?'

'Bah, bloody priests.' With his right hand on the Holy Book, he whispered. 'All true, except for the bit about dawn.'

'I'm sure your wife doesn't look like a man.'

A smile curled Charles' lips. 'My wife, even in the autumn of her life, is one of the most beautiful women on these islands.'

'Are the rest of your family barmy?' James said.

Charles chuckled. 'Grandfather Cecil was the first lamb in a long line of black sheep. Truth be told, his four elder sisters were manlier. On the birth of Cecil, his father, Harold, filled the wine cellar with the finest of French wines. It is said, the party lasted a month. Do you like wine, James?'

'I don't drink.'

'Good God, are you dead?'

'I may be by the time the history lesson ends.'

'Cecil, or Cecily, as our family called him, liked playing with his sisters' dolls. When Harold tried to teach him to shoot, he dropped the gun, darted inside, and hid under the bloody bed. A Drumcreevan poof. Harold castigated his wife's bloodline, and she blamed the wet nurse. Between bouts of gout, Harold took up residence in the wine cellar, convinced he would never hold a grandchild bearing the Drumcreevan name.'

'See, you shouldn't drink,' James said. Despite his reluctance, he'd succumbed to the charm of the stranger.

'Ha! Cecily turned out to be more Cecil than many of my shadier ancestors. Thinking their virtue safe, enchanted by his poetry, ladies and wenches were lured to his bed. It seems all those years of undressing dolls paid dividends, the randy bugger. I've numerous uncles and aunts who do not exist on the official family tree. Paying them off nearly bankrupted the family. Records of them have been kept.'

'Really?' Surprised at this, James posed the question more in disbelief than curiosity.

'Damn right, we kept records. Drumcreevan started the practice hundreds of years ago. He insisted his offspring spread their lust, and paid the families of any progeny handsomely. "Every clan needs an army." That is our family motto, generally not mentioned in public, of course.'

'Have you many children?' The moment he asked, he knew the question carried unintentional daggers.

Charles stared out the window. 'Not Wimpy's fault. It seems the Drumcreevan line stops with me.'

'Sorry.' James wiped a bead of sweat from his brow. 'I can now answer your first question. Protestants talk more than Catholics.'

'Touché,' Charles said. He swivelled as the carriage door opened. 'Refreshments arrive.' He stood and stuck his hands in his trouser pockets, searched through his jacket and slumped onto the seat, seeming quite perplexed.

'Charles, will you dine with me?' James pulled a five-pound note from his wallet and dropped it on the table. 'Coffee and cake as a down payment for amusing stories, well told.'

'Even in these troubled economic times one can always depend on the charity of Rome. Thank you.'

Charles placed the order, handed over the fiver and graciously accepted the change which he slipped into his shirt pocket. He pulled a battered silver hip flask from his jacket and screwed off the lid. 'It's the last of the family silver, old boy. A nip of brandy in your coffee?'

'No thank you, Charles.'

'Tickets please.' The uniformed ticket collector shut the door with a thud.

Faster than a seasoned Guinness drinker, Charles downed the coffee, stripped off his jacket, folded it neatly, and laid it against the corner of his seat. With his head lying against the jacket, he crossed his arms, winked at James, and closed his eyes.

Glad to accept a moment of silence, James stared out the window, watching the countryside whiz by to the clicketty-clack of the wheels beneath. So much adventure in a single day, the day he had planned to die. Perhaps destiny had sent Charles to distract him during the journey home. A colourful character, from a once wealthy background, relying on his wits to survive. *I too must grasp opportunities, seize them, and live life as it is meant to be lived.*

'Hi,' James said.

'Sleeping beauty,' the ticket collector said, taking James' ticket and punching a hole in it. 'Sir!' A gentle nudge. 'Ticket please,' he shouted, shaking Charles.

'What? What?' Charles slowly opened his eyes and delivered the grand finale. 'Blast it, man. Must you be so rude?'

'Only doing me job,' he said, extending his hand. 'Ticket please.'

Out came the hip flask, a half smoked cigar and a handful of business cards, all dropped onto the table. 'Here we are,' Charles said, jubilantly, sliding a gold card across to the ticket collector. 'Father Brennan, you take this one.'

Lord Charles Drumcreevan. Drumcreevan Manor, nestled under an embossed coat-of- arms. The card impressed James, but he wondered how the railway employee would react.

The ticket collector pushed up his peaked cap, scratched his head with the ticket-punch, and tossed the card back on the table. 'I'd only ruin your card if I punched a hole in it. Twenty-eight years' service, only two more till I retire, and my unblemished record will remain that way. Ticket, please.'

'My good man, if you don't accept my card, I'll be doing the punching.'

'Shirr, either you have a proper ticket or ya buy one.'

'Lord Charles, permit me,' James said, pulling out his wallet. 'Ouch!' He reached down and rubbed his throbbing ankle that Charles had kicked.

'My dear ticket collector, rest your overworked legs for a minute,' ordered Charles, smoothing the faux-velvet seat beside him.

'Ticket, please, me Lordship, Shirr.' Clack, clack sang the punch.

'Which railway line is this?' said Charles.

'Dublin-Sligo, Shirr, as, your Lordship, well knows.'

Sipping his coffee, James observed the master craftsmen at work, the determined twinkle in the ticket-collector's eyes. Charles probed in a casual, assured manner. This railway employee had likely seen every trick possible, and stood stoically, resolved to deflect any suggestion other than the purchase of a ticket.

'*The Drumcreevan Line* is its original and more romantic name. Designed and built by my great, great-grandfather. Good God, he would turn in his grave, if he knew one of his kin was expected to carry cash about their person.'

'I am due a break, about . . . now,' the ticket collector said. He dropped onto the seat beside Charles. 'I'm Dan Flynn, a student of history during my free time.' To emphasise this sudden, unexpected civilian status, he removed the cap and laid it on the table. 'Now, Charles Hector Harold Drumcreevan, you were saying?'

'Ahem, my bloody throat is a little dry,' Charles rasped, reaching for his flask. 'Bugger, what was I saying?'

'Sir, your great, great-grandfather built, as you would say, bugger all. His coffin contains empty wine bottles. The good Father should take your confession.'

'Rubbish,' Charles said.

Flynn lifted his cap and wiped the railway badge with the sleeve of his shirt. 'His body was never recovered after he fell overboard whilst bound for South Africa.'

'You seem to know more than you should. Where are you from, Flynn?'

'Boyle, County Roscommon. I'll disembark there, as did my father and his father.'

'As you are a history student, I should imagine you can trace your family back a long way.'

'I can, Sir. Back as far as....'

'To Drumcreevan,' Charles said. Taking one sip, he handed the flask to Dan, who repeated the toast.

Dan lifted the gold card, punched a hole and stuck it in his shirt pocket. 'Take care, Father. Don't believe anything that comes out my distant cousin's mouth.' Locking eyes with Charles, they shook hands. Sticking his cap back on his head, Flynn left, calling, 'Tickets, please.'

Charles looked at James, and they both burst out laughing. With his aristocratic nose inches away from James' ear, he whispered. 'Brennan's Bread. Bring two loaves with you when you and your gorgeous girlfriend come and visit Druncreevan Manor. My castle is at your disposal, a refuge from those who would gaze down their snouts at you. Bring extra clothes. The bloody place is artic even in the summer.'

'I don't...'

'You do, and she is very pretty. Good God, what you do or don't do is no concern of mine. I've an empty, decaying bloody mansion in dire need of many things, above all, the sound of young people laughing. Do you fish?'

'Yes.'

'Good. Does your, ahem, sister drink wine?'

'I think she might.'

'It's decided then. Call me in the next week or two,' ordered Charles, as he pulled on his jacket. 'Agreed?'

He nodded.

'Boyle is the next station. Au revoir, Padre Brennan.'

He stood and turned to the elderly women in the adjacent seats. 'I can't sit with a homosexual priest for a moment longer. Buggering buggers, the lot of them. Good afternoon, ladies.'

Chapter 14

Alone again, James closed his eyes and tuned out the hubbub of the rumbling train. Surreal could not describe the day's events. Father Sweeney had cracked open Pandora's Box, and smothered James' innocence with his web of deceit. Facing such evil had nearly consumed him. Somehow, fate had intervened and steered him from self-destruction.

Determined to embrace life, with the image of Summer at the forefront of his thoughts, he dreamt of a future outside priesthood. Unable to formulate a plan, but believing their love would overcome any obstacles, James was convinced he could control his own destiny. Now his mind turned to the enormous hurdle he would soon have to leap over. How could he deal with his stubborn, colossus of a mother? Courage alone seemed an inadequate weapon.

Picture perfect, the tranquillity of Colooney Railway Station contrasted with the chaos encountered when embarking at Connolly. A uniformed employee stood outside the grey-stone station house, a green flag held against his leg, watching the train come to a halt. James stood, slung his rucksack over his shoulder and ambled toward the exit. He waited until the train lurched to a stop. Yanking the door open, he jumped onto the narrow flagstone platform, and slammed the door behind him. A crow, engrossed with pulling a worm from a gap in the stones, hopped away as James approached. It took flight and disappeared over the incline on the far side of the single track. A whistle sounded as James pushed the bright, red spring-loaded gate that gave access to a small car park.

As on every occasion when he returned home, the welcome sight of his father standing at his car, with the boot held open, gave him a sense of being part of this place. Michael Brennan, Mick to his small circle of friends, reached for his son's rucksack and dropped it in the boot. He pushed his cap upwards and scrutinised James, before breaking into an enormous grin.

'Welcome home, James. Skinnier, you've got. Mother will put meat on yer bones.'

'Da, ya don't look a day over seventy.'

Though it was an age-old joke between them, his father's frail appearance startled James. Many years of hard toil on the land had weathered his face and hunched his shoulders, but now as he approached his sixtieth birthday, the lack of sparkle, once so evident in his eyes, suggested old age loomed earlier than James expected. Affection was never mentioned in any conversation between them, nor an unnecessary cross word said in temper. A handshake, a reassuring pat on the back, or stopping for an ice cream on the way home from the mart, these forged the bonds that left James in no doubt of his father's undemanding love. Living under the shadow of his domineering wife, Mick shielded himself by his devotion to farming the land of his forefathers.

Mick turned the key, pumped hard on the accelerator, and swore, willing the stuttering engine to start. James tapped his father's shoulder. 'Can we talk?'

'Sure, son,' Mick said. He removed his hand from the gearstick and scratched his knee.

'I've met a girl. Her name is Summer. I'm leaving the priesthood.'

Mick turned to James. A quizzical look given, his forehead furrowed as he started the car, and drove out onto the main road. He remained tight-lipped.

James fidgeted with a button on his coat. Sorry for revealing his plans, yet determined to see it through, he remained calm, waiting for his father to say something. Anything. A single word of support would suffice.

Mick remained silent. Pulling off the main road to Sligo, they continued along a narrow, twisting country road, swerving occasionally to avoid the potholes. James panicked. Within three miles of home, and still his father had not uttered the words he longed to hear. Gears ground, and the exhaust pipe rattled in tune to Micks swearing as he urged the car up a steep hill. Both pulled down their visors to block the sunlight at the top. In continued silence, they descended into a narrow fertile valley, an oasis compared to the rugged landscape behind and in the mountainous distance beyond.

Ahead, James could see the winding course of the river that marked the boundary of his father's farm. Twisting along the edge of the distant wood, the watercourse straightened once it passed the far meadow, and vanishing from sight, reappeared as it neared the road. The car slowed. Mick steered it to a gravel verge near the bridge, switched off the engine and opened the door.

'Follow me,' he said.

Eager to look into *his* river, James hopped out and strode to stand on the bridge beside his dad. Shielding his eyes from the glare, he peered down into the rippling water. The barest shadowed movement of a small trout gladdened his heart, for nature's beauty always lifted him beyond the cumbersome realities of existence.

Mick cracked a match. His pipe lit, he lifted an arm, and pointed to the distant oak woods. 'Those trees were there when I was born. God willing, they will be there for more generations of Brennans. Do you know, someone offered me a small fortune for them?'

'No. You never said.'

'No matter. You love the girl?'

'I do.' James shuffled his feet on the gravel. 'There's something else you need to know.'

'Oh?'

'She has a six-year old son.'

'Yours?'

'Of course, it isn't mine. But... he will become Callum Brennan as soon as we get married.'

Mick hawked and spat into the river. 'James Patrick Brennan, my prayers have been answered.' Reaching over, he wrapped his arms around his son and hugged him for the first time since James was an infant. 'I have something to live for. I'll pray to God, you and Summer will have more children. One of them will inherit this farm. If not, then it will go to Callum.'

There were a thousand things James wanted to say, to tell his father. No explanation was required or wanted. 'How can I tell my mother?'

'Leave her to me. She will dress in black for a month or two, and the neighbours will make hay of it. No matter what she says or does to make you change your mind, be as stubborn as a donkey.'

† † †

One hurdle crossed, the car rumbled over the bridge, and they turned onto the stony road leading to the back of Brennan's two-storey, ivy-clad farmhouse. Halfway along, James spotted the expected movement low against the driver-side ditch.

'Go, Lad,' he shouted, excited.

Lad, their black sheepdog, waiting until the car drew level, darted out in front of them, barking, twisting, and tail wagging. James remembered the day he found him, lying on the road near the bridge. Little more than a pup, Lad was skeletal from neglect. He'd wrapped him in his coat, carried him home and nurtured the pup back to full fitness. That was the summer he boarded the bus bound for Maynooth. They rounded the house and stopped in the yard. Lad pawed at the passenger door, and once it was opened, fought his way onto James' lap to deliver a drooling welcome.

'Get out, ya daft beggar,' Mick said.

Outside the back door, Máire Brennan tossed handfuls of corn from a well in her gathered apron to her hungry flock of chickens. 'Chuck, chuck, chuck,' she sang, as she always did, joining the chorus of clucking from her appreciative birds. The hem of her apron lifted, she swung it in a wide arc, scattering the corn across the yard. James wondered whether one of their brethren roasted in the oven for the soon to be prodigal son.

Throughout his childhood, he paid scant attention to his mother's peculiar nodding when she spoke. For the first time, he realised she mimicked the movements of a pecking hen. Silvered hair draped loose over her shoulders, resembled the plumage of the bantam cock who eyed them suspiciously from his roost by a water barrel. Containing a grin, James looked at the ground as he approached her.

'Father James has come home to see his mother.' She made the sign of the cross and opened her arms to receive her son. 'God bless ya, Father James. 'Tis skinny you are, and what are those black rings around your eyes?' She tugged at his cheeks, nearly head butting him. 'Come inside, I've a lovely leg of lamb and your favourite roast spuds for ya. Michael, fetch a jug of spring water. Father James must be gagging for a sup after that long journey.'

'Mammy, you're looking well. How is Aunt Maggie? Should we go to the nursing home straight away?'

She dragged James inside and pushed him onto a chair at the kitchen table. 'Father, sit down there now, and don't be fretting about me. I'm as well as can be expected. Sure, isn't this life penance to get to the next?' She grabbed a plate before Michael had the jug on the table.

James stared at half a chicken, a side plate of vegetables and spuds, wondering what had become of the leg of lamb.

'Get that into you.'

Michael shrugged his shoulders as James gawped. 'Eat what you can. The dog will take what's left over.'

'I was thinking,' crowed his mother, placing her own meagre plate of food on the table, 'Ya might as well give Aunt Maggie the last rites while you're visiting.'

'Isn't she well?' asked James, winking at his father.

'These watery spuds need a pinch of salt.' She fetched the saltcellar and sprinkled every potato on the table, even the extra ones in the large saucepan for the hens. 'Poor Maggie, she's somewhere between this world and the next. I warned her not to be putting salt on her meat. The doctors told me as much after her last stroke, in confidence ya understand. Look at your poor father. The two of us are worn to a thread from the worry. If God doesn't take her soon, there won't be enough money left to bury her.'

'What age is she now?' James said, slipping a sizeable slice of chicken under the table to the dog.

'Sixty-four, and this morning she looked a hundred, till I brushed her hair. Those feckin' money-grabbing-bandits up at the nursing home couldn't look after a sick cat, never mind yer poor aunt.'

Mick coughed. 'She asked for you to say the last rites. Would you be able to do that, James?'

'Of course he will. Jesus, would ye get that dinner into ye or we will be too late.' She bolted to her bedroom, wardrobe doors slammed, and her cackled singing sent Lad cowering behind the turf bucket by the range. She reappeared minutes later dressed in her Sunday best. 'C'mon slow coaches. I'll re-heat dinner later for ye,' she said, dropping fresh tea towels over the steaming dinners.

Quicker than he had been dragged inside, she shoved him outside to the car.

'Wait a minute, me bladder is bursting.' James raced behind an outhouse. Even as he took aim at some nettles, and relief graced his face, he could hear his mother calling him to hurry. While pulling up his zip, James eyed the purpled clouds overhead. 'God, give me the gift of patience.'

'Father James, you sit in the front ... Now, tell your poor mother something. How long will it be before you become a bishop?'

Chapter 15

Máire warbled on about the lack of rain. His father took refuge beneath his peaked cap. James wondered had their conversations always been one-way traffic? Like the crops in his field, Mick yielded to whichever way the wind blew, went along with whatever she said. Yet, for all her faults, she was his mother; the glue which held the family together through the harsh years of the sixties and seventies when money was even scarcer than consecutive dry weeks. Eggs, chickens and apple tarts, sold once a week in a nearby village, supplemented his father's irregular income.

While Máire Brennan believed in the power of penance, chastisement and the church, Aunt Maggie rarely darkened its door. Life had dealt her a cruel blow, taking her husband a few months after they married. She cursed God, and swore an oath to taste all that life offered. Even while growing up, James knew of her reputation amongst the men of the parish. If mother had scolded, or taken the sally rod to his bare legs, Maggie miraculously appeared with sweets or some other treat. No two sisters could be so different. He loved them both.

'It's a sad day,' Máire said, pulling James away from his thoughts.

'We all die, sometime,' replied James, instinctively. 'Aunt Maggie will have few regrets. Don't you dare turn to keening while she still lives.'

A missed gear change followed his father's chuckle.

'Priest or not, I'll take sally out from behind the range if you order your poor, arthritic mother around. If your pestering aunt hadn't interfered in your upbringing, I'd have skelped more manners into you. Isn't that right, Michael?'

'Yer right, Máire. If Sally had swished more than she did, before you sold him to the bloody church, he might have run away and joined the army.'

'Michael James Brennan. Only the fear of snapping your twig-like legs prevented me from giving you as many lessons as James. Do ya hear that, Father James?'

'I do.'

'Have ya yer stole with you?'

'I have.'

'Holy oil?'

James groaned. 'Yes, Mam.' Groans turned to growls as one hand rounded the seat, pinning his head against the backrest, a second digging a comb into his scalp as his mother clucked.

'When did ya shave last? Maggie is nearly lying in repose, and you look like a homeless lad.' She yanked his head sideways, plastic teeth scraping flesh, as she sought his sideburns. 'We will be burying her on Tuesday. I've checked the weather forecast; hazy sunshine in the morning. After ya collect the suit and black dress from the cleaners tomorrow, yourself and your father will visit the barbers.'

Mick swung the wheel and nosed the car up the tarmacadam driveway to the nursing home. Handbrake pulled, engine switched off, he turned to Máire. 'Behave yourself woman, or ya will be walking home.'

James almost convulsed, shot his father a look of admiration and glanced at the rear-view mirror, seeing an open mouth squawk a plethora of obscenities that no decent Christian woman should manage in public.

'Holy Mary ...' Máire's flapping hands crisscrossed in a blessing. 'Michael Brennan, if I have to walk home, it will be to pack your battered suitcase.'

'Nonsense! woman, I packed it years ago.'

James laughed. The power of the troll beneath the bridge had diminished somewhat, suggesting his crossing should be easier when the time came.

Originally a three-bedroomed bungalow, the nursing home boasted multiple extensions, all erected with little thought beyond need. Yellowed paint flaked off the outside walls. A well-tended garden, its flower beds a swathe of colour surrounding a neatly cut lawn, almost made the place look hospitable. Mother led the way, pushing open the front door as though she owned the place. Mick followed in her shadow.

James, having forgotten his rucksack, retrieved it from the car and hurried after them. The aroma of disinfectant, mixed with bacon and cabbage, assaulted both his sense of smell and place. A picture of the Pope hung inside the door. A St. Brigid's cross lay on a table beside a vase of dahlias. His thoughts darkened at the similarity to the presbytery.

Rounding a corner, ahead, a frail old man hummed a tune as he inched along the corridor, frustrating Máire. She attempted to pass, but the walking-frame slid sideways blocking her. A rasping cough brought on by a bout of laughter, left the old-timer doubled over. Máire shot him a look so cold his teeth should have rattled.

'Bossy Brennan, went to town, riding on a donkey. Stuck a feather up her arse and thought she was a chicken.'

Though his legs wobbled, and his lungs wheezed from the effort, his aim was true. As Máire tried to push past his walking aid, he reached out, grabbed her bum and squeezed. 'Jesus,' he said, 'yer a sex bomb. Will ya give me a rubbing, ya fine thing, ya?'

James noticed the semblance of a smile curl his mother's lips. He grimaced when the old fella's shoulder caught the full force of her imitation-crocodile handbag.

'Go away ya dirty thing, Paddy O'Brien,' she cackled. 'Haven't ya better things to be doing, like dying or something?' Faster than should be possible in high heels, she tore off down the hallway and rounded another corner.

'Did ya see that assault on a pensioner, young man?' he croaked, looking directly at James through jaundiced eyes. 'When she was a slip of a lass, I wished I were ten years younger. Isn't that right, Mick?'

A small bottle pulled from inside his jacket, Mick slid it into the pocket of the old fella's dressing gown.

'Sláinte, Mick. I'll miss sharing a drop of this with Maggie. By God, even the stroke didn't prevent her from getting fierce randy with drink on her. I sat with her for an hour last night after the nurse fell asleep. It won't be long. Catch up with yer missus or there will be hell to pay.'

Mick nodded, gestured to James to hurry and followed the echoed tapping of heels on cheap Italian tiles.

Paddy tugged at James' sleeve. 'She has clung to life waiting for you, Father. Hold her hand when she passes.'

Death being a regular event in the life of any priest, James had become accustomed to consoling others. A sudden shiver unnerved him. The finality of Paddy's words shocked him into realising Aunt Maggie would be the first real loss in his life. 'I will,' he whispered, placing his hand on top of Paddy's. He scurried around the corner and saw his father standing at an open door, waiting for him.

Most succumb to silence in such circumstances as though the dying should spend their final moments lost in a sea of whispering. Not mother hen. 'Idiot nurses,' she screeched. ''Tis no way for anyone to die.' Light streamed into the room after she yanked the curtains open.

Aunt Maggie lay motionless on the bed, her face the colour of a duck egg. Shock rooting James to the spot, he tried to control his muffled sobs. In his mind, he always pictured a vibrant Maggie, smiling beneath tangled fair hair. Her quick wit and mischievous bent, ready to challenge any situation with zest. Could this fragile thing, this picture of gauntness beneath wisps of white hair, really be his aunt? Could this be the same woman, who had pelted eggs at the local priest, after he preached about harlots breaking up marriages?

He swallowed hard, listening, her shallow breaths cutting like daggers into his heart.

In a daze, James opened his rucksack, took out his stole and oil, and placed them on the end of the bed. Moving around to the side, he edged his way onto the duvet, and prayed silently for the strength he knew evaded him. 'Mam, Dad, please wait outside.'

Plucking dead leaves from roses in a vase near the window, his mother shot him an incredulous look. 'I'll be staying right where I am.'

Mick grasped his wife's arm and ushered her to the door, manoeuvred her outside, and closed it behind them. Her squealing drowned out, James pulled the stole over his shoulders and opened the jar.

A tender hand placed under his Aunt's skeletal fingers, he stroked the back of them with his thumb. 'Aunt Maggie,' he whispered, then louder. A slight tremor in her fingers, her hand tightened on his with an almost imperceptible squeeze. Dry, wizened lips widened, her eyelids twitched, but could not open beyond the width of blade of grass. In that moment, James knew that of all the wonders of the world, none compared to life itself.

Her lips trembled, the gap between them widened and, with breath gasped by lungs ready to yield to stillness, she whispered. 'Oh James, I cannot ... cannot see the blueness of your eyes.'

His body quivered as he leant closer. Painstakingly slow, her free hand worked its way to her neck, a finger sliding under her chain, revealed an engagement ring.

'Take this for your girlfriend.' Her eyes opened for an instant, merriment evident in her futile attempt to laugh.

Gobsmacked, he stared at the diamond, watching the fading light dance as the ring moved with each struggled breath.

'God loves sinners.' Her eyes opened a fraction, her voice firm. 'He guides all that you do.'

'What do you mean?' he sobbed, clutching her cold hand.

'Remember m ... me'

A decade of the rosary, said with jittering words, her forehead anointed with oil, he pressed his tremored lips to his stole, and then hers. 'How could I forget you?'

James sauntered to the window and gazed out at the setting sun, watching amber shadows creep eerily over the distant mountains. 'So long,' he said, drawing the curtains partially shut. He took a red rose from the vase and placed it by her still hand. His fingers shaking, he fumbled with the chain's clasp. Drawing it from her neck, he held the golden links and the ring in his fist. 'How could you know?'

I guide all that you do.

The voice, still echoing in his head, he opened the door.

Mother peered over his shoulder. Bringing her hand to her mouth, she blessed herself. 'Merciful Jesus.' She tore into the room, fell on her knees by the edge of the bed and began a decade of the Rosary, pausing after the first Mary. 'Mick, come here!'

James remained outside clutching the diamond ring, wishing Summer was by his side. In some ways, though more innocent than Maggie, they both exuded a similar joy for living.

His mother's wails, practised at a hundred wakes, followed his footsteps along the corridor as he searched for Paddy. Maybe, more in hope than certainty, Paddy had answers to impossible questions. After knocking on several doors, he eventually found the right room, and discovered him dozing on his bed.

'Paddy!' he called, tapping him lightly on the shoulder.

The old man stirred, pulled himself upright with a grunt. 'Is my Maggie gone?'

'Yes. Moments ago, without fuss and our goodbyes completed.'

Turning to gaze out his window, Paddy murmured, 'Buíochas le Dia. Thanks be to God.' He reached under his pillow, opened the bottle and nearly arsed the naggin of whiskey, offering James what was left.

Declining the alcohol, James opened his fist and showed Paddy the ring. 'She gave this to me. By any chance did she say why she wanted me to have it?'

A guffaw, followed by a wheezing cough, Paddy sunk the remaining whiskey. 'Here, take this bottle when you leave. Nurse Sweeney has a nose on her like a bloodhound.'

James stuffed the bottle in his rucksack. 'The ring?'

'She will be riding the Devil before the day is out.' He convulsed with laughter, then regained his composure.

'You mean dance with the devil, Paddy?'

'No. I cannot lie to a priest. Only last Thursday, two days before Maggie took a turn for the worse, we were enjoying a small tipple, and a wee cuddle. I made a fiver bet with her she would be riding the Devil before the month was out. Sure, we have been making bets like that for months, harmless fun to pass the time in this shithouse ...'

'And?'

'And! Bloody and, such a small word, loaded with a thousand questions. And, my young Bishop, the next day when I suggested amending the bet to a tenner, she flung a plate at me. Called me a heathen gobshite. Told me to beg God for forgiveness.'

'But ..'

'Exactly, Father. But, but, but. Did ya see the picture of the Pope inside the front door?'

James nodded.

'Well, that's the fifth one hung there in the last six months. Maggie disposed of the first five. The one there now was destined to be flung into the field behind here. Then she goes and finds God, or more likely, He found her. That's not only a miracle; it defies the feckin' laws of gravity, physics and goddamn common sense.'

'Did she mention the ring?'

'Mention it. She ranted on for an hour and a half that the ring was for your girlfriend, and if anything happened to her, I was to ensure your mother didn't get her hands on it. God told her you had one. Bonkers, she went bonkers. You better have a lady friend. And?'

James' mind raced, not able to comprehend what Paddy was trying to say, he tried to be funny, like Maggie. 'And, and if I knew you could keep your gob shut, I might say yes.'

'If you bring me another bottle, I'll not be one to spread rumours about a randy young priest, whom his aunt would be very proud of.'

'I'll make sure my father visits once or twice a month. God bless, Paddy.'

Hearing a commotion outside, James bid him farewell and made his way to the hallway. Arms flapping wildly, Máire screamed at a middle-aged nurse. 'One of ye robbed her engagement ring. I'll have the Garda in here tomorrow if it's not in my possession by midnight.' She jabbed her finger into the nurse's fob watch, and stormed to the front door.

Outside in the car, she continued with a volley of abuse, a tornado that no intervention could abate. A mile up the road, James could not listen to any more. Unclenching his fist, he dangled the ring and chain in front of his mother's nose.

'Thank God. Father James has brains. Give it to me.'

The diamond swinging from his fingers, disappearing into his closed palm, she snatched at air.

'Stop playing games, ya scallywag.'

'No games. I'll be keeping the ring.'

Máire giggled and punched Mick on the shoulder. 'Father James wants Maggie's ring. Did ya ever hear anything so daft? Sure, won't they give him one when they make him bishop?'

Mick glanced at his son, reached up and pulled his cap as low to his ears as it could go.

'Mam,' James said, swallowing twice before the words gushed from a mouth he could no longer keep shut, 'I'm engaged. The ring is for my girlfriend. I'm leaving the priesthood.'

He turned, ready for the expected onslaught. On the back seat, clutching her handbag, Máire folded her arms. Her lips crunched together so tight, they seemed like a single thread of rouge. Eyes which were usually set with accusation, looked right through him without as much as a blink to indicate he or she were still alive.

   Mick turned on the radio.

Chapter 16

Mother had the key to the back door. Determined to leave them standing for as long as possible, she rounded up the hens, and shooed them into the henhouse. Standing there for an age, she counted, under her breath, before closing the inner mesh gate, and slamming the outer door shut. At her approach, the bantam cock took flight, landing behind a bucket, and that was his first mistake. The second was to streak to the left when she feigned to go right, her outstretched arms and the bucket preventing an aerial escape. One step at a time, their mirrored waltz pushed the cockerel ever closer to the corner. Máire lunged, he squawked, and a flurry of feathers floated downwards as the captives' wings quietened into submission. Silence, no good night to her children this evening, no shout to warn the family of foxes down by the river that a shotgun would be their only welcome. As though they were invisible, she brushed past father and son, slipped a key into the keyhole and walked inside the house, soundless as a ghost.

No grin crossed their faces, though both glanced at the kennel by the sparse hedge, with similar thoughts. The doghouse they were about to enter seemed less hospitable. They were right.

Dishes clattered, cutlery rattled, and chairs moved backwards and forwards at a rate that would unsettle a poltergeist. Mick had the good fortune of being able to stoke the range, while James shifted uneasily on feet that knew not where to tread.

'Sit down, Son,' Mick said, shoving the cat off his own armchair. Back bent, he untied his boots, wriggled his toes and reached for his pipe.

James glowered at the apparition who zipped across the kitchen floor, her high heels playing a troubled tune on the flagstones. He collapsed onto the chair opposite his father, sighed, and waited for the dam to burst. What else could he do?

Sausages sizzled in the frying pan. A knife wielded with fury, sliced through homemade soda bread, and butter softened as she slapped it onto a dish. Eggs cracked, bacon crackled. Máire, in a haze of perpetual motion, scorned the men she loved, neither looking at them, nor acknowledging their existence. No Irish mammy, no matter the circumstances, would allow her menfolk go unfed. Duty, however, could morph into a lethal weapon. She wielded it with aplomb, and they knew it. The kettle whistled on the gas stove.

They sat in silence, broken only by forks scraping plates, cups clinking saucers, teeth grinding, and tongues licking runny egg yolk from lips. The antique clock, high on the mantle above the range, ticked. Father looked at son, son gazed at a fly buzzing around the light overhead, and mother, sitting as erect as the Queen who was not amused, scowled at both. Someone had to say something, and soon.

Guilt soured every morsel James chewed. Tea swallowed, swirled around with anxiety in the pit of his stomach. He placed a hand on the bulge in his trouser pocket, taking comfort from Maggie's ring beneath the cotton twill. Summer dancing through the meadow, the ring sparkling from her raised hand, her smile ... she waved at him.

'Damn you,' James shouted, shoving his plate to the centre of the table. 'Seven horrible years wasted just to please you. For what? So you could boast about your son, THE PRIEST. Not one day passed that I didn't want to quit. But, I couldn't. You, who burdened me with sufficient guilt to supress a lad for ten lifetimes, made sure I couldn't.'

Tears as false as her teeth flowed down Máire's cheeks. Sobs, the likes of which no Broadway actress could conjure, rose to a pitch that had the cat flee under the range. James squirmed on his seat, ashamed he had upset his mother, but remained resolute. Mick reached out, took her hand and held it.

'Why did you do this to me? And, poor Maggie, my only sister, gone this day. It must be God punishing me for your wickedness. It would have been better had he taken me instead of her.' She wiped her nose with the sleeve of her best dress, sniffling, sobbing and occasionally wailing. 'What will the neighbours think?'

Knowing someone intimately is to understand all they feel and how they think. Mick leaned toward Máire, placed a hand under her chin, and raised it. 'Summer is her name. She has a child, not James', but he will still be our grandchild, the first in a new generation of Brennans. Maybe the crib, hidden away in the corner of the attic, should get a new coat of varnish. What do ya think, my sweet?'

'Who is the father?'

James shuffled on his chair, 'She ...'

'Dead, Máire.' Mick glanced at his son. 'The poor lad was a missionary in Africa. Malaria took him, leaving poor wee Callum homeless, and Summer a young widow. Isn't that right, James?'

'Oh, that's so sad. Why didn't you say so, James? A saint ya are, giving up the chance of becoming the first Irish pope, choosing to rear an orphan instead. Come here and give granny a hug. I'll have a glass of sherry, Michael.'

James knew the truth needed to be told, but for the sake of peace, he would say nothing until after the funeral. If ever he needed a drink, it was now, and he almost accepted the whiskey his father offered him.

'To Maggie,' James said, raising his glass of orange juice.

Mother sipped her sherry, a picture of contentment. Then reality reared its head, calling her back to the present, and her position as chief mourner at Maggie's funeral. Her plans formulated months ago, she pulled a notebook from a drawer and put on her reading glasses. Phone calls made, one after another, spread the sad news of Maggie's passing. Those tasked with helping with the arrangements were given precise instructions, often repeated.

His father dozed on his chair. How much older he seemed to have become since his last visit home. As far back as James could remember, everyone told him he was the spit of Mick, except his mother, who claimed he was the image of her father.

Thinking his revelations and his father's little lie had been too easily accepted, he eavesdropped on his mother's nattering on the phone. With each call, his suspicions gathered form and the edgier he became. Mother never mentioned him or Summer, nor the possibility she could quite soon become a grandmother. Mother rarely missed Mass, and never, ever, spurned an opportunity to boast. Now, her shadow loomed larger than ever over his conscience. Thinking he would need to probe a little, he asked himself, what would the scheming Drumcreevan do in such circumstances? "Bugger it, Mother, the silly wench has got herself pregnant. How? I don't know. Had WE any money, I'd pay her off and avoid scandal. We shall have to pull a wedding dress from some dusty wardrobe. What a bother."

'Mam,' James said standing up, 'I'll be off to bed if that's okay.'

Máire peered at him over her glasses, a fleeting scowl replaced by a kind look. 'Sure, you must be knackered. Would you like a cup of hot milk?'

'No thanks. It will be hard to sleep, thinking about Maggie.' Legs numbed from sitting, he stumbled over to where she sat, leaned down and kissed her cheek. Goodnight, Mother.'

'Goodnight, ... Father Brennan,' she replied, turned away and lifted the receiver to make another call.

No probing would be necessary. With that niggling thought, he grabbed his rucksack and trudged upstairs to the bedroom which had been decorated by his mother. A picture of the sacred heart centred on one white wall, faced a wooden cross hanging above the bed. Beside the bedside lamp on a wooden locker, arranged square, a leather-bound bible, recently dusted by the look of it, made James wince. The rucksack dropped to the floor, he stepped to the window and stargazed, as he had done so many times as a child.

He grasped each curtain, drew them shut with such venom, he risked yanking the pole from its fastenings. 'Bugger.' He slumped onto the bed, reached into his pocket and withdrew the ring and chain. 'Goodnight, Summer.' Exhausted, sleep came quick.

Chapter 17

Muffled voices, Lad barking, and the distant braying of a neighbour's donkey stirred James. Reluctant to lift his head from the goose-feathered pillow, he stared at the ceiling, tracing the path of a hairline crack. Like his life until now, controlled by outside forces, it ran a jagged route from the door toward the window. Certain of a busy day ahead, he swung his legs off the bed and stretched. Jeans and tee-shirt chosen, he yawned as he made his way to the bathroom.

'Is that you, Father Brennan?' shouted his mother from downstairs after the floorboards creaked.

'No, it's James.'

Mick, sitting by the range, nodded as James entered the kitchen. His unlit pipe held between clenched teeth, he polished his black shoes. Over and back, twisting and turning the brush until all but the soles were coated. A ritual James had witnessed a hundred times as a child, his father placed the shoes under the range, lit his pipe, and settled back into the armchair.

'Son, look after your shoes and they will look after yer feet. I'll do yours if you fetch them for me after yer breakfast.'

'Thanks, Dad. Where's mother?'

'Letting out the hens.'

'Someone has to work around here,' she cackled, standing at the kitchen door. 'Good morning, Father James. While I'm cooking ya a nice breakfast ya can go back upstairs and get dressed.'

'I am dressed.'

'Yer not. The neighbours will be calling within the hour to pay their respects, and if you have any for me, you'll do as yer told.'

'No.' The word had escaped despite his instinct to comply. Bravery shrivelled at the narrowing of his mother's eyes and the disbelief on his father's face. 'No need to panic. I'll dress suitably after I've had breakfast and shaved.'

He returned upstairs and retrieved his shoes. Dropping them on the floor in front of his father, he noticed a few lipstick-smudged cigarette butts by the side of the solid-fuel cooker. Either his father had a girlfriend, developed a strange fetish, or ... Mother who ... who was without sin...

Michael kicked James on the ankle, and shook his head. 'Say nothing.'

James pulled out a chair from the table and sat, his appetite teased by the sizzling rashers. She pushed them to the rear of the pan. Then, with a deft touch, she cracked open an egg and discarded the shell. James noticed the change in his mother. She appeared to stoop more than his last visit. Her steps had become slower, more measured. Like Aunt Maggie, as his grandfather often said, she had legs like a stork. While Maggie kicked her skirts a little higher at the dances, both sisters could glide across the floor as though carried by fairy dust or vodka. James could imagine the short-trousers on the boy he had been, sipping a cola in the corner at some event, perhaps a wedding. Out on the dance floor, beneath the crystal ball, the adults waltzed and jigged. He recalled becoming dizzy watching them. Too much sugar from the fizzy drink.

'What's that older priest like?' asked his father, peering at James through a cloud of smoke.

'A bastard. Apart from that, he looks the same as every other priest.'

'That's a terrible thing to say,' Máire said, placing the plate in front of James. 'I taught you to have respect for your elders. Didn't I, Michael?'

'Ya did, Máire. But, when you weren't looking, I taught him to be honest. Sure, half the feckin' priests between here and Rome think they are more important than the likes of us. And, some of them are queers. At least we know James likes girls.'

'Shut your foul mouth, Michael Brennan. Me poor sister is dead, and here you are saying daft things about the clergy. Have ya no shame? And yer own son a priest.' She leaned over the table and plopped a second egg onto her son's plate. 'Eat yer breakfast, Father James, and put your collar on.'

An hour later, the sound of car tyres crunching on gravel reached the backyard. Máire, in a flurry of skirt, raced inside. She tore off her garish apron, shoved it under the cushion on the armchair, and dragged the chair close to the range. A large box of tissues taken from a press, she teased one out, sat, and clutched it as though her life depended on it. Like their car, she struggled to get started, but soon she keened as well as anyone with the gift. A small mound of crumpled paper on the top of the range greeted the first neighbours, who were considerate enough to bring their own supplies.

'It's a sad day.'
'It is.'
'I hear she went peacefully.'
'She did.'
'It's a good turn out.'
'It is. Sure, it's nearly as good as Nancy O'Brien's last year.'

James rolled his eyes as his mother wailed, aided by the older neighbours and friends. When a lull descended and everyone wiped their eyes, someone told a funny story about Maggie. One after another, tales washed clean of her irreverent lifestyle, were told.

'She is in heaven with her mother.'
'She is. Thanks be to God. *Buíochas le dia*. Máire will be lost without her.'

Loaves of buttered bread moved down the conveyor-belt of hands at the kitchen table. Thick cuts of ham awaited a smear of mustard. Square cheese slices, removed from plastic wrapping, were placed between slices of white bread. Kettles boiled, teapots steamed. The younger girls, ordered to keep the dishes washed, giggled each time James passed them dirty crockery and glasses.

Men surrounded the back door, half in, half out, ready to escape. They could well have been at Mass. Cigarettes were held behind their backs and a glass of whiskey in their drinking hand kept conversations lively. Between discussions on the weather, the price of cattle and football, Maggie was remembered, fondly by most of the menfolk. A few wept in public.

Some ladies, the wives of these grief-stricken gentlemen, were chirpy given the solemnity of the occasion. While their tongues said nice things about Maggie, the sarcasm in their voices peeled louder than the church bell.

James shook many hands, promised to say a Mass for half the parish and, at one point, nearly cried. That would come later. He cringed at the reverence with which they treated him, wishing they would see him as James and not Father. Soon they would have no choice.

Midday came and went, and with it, a changing of the guard. Younger mothers left, needing to get dinners ready for children. The matriarchs of the parish arrived, most driven by their sons in various outfits of work clothes. With one foot of theirs in the grave, old scores were aired, settled and put to rest. By early evening, all concerned, agreed Maggie was a saintly woman whom the gossipers had bad-mouthed – which was just as well, for Father Hickey arrived at six PM to say a decade of the Rosary.

Máire shoved James toward Father Hickey, her makeup-streaked face glorying in the moment. Her only son was a priest.

Hail Mary, full...

Rosary beads placed back in his pocket, Father Hickey sunk the large whiskey Máire poured for him. 'Sláinte,' he said, guiding the glass back to the bottle for Máire to refill. 'I hear,' he said, so loud, all eyes turned in their direction, 'you are still a teetotaller, Father James.'

'I am,' James said. He shuffled his feet. Seeing Eric O'Malley crane his neck around the backdoor and stick out his tongue, he struggled to keep a straight face.

'Good, lad. Sure, a few more years in this job will change your thirst.'

'It won't,' snapped James, seeing in Father Hickey the same bullying attitude as Sweeney. 'I ...'

Michael squeezed his arm. 'We will miss Maggie, Father Hickey. You will too.'

James noticed the slight panic in the older priest as he lifted the glass to his lips. *Oh, Maggie. Had you no shame?* James wasn't the only cleric to fancy someone from the fairer sex. He glanced at his father. Both laughed.

Hickey handed James the empty glass. 'I best be off. God bless you all. Father Brennan, you might walk me to my car.'

Lad raced to and fro, straining against the rope that tethered him to a rusty hook driven into the side of the henhouse. 'Sit,' ordered James. Lad dropped to the ground, and crouched, eager for the next command. Panting, his dark eyes gleamed in the evening light. He inched forward as James approached.

'Good boy,' James said. He reached down and patted the dog's head. 'Do you like dogs, Father Hickey?'

'I loved your Aunt.'

'What?' James said, looking up. 'She hated the church.'

Father Hickey strode toward his car, which he had parked a short distance from the henhouse. He opened the boot and reached inside. 'Come here.'

Doing as bid, James traipsed to the car and stood beside the older priest. Hickey pointed to a neatly folded wedding dress lying on brown paper in the boot.

'What the ...' James said.

'I drove to Dublin to help her choose this dress. She ...' he pulled a handkerchief from his pocket, dabbed his eyes and blew his nose, 'she was so beautiful standing there in front of me, running her hands provocatively down her hips, smirking at my unease. I could have squeezed the life out of her with a hug. I loved the bones of her.'

'What happened? And, why are you telling me this?' James said.

Father Hickey closed the boot. He toyed with the car keys, then faced away from James. His shoulders shook uncontrollably as one muffled sob followed another. Lashing out at a stone with his left foot, he kicked it up the yard, startling the hens.

'Cowardice,' he whispered, twisting about so slowly he could have been the hour hand upon a clock. 'I feared Rome. More than that, I could not face the gossip and the hate that would surely follow us. I was too weak. Now ... now she is gone, forever. That was over twenty years ago, yet the pain and regret never left me. God forgive me. That's why Maggie hated the church. It robbed her of a second chance at love. Every affair she had after that, mostly with married men, made me weep. Each one cut like a crown of thorns.'

James placed a hand on Hickey's shoulder. 'If Maggie loved you,' he said, his voice filled with kindness, 'you must be a good man. You cannot carry the guilt any longer. I understand the dilemma you faced.'

'I don't,' Father Hickey said. He wiped his eyes and smiled. 'We sort of wed three weeks ago. Just Maggie in that dress, me without a collar, and Paddy O'Brien in his dressing gown saying the few words I wrote for him. No, we didn't, in case that's what you are thinking. God knows. It will cost me a bottle of whiskey a week to buy Paddy's silence.'

A chair, a stool, even a wooden box would do. With nowhere to sit, James edged to the front of the vehicle, and rested his arms on the bonnet. He dropped his chin onto steepled hands, and gazed over the fence, across the darkening fields beyond. Cattle grazed, sheep huddled against a ditch, and life went on, the natural world oblivious to the traumas endured by men like James and Hickey. 'Why are you telling me all this?'

Father Hickey flicked a squashed insect off the windscreen, leaving a slight smudge, which he removed with his thumb. His laugh came from deep within, as though he had planned this moment in fine detail. 'Once a rat, always a rat,' he said, pausing to scratch his nose. 'Maggie asked me to look out for you, to keep you safe if I could. I can still smell her perfume. Isn't that strange?'

'Very. And have you kept me safe?'

'Ha! Aren't you alive? I have eyes and ears in Castlebridge.'

'Father Sweeney?'

As dramatic as he could, it seemed to James; Hickey hawked and sent the spiralling phlegm over the fence. 'That would be like having a wolf shepherd the sheep. No, it is someone I trust. When you escape from that place, I'll tell you stories about Sweeney that will raise the hairs on your arms.'

James stood, grabbed Hickey's arm and pulled him close. 'What should I know about that bastard? Tell me. Tell me, now!'

Stern-faced, the older man stared at James, pondering. 'Another time, perhaps in a few weeks after the loss of Maggie is less painful.'

'Okay,' James said, softly. 'Sorry for being so brash. If only you knew ...'

'I know enough. The dress is for your girlfriend. Maggie wanted you to have it. Do not become a sour old priest. Marry the girl.' He offered his hand to James. 'No more questions until the time is right. Agreed?'

'Yes.'

'I'm sorry,' he said, opening the car door. 'Máire is very persuasive and mind-numbingly persistent. Her constant nattering forced me to arrange a place in the seminary for you. Maggie, my dear Maggie, she made the slates on the roof of the church rattle with her cursing.' He shook his head, sat inside and closed the door.

Hands buried in his pockets, James stepped back from the car. The thousand unanswered questions on his tongue would have to wait. Father Hickey started the engine, waved and drove off.

James turned and sloped toward the gate. It clanged as he opened and closed it behind him. From there, lost in his thoughts, he wandered down to the river. In the privacy beneath the branches of a sycamore, he wept, and he laughed. *Summer is so much like Maggie. I'll not let either of them down.*

'James. Father James.' Distant, unmistakeable, his mother's voice carried far in the stillness of the evening. It knocked the breath out of him. His shoulders sagged as he traipsed through the shadowed meadow, past the skeletal remains of an ancient tractor. Duty called him home. For now, he obeyed.

Chapter 18

Conscious of how painful a ceremony it would be for Father Hickey to officiate, but much to the delight of Máire, James offered to assist. Loud coughing, whispered conversations, and an occasional laugh washed over the crowded church. Pews were crammed and standing mourners occupied every available tile of floor space. Many of the men, used to hiding in relative safety near the back, now shuffled awkwardly in the centre aisle. Even though all the doors and a few windows had been opened, sweaty vapours and other more earthly smells from farmers' wellies, added to James' discomfort in wearing a borrowed cassock two sizes too small.

Despite his own sense of loss, James drew strength from Maggie's indomitable spirit, choosing to celebrate her colourful life rather than wallow in grief. She had a large circle of friends and a few enemies, but not this many. He wondered how many had come to gossip and to ferret out the names of lovers hitherto unknown. A swift scan of those with the best seats, revealed a nest of chinwaggers, all nattering, smirking and finger pointing. In front of the altar, her simple coffin remained the focus of her closest friends. James could see the genuine grief in many faces as they stared, dropped their gaze to the floor or dabbed the tears from reddened eyes.

While he awaited the arrival of Father Hickey, a commotion in the centre aisle caught his attention. Definitely masculine, a grey head bobbed up and down as someone barged a route through the crowd. More than one misplaced profanity had the older ladies gasping in shock. Paddy O'Brien, the legs of his striped pyjamas flapping beneath his long winter coat, emerged near the coffin. Probably fortified by whiskey, he seemed oblivious to those smirking at his attire. He clutched a gilt-edged picture frame. Paddy halted at the foot of the coffin, bowed, and then placed the picture onto it. The image faced the bemused congregation. An about turn, heels clicked in military fashion, he marched to the front pew, and squeezed his way between Michael and an irate Máire.

James recognised the signals his mother made. First, her arms flapped wildly, her top false teeth edged out over her bottom lip, and finally, her eyes bulged with a fury no man could calm. Máire jumped to her feet, slapped Paddy across the face and lurched toward the coffin. With both hands, she seized the picture and slammed it down with such venom that Maggie must have heard the racket from the hereafter. While the echo still resonated around the church, she turned and scowled.

Throughout the church, tittering, soft at first, grew louder when Paddy lurched to his feet and faced the people. 'Show some respect.' He shuffled toward the coffin, shouldering Máire out of his way. 'It was Maggie's dying wish,' he said, lifting the photo. 'If anyone touches this photo again, I'll beat the bejesus out of them.' This time, he marched to the side of the church and fought his way onto a seat far away from Máire. Behind him, Sheila Gillespie's flowery hat danced on her head to the beat of her braying laughter. Her elderly mother, clearly disgusted by such a display in church, buried her arthritic elbow into Sheila's ribs. Her squeals sent further ripples of laughter all the way to the font at the back.

'Imbecile,' hissed mother hen as she returned to her seat. Wings folded, head up, she stared at the golden cross standing tall behind the altar.

The storm had passed without drawing blood. James felt like a hare at a hunt. Every sense on high alert, he stepped closer to the lectern, aware his reaction would be scrutinised. Unable to concentrate, he edged his way to the front pew on the far side of the aisle from his mother. 'Thank you for coming.' He shook hands with the Clancy's from Ballisodare, distant relations, whose existence Máire refused to acknowledge. 'God bless her, she is at peace.'

Satisfied no one had seen through this subterfuge, he turned to look at the offending picture. Mirth bubbling in his belly spread to his shoulders and cheeks. He burst out laughing, unable to take his eyes from the photo of the Pope, whose upper lip had been enhanced with a Hitler moustache. *Maggie, you are, were, a gem.*

A diplomat in the making, he turned the photo sideways and returned to the altar. Máire glared in his direction. Paddy howled with laughter. Tempted to stick out his tongue, propriety demanded James respond with a passive, saintly face. The door of the Sacristy closed, Father Hickey took his place before the altar.

† † †

The formalities completed, Maggie lay at rest in the graveyard. Many mourners adjourned to the Broken Jug. Plates of sandwiches and hot cocktail sausages were scoffed, even the crumbs. Elderly ladies sipped tea in the lounge, discussing Paddy's disgraceful behaviour. Many of the men driven demented by thirst, crowded around the bar, shouting over each other's heads at Eugene, the beleaguered barman.

'No point in me asking, is there?' said Rossa O'Flaherty, when James approached. 'Eugene, fill a pint of coke for Pope Brennan. Pull a real pint for myself.'

The nicknames had started at primary school, where James and Rossa had sat side-by-side for eight years. After the Bishop patted James' head during a visit to the school, Rossa gave James the nickname, *Bishop Brennan*. Two years later, James became an altar boy. To celebrate, Rossa and a group of older lads shoved his head down a toilet, and flushing the cistern, baptised him Cardinal Brennan. Upward, being the only route possible, when he was ordained a priest, Rossa declared James the first Irish Pope.

Retreating to a corner away from the din, they sat at a low table. Rossa still carried the scars of a spotty adolescence beneath his scruffy, dark hair. While the welts on James' hands had long since disappeared, Rossa's bore testimony to the cutting edge of a schoolteacher's ruler. They had been inseparable, except when best friend enraged the teacher. Fear of his mother's wrath ensured James vamoosed when trouble brewed. Rossa had flummoxed all his friends when he chose a teaching career.

'Well, Professor O'Flaherty, the summer will soon be over,' James said.

'It is. Three more weeks and I'll be skinning the arses off those reprobates with my recently acquired cane.'

'What?' James said, remembering the image of Sean cowering in the Sacristy, and the mutilation on the bus driver's back. He grabbed his friend's jumper. 'How could you aft—'

'Relax, Your Holiness. I've never laid a finger on any child, never will. Jesus, you are as uptight as your mother.'

Lowering his voice, James leaned in close to his friend. 'I suspect the parish priest in Castlebridge is bullying the altar boys. Sweeney has done it before. Years ago, he tortured at least one lad in an orphanage. I've seen the scarred back of that abused orphan.'

Rossa sunk half his pint, lit a cigarette, and inhaled. 'I deserved to be caned occasionally for the way I misbehaved at school. To tell you the truth, only once did our teacher lose his temper and strike me with any venom. The welts on my hand are a constant reminder of the ass I once was. In fairness to Master Seamus, I'd told him his wife was uglier than Nelligan's goat.'

'And that was one ugly goat,' James said.

'It was. What are you going to do about this thug?'

'I'll see him punished before I get married.'

With the pint glass touching his lips, Rossa spluttered, spraying Guinness across the table. 'What the fuck? Married.'

'Quiet, it's not to be broadcast until I am least halfway back to Castlebridge.'

'Is she pregnant?'

'No.'

Rossa pulled a stumpy pencil from an inside pocket of his tatty, tweed jacket and scratched his stubbly chin with it. 'Is she already wed?'

'Stop it. Of course she isn't married. If she was, I couldn't marry her.'

'True. James and Mrs Brennan, I pronounce you Pope and wife. Holy shit, what did your mother say?'

'Not much. A sudden heart attack followed by a bout of amnesia. As though I never mentioned it. Summer is my girlfriend's name, and Callum is her son.'

At that revelation, the pencil nearly vanished up one of Rossa's nostrils bringing tears to mirthful eyes. 'Hear ye. Hear ye. The Pontiff has a son. In the last days of the Catholic Church, while the seven horsemen of the apocalypse streaked across the heavens, Pope Brennan and his son went fishing. Cardinals cried tears of blood. Meanwhile, Rossa, of the clan Flaherty, sat at the bar drinking his way to oblivion. The end of days is upon us. Amen and all that shite. Dear James, please explain, because thy atheist friend is much confused.'

'Some other time', James said, rising to his feet. 'By the way, how are ya fixed to be best man at the wedding?

'By God, my speech will shake your mother's false teeth from her rimstone gob. I can't wait.'

'Up off yer arses.' Slurred words emanated from someone near the counter. Tables rattled, glasses clinked and a stool overturned as a few stood, raised their glasses, cups, saucers and bottles. 'Get up, ye lazy fuckers.'

Completely out of step with each other, they shouted. 'Maggie. May she rest in peace. Sláinte.'

Down the back of the pub, twenty-six-year old Derek "Duxy" Daly, twisted from the drink and grief, roared, 'She was the best ride around.'

Máire jumped to her feet. Using a technique resembling that of a hammer thrower in the Olympics, she pirouetted and swung her handbag at Daly. Luckier than a black cat, Duxy ducked to pick up his smouldering fag off the carpet. Carried forward by the momentum of her swing, Máire fell on top of him. Entwined in a deadly embrace, Duxy took one look at the assassin's face, hovering inches over his. 'Rape!'

Chapter 19

With his own heartbeat ringing in his ears, bus driver Jack O'Brien listened intently. Beads of sweat formed on his frowning forehead. What was the noise that awoke him from the incessant nightmares?

Someone rapped on the front door. Who?

Exhausted, his cognitive senses barely registered the ringing of the doorbell. A sudden recollection returned him to reality. Pizza, he'd ordered a medium Ham and Mushroom. Always, Ham and Mushroom. But, that was yesterday, wasn't it? Not sure, Jack clutched his head, reaching for a memory that faded before he could grasp it. To and fro, he rocked, whimpering as the bell chimed again, and again. *Pizza. Jack, you ordered one. Pull yourself up, answer the front door. It's not the monster ... he's in Castlebridge. Are you sure? Yes. Dammit. Yes.*

Afraid of cramping, he eased his urine-dampened legs straighter, twisted sideways and, groped for the door-handle. So much easier to curl up into a ball and succumb to the sweet darkness that engulfed him. Jack opened his eyes, turned the handle and pushed open the triangular door. Light pierced his cubbyhole beneath the stairs. Pausing for a moment, his eyes blinked, adjusting. He crawled to the opening, fearful. Inching forward, he watched shadows dance on the wall opposite. None took the shape of the priest, his spiteful whip, or worse. Glancing left, then right, he scanned the front hall of his terraced house.

Sucking air through clenched teeth, and exhaling in measured whispers, he advanced into the vastness of the passage. As usual, using the radiator for support, his knees creaked when he stood. Unsteady, he lurched toward the front door. His right eye pressed against the security peephole, Jack took a deep breath and peered out. Beneath the magnified motif of a chief in full headdress, the legend Indian Pizza in bright red lettering printed on the back of the retreating delivery boy, reassured Jack it was safe to open the door.

One, two, three, he slid the bolts back. One, two, three, he unlatched the chains. He pulled the keys from his pocket, and let them dangle by his side, hanging on a bungee cord. From the hall table, he pulled a cigarette box from a neat line of similar boxes. He tipped the contents into his hand. Four pounds, and a fifty pence piece for the tip. One, two, three, starting at the lowest keyhole, he unlocked the door. One, two, three deep breaths later, he opened the door. Dazzled by the late evening sunshine, he shaded his eyes with a hand.

'Thanks, Ado,' he said, offering payment, and took the box. 'Sorry, I was in the loo.'

'No bother. What's the story? Have ya a dose of the runs lately?'

'I have, caused by your bleedin' pizza.'

'My arse. What's up, Jack? You're not your usual cheery self.'

'A touch of the flu. See ya later.'

Jack surveyed the road outside as Ado returned to his rusty van, noting any vehicles he didn't recognise. Back in the house, the locks, bolts and chains secured him from the outside world. Nothing could shield him from his memories, old nightmares recently resurrected by Father Brennan. For the past three days, he'd not gone to work. Sinking further and further into the mire, into that darkest place, where guilt ruled. Flashbacks robbed his sanity. Taking him back to St. Patrick's Orphanage, to when he was seven.

With a sweep of his arm, he cleared the table, sending the stale remnants of last night's pizza onto the floor. From a corner press, he retrieved a dusty blue metal box, placed it on the table, and sat. His fingers worried his mouth while he contemplated lifting the lid and releasing what lurked inside. Left with little choice, Jack knew he had but one way to purge his guilt, a temporary solution to a lifelong problem. With the fourth and only other key on his bungee cord, he opened the box. A single tear edged from the corner of his eye. One, two, three, he waited, reached for the contents, a diary and a stone. In his right hand, between whitened knuckles, he gripped the stone. He held the diary tight to his chest. No need to open it. He knew its contents by heart. Jack closed his eyes and journeyed back, reliving moments that should never be remembered.

Waking, listening to the whimpering of that night's chosen one, Sweeney's chosen one. Not then, not now, no suffocating pillows could drown out the anguish, Sweeney's lies, or the ticking of the clock in the dormitory.

At first, there were boxes of chocolates, a trip to the zoo with two other newly-orphaned boys, freckle-faced twins from Kilkenny, Sam and Ginger. Then it began. At night. We said our prayers before bed. Something horrible would happen to one of us. We'd heard the others whispering, the screams, the sobbing. We didn't understand. How could we?

Ginger was first. Sweeney smiled as he led him from his bed, holding his hand. An innocent lost to evil. Sam's turn came the following night. Paler than the sheet of his bed, I can see his pleading face turn to his sobbing brother, then to me. I awaited my turn, determined.

Wraith-like, he came like a shadow from hell. The silver cross on his chest shimmered under the light of his flickering candle. Through the thin blankets, it loomed over me, dancing. Petrified, I clutched the jagged stone hidden in my left hand. Slow, slower than the minute hand on the clock, he teased back the blanket, and reached for my sweaty hand, which held onto a corner. Urine trickled down my thigh.

Eyes, evil eyes beguiling me to believe no harm would come my way. I suspected different. He led me away, along the creepy corridor, down the stone staircase to his special, dank room in the basement.

I cannot rid my mind of the foul smell of his tobacco, mingled with cheap aftershave. It suffocates me. Believing I'd succumb, he kissed his cross and tucked it inside his cassock. I stared at the floor, disbelieving a man of God would harm a child.

Soothing words left his bastard lips. "God asked me to love his boys. If you love God, you will love me. I won't hurt you." They were as daggers, each one a lie. "Look what I've got for you to play with", he said, lifting his cassock upwards and off. I didn't look, keeping my eyes on the tiled floor, seeing his shadow approach and the protrusion leading it. Grotesque, distorted hands reached toward me. Behind my back, I transferred the stone to my right hand, a sharp edge gripped between two fingers. Practiced a thousand times in my mind, I struck upwards. Stone meeting bone, chipped a tooth in his spiteful gob, and drew blood. Now, I looked, not at the floor, but his bloodied lip and raging eyes. Showing no fear or remorse, I raised my fist, ready to strike again.

He liked his boys to be submissive. I know that now.

His flaccid penis disappeared under the cassock he pulled back over his head. Hatred, beyond any I'd ever witnessed, creased his brow. Too powerful to resist, he shoved me, belly-first, onto the blanket box. With each stroke of the whip on my back, I knew I'd won. With each bitten sob, I denied him any sexual pleasure. Once a month, as the new moon rose, I paid bitterly for my virginity, but he never removed his cassock in front of me again.

Jack placed the bloodied stone and the diary into the open box, and returned it to the shadows.

Steam rose from the pizza. Ravenous hands snatched a slice. 'I'll return to work next week. Maybe, maybe that nice young priest can deliver retribution.'

Chapter 20

Beneath the ochre-coloured sky, a harsh, rugged landscape in burnt sienna dominated the canvas. The impressionistic interpretation of the surface of Mars, when completed, would join Sapphire McMahon's *Galactic* collection, which she hoped to show in an exhibition. On her left, a second easel held an unfinished commission of Dublin's Mansion House. Silhouettes of walkers strolling along the canal, awaited the artist's life-giving touch. Who were these faceless people? Lovers held hands on a bench, watching an elderly couple, tossing bread to a swan. Two ducks, a male and female Mallard, hid by the edge of reeds. Timeless images capturing the heart of the city and the waterway, this almost photographic piece was bound for an office wall. It would help pay the household bills.

Summer sat cross-legged on her grandmother's ancient, leather settee, sketching her mother. Their sitting room-cum-workshop reeked of oil, paint, and marijuana. She shifted position, uncomfortable. The few springs that remained were content to poke more than fun at any who reclined on the wafer-thin hide. She sucked the end of a yellow pencil.

'Sapph, Jamie promised to call. It's been five days.'

Elegant and striking, Sapphire's aura captivated any in her company. She received regular commissions, while other Dublin-based artists of similar ability rolled out landscapes, which they tried to sell for a pittance in Merrion Square every Sunday morning. A free spirit, she was more a sister than a mother to Summer. Finding a route through the litter on the wooden floor, she slid onto the couch, brought her long, slender legs up to her neck, and rested her chin on her knees. Mimicking the act of pulling petals from a flower, she whispered. 'He loves me, he loves me not. He ...'

'Stop,' Summer said.

'Your father disappeared for weeks at a time. I'm sure your boyfriend will have a good reason. Your dad always did.'

'We're not like you and Dad. Another thing, the free love movement finished years ago.'

Sapphire ran a finger along Summer's arm, smiling. 'We talked the talk like the other hippies, still do, babe. Some guys may have groped my tits and my arse when I was out of it. None, except my Kevin, ever entered the temple of love.'

'You're serious?'

'Yeah, like we made a blood oath during a summer solstice, in nineteen ... when we were in love like you and Jamie are. What's it like to ride a priest?'

'Mam!'

Sapphire leant over and kissed Summer's cheek. As though inspiration blew her from the couch, she leapt to her feet. Humming softly, she mixed paint, and with one God-like stroke of a wide brush, erased the swan.

'I like swans,' Summer said, wistful.

Reciting from Yeats' poem, *The Isle of Innisfree,* Sapphire studied her work, her back turned to Summer. 'Imagine how beautiful his poetry would have been, if he'd smoked a little grass, or even those *wattles.*'

Summer perked up. No matter how foul her humour, she always enjoyed listening to her mother's unique, self-educated opinions on the world of art and literature.

'Summer, Yeats loved Maude Gonne. Time and time again, she refused his marriage proposals, as did her daughter. *Unwearied still, lover by lover, They paddle in the cold Companionable streams or climb the air.* Jack Yeats created poetry with paint, William with words. It's cool, a family nearly as talented as us McMahons.'

Sapphire edged away from the easel, turned and faced her daughter. 'Voilà. My beautiful swans, Jamie and Summer. Ring him, babe?'

Her vision obscured by the tears that now welled in her eyes, Summer marvelled at the beauty of a pair of swans floating on the still canal, their necks entwined. Looking at her mother, she whimpered. 'I can't. Jamie never gave me his parents' phone number.'

Sapphire cleaned her brushes, wiped her hands on her smock, and hollered, 'Kevin, roll us a joint, and get your cutie ass in here with the telephone book for those unfortunates who live outside Dublin.'

A single spark igniting a fire, Summer flung her pad onto the floor, hopped up and hugged her mam. 'Oh, Sapph. You're the coolest.'

Doors opened and banged shut. The dog snarled. Sapphire and Summer giggled.

'Madam called?'

One arm behind his back, Kevin entered the room, balancing a telephone book on a battered silver platter, a comedic imitation of an

English butler. Long grey, unkempt hair, straggled down the back of Sapphire's floral kimono, which barely reached his spindly legs. Behind each ear, a rolled joint for the ladies, both lit. His feet, thrust into pink slippers threaded their way to the couch. Encased in a plume of smoke, his reddened eyes blinked a clear message. *Take these joints.* Summer reached up, seized them before her crazy dad was incinerated.

'The Times,' he said, presenting the telephone directory to Sapphire. 'Will that be all, your majestic?'

Taking the directory, she waved him away. 'Yes. Go feed the weed.'

'Good.' Kevin let the tray fall, and drop-kicked it out of the door. It clattered on the tiled hall, sending their alcoholic bloodhound into a barking frenzy. 'Quiet, Mabel. Otherwise, I'll send you back to the pound, or worse still, make you watch Coronation Street.'

Arms spread wide, the wings of an angel on high. Kevin slumped back onto the couch between the ladies. 'Man, I'm worn out from all this slaving around. What gives with the bible?'

Sapphire dropped the directory on his lap. 'Babe, locate all the Brennans in county Sligo whose son is a soon to be an ex-priest. Our lovesick daughter is lonely.'

'No. Not cool, not now, not ever. My final word,' he snapped, lifting his bum and shoving the book underneath it. 'Not all the grass in our attic could dull my grief if Summer and Callum left us.'

One looked to the other, both giggled and then dived on Kevin, tickling him. Sapphire targeted areas that no mother ought in the company of their offspring.

'Okay,' he squealed, retrieving the directory, and opening it. Squashed between mother and daughter, he turned the pages, one at a time. 'Ouch.' An elbow to his ribs suggested more urgency was advisable. 'Baird, Bourke ... Brady, we're nearly there.'

Three sets of eyes, perused the lists of names.

Summer screamed, 'Stop.' She tried to wrench the directory from his grasp, almost toppling off the edge of the settee.

'*I wish, I wish...*' Kevin sang with all the skill of an alley-cat. 'Sligo is not the Far side of the Moon. After couldn't give a fuck, patience is the coolest virtue. What is his father's name?' Kevin sucked hard on the butt of his joint, held his breath, and exhaled loudly. 'Mars calling Summer. Does St. Jamie have an old man?' Eyebrows raised, ash fell from his goatee beard onto Angela Brennan, Rosemount Road, Longford.

Summer groaned, twisted a lock of hair around a finger. 'Yeah, it's Mick, Michael or ... Paul.'

Sapphire nearly convulsed. 'Hey, that reminds me of Jade. Remember when the midwife asked her the name of Olwen's father? She listed eleven possibilities, and three were called Gary.'

'*Doctor doctor!* No shit! I was devastated. Me, the greatest lover since Genghis Khan, she never mentioned my name,' Kevin said, turning pages so quick, Summer and Sapphire groaned. 'Bingo, Michael Brennan, the first, Galway.'

Summer crossed her fingers, closed her eyes, and listened as her dad read each address, from the kingdom of Kerry in the south, to Buncrana in the farthest north. On and on, he read out the details until Sapphire shrieked. She was a dozen names ahead of Kevin.

'Brennan, Michael, Colooney. Co. Sligo. Where's the phone?'

Summer located it under a cushion in the corner. The knotted, half-chewed cable reached the couch.

'Ahem,' Sapphire said, holding the receiver to her ear, while Summer dialled the number. 'Hi. May I speak with Father Brennan, please?'

There were seventeen named Michael or Mick Brennan in county Sligo who owned a phone. None, however, were proud owners of a priest though a few claimed they knew of a Father Brennan who had died nine years previous.

Summer wiped the tear trickling down her cheek. She sloped off to the kitchen and dropped to her knees on the floor beside Mabel. 'What now?'

A furball of fat, mainly from her overindulgence of hash-cakes, the dog tried to roll onto her back, and failed. Summer's hands roved over Mabel's matted head, thinking. She refused to believe they had been defeated. *Mick, Michael. No, wait, wait ... Máire.*

'Máire,' she said, racing through the door and jumping onto the settee. 'His mother rules with an iron fist.'

'Hello, this is Máire Brennan. A sadder day there's never been. Who is calling?'

'Don't you know,' Sapphire said, in her finest Dublin four accent, 'Sister Bernadetta from the papal orfice in Doblin. Do be a dear and fotch me Father James.'

'Sorry. Oh, my God. Michael, there's a nun on the phone, call James. Sorry, Sister, wasn't I just telling my husband to fetch James. He's not himself from the grief of my terrible loss.'

Three ears fought to be closest to the earpiece. 'I'm sorry,' Sapphire said, yanking the phone away from Kevin's claws, 'did you say you lost something?' She held the phone in front so all three could listen.

'I did. I did. My sister passed away the same day as O'Rourke's milking machine went on fire. But never mind me. Sure, won't my faith in God see me right in a year or two? And, what is having ye calling Father James?'

'Oh, that would be a private matter between Father James and the Pontiff.'

'Jesus, Mary and Joseph. Michael, the Pope is on the phone, and, saints preserve us, he wishes to speak to my only son, James. Hello, your Highness, I shall fetch James.' The patter of feet, a door opening, her voice trailed away. 'James. James. Father James!'

Kevin gawped at Summer. 'Is Father J as fuckin crazy as his mother? That must be some shit she smokes.'

Summer shrugged.

'Sssh,' Sapphire said. 'Hello. Father Jamie.'

'Yes. Who's this?'

'I'm a wife to an impotent husband, and a mother to a neglected daughter. Would you fancy a threesome?'

Kevin guffawed. Summer reddened, grabbed the phone, and slid off the couch onto the floor. 'Jamie. My mam loves to tease. You didn't call. How is your Aunt Maggie?'

'Summer, it's you. She passed away shortly after I arrived.'

'That's sad. Are you okay?'

'Yes.'

'When are you returning to Castlebridge, Jamie?'

'Tomorrow, I hope. Wait a second. I'll see if I can get some privacy.'

His reply barely audible, Summer strained to hear. 'Sssh, Dad.' Turning toward the bay-window, she watched Callum playing marbles on the driveway.

'Nope, I'm being followed. Sorry. I'm getting the early train in the morning. I'll be back in Castlebridge by evening. And you?'

'Cool. I'm packing already. See you at the cottage after Mass, three days from now. I hope you aren't so stuck for words then. Okay?'

'Great! Miss ya.'

'Of course you do.'

The line went dead. She held the phone to her ear for a moment longer, dispelling the sudden sense of loneliness with thoughts of seeing Jamie in three days.

A paint brush held in each hand, Kevin drummed a cushion. *'She loves you, yeah ...'*

'Dad.'

'Yep.'

'Mam.'

'Yeah, babe.'

'Callum and I are going to be alright.'

† † †

'A nun.' Máire bellowed. Yanking the handset from James, she wiped it with the hem of her apron and slammed it onto the receiver.

'Mam.'

'Don't you Mam me, ya selfish pup. What sort of devil-worshippers are ya consorting with? Is it them Jehovah's Witnesses? Maybe it's the ones in orange robes and clanging feckin' bells. Ding-feckin'-dongs. The stink of incense from them would sicken a pig.'

'Mam. Stop the bad language.'

'Stop.' She pulled a half-smoked cigarette from the pocket of her apron, poked a twig into the fire, and lit the cigarette. 'Look at ya, a priest with a prong in his pants. Like one of Morrissey's randy mules, you forgot your vows and shoved it into the first slut that dropped her knickers for ya.'

'Stop. That's not true and not fair. What's got into you? You don't smoke.'

Deaf to his words, Máire pranced thrice around the table, muttering, sucking the guts out of her fag. Lad yelped when she stood on his tail, and tore out the open door, leaving James to deal with his berserker of a mother. 'I'm a nun, she said. A feckin nun. What made her say that?' She seized James by his shoulders, and shook him viciously. 'Why did your whore's mother say she was a nun? Why? Why, for God's sake? Why did the bitch claim to be a daughter of Christ?'

James pushed her hand away. 'It was a joke. Funny. She was only messing with you.'

'Funny! A Dublin comedienne, is that it? Thinking she can pick up the phone and abuse a poor country woman who is in mourning, and, as if that isn't bad enough, claim to be a nun.'

Out of breath, Michael tore through the door. 'What's going on? I could hear the shouting from the bottom meadow.'

'Ask Father Randy.'

'Who?'

Nearly pulling the door off a press as she opened it, she grabbed back issues of *The Farmers Journal,* skimmed though them, and flung them onto the floor. 'There,' she said, thrusting the picture of a stallion mounting a mare, in front of Michael. 'That could well be James and his whore girlfriend.'

Michael picked up the magazines and tidied them away. 'Don't be ridiculous. You're making an eejit of yerself.'

'Am I?' Grabbing the bucket of boiled potatoes meant for the hens, she tossed them into the fire. 'Here, Father. Throw a few oats in this and feed your girlfriend.' Muttering wildly, flinging accusations that made little sense, Máire grabbed the handle of the door, turned and faced James. The edge in her voice reduced to a whimper. 'Why did she say she is a nun?' Not waiting for his answer, she slammed the door shut behind her.

Michael raced after her.

Looking out the scullery window, James could see them remonstrating, Michael managing most of the talking. James retreated to his bedroom and collapsed onto the soft mattress. *It's like Mam has had a mental breakdown. Why? The nun joke was timid.*

After being locked in their house long before the sun had set on the distant mountains, the hungry hens squawked, keeping him awake. As certain as Kerry would beat Offaly in the football final, silence followed the thunder.

† † †

Máire dipped her face into a teacup in a series of rapid movements, mimicking her pecking hens. Sucking the last drops from the china antique, she slurped loud, bedding her false teeth back into position. Across the Formica table, James munched on a ginger-nut biscuit. Lad's head rested on the packed rucksack by his feet. Leonid Brezhnev versus Ronald Reagan, Máire versus James. Frosty war raging in the Brennan household, required diplomatic intervention. Michael, like an experienced referee during a melee at a football match, observed the pair through the spiralling smoke from his pipe.

Anyone, who has clattered a bone-china cup onto a saucer without chipping the delicate surface, would appreciate how difficult a skill it is to master. Three times in rapid succession, Máire bounced the cup, knocking the spoon onto the table.

There was a time when guilt would have weighed heavily on James. Not any longer. In twenty minutes, he would leave this war zone. Behind the veil of his mother's storm-tempered eyes, he knew a reservoir of sadness welled. It showed in the twitching of her wrinkled hands, the slant of her once proud shoulders. Beneath her flimsy armour, afraid of how change would affect her cosy life, Máire stubbornly clung to her self-centred beliefs. James understood. Wanting to reach out and wipe her pain away, he couldn't. A show of weakness would only prolong the ordeal he'd endured for years.

Michael's chair grated on the stone floor as he edged closer to Máire. Taking hold of her hand, he turned to James. 'We support you, no matter your decision.'

Yanking her hand away, Máire spat a last-gasp volley. 'How can you turn your back on God, on your family? Is this what I reared ya for?'

'Enough.' Michael slammed his hand onto the table. His cup and saucer launched skywards, fell to the stone floor, and shattered. 'This is not what we agreed.'

'Agreed?' Her eyes ablaze, she seized the spoon and pointed it at her husband. 'After all I sacrificed for you.' Letting the spoon drop, her hands shot to her mouth, the words irretrievable. 'No,' she begged. Reaching out for his comforting hand, she found a fist. With a muffled cry, she slumped back into her chair.

Michael wiped the spillage from the table with his sleeve. 'James. Your predicament is history repeating itself.'

'What? My father was a priest?'

'Let me tell you a tale,' Michael said. He reached for Máire's hand, and brought it to his lips for a tender kiss. 'A real-life love story that began when I was your age. Would you like to listen to it, son?'

'Do I have a choice?'

'I guess not.' Michael drew a love-heart on the damp table, adding a cupid arrow with a thumbed flourish. 'Picture a doe-eyed schoolgirl, on the front seat in the convent school, her eyes ablaze with religious fervour. In front of her, a handsome bishop made his sales pitch. By the time he'd finished, the life of a nun seemed more appealing, more glamorous than that of a Hollywood actress. Máire was besotted by him. Isn't that true, mo chroí?'

James noticed his mother soften. Leaning into the comfort of his father's shoulder, she giggled. 'I was young,' she said.

'And very sexy,' he said, grimacing at her elbowed response. 'Little by little, my flower's petals, darkened by thoughts of becoming a nun, withered until she knew me not. I was cast aside, the Bishop forgotten. She had only eyes for the crucified Christ, hanging on the wooden cross above her bed. I turned to drink the day she entered the Ursula Convent in Sligo.'

James was surprised by his father's eloquence, confused by the content. So much had been hidden from him. Why?

'One summer's night, drunker than the sailors on the quay in Sligo, I consorted with a bottle of cider by the back wall of her prison. On my fifth attempt to climb the wall, just as I lost grip on the ivy, the light of the full moon revealed the unlocked gate. Isn't that right, Máire?'

'True,' she said, with a sigh. 'The faeries kept their promise.'

'Following the path lined by a thousand statues, each one holier and uglier than the previous, I rounded the front of the building, and charged in though the solid oak door. *Máire, mo chroí* I shouted, racing from room to room, ignoring the squealing women dressed as penguins. Faced with one more door, I sipped the last drop of courage from the bottle. About to turn the handle, certain I would find my true love within, I sensed a presence behind me. Tightening my grip on the neck of the bottle, I turned. I saw a pair of red high heels, and legs encased in fishnet stockings. I followed the ladder running from her ankle up past her knee. Without pausing, though tempted to linger, my bewildered eyes travelled beyond her dignity upwards to the Reverend Mother's devil eyes. Wilder than a ban...'

'Filthy-minded old fool, stop your story telling,' Máire said.

James reached for another biscuit. Had his teetotaller father been drinking? 'I need to catch a train. Does this fairy tale go on much longer?'

Michael sighed. 'A thousand years, were I allowed the time. My head throbs from the pain of a fettered imagination. Okay, I'll stick to the facts. Fixated on becoming a nun, ignoring my pleas to marry me, your mother had moved to the convent in Sligo. Every Sunday afternoon, for four weeks, I waited on the bridge for the nuns to file by. She hid beneath her habit, denying me as much as a look at her eyes, or her shapely legs draped in layers of black. On the fifth Sunday, I concealed myself using the guise of a beggar. Slumped against the wall in a lane, I pinched my nostrils against the stench. When they passed, I gave pursuit. Risking ridicule, and worse, I grabbed Máire. Sleeping beauty awoke to my kiss. That's the truth.'

Máire nodded. James had never known her to remain silent. No, something was being withheld. His interest piqued, he wondered how best to retrieve the ferret from his mother's warren-like brain. Once he had determined the need, the solution became obvious. 'So, I'm the illegitimate son of a beggar and a sinful novice. Was it you and not the Reverend Mother who cavorted in sexy lingerie?'

'No,' screamed his mother, aghast. 'The story about the stockings is all made up. Tell him the truth, Michael.'

Michael pulled his tin from an inside pocket, and filled his pipe. The sparking match, reflected in Máire's narrowed eyes, lit the pungent tobacco. Her hands shaking, she pulled another butt from the seemingly endless stash in her apron pocket.

'Máire left the cloistered life for me. Wracked by guilt, she demanded one thing from her would-be husband.'

He turned to his wife. Ash falling from the cigarette held in her quivering lips, she nodded.

'Before the Statue of the Blessed Lady, we swore an oath that our firstborn would be given to the church. I'm so sorry, James. The stigma of having left the nuns tortured your mother. As you witnessed yesterday, she still carries enormous guilt. What choice did I have? I loved her, still do.'

'Rumpelstiltskin,' James said, rising. He turned his back on his parents. *Guilt could drive anyone to the edge. I've been there.* 'Not as much as a thread of gold for the pain you caused me.'

Máire sobbed. Remorse in every tremor, he knew her to be broken, yet, he remained stoic. 'What now? Do you want rid of me? Who would want to be a mother to a second-hand priest?' James lifted his rucksack and trudged to the kitchen door.

'No.' Máire screamed. Broken china crunched beneath her wellies. 'My son. My only son. Forgive me.' She clutched at his coat.

James turned slower than a spring tide. Towering over her, he steadied her shaking shoulders. 'Only if you promise to love Summer and Callum as much as you love me.'

'Anything,' she said, making the sign of the cross. 'I swear it.'

He was aware she'd have sworn God was the devil, Christ a leper, and lead was gold, but James embraced her, looked to his grateful father, and winked. 'Dad, remove at least half of the holy pictures from the house.'

Chapter 21

James enjoyed the solitude of the return train journey to Dublin. None sought his company, sat beside him or asked to inspect his ticket. Curled up on the seat, he observed the changing countryside roll by, boggy browns changing to myriad greens as they headed east.

Maggie's engagement ring hung on the chain around his neck, a reminder that his days as a priest were numbered, not in years, but months. Consumed by loneliness these past weeks, believing his predicament unique, Maggie's death and Father Hickey's revelations concerning their secret relationship allowed him clarity of thought. None would prevent his marriage to Summer. Some questions remained unanswered, but how did Maggie and Father Hickey know he had a girlfriend? This addled him. Seanie? Surely not, the sanctity of the pub is greater than that of a confessional. Who then?

I guide all that you do.

That bloody voice again.

He'd always known his mother had an unnatural bond with the church. It had never occurred to him his father was part responsible for his enrolment into priesthood. Unable to undo the past, he forgave them both. Although she would continue subtle resistance, he knew she'd fall in love with Summer and Callum once they met. He wished Summer would be at the station in Dublin. Two more days seemed an eternity.

James disembarked at Connolly and strolled to the bus station. His e-yes roving over the crowds, he sipped a coffee in the small café. Each time he spotted someone in a driver's uniform approach, disappointment drew a sigh. None was Jack O'Brien. The more he considered the torture Sweeney had visited on Jack, and probably others, the more responsible he felt for Sean and the other altar boys in Castlebridge.

Skilful anglers study the habits of their prey. James tried to consider the possible horrors Sweeney had visited upon the innocent children, but his mind failed to conjure such images. How could any sane person imagine such abuse? By what means could he hook this vile priest? James smiled. The implement used by anglers to dispatch fish is commonly known as a *priest*. Maybe he should use his own to send Sweeney to the fires of hell. A priest used to rid the world of a bullying priest.

James decided he would become a chameleon, a predator to catch a predator. With one thought on his mind, he finished his coffee, and boarded the Castlebridge bus, regretting Jack wasn't in the driver's seat. *Sweeney must pay.*

† † †

A tea towel slung over his shoulder, Seanie Lavelle scrubbed ashtrays in the backroom of the pub. 'Our traveller returns. James the Father, how fare the people of county Sligo?'

'Grand.' James, placing his rucksack onto a stool, sat on another. 'How did you know where I went?'

Suds dripping onto his shirt, Seanie touched his bulbous nose with an index finger. 'I have my sources.'

'You missed your vocation.'

Sean looked up. 'Did I?' He dried the ashtrays, stacking them one on top of the other in front of James. 'Our jobs are not dissimilar, though I'd argue I have a more satisfied clientele. A coke with ice, I presume?'

'A coke will be fine.' Despite the rigorous cleaning, foul odours emanating from the tower of ash trays made James gag. Lest the skyscraper topple, with one hand on top, he pushed it to one side. 'Whatever similarities you have conjured up, they remain a mystery. Enlighten me, please.'

Seanie strutted on the boards behind the counter as an actor would a stage. His words chosen with care, keen eyes followed their delivery and any reaction they received. Dropped from on high, two ice cubes fell into the glass of coke, splashing James. 'Sorry about that slip of my hand,' Seanie said. His eyes pierced into James.

The chameleon priest feigned surprise, and *nearly* toppling off his stool, swung an arm outwards. 'Sorry about my swinging hand.' James reached over the counter, grabbed the towel from Seanie's shoulder, and wiped the wooden surface, the drenched ash trays, and finally the back of Seanie's hand. 'I'll have another coke. Hold the ice.'

Bellowing laughter followed a fresh glass of coke onto the counter. A nod confirmed the customer was satisfied with the three cubes of ice.

'The country air suited you. You left here a spotty lad, and, having grown a pair in recent days, you have returned a man.' Seanie tossed the filthy tea towel into the sink. 'You offer penance to cure your client's guilt. I, on the other hand, offer an escape from the horrid realities of life.'

James lifted the glass to his lips and held it there, listening to the crackling ice and the popping of bubbles. 'Your offer of escape is temporary.' Proud of his answer, he took a large gulp, almost swallowing an ice cube. Waiting for a response from the barman, he chewed on what Seanie had said. *Yes, he had changed.*

'Take one box of matches, like so. Release from hand, like so. Outcome is predictable, like your indoctrinated answer.' Seanie stared hard at James. Without looking away, he kneeled and lifted the box off the floor. 'You make suffocating rules, force guilt on decent people and then offer to take it away through penance. A circle of deceit. If I stood on a beer keg outside my premises, pronouncing drink as evil, then offered a naggin of whisky to any who agreed with me, I'd be locked up as a scoundrel.'

'You would, and probably should anyway. Your analogy about the whiskey makes little ... actually, no sense. Speaking of which, I need a bottle of whiskey for Father Sweeney.'

'Speaking of your poor memory, where are my flies?'

'I'll bring them tomorrow.'

'That twenty Pound note, peeping out your shirt pocket, will cover this bottle of Bushmills. Seeing as it will take a week for you to get your pea brain around my philosophy, I'll put the two cokes on your slate.'

James opened his rucksack and placed the bottle inside. Slinging it over his shoulder, he swivelled when Seanie leaned across the counter and whispered. 'Be careful, Sweeney can be a nasty shite when he has drink taken.'

'He's the same sober. Thanks, Seanie. I'm slow, but not dumb. Neither are your religious philosophies.'

'On the second point, I agree wholeheartedly.'

James glanced at Seanie, before he left the pub. 'How is young Sean? Upstairs watching television, I suppose.'

'Nah, he's gone to the GAA club to watch the senior team play a friendly match. He's been acting a bit strange, quieter in himself. Sure, I suppose that's part of growing up.'

'Tell him I'm going fishing tomorrow for an hour or two. I'll knock on your door after morning Mass. If he's interested, and you don't mind, I'll teach him how to cast. Has he waders?'

'Interested? My boy will be up half the night polishing the new rod. To tell you the truth, he's told me a dozen times that the new priest is cool. Fair play, James.'

☦ ☦ ☦

On those summer evenings, when night embraces the fading day and the long shadows of dusk snake up through the pools, oily rings on every glide mark the presence of feeding trout. The novice angler, seeing so many trout slashing and splashing, jumps into the pool. Making clumsy casts and wading too deep, only the juveniles continue to feed. Beneath the bushes on the far side, an old trout feels the vibrations, the disturbance within his watery domain. It slides further into the shadows and will not feed that evening. A clever angler waits by the edge, learning the feeding patterns of the larger quarry.

James leaned against the door of the Sacristy, listening. Though the cadence of Sweeney's voice was lost in the heavy oak door, the hairs on his arms rose as though swayed by a chill wind. He'd twenty minutes to unpack his bag and boil the kettle in anticipation of the ferret's return to the presbytery following evening Mass.

In an effort to look casual, James sat at the dining table reading a newspaper. A little off centre, he placed the bottle of Bushmills with its label facing the door. Fastidious, perhaps, but attention to detail being the mark of a true hunter, he'd not make any mistakes. Startled when the clock chimed the hour, James knocked his shin against the leg of the table. Before the throbbing eased, the front door had opened and closed. Eyes glued to the blurred words on the paper, James lifted his gaze when the door into the dining room burst open, the face entering not what he expected.

'Luke, what are you doing here?'

Mouth agape, Luke raised his hands to cover a gasp. The mirth in his eyes turned to utter shock. From the hall came the familiar clang of keys landing on the hall table. Luke turned, just as Sweeney entered the room. An entire gamut of every know emotion flickered in the ferret's eyes; shock yielding to a warm welcome.

'Father Brennan, welcome home. Sit down, Luke. I'll get that book for you.'

'Thanks, Mick,' Father Brennan said.

While Sweeney, making more noise than necessary, rummaged amongst the many books strewn around the television room, James focused on Luke. Shifting uncomfortably on the chair, the red cheeks of his angelic face deepened under James watchful gaze. 'Why are you really here, Luke?' Silence confirmed James's worst fears. 'Never mind,' he whispered. 'I'm a nosey parker.'

On Sweeney's return, Luke jumped to his feet.

'Here ya go,' Sweeney said, handing the boy a leather-bound book. 'Tell your mother, I'll search for the other three volumes. Be off with you.'

Luke grabbed the book and bounded out the door.

'Dafter than a brush.' Sweeney guffawed.

The chameleon stood and laughed so loud that Sweeney eyes popped wide in astonishment. 'Here,' James pushed the bottle across the table. 'Is it any wonder you need a drink now and again? I've realised my behaviour these past weeks has been ridiculous. Please accept this as an apology.'

Sweeney grasped the bottle. 'You are full of surprises. Maybe I had you all wrong.'

'You did. Perhaps we can talk tomorrow. I'm knackered. I'll have an early night and be fit to do the first Mass in the morning. In fact, I'll do them all tomorrow.'

The chameleon's smile vanished the moment he passed by the speechless Sweeney.

Bastard!

Chapter 22

Luke arrived late for Mass, breathless and downcast. Dark rings circled his hazel eyes, which peeped out through the thick strands of hair, partially covering his face. 'Sorry, Father. It took me ages to find my shoes.'

His voice squeaked like the rusty gate at Summer's cottage. Something about the lad made James wish to reach out and give him a hug, to reassure him he would be safe. Now was not the time. Not yet. Trust had to be earned. 'That's fine, Luke. Even if you had been late, I would not have been cross. Let's go to work.'

In his rush, Luke pulled on his cassock back to front. Fumbling and mumbling, his efforts to rectify matters were comical. About to clap, James stared at the unblemished skin on Luke's back until folds of white material cascaded over it. *Thank God. I've been wrong.*

Nearing the top of the aisle, James whispered to Luke, 'Go ahead.' From the bottom of his lungs, he manufactured a cough so loud, Agnes Murphy banged her head on the seat in front as she sprung from her kneeling position. 'Saints be praised,' he said, covering his grin with the billowing sleeve of his vestments. 'I hoped you'd be at Mass. The Bishop asked me to make a list of the needy people in the parish. You know, the elderly, those without work, invalids, unmarried mothers and the like. How would an outsider like me do that job? Would you do it for me, Agnes?'

Straightening her shoulders, she sat back on the seat with her Rosary beads dangling from clasped hands. 'I will, Father, I will. I'll start straight away.'

'God bless you, Agnes. You can be certain I'll make sure the Bishop knows of your tireless work around the parish. Such piety will receive just rewards in the kingdom of heaven,'

The light of a one-hundred and twenty watt bulb would appear as a candle compared to the radiance emanating from her face. 'Thank you, Father. Christ be with you.'

'And with you. Don't tell Father Sweeney. Sure, he'd only take the praise for our work.'

The Madonna, holding her infant within the stained glass window over the altar, held his gaze as he strode to join Luke by the holy table. *Are we not all a complex puzzle of multi-coloured personalities?* Discovering the true character of an individual was a subject that had intrigued James during his studies. He prayed the theories would now hold water, for he would be testing many of them.

All through the Mass, Agnes stared at him, and smiled when he locked his eyes on her. During the prayers of the faithful, he considered winking in her direction, but that would be overkill and could undo the morning's work. Once he finished charming Sweeney's snake, Agnes, would hiss to the tune of two masters.

✝ ✝ ✝

Expecting the ferret to be ensconced at the dining table ready to interrogate him, the absence of his car from the driveway caused James to skip to the front door. 'Ye ha.' In case his nemesis returned unexpectedly, James donned his waders, grabbed his fishing gear and the box of flies for Seanie. One foot on a pedal of his bicycle, he rode side-saddle to Lavelles, laughing each time he fell off the bike.

Wearing waders too long for his short legs, and holding his fishing rod, Sean stood like an army sentry guarding the pub. His wave to James would have earned him a flogging if he were really in the army. Unable to wave back, James grinned.

'Are ya ready to catch some trout, Sean?'

'Yes, Father.'

'Then what are we waiting for?' James said, amused at the contents of the homemade panier on the back of Sean's blue bicycle. Two cans of coke, crisps, and a clear plastic bag, filled with melting ice cubes.

Powered by enthusiasm, Sean's bike raced ahead. A cheesy grin lit his face each time he checked on James. James pedalled slowly. No need to teach the lad any lessons until they reached the river. He remembered his own first two-wheeler, a second-hand girls' bike his father had bought in Sligo. He'd covered the vibrant pink with a paint mixed from leftovers. On the frame, in bright yellow lettering, he'd painted *Silver Streak*. The bike was a dull navy, and only the handlebars were silver. Until the Christmas that Aunt Maggie had given him a fancy bike with five gears, he'd never lost a race against his school friends. *Silver Streak,* now a rusty relic, hung on a hook in the stable at home. The other bike had been discarded. It lay in the heap of rubbish at the corner of the yard.

Sean guided the anti-theft chain through the front wheel and around the pillar. 'You should buy a racer, like mine.' He clicked the padlock shut, and tested the chain.

James liked that, attention to detail defined a person. One bike chained to the other, they climbed the gate and made their way downstream, following the path kept open by walkers. Where possible, it followed the course of the river, cutting through a stand of hazels, wrapping around thicker vegetation. There was an easier route, but it meant cutting through the graveyard. One well-crafted pishogue achieved what a dozen rules could not. Gerry Walsh, late of this world, dared test the longstanding superstition that anglers using the graveyard to access the river would find their rods cursed. From that day forward, he never fished again. Sweeney's drunken mouth revealed to James, the truth of this modern legend. On the longest day, a friend of Gerry's donned a white sheet and hid behind a headstone. When Gerry returned well after midnight, the ghostlike apparition and its wailing cries scared the shite out of him. *Never fish again.*

'What's your favourite fly? How many do you use? Wet or Dry? Biggest trout? Smallest fly?' Sean fired as many questions as there were flies hovering over the river.

On reaching the shallows, overlooked by the ruined Protestant schoolhouse, they halted. Sean unhitched his fly from the keeper ring and ran to the muddy edge of the river.

'Whoa. What are you doing?' James sauntered inland to his thinking stones. Probably left here by the builders who erected the ancient school, they had seated many an angler's arse over the last hundred years. 'Sit.'

James couldn't help noticing the exaggerated hunch in the boy's shoulders, who sat beside him on the stone, his legs swinging in perpetual motion. He opened his fly box and placed it between them. 'Nymphs, Sean. Do you know what they are?'

Sean leaned over and scrutinised the flies. 'No. Can we start?'

'In a moment. These?'

Sean examined at the contents of the second box. 'Dry flies,' he squealed, plucking a drab looking fly from the middle. 'It's very dull. Dad's dry flies are much more colourful.'

'Really,' James said, surprised. 'Does he catch many trout?'

'He used to catch loads of big ones. He's deadly with worms. Worms aren't allowed any more, are they Father?'

'When we're fishing, call me James. Fly fishing only is the rule. Fetch your rod.'

James pulled a spool of nylon from his pocket. Deft hands tied up a leader suitable for a novice, and he completed the rig by attaching a small nymph under a medium sized dry. 'Lift slow, flick, pause, flick, stop, drift,' he said, explaining as he walked to the river's edge. 'Sean, stand by my left shoulder, out of harm's way. The essential rudiments of a cast explained, James flicked the flies upstream. 'Watch the dry, pull in the slack line with your free hand, and lift to make another cast. Got it?'

More confused than many of the men who were dragged to Mass every Sunday, Sean shook his head. James cast again, reiterating his instructions. As luck would have it, just as he described the necessity for keeping a vigilant watch on the dry fly, it dipped under the surface. A quick flick of his wrist and the rod tip bent into a small trout. Not quite the miracle of feeding the ten-thousand, but the look on Sean's face made James an instant hero. 'Wet your hands first,' ordered the priest as Sean tried to grab the splashing trout. After a quick lesson on unhooking and returning the trout safely, he thrust the rod into Sean's waiting hands. 'Your turn.'

James retreated downriver. Sean struggled at first, but with careful guidance, soon had his flies landing about eight yards upstream. With a growing confidence, he edged out further. Although the water was shallow, stepping into holes could tumble a novice. More for reasons of safety than to shade his eyes, James put on his sunglasses before wading up. He stood at Sean's left-hand-side.

'This is the best ever,' Sean said, thrashing the water in front to foam. 'I can't catch anything.'

'See the darker water between us and the mid-stream boulder?'

'Yeah, that looks deep. Is it? Does it hold a monster trout? Does it? Does it?'

James had spent so much time recently in the company of the elderly. Sean's boyish innocence and enthusiasm, made him realise how much fun his life would be when he married Summer. *She and Callum will here tomorrow. Yipee.* 'It might, Sean. Let's find out if it does.' Sean stiffened when he placed a hand on his shoulder, unnerving but not deterring the priest. 'I'll hold the sleeve of your coat in case you slip into a hole. Okay?'

Sean looked at him coyly. 'Jeepers, ya better hold on tight. Me father has a terrible temper. If I went home wet, he'd beat the dandruff from the back of my head.'

'Take small steps, feeling your way forward, and don't cast till I tell you to.' When they reached mid-stream, James took a deep breath. 'I'm going to reach around your back, and grip your rod. You continue to hold it like you are holding an egg. I'll control the cast and you'll experience what a good one feels like. Are you okay with this?'

Sean flicked a fly off his arm, and turned away as though he'd not heard the question. Dark clouds had gathered in the distance, the threat of rain imminent.

James pointed upwards. 'See that, Sean? If you don't make a decision, God will pee on us and we will have to face your father's temper.'

Sean burst out laughing. 'Okay. If you think I'll catch a trout, you make the cast.'

Confident in his flies and skills, James reached around the boy and gripped the cork handle. 'One, two, three, here goes.' The line lifted, driving the flies behind them, 'pause, push, flick.' The line unfurled high above the surface, glided down, and a wee splash marked the nymph's entry into the river. Four eyes focused on the dry, two of them belonged to an excited child. The other two were full of hope. If he gained Sean's trust, he could protect him from the monster, Sweeney. Sean yanked the rod upwards and caught his first trout, a whopper, seven inches long.

'Wow. The dry fly disappeared.'

His heart bursting with pride, James smiled. The first drops of rain fell as Sean kneeled by the river's edge and released the trout. Now was not the time. He'd intended to probe, ask questions about Sweeney. It would be cruel to destroy such a happy moment for Sean. They chatted all the way back to the bridge, oblivious to the pounding rain.

In his rush to get to the river, Sean had forgotten to take the refreshments. As luck would have it, no scallywags had robbed the coke and crisps. Using the parapet of the bridge as their dining table, priest and fishing protégé munched crisps and sipped coke. 'Look there,' James said, pointing to a trout about ten yards below the first arch.

Sean leaned over the edge. 'Where, Father? I can only see stones.'

James dropped a crisp. Both watched it fall down and outwards. 'Wait. It's a yard to the right, now. Can you see it?'

'No.'

'Take these and don't drop them,' James said, handing Sean his sunglasses. While Sean hooped and hollered, spotting trout after trout, James turned and faced upstream, wishing he could glimpse the cottage beyond the trees.

'Come on,' he said, tugging the sleeve of Sean's coat. 'Let's be off. You can keep the glasses. I'm putting a box of flies in the panier for your dad.'

'Really, I can keep the glasses?'

'You can. Get string and make a loop to tie to the arms. Then you won't drop them into the river. And, this box of flies is for you.'

James eased an aluminium case from an inside pocket. Coy at first, something bothering him, Sean stepped closer and reached for the box. Silent, he ran a finger over the engraved trout on the lid. Whatever internal conflict had raged, his grin suggested it had been resolved. Sean flung his arms around the priest, and squeezed. 'Thanks.'

A minor achievement in the greatest challenge James faced, he peered toward the church steeple. *Luke is next.*

Chapter 23

Awake for more than an hour, James lay on his bed, toying with the ring and chain. Light from passing cars chasing shadows across the ceiling and walls, scurried into the darker recesses of his bedroom. A week earlier, these were creepy, clutching, crawling things, ripping at the remaining threads of his sanity, while he skulked beneath his pillow. Now he understood that a life without hope could be a lingering death. Having felt the chill winds of the void and the deep depression they brought with them, James resolved to create a future without baggage, alongside the woman he loved.

Though civility had returned to the presbytery, the odour of its deceit hung heavy in the air. Smiles forced, pleasantries exchanged, both priests avoided looking directly at the other. Polished floors and glasses, even cutlery, became the mirrors upon which James gazed at the distorted images of the monster beneath the Roman collar.

Shadows no longer preceded the sound of a passing car. His futile attempts to catch the dawn, reflected in the intricate faces of the diamond, reminded him of those elusive minnows he'd chased as a child. Smiling at such silliness, he pulled the chain over his head and let the ring dangle against his chest. Time to rise and prepare for Summer's arrival. A shave being a good place to start, he slipped out of bed and headed for the bathroom.

On tiptoe, he crept along the landing. Sweeney's wheezing cough, and the noise of drawers opening and closing, filtered through his door. The ferret usually rose first, always used all the hot water and left puddles on the bathroom floor. There were none today. James stepped into the room and, closing the door, locked it. He filled the sink and reached for his shaving foam. The handle of bathroom door rattled. Muttered curses fading, were lost when the old bastard's door slammed and rocked on its hinges. James grinned at his lathered reflection in the mirror. *Oh, dear. It sounds like someone isn't too happy this morning.* Though he shook with mirth, he managed a clean shave. He cupped his hands under the tap, continually splashing his face until the water ran cold, and a lake had formed on the floor between the frosted window and the door. *Oops. How fortunate, I'm wearing leather slippers.*

James dressed and bounded down the stairs. At home, where no meant yes, two poached eggs on toast was the only fodder on the morning's menu. Mother hen had always insisted he ate a good breakfast. He honoured that tradition, popped a slice of bread into the toaster, filled a bowl with cornflakes, sprinkled a heaped spoon of sugar onto them, and poured in the milk. James knew that slurping while eating had never been traditional, even in those countries where belching is desirable, but for him it had become a way to celebrate being alive. He carried his food into the dining room and sat at the table. *When in Rome, slurp like Sweeney.* Like confetti at a wedding, his uncontrollable laughter sent a shower of cornflakes as far as Sweeney's slippers lying on the floor. *Oops.*

Certain, he couldn't face the ferret so early, he grabbed the slice of toast and escaped from the house just as the top step of the stairs creaked. James munched his way down the lane, nibbled the crust while crossing the road to the shop, and wiped the crumbs from his raw chin before entering widow Mahon's lair. His gaze settled on the apparition wearing a flimsy dress. *Christ almighty, Una isn't wearing a bra this morning.*

'Hmm,' she said. 'Is that expensive aftershave?'

Don't look. Don't stare. Crap. In his peripheral vision, he caught her follow his stare to her cleavage, and her tongue slipping from between moistened lips.

'What?' He grabbed the Irish Times off the newspaper stand and placed it on the counter.

Her hands slid toward the paper, and beyond it. She placed her elbows on the newspaper, allowing an ample gap to develop at the top of her dress. 'Did your girlfriend give you that sexy fragrance?' Una stared up at him, waiting for an answer, and probably more if he were willing.

The chameleon stepped forward, yanked three pennies from his pocket, and dropped them one at a time down the front of her dress. 'Buy a bra, Una. Wear it to confessions after Mass tomorrow.'

Deep pink the colour of her nipples, bright red the colour of her face, she shot upright. Both images enjoyed, James grabbed the paper and retreated to the door. 'Yes, Una. My latest girlfriend bought me the aftershave.'

Her folded arms covered her embarrassment, but nothing covered her shock. The pennies clanged onto the floor.

James strode back down the lane toward the presbytery, swinging the newspaper and whistling as he went. Ahead, Sweeney's black Mercedes reversed down the driveway, smoke billowing from the exhaust. *Good preparation for an eternity in the fires of hell.* The car swung out onto the lane and stalled after a missed gear change. The ferret peered over the steering wheel. James did not miss the manic expression on his face nor the fury in his beady eyes. The engine started and revved from low to high in quick succession like a racing car. *The swine is lining me up, using the badge on the bonnet as a sighter, like a hunter would a rifle. He wouldn't dare.*

Sweeney slipped the clutch, wheels spun, and the car shot forward. James vaulted the wall into the churchyard. As he turned around, the Mercedes skidded to a halt. The ferret wound down the window. 'Jesus. Are you okay, James? My shoes are soaked from the puddle in the bathroom. My foot must have slipped off the brake.'

'No harm done.'

'Good. I've another meeting with Bishop Ryan. Mind the fort.'

James climbed back over the wall and stood with one arm on the roof of the car. 'Is it safe to be driving at your age? Seeing as ya have bad eyesight and a slippery hoof, you should get a taxi. I might get Billy to give me driving lessons. What do ya think?'

'Do that. If you pass the test in a few years, purchase your own vehicle. This classic is not for sharing.'

'Go on outta that. Sure, isn't it paid for out of the collections at Mass. I'll be happy to let you use it now and again.' James banged down on the roof, drowning out Sweeney's mumbled reply. 'Enough of this fooling around,' James said, dipping low so he could see inside the car. 'Please tell the Bishop I said everything is in order.'

'What do you mean, in order?'

'It was a joke, Mick. Have ya no sense of humour?'

It seemed not. Sweeney grunted something unintelligible, started the engine and shoved the gearstick into second. The snarl curling his lips changed to a smirk as he revved the engine. Sweeney's reply was almost lost in the squealing tyres. 'Get your own fucking car.'

The stench of burnt rubber lingered as the Mercedes turned left at the end of the lane. *A nice family car wasted on a twisted moron like Sweeney.*

† † †

A little weary, James yawned and rubbed his eyes with the sleeve of his cassock. Lacking any enthusiasm, he abandoned his normal mental preparations for Mass. Summer was arriving today. Nothing else mattered. In the corner of the Sacristy, the leg of a chair stuck out at an odd angle. After confessions, he'd remind Billy it needed mending. God forbid Father Ferret might sit on it, fall onto his face and break his neck. Amen.

James swivelled as the creaky door opened. Someone, wearing a black duffle coat with the hood pulled up, stepped inside, twisted the key in the door, and locked it. The bare legs beneath the coat were those of a young lad. Both amused and curious, James remained silent.

'Surprise,' shouted the lad as he leapt, and twisting around, cast off his coat. Luke Ahern stood gawping at Father Brennan. Naked from his white runners up, he dropped to the floor, and curled into a ball. Too late for James not to have observed rouge lips, powdered cheeks and shadowed eyes, the face of a harlequin.

Sweet Jesus, no, I never suspected anything more sinister than physical abuse. Luke, forgive me.

James lifted the coat and placed it over the shivering boy. He turned and faced the Blessed Mother.

'Put on your coat, child.'

Numbed, the horrific image burned into his mind. Behind him, Luke whimpered.

Suffer the little children to come unto me. Damn it Lord, it should be the children suffer for me?

'Sit here please, Luke,' he said, his voice gentler than a summer breeze. He pointed to the pine stool beneath the statue.

The child sat crouched, hands in his pockets and staring at his dancing feet beneath the stool.

James knelt in front of him, but far enough away so Luke would not be intimidated.

I guide everything you do.
That annoying voice again. I need to think.

'Was the clown performance for Father Sweeney?'

Luke nodded.

'Did he ask you to wear makeup?'

'No.' Luke folded his arms and glared at James. 'It's his birthday today. You ruined my surprise. I hate you.'

Almost toppling in shock, James stood. 'Has Father Sweeney ever hurt you?'

'No. We ... we love each other. I'm his special boy. Not Sean.' Luke produced a toothy grin; a grotesque caricature of something far different than a twelve-year old boy.

James pulled a tissue from his pocket. 'Wipe away the lipstick and makeup with this, please.'

Ill-equipped to deal with any form of abuse, but understanding the fragility of the situation, James paced the floor. Luke spat on the tissue and removed much of the offensive visage, revealing the angelic face of a child whose innocence had been irretrievably stolen.

'I'm so sorry, Luke. I didn't realise that you were special to Father Sweeney. You never said. Why?'

Luke shuffled on the seat before answering. 'Father Sweeney said what we have is special, from God. Everyone else would be jealous if they knew. Jealousy is a sin.'

'It is, Luke. We should tell your parents. They should know.'

Luke lashed out with his foot, missing James' knee. 'No. If you tell anyone, I'll say you touched me, touched my privates.' With a triumphant grin, his face no longer angelic, Luke sat up straight.

'Okay, Luke. I understand.' James stepped closer to the child. 'If you tell Sweeney about today, I'll say you asked me to ... to make you my special boy. That will make him cross.' *Jesus, what did I say?*

Luke burst out crying. 'I'm thirteen in three months. The last special boy before me was Keith O'Neill. God does not allow boys to be special once they become teenagers. Sean will be the next special boy. I hate Sean and I hate you.'

Luke bounded for the door. James could have prevented him from leaving, but there was no point. 'If you ever need my help, just ask.' His plea was lost in the sound of the slamming door. James sat rigid on the stool, his eyes locked on the crucified Christ, depicted in the picture of the twelfth station of the cross hanging beside the door. No crown of thorns nor blood-streaked face, just the hideous face of a child-clown. 'There is no God.'

I guide all you do. I walk with you always.

No. I walk alone. I will destroy Sweeney, the Father, and protect Sean, the son. You, God, are a ghost who will haunt me no more.

I guide ...

No more.

☨ ☨ ☨

Darkness climbed the stained-glass window as Father Brennan, still in shock, marched to the altar, the hem of his cassock swirling around his leather shoes. The church now plunged into deepest gloom, he turned to face the sparse congregation as Billy Egan darted behind the font. One by one the lights came on, revealing Billy's raised fist and the wrinkled faces of those upset by the lateness of his arrival. On another day, James may have relinquished a smile.

'Regretfully, Mass is cancelled. Please leave.' James turned and faced the window, folded his arms and waited.

I guide all you do ... no, you don't exist.

There is no God.

Ripples of confusion emanated from the stunned parishioners. Murmurs growing louder, developed into pantomime whispers. Footsteps crossed the tiled floor. The inner door swung open and closed. Eyes narrowed, fists clenched, James remained rooted to the spot until the only sound was his heavy breathing.

'They are gone, Father. What is going on?'

James swivelled at Billy's familiar scraping voice. Ten years off the fags hadn't cured his bark. Resplendent in his dungarees, neither grease, nor dirt resided either side of the crease ironed down the middle of each leg. He sat cross-legged on the front pew. 'Nothing. Go home, Billy.'

'Not since a broken pipe flooded the church in nineteen sixty-seven has a priest cancelled Mass. Mickey Nelligan's funeral went straight from his house to the graveyard. Humour me with a worthwhile excuse.'

'Sorry. My reasons are my own. Buzz off.'

A sharp wit and a generous nature marked every interaction James had with Billy. From fixing a buckled bicycle wheel, to directions to where some old biddy lived, he had never sought any payback, never complained.

'Sit here, ya condescending bollix.' Billy thumped the wooden seat. 'Do you think, I've been listening to religious shite every day these past few years for the sake of me health, or for a promise of another bloody life in the hereafter? Sit!'

Stunned by the ferocity in Billy's tone, James slid onto the pew, just out of reach of the retired undertaker's fist, a weapon with which few would argue. 'I don't understand. You come to Mass every day. Single-handed, you maintain the church, the grounds and the presbytery. Why?'

'Why should I tell someone as rude as you? Answer me, Father bloody miserable.'

'It's not personal. Something bad happened earlier. I can't tell anyone, not yet.'

Billy leaned over and jabbed a finger into James chest. 'So, you don't trust me, is that it?'

'I dare not trust anyone.'

Billy stiffened, pinched the bridge of his nose, and offered a half-smile. 'Knowledge is more valuable than cash, or position. I know I can trust you, and that gives me an unfair advantage. I've given much of my time to the church because a young lad is dead, and I'm the only person who knows he was murdered.'

'What? Murdered, by whom?'

Leaning back on the pew, Billy glanced around. 'Nine years ago, Father Hickey, my second cousin, asked me to keep an eye on our new parish priest, claimed he was an evil bastard.'

'Sweeney? Wait, Father Hickey from Sligo. Are you the friend he has looking out for me?'

'Yes, to both questions. I'm sorry about your aunt. Maggie was one of a kind.' He pulled a packet of mints from a pocket, took one, and offered them to James. 'Keith O'Neill drowned in the pond on the edge of the village. I'd known the lad from when he was old enough to blow into a tin whistle. Like his father, he'd the gift to play any tune after hearing it the once. The lad could have beguiled the fairies with his music. Sometimes, when I'm here on me own, I hear a mournful tune coming from the Sacristy. Maybe guilt is playing tricks on me.'

'Why is it your guilt?'

'I witnessed the change in Keith, and never understood until it was too late. From a happy-go-lucky lad, he became a sulky, secretive troublemaker. For feck's sake, he used to help me wash the hearse every Saturday. I thought it was the hormones. But the week before he died, I met him outside the garage. To tell ya the truth, I've seen healthier corpses. Keith told me he was no longer spe...'

'Special,' whispered James, clutching Billy's hand. 'Thirteen when he died?'

'How did you know? Three weeks after his birthday, he leapt into the village pond carrying a concrete block and wearing his altar boy clothes. Sweeney beat him. I'm sure of it.'

'Look at me.'

'Why?' Billy said.

'Because it will happen again if we don't act. Sweeney doesn't beat his *special* boys. He buggers them. He casts them to one side when they reach thirteen. He reserves his violence for those who refuse to be *special*. I've seen his handiwork on the back of someone who denied him twenty years ago.'

'There's a bastard, paedophile priest in this parish, operating under my nose.' The expression of horror on Billy's face matched James feelings. 'I never ... Are you sure, Father?'

'Certain. I'll inform Bishop Ryan tomorrow. Will you drive me to Carlow?'

'No. That would be a waste of petrol. Thinking he would help, I wrote a three-page letter to the dunderhead Bishop. He wrote back a fuck-off note on plain paper suggesting I pray for Keith's sinful soul. His eminence is another bastard with his head up his holy arse.'

This flummoxed James. He'd thought the Bishop hated Sweeney.

Billy hung his head. 'Luke's personality has changed, hasn't it? Is he interfering with him? I've suspected he has hit Sean at least once. Jesus, I assumed he was just a violent bully.'

'I don't know Luke too well, but it's a firm yes to both questions. Luke is his current *special* boy, and Sean, if he succumbs, is next. Luke told me he is in love with Sweeney.'

'Fuckin Nora.' Billy made a fist, and punched the palm of his other hand. 'I'll kill that pervert.'

James rose, paced over the tiles in front of the confessional and back.

I guide all that you do ...

You don't exist. Let me think.

James turned to Billy. Worried they might be overheard, he leant to whisper into Billy's ear, 'We will gather as much proof as we can. Then we will go to the Bishop, higher if necessary. We have three months.'

'Why three?' Billy pushed himself up and off the seat.

'Luke turns thirteen. Don't say anything to him, to anyone. I must face Sweeney without giving the game away. You will, too. Seeing as you've had suspicions for a long while, you should be okay.'

'No problem.'

'Can you do me a favour? I need driving lessons.'

'I've been half expecting such a request. Do ya remember Maggie's yellow Fiat?'

'I do ... why?'

'It's parked in my garage, behind the hearse. Putting it there was Father Hickey's idea. Two days after I told him you had a girlfriend, he drove it up from Sligo.'

'Go away out of that. By the way, how did you know I'd a girl?' James said.

'Give James my passion wagon, Maggie had said. Tell him the back seat is built for bonking, but be careful of the broken spring near the left door. As for Summer, sure, didn't I bury her great-grandmother, Aggie. Isn't she living in Aggie's cottage.'

'Summer and Callum are arriving by bus this evening. Keep an eye on Sweeney. I'll ensure he isn't left on his own with boys in the Sacristy.'

'Grand,' Billy said, putting on his cap. 'It's two and a half heads against one. We'll beat the bastard.'

'We will. Then I'm leaving the priesthood.'

'I would too if I'd a girlfriend like Summer. Do ya know what? I'd love one drag of a fag. Call over tomorrow and we'll see if I can teach ya the difference between the clutch and the accelerator.'

Less traumatised than earlier, James returned to the Sacristy and defrocked. Unwilling to visualise the vile acts perpetrated in this holy place, he left. What could be more abhorrent? A question he couldn't answer. At least he'd found an ally, someone to lean on. Billy's jovial mask belied a courageous spirit.

Chapter 24

Stupefied by the horrific display in the Sacristy earlier, James could not dispel the image of Luke. It clawed at every positive thought, and sucked the joy from any exhilaration he felt at Summer's imminent return to Castlebridge. Luke would require professional help. As much as it pained James to sit idly by for the moment, his immediate concern lay with Sean. He would have to be protected. Dare he inform Seanie without proof? Convinced he should, James scoffed the remainder of his lunch and strode to the kitchen. He spotted Mary through the haze of smoke, lounging at the small table, a bottle raised to her blubbery lips.

Mischievous intent in her bulbous hazel eyes, she drained the sherry as if it were beer, and tossed the empty bottle into the bin behind her. 'Did ya leave a clean plate, Father?' Mary lurched to the corner press by the sink, yanked the door open, reached in, and grabbed another bottle. 'Medicinal,' she said, burping loud.

'I did,' James said, regretting every mouthful. Did she even bother washing the cabbage?

'And, did ya splatter the bacon with tomato bloody ketchup?' She tossed the cap of the second bottle at James. 'Are ya a virgin or another randy young priest?'

More amused than abashed, James knelt and retrieved the aluminium bottle-top from under the table. Rising, he grabbed Mary's wrist and wrenched the bottle free. 'One bottle a day is enough.' He twisted the cap tight.

Spittle landed on his shoe as she lunged for the booze, but James was prepared. Her greedy eyes followed the bottle as it rose above his head. He parried with ease her attempted punch to his gut. 'Stop, or I'll have words with Father Sweeney.'

'Father Fergus knew how to thank me every Tuesday and Thursday,' she said, loosening her blouse. 'Would ya like desert?'

Horrified, James shoved her clawing hands away and took a step back. 'You are a despicable woman. Sober up.'

With her cackling, drunken taunts ringing in his ears, James strode from the kitchen and down the hall. Before he slammed the front door shut, breaking glass was followed by a loud curse. Had Father Fergus been tortured by a manipulative parish priest and possibly goaded into sexual acts with a drunken housekeeper? No wonder he went scatty. Another innocent harmed by these loathsome people. The ring of evil had to be broken.

For a moment, he lingered beneath the porch. Sheets of water cascaded from overflowing gutters onto the concrete driveway, refusing to mix with oil spilled from Sweeney's car. Myriad colours shone from the slick. He stepped down into the mini-rapid. Head bowed, he set his course for the only sane place in the village, Lavelle's pub. Perhaps Seanie was correct in his assertion that a barman is more of a priest than ordained ones. No matter, soon he'd be free from this cursed collar and the morons who'd sour cream with their perversions and ill humour.

Despite the rivulets flowing down his forehead and seeping into eyes, he spotted a red, polka-dot-scarfed head poking out the door of the post office beyond Lavelles. He failed to recognise its owner. *I'll tell Seanie the truth. I will. I won't.* Absorbed in internal debate, he looked up, startled by the sound of squelching plimsolls. Agnes bore down on him like a killer whale to a seal. Thinking he could reach the door of the pub and avoid having to speak with her, he cast his eyes to the pools at his feet, and quickened his pace. Something large and soft slammed into him, and bounced off. He glanced up, shocked at the sight of Agnes, apparently in the process of doing a back-flip. Her hands flailing, her fingers clawed, she grabbed the hem of his jacket as she toppled backwards. She landed on her arse on the wet footpath. James stumbled, and landed on top of her. For a moment, their eyes met. The pure horror expressed on her face denied him his instinct to laugh. Assaulted by her garlic breath, he rolled off and scrambled to his feet.

'Here, let me help you up.'

All limbs and squeals, Agnes ignored his outstretched hand. She turned onto her front and brought her knees up under her dripping chin. Perhaps it was the way her eyes raged, and her teeth gnashed as she lurched to her feet that made James resort to prayer. *God forgive me, she looks more Rottweiler than human.* Once she had stabilised her twig-like legs, straightened her knee-length skirt, and pulled her scarf into position, her customary frown replaced the scowl on her ashen face.

'Sorry, Agnes.' He pushed sodden hair from his forehead. 'I'd my eyes on the footpath to avoid the deluge. You must consider me an idiot.'

'Oh, my God. No, Father. I'm the clumsy one.' Dipping a hand into her bag, she rummaged around and pulled out a brown envelope. 'Take it quick or this blessed water will smudge my endeavours.'

'What is it?'

'The list ya wanted of those in need.'

'God bless. You are a miracle worker.' The chameleon forced a wide smile as he accepted the results of her diligence. *Hmm. Her skills may prove very useful.* 'Would you be able to do another small errand for the parish?'

Hunched against the murderous raindrops, a gasp escaped her thin lips. Like a hyena guarding a kill, she glanced left, then right. Bedraggled or not, there was no mistaking her nodding head and the drips falling from it.

'I'm organising a surprise party for dear Father Sweeney. Apart from you, and a few other special people, I'm inviting all the lads who were his altar boys over the years. Could you make a list of their addresses and telephone numbers? Also, find their dates of birth.'

She whipped a small leather-bound notebook from her handbag. Holding it beneath the wide lapel of her sodden coat, she ripped out the pencil concealed in the spine of the book, and scribbled on a page. 'I'll have those names before the gutters are dry. Father Sweeney will be thrilled.'

Prepared to suffer the remnant stink of her dinner upon her breath, James leaned closer. 'Be discreet. We wouldn't want the surprise ruined, would we?' *The bastard will know before the day is out. He'll have palpitations while trying to figure out my intent.*

'No, Father James,' she said, returning the notebook to her bag. 'Goodbye.' Fuelled by conspiracy, she rocketed back to the post office, the epicentre of gossip.

Amazed at his newfound deviousness, James waited until she was out of sight, before he pushed open the door, and scuttled inside the pub. Muted greetings through the cloud of smoke marked his entrance. He nodded to those gathered in the bar. Apart from one of the Kellys, he recognised none of the drinkers, nor did he attempt conversation. Four strides later, he walked through the wainscot archway into the smoke-free snug. Muffled laughter following him, suggested he was the butt of their derision. Weeks earlier, he'd have cringed and slumped onto the stool.

Humming a cheerful tune, Seanie staggered in through the rear entrance, carrying two cases of soft drinks. Sweat beaded his brow. 'Sit down, James. Take the weight off your pious soles. Jesus, you're drenched.' He heaved the crates onto the counter, and hitching up his trousers, strolled off to the public bar. James pushed a stool to the right, allowing him a narrow view through to the front. A few faces were perused before Seanie appeared in his line of sight. 'A large coke.'

Seemingly bemused, Seanie grabbed the cases of drinks and placed them on the floor. Still humming, he pulled the towel from its holder, wiped his brow and kneeled. One by one, he towelled each bottle and placed them in rows upon the shelf, their labels facing forward. 'You will be a bishop someday.'

'What did you say?' James said, leaning over the counter.

Seanie pushed the empty crates under the sink and stood, facing James. 'Give us this day our daily bread. Why is *please* omitted from your prayers, as it was from your request for a coke? I suppose, if you can't use it when speaking to God, a poor feckin barman has no chance.'

'Padre, Seanie. Perhaps procrastination is a worthwhile pastime when played with your collection of pint-swilling layabouts. I, on the other hand, am in need of a large coke ... please.'

Seanie scratched his chin. 'Pro-feckin'-what? Is that one of them new drinks from the EE-bloody-C?'

James tossed a fiver onto the ashtray, while Seanie poured two cokes into a pint glass. 'Do you know much about Keith O'Neill?'

Seanie stiffened, turned, and thrust the glass in front of James. 'Know much? I know fear drove him to the pond, poor lad. Your delightful Father Sweeney raised the rafters of the church with his condemnation. Ye blasted clerics call it a sin. A decent person calls it a tragedy. Are ya decent?'

'I'd never call an act of such finality a sin. When hope is absent, despair can blind anyone. Some see it as the only option.' *I should know.* Lost in thought for a moment, James ran his fingers through his damp hair. *I wonder, does Seanie suspect anything malicious?* 'Does anyone know why he took his own life?'

'My suspicion is that he had issues with his sexuality.'

'Are you sure?' *So, people knew what had happened.*

'Not certain, but I reckon I'm right. Young lads inclined that way often can't admit they are queers, or face the abuse and jeering from wankers like those idiots behind me. Only recently, I got rid of the nightmares as a result of seeing his makeup-streaked face when we pulled his corpse from the pond. Smudged mascara and other coloured shite surrounded his staring, lifeless eyes. Why are ya asking me these questions and resurrecting the past, you pesky priest?' Seanie leant over the counter and grabbed James's left arm, and held it for a moment. 'Answer me.'

James took a sip of Coke, buying time to think. 'Relax. Billy mentioned his name. I was curious, that's all. Poor lad, I'll say a prayer for his soul.'

'Do that. Sorry for shouting at you, and I'm sorry for your own loss. I met your aunt once. If Maggie wasn't so attracted to weirdo priests, I'd have whisked her off somewhere foreign.'

Telling Seanie what I know is too risky, he is too volatile. James concluded a less than direct approach would be required.

Still looking edgy, Sean poured himself a whiskey.

'Wine has gone missing from the Sacristy.' *I'm getting good at this.* Seanie leaned across the counter. 'What are you saying?'

'I think Luke has been stealing it. Can you ensure Sean is unavailable for altar boy duty until I'm certain it's Luke?'

'I've been meaning to talk to you about that. When Sweeney asked Sean to help at Mass, I only relented because my late wife would have wanted it. Sweeney is a twisted bastard. I'd be as glad as any to see the Brits gone from Ulster, but I don't want Sean listening to his version of republicanism. My son will never wear one of your feckin cassocks again. An dtuigeann tú mé[I]?'

'Yeah, I understand, but there's a condition.'

'What?' Sean reddened, but held his temper in check.

'Do not judge me by the actions of Sweeney, or because of your own prejudices. An dtuigeann tú.'

Seanie lifted a glass and poured a liberal measure of whiskey into it. Eyes locked on James, he brought it to his lips and downed it in one go. 'Don't presume me to be an idiot. If I could prove my suspicion that Sweeney struck Sean, the bastard would already be dead.'

'You think him a bully?'

'Think? I know he is, especially when he has taken drink. You, I trust.'

'Sláinte[II].' James tossed back the remainder of his coke. 'Enough said.'

'About that, yes.' Seanie smirked and pointed at the clock.

'What?'

'The bus from Dublin will arrive any minute, lover-boy.'

'How did ... never mind.' James skedaddled before Seanie had a chance to jeer at his embarrassment.

Emerging onto the pavement outside, surprised the rain had ceased and the footpaths were steaming, he blinked at the intense sunlight coming from a cloudless sky. It seemed half the men, women and children of Castlebridge had abandoned their homes to enjoy its warmth. *Blast. I can't be seen waiting for Summer at the bus stop, or can I?* Shoulders slouched, and hands deep in his trouser pockets, responding like an automaton to those who greeted him, James

---

[I] Do you understand me?
[II] A toast. Good health.

trudged toward the presbytery. A young couple holding hands giggled when they parted, allowing him to pass between them. He turned. Something snapped when he witnessed them reunite and nestle against each other. *Man up.*

Head raised, shoulders back, James marched across the road, and stood near the bus stop with his eyes fixed on the corner of Una's shop. *I hope Jack is driving the bus.*

Chapter 25

Convinced dozens of eyes queried his presence beside the bus stop, tentacles of guilt rooted James to the footpath. *What am I afraid of? Love can never be a sin. Grow up. Why is the bus late? Maybe I'll walk out to the cottage and wait for her there.*

The bus lumbered around the corner, a prehistoric monster in metal. Plumes of filthy fumes spewed from beneath the behemoth's belly, and the grinding gears growled a warning to those who considered the middle of the road a suitable place to chatter. James thought it the most beautiful sight in the world. Passing Lavelles, the beast winked its indicator continuously, declaring its intentions. Pneumatic brakes hissing loud, the bus rumbled to a halt. He scanned the darkened windows, seeking a glimpse of Summer or Callum.

Whish, clunk. The door opened. Slouched over the steering wheel, Jack stared straight ahead. Nervous, exhilarated, and impatient, James' leather sole squashed a stranger's cigarette butt and tapped a lively tune on it. An elderly man grasped the rail with gnarled hands and shuffled his way down the steps, struggling with the luggage he carried. Stepping forward, James reached for the bag, set it down, and placed a hand on the old fella's elbow. 'Lean on me.'

Once on terra firma, his breathing shallow from the exertion and his eyes twinkling like fairy lights, the man wheezed a laugh. 'Most unusual, a Catholic good Samaritan. Thank you, Father Jamie. Your wife and child are lovely.' Still laughing, he stooped and lifted his bag. 'Don't worry. I'm a Protestant. Secrecy is second nature to me.'

What?

'Father Jamie. Father Jamie.' Callum raced down the steps and launched himself from the bottom one. 'Can we play football?' he said, after a startled James caught him.

Easing the lad onto the pavement, James tousled Callum's curly hair. 'You bet we can.'

More beautiful than he remembered her, Summer glided down the steps and slung him her heavy rucksack. 'Hi, Jamie.'

Not caring which gossips scrutinised them, Jamie took her in his arms, twirled her round like he had seen in the movies, and whispered, 'I love you.'

'Cool. Butterflies invaded my stomach these past days. Their constant fluttering keeping me awake, only by picturing you could I get to sleep. How cool is that?'

'Cool cool. Wait here Summer. I need a quick word with Jack, and then we'll walk home.' Reluctant to let her out of his sight, he turned and bounded onto the bus.

Jack grunted, and tilted his head. 'You like young boys, do you, priest?'

'What do you mean?'

'He's pretty, the lad outside with your friend.'

'Girls are pretty, boys play football. I made you a promise.'

Jack stared resolutely ahead. 'In my book, every priest is a Sweeney until he proves different.'

'Fair enough, I suppose.' Not built with brick nor mortar, it was obvious to James that the wall protecting Jack from the world and the horrors of the past could not be scaled or sundered. Only trust could open a doorway. 'I've gathered some evidence against him, and will continue to do so. Can you write?'

'Why?'

'Can you write about your time in the orphanage?'

Jack spat onto the floor and started the engine. 'I've already written it. Meet me here Friday week. I'll give you a copy, maybe. Fuck off, priest.'

James leapt off the bottom step as the bus juddered forward. 'Now, Mrs. Brennan,' he said, heaving her rucksack onto his back. Linking arms like a married couple, they giggled like schoolkids. 'What tales have you been telling old men on buses?'

'My mam always told me to be truthful to my elders.'

'I'm older than you.'

Propriety, in the form of Callum, intervened in James' foolhardy show of affection by wiggling his way between them. Many narrowed eyes following them up the street did not go unnoticed by the lovers. Summer waved at two ladies whose guarded smiles suggested wagging tongues would soon be about their business. 'They must think I'm pretty. Why else would they gawk at us?'

'You're witty as well as beautiful, my kind of girl.' He turned and saluted, leaving the ladies little choice but to wave back. 'What lovely people. Most of the villagers still refer to me as the *new priest*. We'll deny them the chance to refer to me as the *old one*.'

'Saintly, but not cool. Kevin calls them sneaky snots.'

Who?

Past the garage, the images of handsome men surrounding Summer a whirlpool in his mind, they crossed over to the primary school. They avoided many of the puddled potholes Callum insisted jumping into. The road widened past the school. Callum ran ahead, hopping, skipping and hollering.

James stepped in front of Summer, turned and blocked her. 'Who's Kevin?'

'Oh,' she said, tilting her head a little, looking at the grassy verge. 'Just someone I know.'

'Close?'

'Very close.' Summer raised her hands, concealing her face.

Apart from a domineering Mother and a mad Aunt, James had little experience in the ways of Eve. Her reaction unnerved him. 'I'm sorry I asked.' He took a step back, turned, and strode up the road after Callum.'

Self-pity raced through the byways of his brain until he felt her warm hand clasp his. Pride suggesting he ought to pull away, he could not. Callum paused at the bend in the road. An impish smile lit his face, before he skipped onto the path leading to the cottage and disappeared. Summer pulled Jamie's hand. 'C'mon, we must catch my son. Kevin is my Dad, you jealous oaf. Callum will hide at the first gate. Pretend you cannot see him, just walk past.'

Our son. James halted again.

'What now?'

'Callum will be *our* son, won't he?'

'Jamie Brennan, I'm looking for a husband and lover, not another child to mind. Once we are married, he will become your son, Callum Kevin McMahon-Brennan. Like, you will become Jamie McMahon-Brennan. Got it? Good.'

'That's a mouthful of a name. Close your eyes.'

'Cool, I love surprises. Are you going to kiss me or ravage me?'

Reaching inside his collar, he eased Maggie's chain and up over his head, and held it within his fist. *Best get around the corner.* 'Keep them closed.' Holding her hand, he guided her off the main road, away from prying eyes. Excited, nervous, he struggled with the clasp. Once open, he brought the chain up under her chin. He pressed against Summer, lingered there for a moment and, sensing her quickening breath, he held his own.

'Keep them closed.' Her lips tremored and he would have stolen a kiss if the blasted chain had been easier to close behind her neck.

'Do you need help?'

'No.' His barked response and her resultant shaking made the task impossible. *What am I doing, idiot. Which finger? Eenie, meenie ... Bishop O'Rourke's, the one I kissed a few weeks ago ... right hand, ... little finger ... no, the one next to it.* James eased the ring off the chain, took her right hand and, gripping it, separated her index finger from the others. Summer gave a muffled giggle and, wrenching her hand away, offered the ring finger of her left. With a gentle twist, he slipped the ring over her knuckle. The shank of his declaration of love uppermost, he twisted it round until the gem sat perfectly at the front for the entire world to see, sparkling like the future he knew would be theirs.

'Open sesame.'

Her eyes blazing with excitement, she blinked twice, before focusing on the engagement ring. As if it were a trinket from a pound shop, her expression changed to one of dismay. 'It's not as cool as the ones from previous lovers.'

The tsunami insult could have drowned his enthusiasm, dampened the desire pressing his pants. 'The previous owner did not find it, or me, wanting.'

The gem flashed before him as her arms swung up and wrapped around his neck. 'It's so ... real. Is it?'

'I borrowed four thousand from the widows and orphans fund. That's a three hundred carat diamond.'

'Wow.' Summer stepped back and traced the outline of the gem. 'I so love you. Come here, my lover.'

Passion rising, James found her lips. Felt her hands press him closer, closer, firmer. Her fingers slid between them, teasing, pulling at his leather belt. She raised a leg slowly, her thigh massaging his. An explosion of pain, starting in his big toe, shot up his leg and watered his disbelieving eyes.

'What the f ...?'

Arms folded like a wronged woman, Summer's grin suggested she enjoyed watching his discomfort. 'Would you care to tell me the truth?'

James wiggled his toes. When the throbbing diminished, he hobbled in front of her, out of arms reach in case further violence was intended.

'On her death bed, Aunt Maggie handed me the ring and told me to give it to you.'

'But she didn't know I existed.'

'She did know. Maggie wed the local priest in a private ceremony before she passed. He is related to Billy Egan. That's the connection.'

'An engagement ring inherited by one priest, from the wife of another priest. Cool. I love it and you.'

Callum shouted. 'Father Jamie. Father Jamie. Come and find me.'

'Our son needs us, as much as I need you. Catch me if you can, Summer Brennan.'

Hopping from one hiding spot to the next, it took twenty fun-filled minutes to reach the cottage. Once they arrived, Callum remained outside playing in the sandpit. Surprised at how unfit he'd become, James collapsed onto the armchair. 'This is crazy. A few minutes running makes me wheeze like a punctured accordion. I'll have to get some exercise.'

Summer filled the kettle, and flicked the switch. 'I've plans on us getting fit together. Would you like me to tell you about them?'

'I'm up for anything.' James twisted his neck back and forth, trying to ease the pain from giving Callum a piggyback ride. 'Ouch!'

'Poor, Jamie' Summer knelt in front of him, smiling as she massaged his thigh. 'Where's it sore babe? Higher?'

Teasing eyes and sensual hands, his pleasure mounting, James covered her hand with his, urging it upwards, higher, higher. Summer's puzzled eyes followed it to his collar. 'The day I remove this manacle from my neck, I will bed thee from dawn till dusk, wench.'

'Wench?' Climbing onto his lap, she trapped his legs between her thighs, leaned close and nuzzled his ear. 'Be thee man enough?'

'What,' he said, pointing to the steaming kettle, 'what is the sizzling sound?'

'Sssh. It's only sparks from the plug playing a tune.' Her fingers slid under the collar and tugged. 'Can we do a trial run?'

I wish ... 'Isn't that dangerous?'

'No, it's exciting.' Lips pressing hard on his, her tongue teased an opening.

Oh ... In tune with the whistling kettle, he grasped her buttocks, and clambered to his feet. For an inexperienced lover, his next move drew expectant moans of pleasure. Taking her full weight, he aimed for the kitchen table, and slid her onto it. Gripping her hands in his, he forced them onto the table behind her head, his lips inches from hers.

Summer closed her eyes. 'I like my men strong.'

'Priests like their wenches to behave. I was referring to the danger of the kettle exploding, not the risks of sex before marriage. I'm off to say Mass. See ya tomorrow, wench.'

Writhing like someone possessed, Summer lashed out, but could not break his grip on her wrists. 'Wimp. Would you deny this damsel a little pleasure while she awaits her Knight?'

'This celibate armour renders me impotent.'

'And leaves me neglected.'

'Beautiful wench.'

'Handsome wimp.'

'One kiss for the road.'

'Two, please.'

Maths was not their strong point.

James staggered from the cottage to the main road, jogged downhill to the village, wheezed his way up Main Street, and fell in through the Sacristy door as the clock chimed seven. *Feck the pervert, if he can't take a joke.* He lifted Father Sweeney's black jumper from the window ledge, and for the second time that evening, he wiped sweat from his brow. *It really is a sweater. Hah, ha.* James crumpled the garment into a ball, tossed it onto the ground, and used it as a doormat.

Saying evening Mass will soon be a distant memory, as will Sweeney.

Chapter 26

Despite being disturbed by the drunken ferret in the early hours, James awoke refreshed, and hopped out of bed. On the rare occasion he'd consulted the full-length mirror, hung on the inside of the wardrobe door, he'd been fully dressed. Wearing only a lovesick smile, he checked himself from head to toe. Wilder than the bristles of Mary's brush, hair on the top of his head refused to yield to the sweep of his palm. James Brennan needed a haircut. An ungainly half-inch of fat, layered around his waist, wobbled at his touch. *Bacon and bloody cabbage. I'm a disgrace.*

James dropped to the floor and executed twenty press-ups. Risking carpet burn, he struggled to achieve an equal number of sit-ups. *Summer's husband will be the fittest in town.* Stirrings not befitting a priest abated at the sight of the dog collar lying on the floor. His thoughts turning to his duties, James dressed. He would take the morning and evening Mass, but Sweeney would officiate over the christening of twins in the afternoon. James winced at the image of him drooling over the male baby.

Without sugar, the cornflakes were as tasty as the Eucharist, the tea no better than bog water. Both were discarded. Laden with two dry slices of brown bread and a half-mug of black coffee, the would-be sexual athlete trudged to the dining room, determined to lose the lard that girded his loins. At the sound of creaking floorboards, James reflected on how best to deal with the abuse. As soon as Agnes provided the list of names, we would somehow determine how many of them had been *special,* and make contact with boys grown to men. Thanks to Seanie's decision, Sean would no longer be part of Sweeney's plans.

There's always a downside. James had little doubt, Sweeney, the devious bastard, had already begun his search for a replacement. Who? As far as he knew, most small parishes would have at least four altar boys. Why did Castlebridge have two? On reflection, he should have asked Sweeney this question sooner.

The pipe leading his sharp nose, his snout dragging his bloodshot eyes behind it, and his entirety encased in a cocoon of smoke, Sweeney lunged into the dining room. 'Brennan. Christ, you look uglier than usual this morning.' Hacking and laughing, he reached down, pulled new slippers off smelly feet, and dropped them onto the table. 'Everything and everyone is replaceable. Three quid from a market in Dublin, what do you think?'

James poked them with the handle of his spoon. 'By the looks of them, I'd guess they're from the flea market. Waterproof soles? A perfect fit for you, I'd say.'

'They had great value in hiking boots. I considered purchasing a pair for you. You'll need rugged soles when O'Rourke sends you to the missions in Africa.'

A reply laced with raging indignation or a more subtle response, which one? 'Forced early retirement is humiliating, resigning is less so. Either way, I will become Castlebridge's parish priest.'

'Over my dead body.'

Sweeney returned his pinkies to the slippers and slithered from the room. His hacked laugh continued as cupboard doors opened and clanged shut in the kitchen. On his return with a mug of coffee, he stumbled, and banged against James's chair. Thinking it intentional, James clenched a fist, then realised the bastard was still drunk. As usual, granules of sugar dropping from Sweeney's shaking spoon submerged into the pools of amber on the table.

Why must sourness always conspire to consume that which is sweet? Despite the sour taste of his beverage, James took a final gulp, and stood. 'Make sure you've sobered up for the christening. It's a *special* day for the parents. Is Sean assisting?'

'No,' said Sweeney, lifting his pipe and matches. 'I've spoken to Lavelle. We've agreed the lad is not suited to the job. I'm sure you'd agree he's too unpredictable and unreliable.'

Sweeney could lie his way into a harem and out of a coffin. 'We'll have to find more altar boys. Luke is getting too old. I'll have a word with one of the schoolteachers.'

'You won't.' Sweeney banged the table. 'I'm the parish priest. I'll decide on suitable candidates. What would you know? You're not much older than them.'

'Maybe you're right.' An envelope lying flat on the mantelpiece caught his attention. 'I'm too young and you're too old.' While Sweeney snorted a rebuke, James grabbed the envelope. The last thing he expected was a coat of arms stamped on the top left corner. On the rear flap, embossed in gold, the letter D had been made with a flourish. *Drumcreevan. What does that scallywag want?*

Curiosity drew the skin on the ferret's nose tauter than the hide of a goat's stretched for the making of a Bodhrán. 'Is it from a fancy friend of yours? One of them queers?'

'That's right.'

'Anyone I know?'

'No. I better get to the church, it's nearly ten.'

† † †

James retreated to the confessional at the end of Mass. He teased open the envelope and slid out the single page letter. Designed to allow sanctuary for the sinner to seek absolution, the confessional also provided a safe haven to read private correspondence. Relying on the glimmer of light coming through the narrow gap in the doorframe, James squinted at the cream paper.

Drumcreevan Manor
Roscommon

My dearest James,

The charlatan baker has gone and done it. Whipped up a storm and refuses to supply the manor with as much as a stale crumb. Man cannot live by bread alone. You buggers spout such as this from the moral high ground you believe you tread. Try making toast without some. Poor Winfred, she laboured over the stove for several days making marmalade. What shall we do with it now? I'd rather die under a stampede of Wildebeest than be reduced to kneading dough.

The solution is obvious.

James, you and your SISTER will visit next weekend. I have recently, ahem, obtained a case of the finest port. Port and toast, old boy. Bring as many loaves as you can carry. Arthritis and God conspire against me, but I can still work the miracle of the fishes with a spot of angling, Drumcreevan style. My man will meet you at the railway station in Boyle at eight-thirty PM on Friday week.

My dearest wife is preparing the finest four-poster in the Manor. While Lizzy, the First, sat her royal bum on the throne, Gráinne Mhaol and The Drumcreevan bared theirs on this fine bed. Springy, but it remains in fine working order. Wimpy and I tested it thrice on a St. Patrick's Day long ago — I would have been about your age then.

Don't forget the parable of the loaves and the fishes. And, for God's sake, man, bring some proper clothes, not those dour, castoff rags from Rome.

Charles.

James shredded the letter, and stuffed the remnants into the inside pocket of his rags, to be scattered onto the first fireplace, bonfire or erupting volcano. Perhaps, the cremation of his priest's garb would have to wait a few more weeks. Scoundrel or not, James could not refuse Charles' tempting invitation.

Arms folded, he closed his eyes and visions of standing alongside Summer in a ruined castle swirled through his thoughts. Snarling gargoyles loomed over them. Drumcreevan stuffed chunks of toast in his mouth. Marmalade dripped from his aristocratic chin, turning blood-red as it hit the table. Night came. Lying naked beside Summer on the silken sheets, with cherubs guarding the corners of the four-poster bed. Flashes of lighting overhead illuminated a forest. He is a red deer, crashing through a thicket, flanked left and right by a pack of wolves. Trapped by the edge of an abyss, James stared at the swirling mists beneath. The grey alpha-male howls, reveals his fangs and moves in for the kill. Only yards away, his face is transformed. It is Sweeney. James leapt into the void.

'Jesus.' James' head-butted the slatted wall. 'Ouch.'

'Who the hell's in there?' a panicked voice shouted. 'Father Brennan, is it you? Are you hurt?'

Startled, James emerged from the confessional, a little dazed. Billy raised his sagging eyes and slid across a row of seats toward him.

'I almost fell asleep in there waiting for a penitent.' James grinned. 'Bumbling twit that I am, I slipped off the edge of the stool and whacked my noggin.'

'Ya scared the shite out me, Father. Have ya time for a chat?'

'I do.' James glanced around. 'Not here, somewhere more private. If I called to your house in an hour or so, would that suit?'

'Perfect.'

'Great. Is my forehead bruised?'

Billy leaned close. 'Do ya mean the red blotch on your temple? It looks sore, like the arse of a baby with nappy rash. Go over to Una. She'll rub some cream on it.'

'You must be joking. This sheep needs to be sheared. Maybe that new barber will have some lotion.'

Billy scratched his chin, pensive. Linking his arm in James', he guided him to the Sacristy. 'Be careful. Josh, the new barber, is a northern Protestant. No telling what snake oils he might have.'

'Stop yer nonsense.'

'Have it yer own way. If you're still alive, I'll see ya later.'

Alone in the Sacristy, the image of the wolves haunted James. The loathsome howls of the pack echoing in his mind, he changed out of his robes. Suffocated by an overwhelming sense of foreboding, James tore out of the Sacristy, and slammed the door shut. *Evil lingers in that room.*

A new barber's shop had opened adjacent to Lavelles. This delighted some of Castlebridge's residents, James included. Few men risked the ladies hairdressers. Most trekked to the neighbouring town of Allenwood.

James made a bee-line for the red and white barber's pole extending over the street. Greeted by the aroma of fresh paint, he opened the white door and stepped into an unexpected sauna. 'Hello,' he said, peering through the steam.

From somewhere in the misty beyond, a masculine voice choked a response. 'Leave the door open for a minute.'

Wisps of steam curled and raced for freedom, only to vanish into another dimension upon crossing the threshold. A shadow moved through the vapour, a fleeting thing, neither man nor beast by the shapelessness of it. Something flapped in the billowing whiteness. Batman emerged. The cape shimmering in front of his head shielded his face, but his damp blond hair proved him an impostor.

'Sorry.' The barber's cape falling to his side, he proffered his sweaty hand. 'Josh Allen. You must be James. Father James.'

A handshake and a loud laugh shared, James followed Josh inside, and sat as directed on the burgundy-coloured leather chair. *Posh.* A steamed mirror ran the length of the setback section of the wall in front of James. In the centre, a washing basin with a grooved headrest awaited those requiring a wash. Given the humidity, a dry cut was now out of the question. On each side of the sink, lined up like surgical instruments on the short sections of counter, the tools of Josh's trade dripped with moisture. Rivulets chased their way downward to the tune of gravity.

To his left, another mirror ran from floor to ceiling, extending as far as a row of plastic seats placed against the sidewall. Josh pushed the mirrored wall. A door sprung open, and he stepped inside. Compared to any other hair salon James had visited, this was the Ritz, though a little steamy. The barber returned with two bath towels and dropped one onto James' lap.

'Rub a dub, dub.' Josh dried his face, then wiped the mirror until it squeaked. 'You're quiet for a priest, much quieter than your older colleague.'

James leaned forward, allowing the barber to wrap the cape around him. 'Do you mean Father Sweeney?' Both actor and audience, James watched the mirror as though it were a television screen. Like John the Baptist's on the platter presented to Herod, only his head remained visible. Every movement was captured and replayed back to him. It took James a moment to register the reflected poster of Culture Club on the back wall. Perhaps this chameleon could learn a trick or two from Boy George. The lyrics from their hit single played over and over in his head, refusing to stop like it always did.

'What style would you like? Scalped or layered? Short back and no sides is a common request. By the way, Father Sweeney thought I was Jesus when I asked him the same question.'

'How so, you have different hair styles?' Amazed his eyebrows shifted up as he asked, James tried mouthing the words again while holding them in check. *Hmm, I need to work at not showing what I'm thinking.*

'He wanted a miracle.' Josh combed James' hair, pushed any wayward clumps into their natural position where they remained. With his hands rested on James' shoulders, he peered at the young priest in the mirror. 'Sitting where you are now, Sweeney suggested a good barber could hide the bald patch infiltrating his crown. My face frozen in the same serious mask you now wear, I locked my eyes on his image in the looking glass. Is vanity a sin in the Catholic faith? Mirror, mirror on the wall ...'

'Did he answer you?'

'He scowled.'

Do I scowl? 'Josh, are you an Agatha Christie fan?'

Deliberately slow, the scissors twisted in the barber's hand. The point now aimed at James' throat answered the question. '*The Mirror Crack'd*, as did Father Sweeney's temper. It seems the spirit of ecumenism flew over his head and kept going.'

'It was a great movie. What do you mean?'

'Exploding like a firework, he hopped from the stool and spat on the floor. "No fuckin Protestant will cut my hair." It's a wonder all of my feckin' mirrors weren't shattered when he slammed.' Maintaining a poker-face proved difficult for James. Control over twitching facial muscles requiring distraction, he concentrated on Boy George's lyrics. 'So you are a Protestant. Why are you telling me about Sweeney?'

'Because Seanie Lavelle swears you were born with a frown on your face and Rosary beads stuck up your arse. He has tasked me with the removal of the lemon-sour expression, including your hair.'

'And how will the beads be removed?'

'He mentioned something about a young lady.' Josh smiled. 'Gotchya.'

James wanted to laugh. 'Were your ancestors with King Billy when he crossed the Boyne? Is your own behind so stuffed with your orange sash you talk only in riddles of excrement?'

'Touché. I suspect arse and shite were the words on the tip of your tongue, but Rome denies you permission to use them.'

James shuffled in his seat. Stony-faced, while his hand sought a path out from the cape, he observed the smiling hazel eyes holding him in their gaze. Josh appeared of similar age and stature to James. Assured, yet his demeanour suggested he could be trusted. Like James and Seanie, Josh's profession demanded he kept good counsel or would soon be bereft of customers. His blabbing about Sweeney was justifiable. *I need friends. Why not Josh?* Extending his hand upwards, James burst out laughing. 'I needed a laugh, so thanks.'

Giving a low five rather than a shake, the barber resumed his position, poised to deliver unto Caesar what was rightfully his, a professional haircut.

'Do you usually have a sauna when the place is quiet?'

The comb pointed to a glass-fronted box sitting on the counter. 'That's for steaming the hand towels used on those desiring a close shave. There are gargoyles in the works and it has stopped steaming. I tried using the kettle, but the switch got stuck. Sparks flew, and I panicked. On my knees out back, searching for a screwdriver, I cursed you for arriving when you did.'

'You mean gremlins not the grotesque sculptures hanging on buildings.'

'True, but that unit contains a monster's face.' Josh trod to the steamer and flicked a switch. A faint, red light illuminated the interior, increasing in intensity until it glowed bright. 'Watch the glass.' Within a minute, etchings appearing haphazardly on the surface formed something resembling a red-eyed gargoyle.

Held in check these many years, wit bubbled to the surface, surprising its owner. James laughed before the words spurted from his quivering lips. 'That's not a gargoyle. It's Father Sweeney.'

'You deserve an ear clipped off for such impertinence.' Josh switched off the steamer. 'Lucky for you, my reputation as a barber depends on ensuring my clients do not leave lopsided. I shall clip both sides after my hand steadies.'

'Are you from Castlebridge? You seem well educated for a barber.'

'And you for a priest. Stop it, Josh. Sorry, James, I couldn't resist a silly retort.'

James acknowledged this with a smile and a nod.

'Third generation if you must know. My grandfather moved here from Tyrone in eighteen sixty-four. And you?'

The door slid open, silent and slow. Unaware of the head and feminine fingers edging around the frame, Josh continued to snip. James smirked. Only a professional eavesdropper could execute this manoeuver with such skill.

'Come in, Agnes. We won't eat you, will we, Josh?'

Josh swivelled as Agnes stumbled inside, her demeanour that of a child caught with a forbidden bar of chocolate.

'I ... I'm looking for Father Brennan. Una Mahon swore she saw him sloping in here earlier.'

'Sloping?' Josh's over-emphasis of the *S* made it sound like a dirty word.

Agnes spotted James reflected in the mirror. 'That's what she said. Sure, ya know Una, an awful gossiper and always saying the wrong thing.' Her hands a flurry of anxiousness, she stepped forward and dropped an envelope on James' lap. 'Here's the list for the party.' Like the steam earlier, she evaporated before James could thank her. The door closed silently behind her.

James stared at the envelope. His heart thumped in expectation of reading the contents. He invoked the resolve only someone who observed Lent with honesty could achieve.

'Breeding.' Josh grinned. 'To answer your earlier question, I'm a historian by nature, a barber by trade. Agnes Murphy, daughter to Paddy and Sheila Murphy. An interesting lineage, in so far as little has changed in the behaviour of the four generations of Murphys I've had the misfortune to study. Purveyors of information and consumers of alcohol, they were as thick as thieves with a plethora of parish priests. It seems Agnes and you are quite close, so the tradition continues.'

Caught in the act. James allowed Josh to observe a look of horror followed by a whisper of a smile. 'Historians are, in my experience, a little odd. At least, the religious ones in Maynooth are.'

'True,' Josh said, pushing James' head forward. 'Many become time travellers who forget to or cannot return to the present. Early in my studies, historical anomalies tested my sanity. Documented historical facts consist of not only factual ones, but also those the author perceived had occurred, and quite often, those the writer wished had been the case or some other flight of fancy.'

'I like the time travel metaphor. It explains the weirdness of some. How well up are you on the Anglo-Irish landed gentry?'

'No metaphor, I can assure you. Ah, it might surprise you to know Father Gargoyle also asked me a similar question, moments before he stormed out. Though in his case, he showed me an envelope bearing a coat-of-arms.'

Eyebrows held in check, James wondered if the bastard had steamed open the letter from Drumcreevan. There had been no visible sign of interference. 'Did he, indeed?'

'Would you agree it was careless of him not to cover the addressee?'

'Very. You responded to his query?'

'Did I fuck.' Josh slammed the comb and scissors onto the counter. 'I've finished cutting your hair. Wait here a minute.' Fury in his steps, Josh tore from the salon.

Confused by this sudden outburst, James stood. He reached back and freed the Velcro fastener, allowing the cloak to slither onto the floor. *What is Josh up to?* Choosing a chair at the side, James sat, contemplating Agnes' list. *These names might be enough.*

Minutes after leaving, Josh walked backwards through the door, carrying a pint of stout and a glass of iced coke. After handing James the soft drink, he locked the door. 'My apologies. History is littered with pricks like Sweeney who think their collar should make them beyond reproach. He's rude. I don't converse with such people willingly.'

The drink was a welcome distraction for a moment. 'Did you see the letter D on the back of the envelope? The coat-of-arms I believe is from the Drumcreevan family.'

Josh wiped the creamy mess from his lips. 'What do you wish to know, and why?'

I'll not mention Summer, not yet. 'The scallywag has befriended me and invited me to visit his castle. Seeing as you are a historian and a Protestant, I thought you might know something about him.'

Josh sat on a chair alongside James and stared at the tiled floor. It seemed he'd indeed travelled back in time, for not a sound escaped his lips for a full three minutes, which James measured by watching the wall clock. When he stirred, he downed the pint. 'Knowledge is a commodity I refuse to trade in. The validity of some information I have garnered through dedicated research cannot be proven, unless revealed by those close to, or descendants of those involved with past events. This is such a case.'

'Oh. I'd hoped you would tell me they were one of the better Protestant landlords. Not that it really matters now. The past is the past.'

'Not so. The past is the foundation of the future. Never underestimate it. If I was Catholic, I'd be proud to shake Lord Drumcreevan's hand.'

'Really. Why?'

Josh pointed to the tip of his nose. 'There is a glaring anomaly in the Drumcreevan past. Ask him this, and you may mention my interest in the answer, if he can provide you with one. Grace O'Malley, the pirate queen of Mayo, would slit her own throat before lying with an English Lord. Would Drumcreevan have slit his own throat if asked to bed the virgin Queen?'

'Very cryptic, isn't it?'

'Lord Charles Drumcreevan may refuse to be baited, and I may never learn the truth. If you confirm my suspicions, you'll never pay for a haircut or a shave in this establishment.'

'Do I get a free sauna as well?'

A knock on the door ended their conversation prematurely.

Before leaving, James slapped Josh on the back. 'Can you be a friend to a priest?'

'Do I have a choice?'

Chapter 27

James gripped the envelope in his left pocket as though it were the winning ticket to a lottery. Soon, the extent of Sweeney's abuse would be discovered. Each time he opened his mind to the depravities the monster may have inflicted, queasiness invaded his gut and instinct transformed the images into matchstick-men and boys. Try as he might to block the bastard from his mind, every time he considered his relationship with Summer, Sweeney infiltrated and darkened his thoughts.

Sweeney believed himself to be untouchable. James had met his ilk in the Seminary. Driven men, who were so eager to suckle from the breast of infallibility, they had set their sights on the powerhouse of their faith. Xavier O'Loughlin, a prime example, had trampled on the other Seminarians, and bullied James' best friend, Mick *The Mouse* Flanagan. James reckoned Xavier's ambitions extended beyond sitting at the right hand of the Father, he wanted the throne. Such men were opposites to the majority of priests who tried to live according to Christ's teachings. James knew he should have protected his friend and faced down the bully. God, if he still believed in such an entity, may have forgiven his cowardice, but he could not forgive himself.

Billy lived in a bungalow, set back from the road, beside the GAA club[1]. Mature pine trees, sculpted and uniform, lined the perimeter of the property. On each side of the driveway, well-tended flowerbeds offered visual splendour, but the scent of mint caught James' attention as he strolled along. Spying the herbs growing in gaps between the blooms, he grinned at his own witty thought. *Billy-no-thumb has green fingers*. Nearing the house, he admired a small pond in the tear-shaped lawn. A little Buddha, mounted on a marble plinth, overlooked watercress and lilies.

---

[1] Gaelic Athletic Association.

The front door opened, and Billy scurried outside to meet James. 'Come this way,' he said, grasping James' arm. 'My wife is having a nap.' The retired undertaker's stumpy legs zipped along the path to the enormous block-built garage at the rear. 'Welcome to my haven.'

More like a bank vault than a retreat, three locks had to be negotiated to gain entrance. Billy closed the door behind them and switched on the lights, revealing a spacious open-plan interior. Gleaming brighter than when new, Aunt Maggie's yellow Fiat sported a new set of chrome spotlights and racing tyres. James walked to the driver's side. 'Holy, God. Go-fast stripes as well. You have been busy. How can I repay you?'

Hands on hips, Billy beamed. 'Retirement is what you make of it. Sitting around being idle is an early death. I added the stripes and spotlights for fun, and will remove them when it becomes a family car.' He winked.

'Thank you. Two months ago, I was alone. Now, it seems I have several friends in Castlebridge.'

'I'd offer you a coffee if the switch on the kettle wasn't broken.' Billy pointed to the chrome dome sitting on a counter in the far corner. 'It sparked and shocked me last week.'

'Similar to Summer's. Wait, it's identical, and so is Josh's. That's weird, isn't it? At the first opportunity, I'll buy three new kettles.'

'Nah, they're probably from a faulty batch, that's all. It happens. Come,' said Billy, edging his way toward a pair of funeral caskets on a stand, which James hadn't noticed.

'A bit morbid, isn't it?'

'Look around, James. This garage is me. Look at my *Noah* tools, which my wife nicknamed, on that workbench. Two of everything arranged in order. Two spare gas cylinders, and yes, two coffins. One for *moi* and the other was intended for my dear wife. Alas, she wants to be cremated, and have her ashes tossed over my tomato-less tomato plants.' He lifted the lid of the nearest coffin, slipped his hand inside and pulled out a cigarette and an ashtray.

'I thought you didn't smoke anymore.'

Billy lit the cigarette. 'I don't,' he said. 'My schizophrenic alter ego does, usually twice a day. To remind me of how disgusting the habit is. I'll have a word with him later.'

'You're joking.'

'No. I am lying though. Of late, he's been going through a pack of ten a day. All this business with Sweeney has him agitated. We can't sleep at night. He gets up for a fag, me for a coffee.'

'That, I can understand,' said James, pulling the crumpled envelope from his pocket. *Dare I open it?* His steady hands now trembled.

'What have you there?' Billy tossed the cigarette butt into the ashtray. 'You look like you've seen or heard a banshee.'

'It's a list of all the altar boys since Sweeney came to the parish.'

'Oh, clever priest,' Billy teased. His face fell, 'Jesus, do we really want to know?' He reached into his final resting place and grabbed another cigarette. 'What are you waiting for, divine inspiration?'

There is no God. Taking hold of the corner, James ripped the envelope open and removed the single sheet of lined notepaper. 'Here goes.' James unfolded the document and placed it on the coffin.

Billy whispered the names as he read them. 'Joe Wall, Conor Heffernan ...'

'Keith O'Neill – deceased. Michael Reilly – deceased. Eoghan Jacob – five years he is missing.' James gasped. 'Thirteen names. Sean is the last one, and possibly the luckiest.'

'Two are dead. That's not natural.' Scanning the list a second time, Billy pulled a red pen from his pocket and put a question mark beside Conor's name. 'Only Joe Wall still lives around here. Conor Heffernan is in jail. I always wondered why such a good lad turned bad, and why his crimes and sentencing were shrouded in secrecy. Rumours festered for months, but even the Murphys, bored from scraping the bones of that scandal, chalked it up as a government conspiracy.'

'You think Sweeney is to blame?'

'Don't you?' Billy pulled a notebook from his pocket and copied the list of names.

'We know about Keith, Luke and Sean,' James said. 'That leaves ten other possible victims of abuse. Find out what you can about Conor, Michael Reilly and Eoghan Jacob. I'll visit Joe Wall. Then we'll regroup.'

'Fuck!' Billy smacked his forehead. 'I knew the name rang a bell with me. Joe Wall overdosed at seventeen and is locked in his own world, barely alive. Kate, his mother, rarely leaves the house.'

James and Billy stared at each other, both aghast at the implications.

'Why has no one else questioned Sweeney's activities?'

Billy spluttered, and barked several coughs into a handkerchief pulled from his pocket. 'Most around here grew up fearing the rule of the Church, doffing their hats to Priests and Bishops. Hell is a mighty deterrent, and belief an iron shackle when faith is compulsory. The English, the Famine and the Church, in no particular order, painted the landscape of our lives and made sure the laws of the land and God kept us in check.'

Perhaps some parishioners posed questions, but were silenced by Sweeney. Did the Bishop snub any others?

James nodded. 'You're a philosopher as well as a gardener.'

'When you spend your entire life tending corpses, it's difficult not to reflect on the bigger picture. Occasional strange noises make you jump. Apart from passing wind, cadavers do not speak.' Billy paused for a moment, and blew ash off his casket. 'The mortal remains of Keith O'Neill screamed at me as I sponged the makeup from his bloated face. Jesus, I should have been more aware of his angst.' Billy plucked a hair from his bushy nostrils, dropped it onto his palm to examine it before flicking it away. 'Hair today, tomorrow turns to dust. I never philosophise, preferring to observe with a little homespun commentary.'

'Why not give more worth to your opinions?'

Another grey hair, this time teased from the opposite nostril, he held it up for James to view. On releasing it, he blew hard, sending the wisp spiralling until it faded from sight. 'Balance, James, is the order of the universe. Besides, who'd want to be buried by a clever shite who plucks hairs from his nose in public?'

James leaned against the casket, and running his finger along a brass handle, contemplated on their investigation. To wade into rapids and dare to brave a raging river presented an easier task than the one they faced. To know of Sweeney's treachery was one thing, to prove it beyond all reasonable doubt, demanded hard evidence, backed by more than one person. If he or Billy unearthed a single victim who spoke out, and Jack provided written documentation of abuse from the orphanage, combined with their suspicions, this must convince the Bishop.

Billy returned the ashtray to its hidey-hole. From the same place, he pulled a bottle of aftershave, and applied a generous drop to his chin. With a grunt, he closed the lid on the evidence of his addiction. 'Sarah-Jane would kill me if she knew.'

James swung by the car on the way to the door, glanced inside and imagined himself behind the wheel. *"Vroom, vroom,"* he said.

Billy wheeled around, smiling. 'What did you say?'

In James' head, sunlight beamed through the stained-glass windows of the church onto the child whose mother he now loved. 'Summer's son, Callum, says vroom when he plays with his toy car.'

'Do you love her, James?'

'Yes.' He stepped close to Billy. 'I can't bear being separated from her.'

Tears haunted the corners of Billy's eyes and refused to be blinked back. Once again, he pulled his handkerchief from his pocket and, this time, wiped them away. James felt uncomfortable for the first time in his company.

'Sarah-Jane is dying. I'd die twice to save her. She is my summer, my winter, my autumn and spring. Without her... I'd wither.'

I guide all that you do. Pray for her. 'That bloody voice again.'

'What?' Billy sobbed. Embarrassed, he shuffled his feet, and turned toward the exit.

Sorrow watering his own eyes, James clenched his hands in the attitude of prayer as Billy left the garage. James traipsed after him. Unable to help himself, he intoned, 'Hail Mary, full of grace, the Lord is with thee ...' Intending a full decade of the Rosary, Billy's loud laughter halted his devotions.

'James, in your innocence, you have cheered me up. Thank you for the prayers, but no thanks. My wife is a Buddhist, and is prepared. After she's gone, I'll need your support.'

Programmed to respond in a particular manner, with the love of God and the Saints on the tip of his tongue, Father James unshackled his mind and allowed James Brennan to reply. 'I can't cook.'

'That's because your mammy and your housekeeper spoil ya.'

'Not for much longer. If we can gather the evidence against Sweeney, then I can marry Summer. Where does Joe Wall live?'

Bill scratched his chin. 'One, two ... eleven,' he counted using the fingers of his left hand. 'Eleven from eighteen equals seven. Isn't that right, Father?'

'Yep.'

'The Walls live at number seven on the red-brick terrace behind the church, around the corner from Murphy's ministry of gossip. Light cannot bend around corners, but Agnes and her clan can see around one. Beware of them sussing out your intentions. One and one make three in their world.'

'Not if I knock on Murphy's door first and provide an excuse to visit number seven.'

† † †

On more than one occasion, James had spotted Agnes and her mother entering one of the houses on the terrace behind the church. Stopping halfway along the pavement, he pulled out the only coin in his pocket, and tossed it in the air. *Heads it's the third last house.* Gambling was frowned upon in the Seminary. The penny rolled along the footpath, slid over the edge and disappeared down a drain.

Penniless, he knocked hard on the black door of the second last building. Lace curtains twitched behind the sitting-room window and shadows darkened the frosted panes each side of the front door, but the way remained shut. Seven more times he rapped, much to the chagrin of his knuckles. Agnes and her family were strange people. As entertaining as it was to play cat and mouse, James abandoned Murphy's unfriendly doorstep.

Trudging around the corner, he sucked his throbbing knuckle and gazed ahead. Two ladies deep in conversation ignored his approach and his greeting. Perhaps living in the shadow of the granite chapel chilled the inhabitants of Church Row. Nearing Wall's house, he wondered about Joe. How disabled was he? Would he be able to recall his time as an altar boy? How would he approach the topic without alarming them?

Number seven showed more promise than the ageing paint on the entrance suggested — it had a brass knocker. The door opened moments after metal clanked metal three times. A middle-aged woman, wearing a frown and a flowery apron, peered out. Instinct suggested a wide smile would bring a warm welcome. For the second time in as many minutes, his gamble failed.

'Priest.' The snarling tone of her voice confirmed he was less welcome than a cuckoo to a blackbird's nest. 'Fuck off.' Timber crashed against timber. A solitary blue flake of paint flew from the uppermost panel and floated to land on the ground by his feet. Head bowed and sucking in his cheeks, James stared at the fragment, as if it could explain why he was being treated like a leper. Undeterred by the profanity and the ringing in his ears, driven by a purpose to which he had bound himself, James lifted the tarnished knocker again and rapped hard.

Somewhere inside, Mrs. Wall responded with either 'Feck off' or 'Fuck off.' Left with little choice, his knees, trained in the art of supplication, he bent until the letterbox became level with his lips. He poked the spring-loaded flap back. 'Mrs. Wall. Please, may I talk to you and Joe?'

James stooped lower, leaned against the door, and peeped through the letterbox. His eyes adjusting to the gloom he spied movement too late. Blinded by the liquid splashing through the opening, he fell backwards. 'Damn.'

Cold tea being a remedy for eye complaints, he should have been grateful to Mrs. Wall for her generosity. The door opened. Prepared to scramble away on all fours, he tried to focus. His vision blurred, James caught a hazy image of something about to smack into his face. He put his hands up to ward the missile off and his fingers closed upon a cloth

'Get up off yer arse and wipe your face. Priests aren't welcome here.'

James dried his face, almost grateful she didn't put sugar in her tea. At the sight of the frying pan materialising by her side, he slid backwards on his bum to the edge of the footpath. Ninja-like, he twisted and sprung to his feet, coiled to meet any challenge or weapon. 'Truce or I'll tell the Murphys you attacked me.' Plucked from the ether with no intelligent thought or weighing up of consequences, his threat softened the defiance in her eyes. *So like my own mother.*

'Would you come in and have a nice cup of tea, Father?' Not waiting for his answer, she grabbed his arm and dragged him inside. Astounded, James allowed her to march him along the hall, and shove him into a dark room. 'Take a seat.'

Silhouettes took form as his eyesight adjusted. Light from the television flickered across faded wallpaper peeling at the joints. Tom chased Jerry across the screen. James faltered, his gaze locked on to the wheelchair parked beside a two-seater couch. *Joe?*

James stepped around the chair and gazed upon a lad not much younger than he. Joe's head slumped sideways on a navy cushion, his dusty brown hair tied back in a ponytail, hung limp and lifeless. Drool dripped from the side of his mouth onto a flannel towel. The corner of the tartan rug wrapped around his legs and hips, trailed onto the floor and under a wheel. James stooped and teased it free. Seeing the vacant expression in the young man's eyes, James spoke. 'Hello, Joe. My name is James, Father James.'

For a moment, James dared not move, rooted to the spot by an overwhelming sense of sadness, numbed by the pervasive silence. Names scribbled on a sheet of paper were but a means to garner success in his mission to break Sweeney. Joe and the others existed, real people, not actors playing victims in an investigation.

The lingering aroma of disinfectant reminded him of Maggie's nursing home. Anger replacing sympathy, James clenched his fist and banged the arm of the settee as he sat. *If this is Sweeney's work, I'll kill the bastard.*

Mrs wall entered carrying a tray. 'That's good, Father. Make yourself at home,' Mrs. Wall said.

Short in stature and a touch plump, her muscular arms placed the refreshments on the glass coffee table in front of James. Though she smiled, her sunken eyes betrayed the hardships she endured in looking after Joe.

'You didn't like my tea.'

Her narrowed eyes watching him for a reaction, James grinned. 'I've washed in worse.'

'Tea is off, I made us black coffee.'

James reached for the cup. 'Thank you, Mrs. Wall.' *No hint of apology from her. A formidable woman?*

'Stop calling me Mrs. I'm Aoife. Help yourself to the biscuits, they were Joe's favourites. What do they call you apart from the new priest?'

'Many names I'd not repeat. I was christened James.'

Aoife plucked a tissue from a packet stuffed down the side of Joe's wheelchair. Placing a hand under her son's chin, she wiped away the string of dribble. 'There ya go.' With her legs straddling Joe's, she leaned forward over him. She cupped her hands and slid them down behind his neck to the middle of his spine. Grunting from the effort, she pulled him towards her. One arm held him, while the other adjusted the rug. She eased him into a comfortable position, then kissed his forehead.

'Can I borrow a tissue?' James reached for the packet, took two, and brought them to his nose. Simple tasks, which he took for granted. These were as mountains for this woman to ascend every day. 'How do you and your husband get Joe in and out of bed or wash him?'

Aoife sighed. 'Paddy is dead these eleven years. I'd be lost without my son, Cormac. Every day at lunchtime, he drives back here from his job, a nineteen mile journey. Without ever complaining, he helps me get Joe dressed, washed, and out of bed. Nine miles there and ten miles back ever since they put in the one way system in Allenwood. He's a good lad.'

'Thank God you have help. You must be proud of Cormac'

Aoife shrugged. 'I'm proud of them both. God has nothing to do with it. Joe,' she said, patting her son's knee, 'loved being an altar boy, and until his accident, I never missed Mass.'

'Really?'

'Father Sweeney perched on that very settee. Preening himself like the cockerel he is, he sneered at me when I begged for help.' Aoife sobbed for a moment, grabbed a tissue, and wiped her bloodshot eyes. Do ya know what he said? "Joe sinned and got what he deserved." Those cruel words near sliced me in two.'

What? Stay calm. 'I bet they did.' James gulped back the remaining coffee. 'Father Sweeney is a horrible man. What did he mean?'

'Mean? Word for word, this was his reply when I screamed the same question. "Your perverted son seduced another into lewd acts. God has punished him." When I pressed him further, he zipped his lying lips by saying the seal of the confessional cannot be broken.'

Sweet Jesus. He blames his victims for his own perversions.

Threadbare like the carpet, his repertoire of words to express his horror and shame proved inadequate. Left only with the tools of his trade, James reached across and placed his hand on Joe's head. 'Father, mind this child. He is guiltless.' *I wish I could tell her the truth. She's suffered enough, and deserves to know why Joe tried to overdose.*

Her eyes lit with a joy he'd imagined impossible for her. 'Joe,' she said, running her hand along his cheek. 'He is innocent. Isn't he?'

'Yes, Aoife.'

'Even though Sweeney said otherwise, I knew Joe could never hurt anyone. A mother knows these things.' Aoife turned to face James. 'How do you know? You've never met us.'

'You've waited a long time to hear the truth. It pains me to say, you will have to wait a short while longer. Soon, the world will know of your boy's innocence. I swear.'

'How do I know ...?'

'I'm not like Sweeney? Trust me. Please.'

'I'd like to take Joe to your Mass someday. Miracles can happen, can't they, Father.'

'I'm sure they do.' *Only if you believe in the tooth-fairy.* James stood. 'Send a message to me when you want to go. I'll push the wheelchair to the church and home again afterwards.'

Aoife nodded. 'I'm sorry for my earlier behaviour. Trust does not come easy. When the light of hope is extinguished by false promises, what's left?' They walked down the hall. One hand on the handle of the door, she turned to face James. 'Let me down and I'll see you castrated.'

The door on number seven closed quietly behind him. James stepped into the shadow cast by the church and shook his head. Evidence may be harder to find than he'd envisaged. Someone on the list must share their *special* secrets. Who?

He shivered at the thought of failing Mrs. Wall.
I'll not tell Summer what I risk in my search for the truth.

Chapter 28

The troubles in Ulster dominated the news programme on the television. Pie-eyed, Sweeney swayed on the edge of the armchair in the sitting room, whiskey sloshing around the tumbler as his hand gesticulated. Determined to maintain a semblance of normality, James feigned an interest in the latest scenes of petrol bombs bombarding RUC vehicles in West Belfast. Shielded behind a barricade of two burning cars, kids launched stones, piping, and a host of other missiles. Older lads, wearing balaclavas and surplus army jackets, lobbed more lethal cocktails over the barriers. Scenes such as these, a nightly occurrence in Belfast and Derry, no longer shocked James and those living in relative harmony south of the border.

'Yes!' Sweeney hissed. 'That's the seventh direct hit.' Slurping a mouthful of whiskey, he turned to James as though they watched a football match. 'Seven nil.'

He's easily amused. I wonder if I can light the fuse on his temper without striking a single match. More interested in analysing Sweeney than the news, James changed position on his armchair to get a better view of the old priest. 'They have a great aim.'

'Ha! Look at the Brits hiding down the street.' Sweeney tossed back his drink. 'Er? What did you say, Brennan?'

'I said those lads should take up cricket.'

'Cricket! I suppose you would have them play against the Prods?'

'Why not? It's a non-contact sport. Nobody would get hurt.'

'And maybe, we'll sing God Save the Queen at half time, if there's such a bloody thing in that daft game. Suck a few oranges like those ponces at the rugby matches. Is that it? I've a mind to thrash you with a hurley for uttering such nonsense.'

'You'd enjoy that,' James said, rising to his feet. 'Did you find fresh altar-boys?'

'All is in hand, young man.' Sweeney removed his glasses and pulled a handkerchief from his pocket. Focused on polishing the lens, he stopped mid-wipe, and growled. 'What do you mean by fresh?'

I've touched a tender spot. Look the bastard in the eye. 'Fresh, as in new or ... I don't know the dictionary inside out. You do crosswords.' Pausing for a moment, James noticed suspicion furrow Sweeney's already wrinkled brow. *Now, take him to the precipice.* 'There must be more words. How about, untrained, unspoiled ... virgin?'

Sweeney's wolf-eyes widened as he assumed the appearance of a bedraggled teddy bear. Cuddle me, his smiling face suggested. *It took less than a heartbeat for him to adopt a persona that fools most people, but no longer me.*

'Neoteric is a great word. Everything immature becomes experienced, curates even become priests. Do you consider yourself neoteric, Father Brennan?'

Despite his disgust, James couldn't help marvel at the surreal transformation of this arrogant predator. 'Did you know, if you mistime when you're bowling in cricket, the ball is likely to return from the bat like a missile? I'm going for a quick walk by the river.' *Two can play the innocent jester.* 'Would you like to come with me?'

'No thanks. I'll enjoy another whiskey and test myself with a cryptic crossword.'

James eased himself off the couch and lumbered to the door. The image of Sweeney, dressed in a white jumper and trousers, standing on a cricket crease tossing petrol bombs at a bewildered batsman, tickled him to the extent he wondered if Summer could replicate it on canvas. She could paint a series of pictures similar to the Stations of the Cross. The run up, followed by the overarm bowling of a fiery bottle, and the final one, and with whatever artistic licence was necessary, depict Sweeney crucified on the stumps. As soon as he reached the cottage he'd ask her.

James missed the mountains of his youth. The pleasure of sitting beside the stream at dusk, watching shadows chase gold and amber fingers over the bog and up the distant glens to the jagged peaks. He'd imagined the fairy folk coming out at twilight, dancing around their glowing fires, ready to whisk away naughty children. To ward off evil, James had always turned his jacket inside out before nightfall. An apotropaic jumper is best, but a master angler had no need of one.

One calm autumn evening, he crossed the fields on his way home carrying three plump trout. An unexpected breeze plucked at the tail of his jacket. Louder than the keening of a thousand mothers, the mournful wail of the Banshee sounded from the distant woods. In fear of his life, he dropped the fish and fled to his parents' farmhouse. His father said it was a fox. Not for the first time, his mother disagreed and insisted on saying a decade of the Rosary. The death of Daniel O'Kane that night, a neighbour, left James terrified for months. It was a time of innocence and he was a sponge for myths and folklore.

Lost in time and place, James reached Summer's home quicker than he expected, whisked there by the good fairies of his dreams. Having only viewed the cottage through lovesick eyes, the decay and neglect had been invisible to him. Above the broken gutter to the front, several roof tiles were askew. One at the butt of the chimney was definitely cracked. Paint flaked from walls and windows, which required fresh putty to hold the glass panes in place. Weeds had the run of the garden, the boundaries, and most of the gravel path. This ramshackle cottage in a wilderness would soon be his responsibility. James stared necessity and obligation in the face and, like a good Christian, turned the other cheek. *I'll worry about the cottage when I move in.* Decision made, problem solved, he opened the back door and stepped inside.

His lady in waiting readied the manor for her knight in mournful black armour. Standing near the wall, amidst mounds of wallpaper strips, paint flakes and lumps of crumbling plaster, Summer trowelled filler into holes the size of a man's fist. James sneaked up on her, placed his hands on her hips and leant over her shoulder. Lost in the scent of jasmine, he whispered. 'Guess who?'

Working another slab of filler into a crevice, she swapped the trowel for a scraper, using the smaller tool to flatten the mix and render a smooth finish.

'Are you ignoring me?' James said, nuzzling her ear. He shadowed each step she took, enjoying the swaying of her hips as she moved away and back against him. 'Shall I have to force myself upon you, wench?'

His tease had the desired effect. Trowel and scraper clattered as they bounced on the floor. Summer swivelled, reached around his neck, and brushed his lips with hers. 'Were you invited?'

Stepping backwards, he slid onto the couch, enticing Summer onto his knee.

'Yes. I'm engaged to a beautiful woman. She insisted I tuck her into bed every night.'

'Really? Cool. And will you be staying for breakfast?'

'Yes. Soon.' He ran his fingers through her hair as she lay her head against his chest, gazing up into his eyes.

'Would you like to stay with me in a castle, the weekend after next?'

'In a castle, do you mean a real one with a moat?' Her fingers stepped up his neck, tracing a shiver of pleasure on his stubbly chin.

'That's the plan. Lord Charles and Lady Winifred Drumcreevan have invited us to their estate in County Roscommon.'

'I'd love to, you know I would. Callum will be thrilled.' Her eyes danced like the wee folk in his dreams.

'The invitation is only for us. Can Callum stay with your parents?'

Her reaction startled James. Hands that moments before caressed, pounded his chest. 'You only want me for sex? You joke and call me a wench, then treat me as one. I've not been parted a single night from Callum since the day he was born. And, I'll not be anyone's sex slave.'

'Stop hitting me, it hurts.'

'Good,' she said. Fists becoming palms, anger turning to tears, she fell against his chest, and sobbed. 'I thought you were different. Where is the man who showed compassion to my son at Mass? I'm so afraid you will think Callum is a hindrance.'

'I'm still here and am sorry for being inconsiderate. Callum will come with us.' Tender in every movement, he slid a hand under her chin and eased it up so their lips touched. Feeling the tremors cease, he whispered. 'I'm sure the four-poster can sleep three. Will I be forced to lie like a dog at the end of your bed?'

'Do you bark?'

'Woof.'

'Beg.'

'Please. Summer, please, will you and Callum come with me. I love you both.'

Summer rose and paced around the room, searching through the chaos. She reached behind a paint can and lifted her pouch of tobacco. James locked her in his vision. Every movement she made, he found enticing, sensual. Deep in thought, she twisted and turned, stepping over the rubbish on the circular path she followed. A cloud of cigarette smoke spiralled over her head.

'Jamie, Callum will stay with my parents.'

'You'll come with me?'

Summer giggled. 'Often, I hope, after we're married.'

'Huh?'

'Yes, Jamie.' Her hand holding the hem of an imaginary dress above her boots, she waltzed round and round, scattering damp strips of wallpaper before her. 'Prince Charming is taking Cinderella to the ball at the castle.' Midnight in fairyland, a magical clock chimed an end to the dance. She swooned onto his lap and smothered him with kisses. 'When will the carriage collect me?'

'Your prince shall meet you at six next Friday evening, beneath the clock in Connolly Station. If we are early enough, you may choose the carriage.'

'Cool. Can I bring my artist's kit?'

'If you make me a coffee.'

Summer raised an index finger, pointed at the kettle and twirled her imaginary wand. 'Magic time is over, and I like to share chores. You fill the kettle. I'll do the rest.'

Laughter filled the kitchen as they wrestled for control of the tap. Jamie yielded before they were drenched. While Summer dried two mugs, he filled a jug of water and poured it into the domed kettle. The switch sparked when he pressed it.

'What the ...' James shot backwards.

'Oh. I use that long plastic toy screwdriver to flick the switch.' Summer grasped his hand and kissed each finger, one at a time. 'Poor, Jamie. Did you get a shock?'

'Stop. I'll buy you a new one. That thing is more dangerous than Sweeney.' Leaving the kettle to boil, and Summer to make the coffee, he retreated to the couch

'He's not cool. I don't like him. Remember what he did to Jack's back?' Summer dropped a spoon of instant coffee in to each mug, filled them with boiled water and topped with milk. 'How many sugars?'

'Have you forgotten already? I always have two.'

'He's a paedophile.'

Summer handed him a mug. 'What's a pedo... thing?'

James pursed his lips before replying. 'A paedophile is someone who has sex with children.'

Summer sipped her coffee. Then, as though his words had taken a trip around the moon and returned to hit her in the face, her mouth opened and her hand rose to cover the gasp that escaped. 'How can ... that's disgusting, sick, perverted.' Coffee spilling from her mug, Summer paced the floor. 'You cannot go back there. Stay here. Call the Gardaí[1], the Bishop, the Pope. Fuck's sake, Jamie. He's evil.'

'I know. Billy Egan and I are gathering evidence. We'll stop him.'

A little calmer now, Summer sat. 'I like Billy. He's been kind to us.'

Summer remained quiet as Jamie recounted events. Her expression shifting from shock to horror, to total revulsion, mirrored her feelings to each harrowing detail.

When he finished, they clung to each other, weeping.

---

[1] Irish police force.

Chapter 29

James wended his way to the corner shop, avoiding any who would delay him. His rucksack, loaded with two shirts, new underwear and socks, thumped against his spine. Before entering the widow's lair, he donned his sunglasses. Once inside, the gaggle of chin-waggers deep in conference quietened at his entrance. James smirked. In his peripheral vision, their heads bobbed up and down in unison with each loaf he lifted. Balancing six proved difficult, and the route treacherous, but with the luck of Moses on his side, the Red Sea parted. He dropped the bread onto the counter in front of the shopkeeper. 'Thank you, ladies. I'll need bags for these, Una.'

They glanced one to the other, back to the loaves and then to their chairwoman. Una took two large, blue plastic bags from a box behind her. 'One, two, three sliced pans for Father Brennan.' She twisted the two handles, made a knot and pushed the filled bag to the side. 'Three fresh loaves of Brennan's Bread for Father Brennan. That makes it six in total. Isn't that right ladies?'

'It is,' Mary Judge decreed. She raised six fingers for all to see she had done her math, and her nails.

Sheila Murphy slanted her head to have a gawk, as if she were looking into the pram of a new-born. 'What is a priest going to do with six loaves of bread? Well, are ya going to feed the five-thousand with them, together with a few trout, Father Brennan? Sure, Jesus only needed two, but I suppose you're hardly up to his level.'

He took a five pound note from his back pocket and handed it to Una. 'My girlfriend and I are spending the weekend at a castle. The Lord of the Manor has a penchant for Brennan's Bread, his exact words. Now, ladies, I must catch the bus to Dublin. Keep the change, Una.' Before they could utter disbelief or decipher the meaning of penchant, James slotted his index fingers into the loops of the carrier bags, turned, and strode to door. 'That got ye going,' he said, swivelling to face them. 'I'm afraid Father Sweeney would have a seizure if his curate was up to such mischief. For your information, the bread is for the ducks I'll be feeding by the canal in Maynooth. I'm off on a celibate retreat.'

For all the interest he had in their responses, they might have quacked as he closed the door behind him. An apparition, shadowing him from the other side of the street, captured his full attention as he headed for the bus stop. At the first break in traffic, Billy scuttled over the road and grabbed James' arm.

'Father Brennan.'

'Billy. What news?'

'I can't delay. Sarah-Jane is having a bad day.' Billy plucked an envelope from his shirt pocket and shoved it into James' rucksack. 'Read this as soon as you can. It's a photocopy. The original is in my safe.'

'What is it?'

'A birthday present from a jailbird.'

'Jailbird? Conor?'

'Yes. It's all the proof we need to sink Sweeney. My phone number is on the back. I have to scoot.'

Billy skedaddled before the bus juddered to a stop alongside James. The door hissed open. He clambered up the steps, and walked a short distance down the aisle. He dropped his luggage onto a vacant seat, and returned to stand in front of the driver. 'Hi, Jack. May I have a ticket to Dublin?'

'Father Brennan. You may have a ticket to Dublin, but your soul is bound for Hell.'

Jack had changed. The dark rings around his eyes had reduced to faint shadows, and his hair had been cut shorter. 'Why is ... wait, you didn't call me priest, or to be precise, fuckin' priest.'

'Yeah, yeah, yeah. Priests miss fuck all.' Jack printed the ticket. 'Return, I presume.' After they settled payment, Jack started the engine. 'You've paid for a seat, what more do you want?'

'Evidence against Sweeney is what I want. What do you want?'

'Me,' Jack said, reaching under his seat, 'I want to sip cocktails on a Caribbean beach with a gorgeous chick each side of me. Not going to happen on this salary or with my messed up head.' He tossed James a brown paper package. 'That's my diary. I never wish to see it, or you, or this village again. I'll be driving a bus in London a month from now. Thanks, Father Brennan. You've given me hope and a reason to forget. Now, fuck off, before I remember what's best forgotten.'

James proffered his hand. The bus driver grinned for the first time in James' company, shook his head, and released the handbrake. James fell back against the rails alongside the baggage section. Stability returned when he planted his feet wide apart. 'I hope Londoners don't get seasick with you at the helm. God, go with you.'

After settling onto a seat, James pulled Conor's envelope from the rucksack. Disappointed by the outcome when he visited Joe Wall, he needed solid evidence. To remain calm, he teased open the envelope and drew out the single page letter. Resting it on Jack's diary, he read.

Loughlan House – August 1982

My name is Conor Heffernan, aged 15 from Castlebridge.

When I was eleven, Father Michael Sweeney pretended he was my friend. He called me special. My stepfather didn't like me. Sometimes he hit me, and called me a Nancy boy.
Father Sweeney told me my step-father was evil. I believed him. I trusted him.

When I turned twelve, I found out what special meant. He pushed me over the table in the sacristy and pulled down my trousers. I screamed. He tried to shove his cock into me. I grabbed the scissors lying in front of my face. I stuck the scissors into his thigh and fled.

Father Sweeney said he'd caught me several times stealing wine, and that I stabbed him because he had decided to report the thefts to the Gardaí. No one believed my story. Bishop Ryan pretended to listen to me. Then he arranged that I be convicted of theft, and they sent me to this young offenders' prison. I didn't even get to go to the court in Cork. Why Cork? That is the far end of the country.

Twice a prison officer has tried to bugger me here. Father Sweeney tried to bugger me, and the Bishop may as well have buggered me.

Please, please help me.

Someone must believe me.

Conor.

Smudges dotted the page. *Tears, or marks caused by a poor photocopier?* Twice more James suffered a seesaw of emotion as he reread the document. Taut with anger from the shock of such alarming content, sorrow consumed him when he considered the plight of Conor, dumped into an institution. How many more Conors are locked away at the behest of these beasts? Mulling over the letter, gilt-edged proof dissipated into fragments. A jailbird is looking for revenge, no case to answer. *Damn.*

Unable to contain his outrage and frustration, he ripped open the brown paper package. Gold lettering on a leather-bound journal was not what James expected. *My screwed up head. By Jack O'Brien.* Nor did he expect the contents to be delivered in exquisite calligraphy and flawless script handwriting. Looking up, he gazed at the back of the man whose artistic skills were hidden from the world.

My mother was a whore, and I, her bastard son. Act 1 of my life was the happiest. I had a mother, and she loved me. She wore red lipstick and high-heeled shoes at night. When she closed the door on our flea-infested room, I hid under the coarse blanket, dreaming of the pirates from her plays. Mam never took me to the theatre to see her perform. How could she?

On my sixth birthday, I believed myself a man and followed her to work. Her stage was an alleyway behind a pub, a cesspit of piss and vomit. Sailors from Russia and scumbags from the docks were her leading men, and one of them was my father. Before I reached seven, a coward plunged a knife into her heart, and mine broke forever. That cursed communist blade severed my childhood and cast me at the feet of a monster. The only picture I have of her is framed in my mind.

Dublin's most charitable sent me to St. Patrick's Orphanage, where our patron saint had hidden his snake, Father Michael Sweeney.

Unable to read any further, James inserted Conor's letter inside the cover, and closed the diary. It would be safe, buried deep in his rucksack. Billy would have to get the diary copied. He leaned against the window, willing the bus into potholes so the vibrations hurt his head. His pain, their pain — he had to suffer for Jack, for them all. *I guide all that you do, my Son.*

You don't. You don't exist. There is no God.

James woke to the hissing sound of the door opening. The bus driver rose and turned. His face in shadow under his peaked cap, Jack raised a hand and saluted.
'Goodbye, Jack.'
James grabbed his rucksack and disembarked. In the distance, Jack swung away from passengers and left via a staff-only exit. He doubted they would ever meet again, ashamed they had met at all. Worried the last Act of Jack's play would not be the fairy tale ending he deserved, tears threatened to flow. James shielded his eyes from scrutiny beneath his sunglasses. Shunting the rucksack onto his back, he

rushed to the railway station. Somewhere along thronged pavements, thinking of Summer expunged the miserable introspection that had dogged his journey from Castlebridge. *Drumcreevan Manor, here we come.*

† † †

'Ahem. Tickets please.'

Summer having chosen the furthermost carriage along the platform, fixed her tee-shirt as James withdrew his hand and twisted back onto his own seat. More embarrassed than he'd ever been, he rummaged in his jeans pocket, discovering it less roomy than normal. Beneath his excitement, he located the tickets, yanked them out and placed them up on the table. Summer giggled. Concealed from view, she ran her hand along his inner thigh.

'Thank you.'

James gulped and raised his gaze to the ticket collector. 'Dan Flynn.'

'Indeed.' As he'd done when faced by a ticketless Drumcreevan, Dan lifted his cap from his forehead with the ticket-punch. 'Nice day for it.'

'What?'

'Cavorting on a train, that's what, Father. An empty carriage does not confer matrimonial rights to travellers. Be a good girl and keep your hands off his communion until you get to Drumcreevan Manor.'

Summer raised her hands above her head. 'Spoil sport. How do you know our destination?'

'Nice engagement ring.' Dan eased back the sleeve of his jacket and glanced at his watch. 'I was celibate myself for six long months when my wife had a slipped disc, and I wouldn't recommend either condition. We spent a fortune going to doctors and faith healers. I'd swear half the men in Connacht were feeling Mary up and charging for it.'

'Is she okay now?'

'She is. Poitin did the trick.'

James returned the tickets to his pocket. 'I've heard poitin is great for arthritis.'

'Is it?' A grin gathered around Dan's dancing eyes. 'I drank a skinfull and wouldn't take no for an answer. I clicked, Mary clacked, and the disc shot home. That was twenty years ago and we've tested the repairs every second night since.' The studs on Dan's punch snapped together. 'Boyle is ten minutes away. Tell that rogue Drumcreevan he still owes me a tenner.'

Laughing at Dan's story, Summer leaned against James. 'We will, and I'll also tell him he's not the only scallywag around.'

Midstride to the sliding door, Dan turned and fixed his cap back into position. 'You're a sweet girl, the image of your mother, and the paint brushes peeping from your bag suggest you're an artist like she is.'

'I don't understand.'

Dan opened the door. 'The cellars at Drumcreevan are an Aladdin's cave. Find your lineage amongst the portraits as I did mine when I was your age.'

† † †

Mounted on newel posts, the grey cast-iron bridge at Boyle railway station afforded safe passage between platforms. Their footsteps clanging on the steps, James and Summer descended onto the main concourse, the only passengers to disembark. They scanned the deserted station, expecting to see the driver Lord Drumcreevan had promised would meet them.

'Look there,' Summer said, pointing at a bench near the exit.

Slouched over and dressed almost entirely in grey, the man would have melded into the station-house but for his white socks. At their approach, he raised his gaze, and a sheet of paper bearing a single word, *Brennan*. Their hands joined, and swinging to the rhythm of their excitement, James and Summer raced to where he perched on the edge of the seat.

'Hello. I'm James Brennan and this is Summer.'

The man rose, shoved the paper into his pocket. Blue eyes, watered by age, gazed at their navels through a mass of grizzled hair. Two bony hands appeared from his sleeves and reached forward.

'I'm Donal O'Flynn. I'll take your luggage.' He stabbed a gnarled finger at Summer's rucksack.

'No need, we can manage.' James doubted the man could carry the bread, never mind the rucksacks. 'Wait, are you related to the ticket collector on the train?'

The sound of Donal scuffing his feet upon the gravel path, reminded James of mice scurrying under the floorboards at the Seminary. Unable to tilt his spine or head sufficiently to look James in the eye, he rotated his peaked cap and took two steps backwards. 'No relation, thank God. If young Sir and Madam could stop fannying about and hand me their bags, we can be on our way.'

Summer nudged James. 'He's too old to carry them. His accent is weird.'

'Eighty-six next month. I'll have ya know, the doctor advises the use of condoms as my sperm are still viable. Perhaps Missy would like to prove the doctor wrong.'

'Not necessary,' James said, appalled. 'Your hearing's as good as mine. It's your back and foul tongue that worries me.' He dropped his bag of bread on the ground, unslung his rucksack and tossed it alongside. 'Summer.'

She placed her bags in front of Donal, stepped closer to him and whispered. His bushy eyebrows rose to meet the ancient crevices lining his freckled forehead. Something resembling a laugh wheezed from his chest. Already bent, he dropped his hands to lift the luggage. He tottered to the exit with the baggage swinging inches from the ground.

Summer and James linked arms and waited until Donal was beyond earshot.

'What did you whisper?'

'I gave him my telephone number.'

'You don't have one.'

'I gave him yours, Mr. Too-Serious.'

Summer dragged James in pursuit of their chauffeur.

Donal stopped at the boot of the only car in the carpark. The glint of chrome accentuated the recognisable lines of a vintage Rolls Royce. He fumbled with the lock, elbowed it, hammered the lid, and fumbled some more. A grunt suggested he had an alternative plan. He hobbled to the front. Both hands gripping the handle, and with his leg planted on the running board, he wrenched the driver's door open. 'Palpi-bloody-tations,' he said, clutching his chest. 'Blast this ancient crock of shit. I need a new heart.' He flung the baggage inside, and opened the rear passenger one. 'Mind your step getting in, also while inside. C'mon, at this rate it will be the witching hour before we get there.'

'Wow. Nice car, Mrs. Brennan.'

'Stylish, Mr. Brennan.'

Summer climbed into the vehicle, slid across the leather seat, and beckoned James to follow. The interior did not match his expectations. Mouldy seats and mouse droppings in the ashtray were minor issues compared to the football-sized hole in the floor.

The stench of neglect in their nostrils, Summer's nose wrinkled. She reached for the handle to open the window. 'It's stiff.' She gripped it with both hands and yanked it upward. 'Oops.' Unnoticed by Donal, she failed to reattach the handle. Sealed lips containing her laughter burst open when the engine spluttered into life, and backfired. She dropped the handle onto the floor and kicked it under the driver's seat.

James had become accustomed to her cheeky grin. Her uncomplicated Bohemian sense of freedom teased him, whispered to the chains of conservatism, which shackling his thoughts, impinged on his sense of propriety. *Damn, why can't I just let go and laugh all the time, like I did in the shop earlier.*

Donal eased the car onto the street, and continued at a smooth pace past closed shops and terraced houses. He proved his credentials as a driver, but not as a chauffeur. With the breeze licking their feet, they grinned at each other. Pedestrians waved as they walked past the car. Summer waved back. A mile or so beyond the town, she elbowed James and pointed to the hole beneath. They could have reached down and touched the road marking.

Donal hunched over the steering wheel. It seemed he lined up The Flying Lady on the bonnet with the centre of the road. James leaned forward and glanced at the speedometer. At eight miles an hour, hogging the white line didn't put them in mortal danger. Regretting not using the toilet on the train, he shuffled his legs. 'Donal, how far is it to the castle?'

'It's three miles if you are a goat, eight if we take the safe route.'

James slumped back into the seat. *An hour.* 'My bladder is bursting, Donal. Can you pull over somewhere suitable?'

'No.' Donal guffawed. He plucked a cushion from the passenger seat and flung it back to James. 'Cover the hole and belt up.'

'What?'

'See the hole in the bloody floor, ya muppet. Put the cushion over it and hang on to your bladder. Hold on tight, Missy.' Donal turned and winked. 'Enjoy a ride with a real man.'

Eight to eighty miles per hour in as long as it took James to brace his knees against the front seat, they covered the same distance in the next minute as they had in the ten since leaving the station. Driving like someone possessed and sixty years younger, Donal used the full width of the road, slinging the car hard into corners and even harder out of them.

'Cool,' Summer shouted. She leaned into each bend, dragging James over and back. 'Faster, faster.'

'Stop encouraging him.'

'Relax, Jamie. Can't you see he's a great driver?' Summer clapped after they swerved to avoid an oncoming lorry.

When the speedometer hit ninety, James grabbed the headrest. 'He's a homicidal maniac. Slow down.'

'In about thirty seconds I will, Master Brennan.' Donal lifted the handbrake and spun the steering wheel. When the car skidded to a stop facing a side road, thrown forward they jerked against the seat belts. 'You may hop out here and do the necessary behind a bush.'

A flock of butterflies leaving his gut, James took a deep breath. 'For some reason I no longer need to. Just get us to the Castle, preferably alive.' Incensed by such reckless driving, he folded his arms and stared out his window. Jealous that Summer enjoyed the trip, one over which he had no control, he sulked.

'No need to wee? Has Master Brennan had an accident?' Donal said.

'Drive.'

They followed the narrow road skirting the edge of rugged terrain at a more sedate speed. From shadow into half-light, moments later blinded by the glare of the evening sun, they wound onwards and upwards. Hugging rocky outcrops and sheer cliffs, James envisaged the car tumbling down the steep incline yards to his left. *One mistake and our goose is cooked.* The butterflies returned in even greater numbers, flapping to the beat of his racing heart. Summer took no notice of his angst, buzzing around the seat as she soaked up the changing scenery, its beauty for the moment lost to him. *It's the artist in her, I suppose.* James leant against the window and closed his eyes.

'Look, Jamie.'

On his side, the land sloped away into a lush valley, undulating in gentle hillocks with no walls or fences to tame the natural landscape. Gliding on unseen currents, a sparrow hawk swooped low over trees guarding the meandering river, its screech as silent as the small bird it now clutched. James sat upright, focused on a scene that heightened his expectations. *Charles asked me if I fished.* Summer tugged his elbow and pulled him to her side, to the window she wiped with her stained sleeve. Set back a short distance from the road, framed by twin towers, Drumcreevan castle loomed over them. A fortress wrought from the mountainside.

'Wow.'

Donal brought the car to a stop in front of the great oaken door; the portcullis guarding it raised and ominous. He switched off the engine. 'Off ye go, children. I'll bring in the bags. Leave the door open.'

'Thanks,' she said.

James locked his gaze on the smirking face in the driver's mirror and waited until Summer had exited. With one hand holding the cushion covering the hole, he tapped the driver's shoulder with the other. Donal swivelled.

'Here's your cow-shit splattered cushion, Quasimodo.' James shoved the cushion into the leering face. 'The last laugh is on me.'

The skin on his jaw pulled tighter than the string on a bow, Donal scowled and fixed his cap back into place. His voice like a whisper on an evening breeze, his eyes bored into James. 'Dead men walk these halls.'

'Ya mean old fellas like you.' James threw open the door and sped to the sanctuary offered by some trees. A deep sigh escaping his lips, he gazed up at the Castle.

Chapter 30

Summer ran a finger along each of the three charcoal-coloured iron hinges of the front door. 'I'm puzzled,' she said, turning her attention to the portcullis looming over them. 'This Castle is of European design, with French and Austrian medieval influences. I'd guess it's early renaissance.' She pressed her thumb against one of the many studs riveted into the door. 'Look at the heads on these. Normally they're square or round. These are multifaceted, like the diamond in my engagement ring.'

'Huh?' James glanced back at Donal, more concerned about their luggage than the architecture. 'Maybe Drumcreevan is a vampire.'

Oh, Jamie, no need to fear, I'll hold you close against my breast tonight.'

'How do you know so much about castles?'

'I studied late-medieval history and renaissance art for a year, just before Callum was born. Have you a silver cross to protect us against vampires?'

'No, but I've got a male chastity belt supplied by the Bishop. Where's the door handle?'

'There isn't one, silly.' Summer leaned against the door and pushed. It creaked and opened wide enough for James to peer around the edge.

'Hello. Is there anyone at home? Count Vlad, are you there?'

In the gloom beyond, someone coughed. James sniffed the sweet wood-smoke, reminding him of times spent clearing trees from their farm. A spluttering wheeze rasped from within, he waved his hands in the futile belief he could ward off the evil fumes. He stepped back, gripped the edge of the door and heaved it open. Wave after wave of wood-smoke rushing by, lapped at their faces, tickling the backs of their throats. Summer and James retreated outside until the smoke thinned.

'Blast this buggering free timber I borrowed. Brennan, is that you or your ghost? Come in and leave the bloody door ajar.'

Drumcreevan stood by the smouldering fireplace of the great entrance hall, a lit cigar in one hand, the other resting on the head of an Irish Wolfhound. Dressed with the same casual respectability as when they had met on the train, exuding calm, presented a prefect image of a country gent.

Beneath an ornate, iron wagon-wheel chandelier, a vase of flowers stood on the great table inside the door matched its twin, twenty feet distant. The colour of the blooms as vibrant as the oil paintings lining the walls, their scent lost until the light breeze had sucked the last of the vile smoke away. In awe of the splendour and vastness of the hall, they sidled over the flagstones, pausing here and there to capture the wonders of the place.

'Charles, this is my Fiancée, Summer.'

Drumcreevan tossed his cigar into the fireplace, and then glided toward them. 'Fiancée, eh? I recall, you suggested she was your sister. Summer McMahon, you are even more beautiful than the girl I spied in the arms of a Catholic priest. Welcome to Drumcreevan Manor.'

Summer curtseyed. 'Thank you for inviting us to your castle. A manor it most definitely isn't. Your pet is most unusual, bald in places?'

Charles laughed. 'Feisty. I knew you would be. Cullen hasn't barked in several hundred years, have you lad.' He stepped back and directed them to the armchairs surrounding the hearth. 'Please sit. Winifred will join us shortly.'

Summer tapped James' arm, and pointed at the portrait above the fireplace. Much larger than the others, its gilded frame more complex, it dominated the place.

'That is *D* as we like to call him, *The Drumcreevan*. Those other reprobates hung on the walls are his male descendants, my ancestors.'

James laughed. 'Yes, you described him as a rogue. Not much family resemblance, apart from the roguish trait.'

Summer, nodding her appreciation of the artwork, flopped onto the chair next to James. 'The two gaps on the back wall, were they disinherited?'

'Very observant,' Charles said. The ripe, green bark on the logs hissed their anger at prods from his poker, as seasoned timber underneath sparked at its touch. Reclining on a chair, he crossed his legs and dropped his arms onto the padded rests. 'Enough history lessons for the moment. We shall have the entire weekend to poke fun at the ghosts of my ancestors and their interesting take on commerce.

I presume you had a semi-pleasant journey in the roller. It hasn't been used in years and is in want of an overhaul, though Duncan insists the engine is perfect.'

As James expected, on meeting his puzzled gaze Summer shrugged her shoulders.

'Who's Duncan?'

'Ah, up to his old tricks is he? That's Duncan, placing your luggage on that lump of a table behind you. Come, and join us, my old friend.'

Duncan strode across the hall, his back as straight as the expression on a face that had undergone an equally miraculous change. 'James,' he said, winding his way to the fireplace. 'You ought to loosen your bolts. Life is too short. I'm sorry, if I rattled your sensitivities. Your lass knew I was an impostor. What gave me away, Summer?'

His hand gripping the edge of his chair, James turned to his girlfriend. 'What?'

Unflustered, she ran her fingers through her hair. 'An artist captures a person's soul onto canvas by interpreting their eyes. Yours watered like a fountain. Next time you pull that trick, don't eat the onion. The barest hint of one makes me nauseous. Mind, your Scottish accent is very sexy, much nicer than Donal's bastardised bark.'

Rage burning his gut, James felt it rise and bubble upwards, twisting words around the tip of his tongue. He bit hard on his lip. *Am I so square and so thick?* 'Fuck it.' He leapt to his feet. 'I haven't cursed in nine years. I don't want an apology, I want a drink.'

'But you don't drink.' Summer frowned and lit a cigarette. 'Don't start now, it will ruin ...'

Her voice trailed off into a laugh as infectious as it was naughty. James shrugged, and sat.

'Can I have one of your cigarettes?'

'No.'

Drumcreevan grabbed Duncan's arm. 'Sit down, man. You make me nervous standing there as if you owned the place.'

'No can do, Charlie. I'm off to watch a young Brazilian driver tomorrow in a Formula 2000 race. Senna will win, he's a wizard behind the wheel and there's no more I can teach him.' Edging his skinny frame between the chairs, he cuffed Drumcreevan behind the lug. 'Because you can't pay me diddly squat, I got to earn a crust elsewhere. I'll see you guys on Sunday for the return trip to Boyle.'

'Cool.'

James relaxed after he left. 'Who is he?'

'He, my young friend, is the Laird of Drumcairn.'

'Not a servant – or a chauffeur – nor your man?'

Drumcreevan shook his head. 'Duncan's castle is to the north of Oban on the west coast of Scotland. The Drumcairn peers down on their entrance hall, on their Wolfhound. They have been our allies since that hound was a pup. Apart from Duncan being a rapscallion, the other thing we've in common is he's also skint.'

'Shit. Made a right fool of myself, so I have.'

'Jamie, stop cursing.' Summer plucked a loose thread from her armrest, balled it and flicked it into the flames. 'This would have been an unusual alliance, considering the religious uncertainties of the times. When did D build this fortress?'

'You seem well versed for an artist. If you must know, work started on both castles in fifteen-sixty-eight, the year following the forced abdication of Mary Queen of Scots.'

Summer twiddled her fingers, gazed at Charles and then his forebears. A smile turning to a smirk, she spoke. 'You are a fox, Lord Drumcreevan. Your answer is misleading.'

Charles fumbled with the poker, and shoved a log back into the heart of the flames. 'You mean the ladies find me attractive?'

'No.' Summer leaned over and patted the back of his hand. 'No offense, you are sweet. Fifteen-sixty-eight is ten years after the crowning of the last Tudor monarch. Elizabeth, The Virgin Queen, was Anglican, as you are.'

'Wait,' James said, sliding to the edge of his seat. 'My friend, Josh, is an amateur historian. I hope I can remember his words. "Grace O'Malley, the pirate queen of Mayo, would slit her own throat before lying with an English Lord. Would Drumcreevan have slit his own throat if forced to bed The Virgin Queen?" I have no idea what he meant, but I'd love an answer to take home to him. Well?'

Summer chuckled. 'You've been outfoxed by commoners, Lord Drumcreevan.'

Charles tossed a log into the fire and stoked the embers. 'If time could rewind the seconds and hours, guests to Drumcreevan would be waited on by a score of servants. Fine wines and whiskeys in the cellars, venison hung alongside pheasant and duck. Children's feet pitter-pattering along the corridors, governesses a-governing and lords a-lording, and young ladies of breeding like you playing the pianoforte before being ravished by suitors such as James.'

Summer clapped. 'We need a deoch dhraíochta.'

'Indeed,' Charles said. 'What magic potion have you in mind?'

'Muisiriún mire[1]. They're my favourite trip. We tried growing them in the attic, but something went wrong. There was no magic in them. Your grasp of Irish is commendable, for an English Lord.'

---

[1] Magic mushrooms

'Never had magic mushrooms, but I am bloody starving. Is that Brennan's Bread, heaped in blue sacks upon my table? I shall remove it to the scullery and find myself a buxom maid who asks less complicated questions.'

'He's adorable,' said Summer, after Charles left. She hopped from her chair and dropping onto Jamie's lap, wound her arms around his neck. 'So are you.'

Pensive, James reached up and pushed her hair back. 'This is so strange for me. I'm so afraid I'll make a fool of myself. When Duncan made you laugh, a devil goaded me into fits of nonsensical jealousy. Even though he's ancient, I despised him for that ability.'

'Poor, Jamie. Don't ever sulk. I'm sorry, I forget you are a priest and this situation is awkward and new for you.' She jumped to her feet and pulled him from his seat, then dragged him away from the fireplace. Holding his right hand, she stepped in front of him and bowed. 'Would you care to dance, my lord?'

The gap between them closed. She guided his anxious hands to her back and shoulder. Coaxing him, she swayed into the first awkward step, then a second. James closed his eyes, imagining the fairies, with their magic flutes and harps playing the sweetest of notes, as they danced by the light of a sparking fire. Enraptured by the rhythm, he relaxed, allowing Summer and the music to steer his steps. Round and round the massive table they danced, faster, faster, their feet gliding over the flagstones. He pulled her close. Her lips moist and urgent, finding his, they pirouetted to a standstill.

James opened his eyes. A few yards away, her arm linked with Charles', stood the most elegant woman he had met. 'Lady Drumcreevan,' he whispered.

'Bravo,' Charles said, leading the lady toward them. 'May I introduce my wife, Lady Winifred Drumcreevan.'

'Please, call me Winnie.' Her hands stretching out from beneath her velvet shawl, she clasped Summer's and held her at a distance for a moment, 'Welcome to your ancestral home, child. And James,' she said, 'Charles has spoken fondly of you. Welcome.'

Summer stepped backwards. 'My ancestral home? Danny Flynn suggested something equally cool, but hare-brained. I don't understand.' She leaned against James and grasped his hand.

'Bugger.' Charles snorted. 'You promised to wait until tomorrow, Wimpy. The soup will taste worse than pigs' piss while you try to explain nearly five hundred years of history over a single course.'

Winifred frowned. 'Why waste another moment? Come, Summer, take my arm. The windbag can follow us to the kitchen.'

'Huh,' James said, wondering what he'd done wrong.

'She's so sexy when annoyed. It isn't easy being Chieftain, as you will discover. One word of advice, bed your woman well and often.'

Drumcreevan chucked two logs on the fire. 'Let me entertain you by showing you around this dump. Some have likened it to a maze. They're not far wrong, so if you're inclined to wander about on your own, it might be an idea to avail yourself of a ball of string.' Charles took hold of James' elbow and guided him out of the hall.

'Like Theseus and the Beast?'

'Good man, it is a Minotaur. I knew a half-educated padre would catch on.'

They entered a gallery as long as a hurling pitch. From the paintings crammed onto the walls, the scornful eyes of Drumcreevan's ancestors looked down their noses as they strolled by. Hopelessly in love and overwhelmed by a sense of history, more conscious than ever of the class-divide, James felt stifled by his discarded collar. A buxom lass sitting side-saddle on a white stallion marked the end. They stepped into a dank corridor, lit by a single buzzing bulb. Chisel marks crisscrossed the rough walls and the low ceiling. At regular intervals, rusty sconces lined each wall, the torches long since extinguished and cast away. Scorch marks showed where flames had licked stone and iron. Conduits, carrying power cables into the depths of the helm, ran along the top of one side of the passage while water pipes snaked along the floor on the other. Stark and foreboding, this damp world of shadows unsettled James.

Somewhere ahead, laughter sounded, and a door closed. Following a sharp turn, the floor slanted downward. The whitewashed walls reflected more light, revealing generations of cobwebs with their entrapped chitinous victims a breath away from disintegration.

'Your silence is similar to many who trod this path for the first time,' Charles said, his tone a touch sardonic. 'Expecting opulent rugs upon marbled floors, a palette of gold in every room, and tapestries hung from ceiling to floor, good manners clamped their tongues, and now yours. Am I correct, James Brennan?'

'Actually, I'm quiet because I sensed your wife dislikes me.'

'What a load of old poppycock. Wimpy does not dislike you, how could she?'

In front of them, the way straightened, and levelled out. James lifted his nostrils to the odour of food, a welcome change from the pervasive wood-smoke that still lingered.

'Whether your nest is feathered with gold-leaf or rough straw is not important. I'm more interested in dipping fingers of bread into carrot soup, catching trout from your stream, and growing a friendship.'

'Homemade from a packet is on the menu this evening. Tomorrow, we shall dust the banqueting table and feast on poached trout with crayfish.' Drumcreevan licked his lips.

He directed James to a left turn. 'The other route leads to the dungeons.'

Faced with another sloping passageway, the staccato of female voices grew louder as they descended to an ash-grey door. James stepped in front of Drumcreevan, closed his fingers around the handle, and raised his other hand like a Garda at a checkpoint.

'I'm not sure what game Winnifred is playing by suggesting Summer is related to you. If either of you hurt Summer, I'll not be answerable for my actions.'

His eyebrows arched, Charles stopped. 'I'm as allergic to pain as I am to manual labour. No harm shall come to either you or Summer. You have my word as a gentleman. By Jove, you priests are a suspicious species.'

'After you.' James twisted the blackened handle and ushered his host inside.

Charles crab-walked past James, keeping a claw length away.

Scant light, filtering from beyond the archway ahead, illuminated the room. They filed past eight long tables, most of them shrouded with flickering shadows. Imagining a line of people sitting on the low bench alongside one of them, James counted ghosts. By his reckoning, each table could seat thirty adults — two-hundred-and-forty guests.

'Wow. This is large enough to sit and feed an army?' With numbers zipping around his head, and not expecting Charles to stop before the keyhole-shaped arch, James stumbled into his back.

'I say, easy old boy, you're not my type. Keep your cutlass in its scabbard for your girl.'

Click, click, click — lights burst from chandeliers of finest crystal, revealing the magnificence of the dining room, and the maritime theme of its design. Bowed clinker-built planks cladding the walls, reached to head-height, where gunwales of dark oak ran from end to end. Models of sailing ships were mounted on top of brassy pedestals, three on each side. Guarding the exit, two cannons sat on wooden frames. Charles sauntered to one, pinched up the knees of his slacks and sat on the barrel. He lit a cigar. 'Do you find the smug look on my face annoying? Walk the plank, James Brennan.'

'I don't get the connection. We're miles from the sea.'

'On that, we are agreed.' Charles chuckled. 'Can you not hear the waves lapping against her ribs, as regular as the beat of your heart? Listen.' He whispered. 'Rope chaffing wood. Wind plucking sail. The sucking sound of a bloodied falchion blade, wrenched from a belly. Gold coins in treasure chests, sliding one over the other in the swell. Can you hear her call?'

'All I can hear are the ramblings of a madman.'

'The fleet of Drumcreevan and Drumcairn privateers met here every two years to divvy up the spoils and toast their successes. Twelve vessels united under a single flag. Miniatures of the

Drumcreevan ships are here, three Carracks to the starboard, Galleons to port.'

'Long John Drumcreevan, you have a wild imagination for a landlubber. Tudor inbred, I'd imagine. I fear for your kin.'

'Ouch!'

James examined one of the models, marvelling at the workmanship and fine detail. An emerald pennant emblazoned each of the mizzen-masts. Unable to read the markings on them, he blew hard, sending a cloud of dust skyward. *Ach-choo*. He rubbed his stinging eyes and stumbled back into Charles. 'I cannot make out the markings on the flag.'

'*DO'M*,' Charles said. 'An dtuigeann tú?'

'What?' James sneezed again. 'Is this some sort of play-room for young aristocratic lords?'

'Perhaps it is a nautical crèche. Never mind.' Charles nipped the end off the half-smoked cigar and slipped it into his pocket. Staring at the red glow fizzling to grey ash on the floor, he groaned. 'My stash of cigars is nearly depleted. We better catch up with the girls.'

They entered a short corridor. Framed between dressed stone, their timbers strapped and studded with iron, and bearing three, black-lock escutcheons, two doors stood to the left and right.

James rapped twice on the one to his left and laughed. 'Is this where you keep the pirate treasure?'

Kicking a door at the end of the corridor, Charles grinned, 'The weaponries, if you must know. Guns and munitions on the port side, swords to starboard.'

'Aye, aye, captain.' *And there's trout the size of Moby Dick in the river.*

Charles opened the spring-loaded door and held it for James to pass.

Four sets of spotlights illuminated the kitchen area, equal in size to the entrance hall. None had a full set of bulbs. A line of black cast iron, solid-fuel ovens and ranges ran along one wall, all cold and dusty to James' touch. Nearest the door, a small mound of ash and soot had spilled from the fuel-box beneath the oven onto the stone floor. A streak of grime leading from it ended by a shovel and brush, joined by tangled cobwebs to a pair of tongs, awaiting ghosts to finish the job someone started in the long ago.

James imagined the hubbub of times past with a butler, resplendent in his finery, overseeing footmen, and scullery maids in their smocks. Platters of venison stacked high, silver serving forks, bottles of French wine, uncorked and breathing their perfume into myriad smells of meat, fish, and antiquity.

An odd mixture of old and new mingled like grannies at a wedding. Chrome against grime, cracked plates from the Orient were set on a pine dresser. A faded poster clung to the wall, its corners peeling.. Elvis strumming his guitar, above an empty cornflake box lying on a three-legged bench as old as the walls.

As welcome as hot whiskey on a bleak winter's day, the sound of Summer's laughter lifted him from reverie. Her voice growing more familiar by the hour, turned his thoughts away from the past.

Winnie ladled soup into deep earthenware bowls. Summer carried them to a round, wooden table in the far corner. Without a shade, harsh light from the low-hanging bulb denied the setting of any semblance of ambience. Stark and functional, like the meal they were about to be served.

'Hmm.' Charles sniffed the air. Pointing to his nose, he meandered to the table, and sat staring at the butter dish. 'What shall I butter, my nose? Bread, bring baker Brennan's bloody bread. My ancestors would have cleaved servants' heads from incompetent shoulders for such disregard. Harumph.'

Summer detoured to intercept James. She lifted onto her toes and dropped a kiss on his lips. 'Hi, handsome.' Before his hands could wrap her up, she skipped away to grab a loaf.

Plonking onto the spindle-backed chair opposite Charles, James straightened his soup-spoon, while Drumcreevan rattled his against the edge of his bowl. Beneath the cold light, flecks of grey hidden amongst the fair strands of Drumcreevan's windswept-styled hair vouched the roots were his own. The veil of lordship seemed as flimsy as one of Summer's cheese-cloth tops. Nonetheless, he played his part with a jaunty finesse that captivated James. Not quite at ease, James ran a finger along the rim of the circular table. 'I suppose Excalibur is in the armoury.' His nervous laugh met deaf ears of a man considering his belly.

'Where the dickens is my crust? Please, Mam, I want some — more would be a bloody miracle. Do ya get it? Dickens, named Charles after me. Please, Sir ... never mind.'

Summer returned with the bread, and sat between James and Charles. Two slices were whisked away before the plate touched the table, one spun through the air and landed in front of James.

'Homemade,' Winnie said, as she slid a bowl across to Summer. 'Carrot and Coriander.' She unwrapped her shawl. After draping it over the back of her chair, she smoothed her low cut, flower-patterned dress, and sat.. The gold chain hanging around her neck could have purchased many a four-course meal.

Words bubbling through masticated dough over frothing lips, Charles smiled. ''S' lovely, my dear.'

'We have guests.'

'I snow, my dear.' He curled another slice into a tight cylinder, dipped it into the bowl, and rammed it into his mouth.

Winnie coughed. 'Perhaps Father James would like to say a few words before you choke.'

Charles' cheeks billowed, his eyes bulged, and through a narrow gap in his lips a single word escaped, 'Yessh.' His eyebrows rising and falling like a stuck lift, he tried to nod at James.

Not relishing the part of playing priest, James stood and blessed himself. Summer eased herself from the chair and ran her fingers across her bosom, making the most provocative sign of the cross James ever witnessed. His Rosary beads rattled in his pocket.

Winnie stood and blessed herself. Eyes locked on Charles, she slid an intricate, gem-encrusted, golden pendant from its hiding place in her cleavage. She brought it to her lips and kissed it. 'Taiseach muintir Uí Mháille, seas suas[I]. Show some respect to God and our guests.'

Charles wiped his sleeve across his lips, gripped the table with both hands and lumbered to his feet. 'Táim ngrá leat freisin, Caitlín Ní Mháille[II].'

'Grace. Amen.' James fell back onto his chair. 'Who are ye? Drumcreevan or O'Malley?'

A lock of hair, whorled around Summer's finger, spun free to the tune of her gasp. 'Both,' she said. 'They are the same.'

Head held high, she sat proud as a victor without a crown of olive branches. James looked on, appreciative of the intelligence behind the coquettish smile, another strand that bound him to her, though what she meant remained a mystery. Rather than profess ignorance or splutter soupy questions, he feigned genius with a dramatic nod.

Charles lifted the soupspoon to his mouth, sucked it clean, and licked the orange streak along the handle. 'Bugger.' As charitable and mannerly as a gourmet interrupted during the main course in a Michelin-starred restaurant, he pointed the tarnished silver spoon at Winnie, and grunted. 'Premature ejaculation is always the woman's fault. You should have waited until tomorrow, like we had agreed.'

The eight crumbs on the table by his soup bowl became the centre of James' universe, and the rearranging of them in his mind a necessary distraction for his prudish nature.

Winnifred slid her spoon from the front to the back of her bowl, brought it to her lips, and sipped from the side. 'Must you reduce everything to your insidiously low version of the vernacular?' The merriment in her eyes laid bare her attempted scowl.

'Smack my botty if it pleasures you, but must we do it in public?' With both hands he lifted the bowl to his mouth and slurped the remaining soup. 'James and Summer, we have prepared Gráinne's infamous four-poster for you. Alas, my wife's indiscretion means I

[I] Chieftain of the O'Malley's, stand up.
[II] I'm in love with you too, Kathleen O'Malley.

shall have to lock you in the dungeons. Tomorrow, I'll reconvene the Drumcreevan Inquisition, and whip the truth from you.'

Summer turned to Winnie. 'I love your chain and pendant, they are so cool. Gráinne Ní Mháille. Jamie and I are confused. Lord Drumcreevan talks in riddles. I never know when he's being flippant. What is your connection to Grace O'Malley?'

'That is sweet of you.' Winnie reached behind her neck and unclasped the chain, letting it and the cross-shaped pendant slip onto her hand. 'Priceless,' she said, handing it to Summer.

'Quite so.' Charles leaned forward, his demeanour serious and uncontrived. 'A gift from Isabella of Castille, better known as Queen Isabella of Spain, to Domhnall Mac Tomás Ó Máille. Not that she knew the beneficiary, or he her. Intended as a gift to a French noble, the emissary carrying it regretted the storm that dragged his vessel into Irish waters. The pendant passed along the line of the Kings of Umaill[I] onto Eoghan Dubhdara Ó Máille.'

Glad the sexual references had ceased, James pushed the crumbs into a small pile, and looked up at Charles. 'And he is?'

'Eoghan Dubhdara is Gráinne O'Malley's father, also the father of twins who never bore the family name. He is Summer's grandfather, on her mother's side, with an extra great in front of it than me. Don't ask me how many greats that is.'

Uncertain whether he could believe Charles, James folded his arms. 'Are you saying Drumcreevan and Drumcairn were Gráinne O'Malley's brothers, and Summer is related to you?'

'I'm happy to be related to Winnie.' Summer winked. 'Not sure about Charles. He's such a fibber.'

'Summer is heir to this castle. She is Tánaiste[II] of the 'Drumcreevan-O'Malleys.'

'What?' Summer shot Charles an incredulous glance.

'Your entitlement is governed by Drumcreevan's stipulation of 1567. He decided his legacy would not be defined by Brehon or English law, or by tradition as was often the case. Eoghan Dubhdara was a cute hoor. Anticipating the collapse of the Gaelic order, he fostered his illegitimate twins to a seafaring Scottish clan. Gráinne's brother, Donal-ne-Píopa, is also thought to be illegitimate.'

Summer dropped her spoon into her bowl. 'To Scotland?'

'Yes. Careful tutelage and masterful subterfuge paved a route into the heart of English rule. Loot plundered by our Galleons came to port in legitimate ships, then stored beneath our feet. While Gráinne plied the seas of the West coast, looting wayward vessels and protecting O'Malley lands, we roamed from Europe to Asia and

---

[I] Umaill is the area around Clew Bay in what is now Co. Mayo.
[II] Tánaiste is second in command, behind the Taoiseach.

Africa, always on a planned venture for known reward. Alas, the world has become too civilised for pirates and privateers. Our fortunes declined with the empire we fed upon. I'd like to think we played a part in its decline.'

Winnie took and held Summer's hand. 'You will make a beautiful bride. Come, I shall introduce you to your ancestors. Summer, we are descendants of Muirisc[1]. You men may follow.'

'That shall be my pleasure. Walking behind pretty ladies is a more stimulating pastime than having to listen to them,' Charles said, hauling himself off the chair with difficulty. 'This bloody arthritis is a nuisance. Thankfully, Wimpy no longer expects me to perform...'

'Charles.' Winifred cast a look of displeasure in his direction. 'We have guests.'

'Sorry.'

Summer grabbed James and dragged him from his seat. 'C'mon, Jamie, I can't wait to get you into the four-poster.' She smothered his embarrassment with a dozen kisses. Still giggling, she coupled her fingers with his, and slid against his shoulder. 'Say something, Jamie.'

'Whatever my Queen commands, I shall obey.'

Charles fell into line behind his wife, the in-need-of-repair heels of his brown brogues flopping on the stone floor. He glanced back at the young lovers. 'Rasputin and Alexandra, James and Summer — the similarities are uncanny. We know what befell the mad monk, and the subsequent fall of House Romanov. Watch your back, James Brennan.'

'And you, yours. Were they daft enough to believe your elaborate tales, the proletariat of Roscommon might tear down your mausoleum to protect the good name of Gránuaile.'

Falling a little behind their hosts as they walked through the ship-shaped dining room, James whispered. 'Do you believe you're related to them?'

'Oh, Jamie, you take everything so serious. Of course I don't. It's like a murder-mystery weekend — they are good fun and want us to have a laugh.'

'Do you think my meeting Charles on the train was coincidence?'

'It was fate. We are meant to be together, forever.' Summer quickened pace, her steps as erratic as the wind that had filled the sails of the Drumcreevan galleons. Infectious excitement washed away James' reservations and dampened his suspicious nature. A hint of wood smoke grew stronger. Charles and Winnie halted at the fork leading to the dungeons. So slender in every regard, Winnie's flowing hair seemed in perpetual motion. Dancing to her slightest movement,

---

[1] Muirisc – legendary seafaring Queen of Mayo before Christianity.

yet perfectly arranged around a warm face painted by fresh air and breeding.

'Hades awaits us, and the lift is out of action.' Charles flicked a light switch, and led them along a short, featureless passage. On reaching a landing a set of steps spiralled down, under one side of a wooden platform. 'Take a peep,' Charles said, directing James and Summer to stand on the woodwork.

Fearful of the unknown, they inched over the solid planks, and peered into the abyss. Summer squeezed James' hand and let go. She reached into his pocket, and, discovering more than the penny she wanted, giggled. 'Make a wish,' she said. The coin pinched between her thumb and finger, she held it over the void.

I wish we could live forever. James squinted as the coin dropped. Its edge sparkling, it twisted, before being consumed by the darkness. Holding his breath, he counted one-thousand, two-thousand... at twelve-thousand he gasped and turned to a grinning Charles. 'It's bottomless.'

'A natural fissure leads to the underworld. My forebears widened it to a depth of thirty feet. Block and tackle hauled ill-gotten treasure up and down this shaft for many generations of Drumcreevans.' He pointed to a pile of dusty ropes and splintered wood lying strewn to one side.

James linked arms with Summer, and descended after their hosts, their footsteps and heavy breathing boomed in the eerie silence. He imagined how treacherous these steps must have been in generations past, when the stairwell was lit by torch and candles. Without a bannister or rail, even though the steps were wide enough for four people to walk abreast, the magnetic pull of the void ensured James planted each foot before raising the other.

On reaching the bottom, Charles hit another light switch, revealing passages running to the left and right. A low circular wall, with fractured slabs of plaster falling away, encased the subterranean fault. James followed Charles' gaze to the engraved crest on the polished wall in front of them. Within a wreath of leaves, a tusked wild boar stood proud above a three-masted galley. Etched below, *Terra marique potens.*

'Powerful on Land and Sea,' Charles said, his chest puffed out like a fighting cockerel. 'The mark of the O'Malleys.'

'Cool. I like the boar,' Summer said, sketching a large likeness in the air with a finger. 'It's representative of the untamed, and an image that suits your family.'

Winnie smiled. 'Yes, he can be a bore, and it's your family too. On the left are the Drumcreevan vaults, owned by the male bloodline. Alas, this comes to an undignified end with Charles and I. Apart from empty crates, worthless bonds, and a few noisy ghosts, nothing of interest remains.'

James clapped Charles on the back. 'You were born a few centuries too late. Have you ever considered working for a living?'

'Good God, are you insane? The battlements have not been breached during my lifetime, nor will they.'

'As I was saying,' Winnie beckoned Summer and James to follow her down the right passage, 'this leads to the Ní Fhlaithbheartaigh vaults, the female bloodline. One-eighth of every treasure chest, every ransom, and any other gains for the past four-hundred years were deposited here. Summer is a direct female descendant of Aíne Ní Fhlaithbheartaigh, Drumcreevan's wife.'

James smirked. *Maybe Rumpelstiltskin will arrive and spin gold thread. If they had such a treasure trove, they wouldn't be begging for crusts of bread or luring strangers to their keep.*

Ahead, looming out of the shadows, an arched door blocked the way. On reaching it, Winnie lifted one side of her dress, up above her knee. She pulled a large key from a leather pouch attached around her thigh.

Fascinated, James watched the dress slide down her shapely leg. Summer's elbow to his gut returned his gaze to Charles inserting the key into the lock. 'Open sesame.' The words sounded hollow, and not as funny as James intended.

The tumblers clicked. 'I'll need your help, James. Shoulder to the door please.'

'Jamie.' Summer placed her hands on the small of James' back, and shoved him forward. 'This is so exciting. I wish I had a camera.'

'I wish I had a cave troll.' Charles said, leaning against the door. 'Heave ...'

James leant at an angle to the door, his face so close to Charles, the whiff of cigars assaulted his nostrils. Believing this to be part of the Drumcreevans' elaborate show, he pushed a little, expecting the door to spring open, while he fell flat to the ground.

'Jesus.' Charles shouted. 'This is a door to a vault, not a ladies boudoir. Heave, ya Vatican poofter.'

Both legs planted on the ground, James bolstered his shoulder against the centre of the door, and shoved on Charles' command. The door creaked. On the second attempt, a gap opened, no more than an inch wide. Their breaths grew laboured with each small gain. Encouraged by Summers' squeals, James wiped his brow. 'One more should do it. What thinks the Lord of the Manor?'

'I think I'll oil the hinges on this door more often. It's been shut for eleven years. I was younger then, as was my accomplice, Paddy Flynn, and he was twice as strong as you. One, two, three, heave.'

With a gap sufficient for a lady carrying triplets to pass through, the men slid down the door, panting like out of condition sheepdogs. Charles pulled his half-smoked cigar from his pocket and lit it. 'These half-cigars are killing me. My lungs aren't used to such deprivation.'

James stood and offered Charles his hand. 'Let me help you up, old man.'

'Huh? Nimble is my middle name.' Drumcreevan sprung to his feet, grabbed James' wrist and bent his arm behind his back, playful yet intent on making a point. 'Never insult or underestimate an O'Malley. An dtuigeann tú?'

'Ouch! Let go.' *I'll remember this. His Lordship is tetchy about his age.*

'Most excellent.' Charles reached inside the vault. 'In my humble opinion, which is more infallible than the Pope's, the age-old saying, "All that glitters is not gold," is utter rubbish. Only gold glitters, Rabbi Brennan.' He flicked on a light switch, stepped inside, and pulled the door wide open. 'Voila. Everything in here that glitters is solid gold.'

Gobsmacked, James and Summer stood hand-in-hand, gawping at her inheritance. *Holy shit.*

Mounted on a rough-plastered plinth, a sarcophagus dominated the centre of what they expected to be a vault. A succession of gold picture frames ran along three of the walls, all containing portraits of women — a timeline of ladies fashion, from dreary shawls in earthy hues to colourful silk blouses and flamboyant, feathered hats. Out of place beneath the gleaming art, a rusty oil can collected dust in the corner near the door,

Summer gasped. 'Hey, the last picture is of Sapphire, my mother.'

'Yes.' Charles leant against the stone coffin. 'It's a self-portrait, which I commissioned her to paint many years ago. She is as beautiful as Aíne Ní Fhlaithbheartaigh-Drumcreevan, is she not?' He pointed a cigar at the first picture. The likeness was uncanny. 'When you reached twenty, the right of inheritance, as stipulated by Drumcreevan centuries ago, passed from Sapphire to you.'

Summer turned to Winnie. 'Sapphire never mentioned you or this place. Why?'

Winnie took Summer by the arm. 'Your mother knows nothing of her lineage or our existence. Most of the ladies lived their lives unware of their Drumcreevan-O'Malley background. She motioned to the second portrait, 'Aoibhinn, their first daughter, was fostered to a family in Dublin, The Pale as it was back then.'

'How awful is that?'

Charles coughed. 'Not an uncommon occurrence in former times.'

Summer examined each likeness. 'So this is my inheritance, oil paintings of my ancestors. Oh, Jamie, this is worth so much more than money, this is priceless.'

James rubbed his throbbing wrist. He could not deny the resemblance between Summer and the ladies, especially with Aíne, the matriarch of the ensemble. 'You wound us up, Charles. I'm glad there is no ill-gotten treasure here, just a wonderful opportunity for Summer to see her ancestors. Thank you.'

'Ha!' Charles indicated the last frame. 'Can you lift this mount off the wall?'

James placed a hand under each corner and pushed up. It shifted a fraction, then fell back into place. 'I can't. It's secured to the wall.'

'It is untrammelled, except for the eighteen six-inch nails it hangs on. What appears as gilding is solid gold.' He returned to the sarcophagus and gripped the head. 'Take hold of the leg-end, and help me lift this off. It's not too heavy.'

Stone grating upon stone, they slid the cover off and leaned it against the wall. All four gathered round the open coffin.

'Is this Aíne's remains?' Summer clasped her hands. 'Say something religious, Jamie.'

'Save your satanic rituals. Charles lifted a bone and wielded it like a double-handed sword. 'My kingdom for a horse and a decent cigar. Aíne is interred somewhere in Mayo. This heap of bones is from her horse and dog, both headless of course.'

'Why build such an elaborate coffin and place animals in it? Your family is crazy.'

'Dear boy, genius and madness are the same commodity. Beneath this nag-o-bones, concealed in the base are over two-hundred gold bars, packed tighter than a virgin's...'

'Drummie, watch your tongue.' Winnie grabbed the bone, and smacked his backside with it.

James laughed. ', I like the name Drummie, it's less formal than Charles.'

'Smirk all you want, lover boy. I estimate Summer is heir to bullion worth seventy-million Sterling. She could have any man she wants. Put that thought in your bible and pray bloody hard.'

'Jamie means more to me than fool's gold.' Summer folded her arms and glared at Charles.

'It's true,' Winnie said. Her smile, almost apologetic, bore no hint of malice or untruth. 'The gold is for you to maintain this castle for your bloodline, those whose portraits will fill these empty frames.'

'No way is any of this true.' Jamie turned and placed his arm around Summer, 'Why have you and Drummie played paupers when you have this wealth at your disposal? This is an elaborate, though enjoyable hoax. I suspect you want to open the castle to visitors and are using us as guinea pigs.'

'Honour is everything, my dear friends. A Drumcreevan-O'Malley would plunder a widow's coffin, a dying man's clothes, and an emperor's harem, but never, ever, would we steal from our family. We couldn't touch what is rightfully Summer's.'

Winnie traced her finger along the edge of the coffin's lid. 'There is a smidgen of truth in your guinea pig theory. We hoped, after you get married, you would live here, and help revitalise the fortunes of Drumcreevan castle. A visitors' centre would make life more exciting, bring in a legitimate income, and Drummie could play the aristocrat daily. What do you think, Summer?'

'Jamie?'

'I've nothing better planned. If there are decent trout in the river, I could spend the rest of my life here.'

Clapping her hands, Summer bounced around the side of the coffin. She hugged Jamie, then Winnie. 'Yes, yes, we'd love that.'

'Excellent,' Charles said. 'In anticipation of your arrival, may I cash in one of the gold bars, and return opulence and fine dining to this morgue?'

James winked at Summer. 'Charles, my good man, would you be so kind as to help me replace the lid on our treasure. We shall ponder upon your request, and provide an answer at first light, before you take me angling.'

'You...'

'Drummie, behave yourself. Come, Samhradh[I], let me show you to your room. The men can close the vault, and fetch your luggage.'

I like that. Maybe I'll whisper it in her ear tonight. Lady Samhradh.

'Never trust a priest,' said Charles. 'Whoever coined that phrase is wiser than the Chinese bloke, Confusion. I suppose, I'll be shown the road like the peasants evicted in famine times.' He grabbed his end of the lid, and lifted in sync with James. They slid the cover back over the sarcophagus, ensuring it sealed the void beneath. 'I'd forgotten how beautiful these ladies were, are. You're a lucky padre to find such a girl. She plays the happy hippy almost as well as I do the bungling Lord. I'd bet all the gold in this crypt, she has the backbone of a lioness.'

Drumcreevan lifted the can of oil and shook it. A few grunts later, the lid clattered onto the floor. 'Oil, not a dog, is man's best friend.' He lubricated the three hinges, heaving the door back and forth until it moved freely. For good measure, he sloshed oil into the keyhole. 'Castle Drumcreevan will be safe for many generations to come, as long as you can get your pecker working, James.'

'Is there any reason to doubt I will?'

Charles muttered an unintelligible response.

[I] Samhradh is Summer in Irish.

They stepped outside. Drummie shut the door, twisted the key, and smiled when the tumblers slid home. He slipped the key into his pocket, plucked another cigar from his stash and lit it. 'Let's fetch your Vatican briefcase, and get thee to the baby-making-bed.'

Stepping in front of Drumcreevan, James squared his shoulders. 'I'd like the key to Summer's vault, please.'

'You mean her chastity belt. Disappoint you, I must.'

'No, I mean the vault.'

'I suppose a priest could no more ignore the lure of riches than a fox could a rabbit.' Charles lifted his gaze and blew a column of smoke over James' head. 'I'd hoped we could become friends. Do you not trust me? Have we not shown ourselves to be honourable by leaving Summers's wealth intact?'

'Would a rabbit frolic outside a fox's den?' James raised his arm, palm up. 'Do you trust Summer to hold the key to her inheritance?'

'Ha! I'm the big bad wolf if I say no; rabbit stew if I say yes.'

Drumcreevan inhaled. The tip of his cigar glowing like a furnace, he concealed his thoughts behind expressionless eyes. His lips forming an O, he blew out a series of smoke rings, each one, smaller than the previous. They oscillated, one gliding into another, and coalesced. Enraptured by the display, James gasped when the key dropped from Charles' unseen hand onto his palm.

'Thank you, Charles.' He closed his fingers around it. Opening them, he observed Charles contrive a nonchalant shrug as he turned away. 'Perhaps you might take this key and return it to Winnie for safekeeping.'

'Good man. My instinct is vindicated.' Drumcreevan snatched back the key. 'I look forward to returning it to its leather pouch on Winnie's thigh.'

Trust established, they returned to the entrance hall and collected the luggage.

'Winnie and I attempted to modernise this part of the castle,' Charles said, guiding James onto a threadbare carpet along the corridor. 'Alas, investments made in stocks and shares by my father, proved to be fanciful gambling. Millions disappeared as our portfolio crashed. Winnie and I lived off the meagre balance, and our wits, for many years. The piss-pot is empty. Summer is our last hope for the survival of the family, and for this historic rock from which generations of my ancestors have carved a fortress.'

It dawned on James there were no windows, no natural light anywhere in the interior beyond the front hall. The walls, the floors and the ceilings, all cast in solid stone. Dark, cold and safe. The first Drumcreevan had to have been a formidable man, one of great vison and determination. He'd more than honoured the O'Malley motto, a family name he dared not use. How fantastical his own future now appeared, far removed from pretending to be a priest to please his mother. *Angels will weep when Máire Brennan boasts of my elevated position to her neighbours.*

Dusty alcoves cut into the walls along their route, held everything from shotguns to heirlooms, porcelain to rat poison. Wooden skittles caked in dust, toy soldiers straddled a homemade sword, just a few of the numerous antique toys waiting for children. A cricket bat standing alongside an ancient hurley, confirming the double identity of the Drumcreevans, hinting at intrigue that James intended hearing in full. Who could resist pirate stories?

Adjusting the rucksack on his back, the corner of Jack's diary dug into his spine. *As soon as Sweeney walks the plank, I'll be free.* Even here, remote from the world of priests and the horrors he'd uncovered, thoughts about that creep made James' skin crawl, while revulsion churned his stomach. So much to do before his new life became a reality.

Charles slowed. 'When we reach the right-angled corner yonder, we shall stop.'

'Medusa awaits me?' James edged forward. 'Do I need a looking-glass or a polished shield?'

'No Gorgon would dare enter my keep. Sinbad Brennan does not require a mirror to sail around the bend, but dazzled you will be.'

There's never a dull moment in this man's company.

James peered at the balding, woollen tufts of burgundy that still clung to the canvas backing of the ancient carpet at his feet. His eyes following a rip line, exposing the stone, he tiptoed forward, and stepped onto the luxurious pile of royal-blue carpeting emblazoned with black sailing ships and wild, red boars. Slower than a trout rising to a spent mayfly, he lifted his gaze. Ahead, covered with the same extravagance, a staircase rose at least three levels. In the centre of each whitewashed wall, a line of swords, arranged tip to handle, running the length of the stairs, were broken by what James assumed were side passages. Stepping onto the bottom step, he climbed. Each blade bore the O'Malley mark and motto, *Terra marique potens.*

Above the line of weapons, oil paintings depicted sea battles. Beneath stormy skies, ships in full sail spewed orange flames from the mouths of their cannons. Others, their broadside a patchwork of gaping holes, masts shattered and the rigging trailing in the water. Many list to one side, doomed to sink below the rolling waves. James craned his neck. Ornate, tarnished brass lanterns hung from the ceiling. Each one linked to the next by an emerald silk pennant. All doubts concerning the Drumcreevan lineage evaporated. It seemed Lord Drumcreevan and Summer shared pirate blood and a hoard of treasure.

Charles caught up with James. 'What is it like to walk in the footsteps of Grace O'Malley?'

'God, these steps are so steep, it feels... it's like I'm following the dreaded ghost of a formidable woman.'

'You are. Your young lady is equally impressive. We'd kept an eye on Summer and Sapphire. When I saw her wrapped in your arms at the railway station, a chance encounter, which came long after Winnie and I had faced up to the harsh reality we'd never have children, I knew I had to take action.'

On reaching the first level, they swung left down a narrow corridor. Deep in conversation, Summer and Winnie turned at their approach. Drumcreevan nudged James. 'Time to lose your, ahem, collar.'

James thought it funny how the notion they would sleep in separate rooms had salved his conscience. Less than amusing, embarrassment knotted his tongue, as though a thousand grinning eyes followed his movements, voyeurs to his anxiety. He fumbled with the strap on the rucksack. Summer's radiant smile distracted him. Like a breeze rustling through autumnal leaves, she skipped to meet him, reached out and took hold of his sweaty hand. She leaned against his shoulder. Their hearts beating to the same excited rhythm, she guided him in silence to the bedroom door.

Winnie nodded at Charles. As though they were performing a pagan ritual, Drumcreevan strode past and stopped at an alcove where perhaps he kept his magic potions. He struck a match. It hissed as flames flickered between his thumb and forefinger. 'Ouch.' He forced his cigar through clenched lips, and illuminated by the wavering flame in the two oil lamps he carried, he marched back. A column of smoke rising above his watery eyes, he handed one lamp to James, the other to his wife. Drumcreevan appeared to withdraw into himself after he opened the door. No smart-arsed quips or smutty advice. 'Goodnight, my friends.' He stepped back and bowed his head.

'I'm sorry,' Winnie said, 'the electrics in here are shot. Perhaps you'll find the orange glow emitted from these lanterns more romantic. The room adjacent is the bathroom, modernised and lit by twin fluorescent strips. I'm afraid there is no hot water until we get the plumbing fixed.'

Summer accepted the second lamp, with its pink hand-painted porcelain bowl raised on an ornate brass base. 'Thanks. I'm sure we'll be comfortable.'

Winnie rearranged the shawl around her shoulders, and linked arms with Charles. 'Oíche mhaith agus codladh sámh[1].'

Huddled together like Victorian explorers in an Egyptian tomb, James and Summer shuffled into the room. James leaned sideways,

---

[1] Goodnight and sleep well.

catching the edge of the door with his foot, he kicked it shut. Amidst shaking hands and giggled whispers, light chased shadows up the walls, across murals, and onto the gossamer drapes of the four-poster bed.

James ran a finger over the nearest bed post. 'Why are there notches cut into this?'

Summer slung her bag onto a chair, placed her lamp on a rickety chest of drawers and laughed. 'Whoever turned that piece of oak was an artisan. A randy ancestor of mine should have noted his sexual conquests elsewhere. How many conquests have you made, Jamie?' She drew back the drape on her side, and slid between the sheets.

Mesmerised by her outline through the veil separating them, unabashed, he stared. Her arms moving upward, she removed her cotton top. Her breasts rose and fell beneath her shimmering hair. Beauty, which he could have only imagined, took his breath away.

James dropped his bag and kicked off his shoes. 'Too many to recall.' Lost in the curve of her buttocks, framed by the half-light, and unable to contain the stirring of his loins, desire broke the shell that had cocooned him for so many years. 'I'd need an entire tree and a sharp axe to record a single year.' His laugh, nervy and stuttering, blurted far too loud. Wary of the heat, he bent over his lamp and blew out the flame. He removed his shirt and jeans, and emerged from the shadows. More nervous than a cat at a dog show, he clambered onto the bed. The boards beneath the ancient mattress complained at his every movement.

'My Lord is experienced. Be gentle. I'm as fragile as the wings of a moth.'

'And you are as beautiful and tempting as Cleopatra. Remember, I said we should wait until we are married.'

'No, my lord. Your lips were sealed when the witches sent you that silly thought.

James eased himself over Summer, her thighs an invitation with their separation.

'Ooh, my lord is too eager.'

In a single movement, he rolled onto the far side of Summer, and reached for the second lamp.

'Hey, where are you going?'

He took a deep breath. Positioning his mouth over the glass chimney, he exhaled. The flame guttered and died, engulfing them in darkness.

His lips nuzzling her ear, he whispered. 'I lied about waiting.'

Chapter 31

James and Summer threaded their way through the plush pile of the staircase, and past the line of swords. Reaching the ground floor, they clung to each other as if this was their last morning together - not the first. Along the winding corridor, layer upon layer of dust had settled on items long discarded by the paint-brushed faces, staring with sightless eyes from the walls of the great hall, and passageways the future owners had yet to visit.

Clawing his way through one area of gloom too many, James stopped at a darkened corner. Overhead, one of many blown light bulbs provided grounding for spider webs and a morgue for insect prey.

'Summer, we must build a house outside, between here and the river. With wide bay windows to fill the rooms with sunlight and starlight. I'll cut a single notch on the bed post and throw away the knife. Living beyond the shadow of this castle could be fantastic, while we trip in and out of the past like time travellers.'

'I never realised you were such a romantic.'

'I'm not.' James brushed cobwebs from the side of an oval mirror. 'This cave gives me the creeps. I'm not a vampire or a long-eared bat.'

Summer ran her fingers through her tangled hair. 'Maybe that's why you snore, Jamie.'

'Do I?'

'I lay awake for yonks last night, stroking your hairy chest, wondering about our future. This is surreal. I don't understand why I'm to inherit so much. I don't think I want such wealth. Gold tainted by blood can't be lucky, can it?'

'From what I've gleaned, big D Drumcreevan made the rules in the fifteen-hundreds. When the last surviving male of the family died, the last female descendant from his daughters would inherit. That person is you.'

Summer shuffled her feet. 'But Charles isn't dead.'

'He might be alive, but he's skint and childless.'

'I'm so cross with myself for not understanding how difficult and painful it must be for Winnie and Charles.'

Her reaction to this surprised James, showing the gulf separating her, as a mother, and he, as a young man who had never considered fatherhood beyond the Church. 'That's why they asked us here.'

'Wait, are you saying they set this up so you and I could...?'

'No — yes. I don't know. If you ask me, they're crazy. Look, their eccentricities might be endearing, but I could no more live under the same roof as them than I could spend the rest of my days in the company of Sweeney.'

'Don't mention that foul man. These are nice people. In my family, being weird is normal, essential. I always thought it was from smoking too much grass, now I understand it's genetic. I'm related to Frankenstein.' She dragged James to the door leading to the entrance hall, and threw it open.

Floundering on a sea of confusion, the last admiral of the Drumcreevan fleet battled the woodworm-infested leg of a full-length mirror, while it teetered on its three good pegs. In danger of toppling, and bringing seven years of bad luck to his Lordship, the fretwork mermaids surrounding the glass whipped their tails to right the valuable antique. Blessed with strong limbs, James sprinted across the floor and joined the fray. Taking a firm hold of the sirens, he steered the wayward vessel north-northwest, while the carpenter, clad in purple silk pyjamas, re-affixed the dainty leg, driving the rusty nail back whence it had drifted loose.

'I say, remove your paws from my girls.' Charles hauled himself from the floor with a grimace.

'Had your ancestors ordered the carpenter to adorn the mirror with images of Poseidon, rather than his daughters, the leg you fondled would have been manlier and sturdier.'

'Too true, James. My dearest Summer, after so many years in the damned doldrums, thanks to you, fair winds once again fill the Drumcreevan sails. I've prepared a canvas on the easel placed in front of the fireplace. It's ready to capture your beauty, Lady Samhradh. The thing is, I've mislaid the resident artist, and am short of cash to commission another. It will have to be a self-portrait.'

'I can paint, but I'm not as good as my mother.'

'Yes you are,' James said. 'Go fetch your brushes. There's a book in my rucksack, can you bring it and my sunglasses? I'll fetch coffee and toast for us.'

'My Lord is very forceful today. Two sugars, please.'

On returning to the hall, James placed the tray of dubious vintage onto the gargantuan oak table, whose elephantine supports were as wide as a tree trunk. So absorbed in sketching on the canvas, Summer did not acknowledge his presence, or the coffee. She had left Jack's diary leaning against the vase nearest the fireplace. Sipping from his own mug, he ran a finger over the gold lettering, building a shield against the horrors he knew lay within the leather-bound volume. He grabbed it, thinking he must find a suitable place outside where he could read its contents undisturbed, donned his sunglasses, and strode to the massive front door.

Maybe Summer's ancestors were giants. Their claim to be pirates, a ruse to hide the existence of their magical goose who laid golden eggs. More likely, when threatened by their enemies, they rode their horses into the castle. He drew back the three inch-thick bolts and hauled the door open. Driven by a gale, sheet rain falling from an angry sky lashed at the flagstone step, and ripping into the gravel outside, whipped at his ankles. Disappointed he couldn't escape from the suffocating castle, he shut the door and removed his glasses. Sealed inside, they were as oblivious to the vagaries of the weather as they were to world affairs, an unnatural existence.

Taking a wide berth around Summer, James glanced at the canvas. Light pencil marks outlined forms that to his eyes were meaningless. Thinking he might pat Cullen's head in passing, he imagined five-hundred-year-old blood-sucking fleas, of Jurassic size, leaping off the beast onto his arm. 'Sit,' James said, passing by the hound. He eyed a cushioned chair leaning against the wall. Its spindly legs splayed in the right formation and number, he leaned heavy on the armrest, ready to right himself should the archaic joints splinter beneath the pressure. Rock solid. Not so much as a creak to indicate possible danger. He eased himself onto the seat, allowing his full weight to settle with his nerves. Cullen's back being in reach of his feet, he considered placing them on it. Glancing up at big D's scowling image in the oil painting, James changed position, and planted his legs on the stack of timber in the hearth. Taking a deep breath, he opened the diary and turned to the second page.

Easons bookshop in O'Connell Street provided me with my weapons of choice; a notepad and a Thesaurus-dictionary. Charity and abuse were the first two words I looked up. I lived under the shadow of the first of these throughout so much of my young life. Each syllable of its deceit leaves a bitter taste any time I force my lips to sound it out. Char-i-ty. Largesse or philanthropy, a hand-out — I followed the trail of words, one leading to another, until like a kitten chasing its tail, I reached a dead end, and returned to the page where I started my voyage. Abuse proved a more arduous trek. It evoked more words to describe its many shades. Twice, my tired eyes slid from the pages as I deciphered its meaning and investigated its disciples, falling asleep in my cubbyhole beneath the stairs with the light on. I always keep it on, a stash of new bulbs close at hand.

Dear diary, the only place I've ever found these two words to be synonymous was in the shit-hole they threw me in after my mother's murder. Perhaps, in time, someone will pluck this diary from my corpse, read my words and rewrite the thesaurus according to my practical findings. Word: orphanage. Synonyms: corruption; exploitation; desecration; injustice; debasement; debauchery. Charity and abuse, these are the two faces of Father Michael Sweeney, and those who turned a blinkered eye to his depravities.

The Gardaí had packed my meagre possessions into a cardboard box. They thrust it into the hands of one nun, me into the arms of another. Marched to the kitchen, they stripped me of my clothes and my dignity. Again and again, they plunged my skinny body into the icy waters of a tin bath, my eyes burning from the carbolic soap that they washed me with. Sponges made from sandpaper. Not caring whether it was a leg, a face, or penis, they scrubbed me till I bled. Though sweat ran down my brow, I shivered while standing naked in front of the furnace. They threw my belongings into the inferno. An angel appeared, shiny and black, with a white collar and a smiling, clean-shaven face. My saviour plucked my teddy-bear by its one leg from the fire, quenched the flames singeing its ear, and handed it to me. He licked his bulbous lips, while his playful eyes drew me in. He examined my hair, probed my ears, my eyes, my anus... those long fingers, calloused, broken-nailed. Declared me bug free and Catholic. He held my hand and whispered. "Jack, you are special. My special boy."

Consumed by the image of the naked child, alone and scared, now unloved, James stopped reading and stared into cold embers in the fireplace, Why weren't the nuns more compassionate? Did they take pleasure in his nakedness or were their minds so bound by servitude to their order and God, they heard no evil, saw no wrong? They scrubbed the child as they would the floors and the walls. Blinded by faith, their compassion only directed to their ideals, those they helped were stepping stones to eternal life with their saviour. Why had they forgotten Christ's words? "Love others as yourself."

These were too many paradoxes for James to consider on his own. He knew he could never solve them, nor understand the motivations behind those who abused, any more than he could decipher the etchings on Summer's canvas. Enveloped by sadness, he twirled an imaginary finger around her golden hair, the way she did. Sitting here under the shadow of her ancestors, he loved her for the way she lit up dark places with her vitality and honesty. Without her...

Duty demands I be in Castlebridge, a Knight defending the children and beheading the tyrant. My heart says otherwise. Stay here, hidden behind that sturdy oak door, with the woman I love.

The sweet aroma of Summer's reefer reaching him, James stirred. She sat cross-legged on the flagstone floor, staring at the mirror. Her head twisted this way and that. She brought the joint to her lips and inhaled. The frown lines on her brow and at the corners of her eyes disappeared behind the column of smoke.

Hey, gorgeous. Her frustration obvious, James dared to speak. 'Is there any way I can help?'

'I can't do this.' She leaned sideways to steal a glimpse of him. 'It's your fault, Jamie.'

'Do you remember last night?'

'Yeah.'

'Don't look at me and don't blush. Face the mirror — funny isn't it, the way everything is reversed?' He slid from the chair onto the floor, and crawled to where she sat.

'I guess so.'

'Shall we forget about the painting and return to bed?'

The mirror revealed a smile that dismissed the anxious expression in her eyes, and the quiver of her lips. James reached forward, wrapped his arms around her, and dropped his chin onto her shoulder. 'It's not the beauty the world can see, but the beauty within you must capture.'

'You would have me in the nude.'

'Later,' he grinned. 'For the portrait, a long tee-shirt over bare legs and pink sandals is perfect. No makeup, no jewellery, except for our engagement ring, partially hidden by other fingers, and smile.'

James stumbled backwards as she jumped to her feet and began to mix paints. Pleased his suggestions had sparked her into action, he returned to his seat and opened the diary.

Others had a lattice of scars on their backs. I knew my own would mirror theirs. The only salve to these wounds came from contemplating the alternative of yielding to Sweeney. We never discussed what he did to his special boys, not in detail. How could we? Nods were sufficient acknowledgement that we knew. Even now, the trauma of visiting the past takes its toll, and must be atoned for by penance beneath the stairs.

The whimpers of the chosen ones always lasted long into the night. Their reward, a trip to the zoological gardens with him and a gaggle of nuns or an occasional ice cream from the shop around the corner. Did the lions retreat to the back of their enclosure when Sweeney approached? Did the snakes slither from dark recesses and lift their serpent heads for him to pat? Treats? Trick or treat? You're a sinner, sing the parrots in my head.

On bended knees, I scrubbed the floors. On bended knees, we bowed before holy statues and begged forgiveness for sins we never committed nor understood. Carbolic soap could not remove the stench of fear that governed our lives from dawn till dawn. Sleep offered no refuge, death no afterlife.

On bended knees, I washed the blood from the tiles in the hall, from the walls where it had splattered, from my hands when Sister Asumpta deemed my work complete. Someone had rolled up the thin, urine-stained mattress on the bed beside mine. Tied with blue twine, the knot formed a perfect bow, a present for the next victim. No one mentioned Fergal's name out loud. In whispers, we wondered whether it had hurt when he slammed into the lower bannister. The fall from the third floor, plummeting through the air like a wingless bird, or did the flailing of his arms mean he tried to fly to freedom? Thump! We all heard it. It still resonates in my mind at night when the world sleeps.

The bells, those bloody bells rang for mass six times a day. Thump! Fergal chose death. On bended knees, beside his empty bed, I cried dry tears, and cursed God and his bastard nuns and priests. On bended knees, we presented our backs and received the whippings, day after day, week after week. On bended knees, beneath my stairs, I write these words.

After an old nun died, a real angel with a freckled face came from the convent. Her name is lost to me. Our hearts sang to her kindness. Cream on the tips of her gentle fingers traced the ridges of my wounds. Her soft voice humming a melody I've long forgotten, but I lie awake hoping it will come back to me. She raised her voice in complaint. They silenced her. On bended knees by the dormitory window, we watched her trudge down the path to the taxi, carrying her own heavy suitcase. I wished she had taken me under her wing and flown me to heaven, to Mam. It was my eighth birthday, the second one of my short life without celebration, without love or the hope of love. Mam never had money. She had so much love to give me she was the wealthiest person I knew.

I still miss her.

But I do not miss the bells.

James closed the diary. *I must return to Castlebridge.*

Chapter 32

The faint scent of patchouli drew James' head to his left. He closed his eyes, allowing the perfume to paint Summer's image in his mind, remembering their tears mingling before they had separated at the bus station. Clinging to each other, she had laid her head upon his shoulder. Consumed by a sense of loss when their fingertips parted, he had dashed to catch the bus for Castlebridge. 'I love you, Jamie.' Her plaintive cry faded beneath the noise of diesel engines revving, but the shape of her words floated in his mind, and the sound of her voice seemed only a breath away. No matter how hard he tried, he could no longer hear her, could not replay her love in any voice but his own.

Taking hold of the diary on his lap, he shuffled his feet, fighting off the threat of pins and needles. Someday, when old age had stooped his back and time had leathered his sensibilities, he'd stoke the fire under the portrait of Drumcreevan, and read the entire diary. On the journey back to Castlebridge he'd dipped in and out of Jack's memories, picking pages at random. Those snippets churned his stomach as they chronicled events that defied comprehension, cruelties beyond the imagination of Nero. James sighed. Rome should burn once again for the behaviour of its servants.

Life at the seminary had allowed monsters such as Sweeney to hide behind collars. Perhaps it spawned them. James recalled the names of his peers and fellow seminarians, and wondered about each of them. *Mouse, where are you now, my friend? You escaped the bullying.* Why had God and the good men of the Church failed the children? Why had he failed his friend?

James glanced at the road sign, one mile to Castlebridge. *How many yards is that? One thousand, seven-hundred and something steps. My next bus journey will be in the opposite direction with Summer and Callum. We'll count from zero until the number is so big, we'll no longer be able to remember the name Castlebridge, and only recall the faces of a handful of its inhabitants.*

After the bus rounded the corner of Mahon's shop at a snail's pace, the church came into view. It's grey stonework, bleak and foreboding, blighted his thoughts, forcing him to shut his eyes. Though muted behind the thick bus window, the sound of the church bells deafened him. At the final peal, he looked out. Agitation stretching her lips, Agnes Murphy scurried along the footpath opposite. She raised her black umbrella above the pillars, before she entered the churchyard by the smaller gate, and charged to the front door. James could picture her eyes darting above crimson cheeks, her head bowed to avoid scrutiny. After mass, Agnes' puppy-like eagerness to please Father Sweeney would be an invitation for him to pounce. That wolf would use her tardiness as an opportunity to blackmail the unfortunate girl into doing his bidding. Out of the corner of his eye, James spotted Luke drop his bicycle near the Sacristy door.

A sigh of inevitability leaving James' lips, he slid the sunglasses off his forehead and over his eyes, as though concealing his thoughts behind darkened lenses. 'Thanks,' James said, to the driver as he exited.

When those bells ring this time next week, I swear Sweeney will be incarcerated or dead by my hands. I owe that to Jack. I, too, hate the sound of the bells.

Marching to the tune of dogged determination, his legs did not falter or break stride on the way to Billy's house. When his friend answered the knock on the door, James thrust the diary into his hands. 'Photocopy this twice and keep it safe.'

Billy scowled. 'Hello doesn't cost a bean. What is this?'

'Sorry, Billy, I'm wound up tighter than a fishing line. It's a diary from one of Sweeney's victims, Jack O'Brien, the bus driver I told you about. To be honest, Dante's Inferno is a comedy compared to this.'

'That good?' Billy turned the book. *'My screwed up head.* Not a title I'd be inclined to pick up in a bookshop.'

'The baleful existence of Jack is a story of unending lamentation. I doubt his tale will conclude well, yet I pray for a miracle. We must end the reign of terror that has blighted too many young lives.'

'One way or another, Sweeney is bound for Hell.'

James scratched his arm for the umpteenth time that day. *Bloody Drumcreevan fleas.* 'I'd be content if he were confined to the inner ring of Dante's Seventh Circle and sodomised by his ilk for eternity. Something tells me the snake would escape. We'll travel to Carlow tomorrow afternoon, if that suits you.'

'I'll enjoy witnessing the jaw drop on Bishop O'Rourke's smug face. Given the proof we've uncovered, do you think the prick will act?'

'What choice has he? All the evidence, when added together, is compelling. Why do you ask?'

'O'Rourke circled the wagons once before, he could do so again.'

Billy placed his hand on James' arm. 'We'll not let that happen. Now, tell me about your romantic weekend.'

'I've little to report, except that Summer, Callum and I will move to Drumcreevan Castle four days from now. They return to Castlebridge tomorrow to pack.'

'You're what?'

'Lord and Lady Drumcreevan-Brennan will be glad to have you visit. I'll not let my lofty title affect our friendship as long as you don't either. I'll tell you everything en route to Carlow. See ya, Billy.' Turning on his heel, James glanced at the statue in the garden as he strode away. *I'll get a Buddha for outside the castle door.* James checked the time. He had ten minutes to reach the Sacristy before Mass ended.

Partially concealed by shelving near the door in the L-shaped Sacristy, James leaned against the cold wall. Arms folded, he hoped he'd not be noticed by anyone emerging from the church. The stink of dirty sportswear no longer lingered. Sean remained safe. The only certainty being his resolve to face Sweeney here, in his place of abuse, James focused on the images from the diary. They washed over him, cleansing him of his fears and inadequacies. Using those horrific acts to fuel his retribution provoked such a strange feeling, James shivered.

Footsteps growing louder, he took a deep breath as the inner door burst open and Luke dashed into the room. Hurrying to the wall opposite him, he removed his outfit and hung it upon a hook. Moments later, his presence chilling the air with menace, Sweeney entered. The door locked behind him, he growled at the child. 'Why were you late?'

'Sorry, Father.'

'You will be. His steps ringing on the flagstones, he strode towards Luke. 'It's your fault I have to punish you.' Sweeney punched the boy in the belly. 'Isn't it?' Sweeney hissed. 'Why make me do this?'

Doubled in pain, Luke turned and grasped the chair with both hands. 'Yes, Father. It's because you love me.'

'Bend over!' Sweeney removed his vestments and stood behind the boy. He flicked the greasy hair hanging over his eyes back to cover his bald patch. 'God loves you, Luke. I am the instrument of His love.' Sweeney unbuckled the belt on his black trousers. 'Pull down...'

James lunged for the old priest, locked an arm around Sweeney's neck, and drove his knee into his back. 'Move, and I'll crush you. Luke, go home. This monster will never hurt you again.'

Sweeney squirmed. Gasping for breath, he tried to kick back, but, anticipating this, James twisted and flung the unbalanced priest to the floor. Sweeney cried out. Clutching his knee, he slid to the corner. 'Bastard. You're a dead man, Brennan.'

James stood over him, his fist clenched. 'Stay there, you perverted shit.'

Luke stumbled over the chair, grabbing the armrest to stop himself from falling. Rising to his full height, he bared his teeth. 'I hate you, Father Brennan.' He charged like a bull, driving James into the wall. Tears flooding the child's eyes, he threw a flurry of punches at the young priest, spat and cursed. What he lacked in strength, he compensated by hatred. Afraid he would hurt the boy, James backed off. With Luke blocking the way, James could not prevent Sweeney from rising. After unlocking the inner door, the ferret kept hold of the handle, ready to escape any further violence.

'That's the second time you prevented me from carrying out my duty. You're finished as a priest. Three slaps from my belt would keep Luke on the path of the righteous. Isn't that right, Luke?'

'Yes, Father Sweeney. Being late for Mass and God is a sin. I deserve to be thrashed, the harder the better.' He pointed at James. 'So does Father Brennan. He struck you and punched me.'

'No, I didn't,' James said, incredulous.

Luke head-butted the wall. 'See what he did to me,' he whimpered, touching the reddening blotch on his forehead. His grin twisted into an accusatory stare.

'Tut-tut, such despicable behaviour makes me sick.' Sweeney limped to Luke and placed a fatherly arm around his shoulders. 'Poor, Luke, a meek and innocent child attacked in a church, by a priest no-less. What are we to do with him?'

'Crucify him.'

'Ha! That's a wonderful idea. Sit at the top of the class, Luke. Did you hear that, James? Your victim demands you be crucified.'

More disgusted by the spittle dribbling down his face than the antics of Sweeney and Luke, James lifted his arm and wiped the filth away. 'If one claims to be the son of God, it's an admirable, though painful way to die. I make no such claim.'

You should.

What? That voice again. There is no God. Distracted for a moment by internal rambling, James scratched his arm. Conscious of Sweeney's mocking eye following his every movement, he raised his eyebrows. 'You studied the classics.'

'Yes. I studied the Irish classics.' A waspish grin replaced his scowl in an instant. 'I paid scant attention to the Latin and Greek rubbish. My preference is Ulysses. You can shove Homer and his bloody Odyssey in the fire. What has this to do with your abject behaviour?'

Idiot, where did Joyce find his inspiration? 'Nothing.' James shrugged. 'Dante's nine circles of Hell intrigue me.'

Luke shuffled his feet. 'He's weird. Can we leave, Father Sweeney?'

'Be quiet.' Sweeney frowned. 'They are vaguely familiar. The rantings of a deranged poet who drank too much wine is of little interest. Are you considering your fate, post crucifixion?'

'No. I'm contemplating yours.'

'Go home, Luke.' Sweeney shoved the lad toward the front door.

James stepped to one side, glanced at Luke, and then faced Sweeney. 'Tell your parents I hit you, Luke. If they don't believe you, tell the Gardaí. I'm not sorry. If I catch you here alone, I'll batter you again and again until you report me.'

'Wait.' Sweeney dug a coin from his pocket and tossed it to Luke. 'Buy an ice cream. If anyone asks, you fell off your bike. I'll deal with Father Brennan. Do not tell anyone. You know the consequences if you disobey me.'

Luke licked his lips. 'I love ice cream.'

Turning the handle on the door, he stuck out his tongue at James. In his own mind, the victor; to James, a child.

'You could fit with ease into many of Dante's circles.' James stepped into the centre of the room. For a moment, Sweeney stood his ground. His eyes darting from James to the door, he edged back in its direction.

'It's the inner ring of the seventh circle that will welcome you.' No reaction, but another step forward had Sweeney adopt a defensive position, the whites of his knuckles a contrast to the grey pallor beneath narrowed eyes.

'Soon you shall be amongst your kin. Bullies and blasphemers shall be your comfort.'

Sweeney's relief palpable, a smirk lit his face like an affront to every child he'd abused. 'If I apologise, James, will you pray for me? My occasional violent outburst is shameful. Will you help me?'

'Yes, Father Sweeney. I will pray. Close your eyes.'

'Bless you, Father James,' he said, keeping one eye open.

'You are beyond redemption. I pray your fellow sodomites bugger you again, and again, until the end of time. There is no escaping punishment, not this time.'

Yellowed teeth bared, Sweeney snarled as he wrenched open the door. 'I'll see you in Hell.'

More nimble than James expected, Sweeney fled, slamming the door behind him.

The statue of Our Blessed Lady, serenity herself, gazed down on James knowingly, as it had done the day Summer came into his life. That naive, young priest, a mere lad collared by church and obligation, no longer existed. The memory of him, just scratchings from a period in his life, best forgotten. He rubbed his arm where it continued to vex him and smiled at her marble face.

My work as a priest is near done. My life as a man begins.

Chapter 33

In the dock, trapped in the unblinking gaze of the packed gallery, the handcuffed prisoner sneers. Beneath staring eyes, his thin-lipped mouth, which refused to answer a single question, holds an unlit pipe. Barristers smooth their gowns and straighten their wigs. Their juniors shuffle papers in the unending game of justice.

'Twelve good men of the jury, have you reached a verdict?'

The foreman stands, and steps forward. He holds a sheet of yellowed parchment in his trembling hands, the result of fifteen minutes deliberation. In truth, their decision took five minutes, the coffee ten. Confused by the directions they had received from the judge, the jurors whisper to each other. Beady-eyed and hesitant, the foreman unfolds his horn-rimmed glasses, but choosing not to wear them, stares at his feet. 'Not guilty.'

Sweeney lights his pipe and cackles like a witch stirring a cauldron.

Judge O'Rourke nods at the Bishop and rises.

'All stand.'

This was James's worst nightmare, played over and over each time he closed his eyes. In the passenger well of Maggie's Fiat, a manila envelope sat pinched between his feet. Behind the wheel, Billy hummed a tune more appropriate to a funeral than Sweeney's hanging party.

James had locked his bedroom door the previous night. The handle of his fishing priest peeked out from under his pillow. Used to dispatch trout, he'd gladly use it to tap Sweeney's lights out if necessary. Kept awake by the drone emanating from the lecherous bastard in the adjacent room, he'd considered not only the contents, but also the envelope. Every detail mattered. Centred, using a black marker he'd written, *To Whom It May Concern*. On the top right, *Copy 1 of 20* in bright red lettering carried a world of threat. A second envelope, containing the only other copy of the diary and the other documents, occupied a place in Billy's coffin alongside the stash of cigarettes.

Just past two in the afternoon, they neared Bishop's House on the Dublin Road. Billy had quietened. Perhaps the river from which he drew a torrent of jokes and stories had run dry. More likely, overwhelmed by the same doubt that plagued James, he battled to remain positive. Billy chose a parking spot a short distance away, between two vans.

'James. *Deja vu* ran across the bonnet and thumped me in the face. My stomach is all rock-n-roll, like Mick Jagger is prancing around my intestines. I better bloody get satisfaction this time round.'

'We will.'

Billy plucked a cigarette from his shirt pocket, lit it, and opened the window. Wisps of smoke swirling around his head vanished, whipped away by invisible forces. James wondered if his own existence was also a fleeting thing, and their evidence as fragile as a dandelion's seed head, to be blown away, spore by spore.

'I'll tell ya something else, James Brennan. Billy boy will only touch his lips against that prick's ring after he kisses my undertaker's bum.'

James lifted the envelope. 'We'll not antagonise O'Rourke or make threats. Bishops are powerhouses within the church, shrewd and intelligent. They expect and demand loyalty. I've learned one important skill from Sweeney, how to be a chameleon.'

'Jesus, aren't they those insect yokes who eat their husbands and children.' Billy yanked open the door. 'Stay away from me.'

Laughter, loud and bellowing, drew strange looks from passers-by.

'That's the praying mantis. Chameleons have perfected their ability to change colour, to blend in with their background.'

'Then Sweeney is a cross-breed. We know what he prays for and preys on.' Billy tossed his cigarette out the window. 'Okay, Lone Ranger, Tonto will keep his gob shut. Let's ride in there and inform Sheriff O'Rourke of his obligations.'

Befitting a prince of the church, the Bishop lived in a palace compared to Castlebridge's presbytery, one protected by a high wall and sturdy barred gates, which were open. Mature sycamores lined the sides of the property. A cuckoo called. Billy replied, their songs indistinguishable.

'Magpies, crows and cuckoos,' Billy said, cawing like a crow, 'were my companions during a lifetime of burials, especially in rural cemeteries. Do you sing, James?'

'Not a note. Three steps and we're there. Are you ready for this?'

Billy scuffed his feet on the gravel. 'No. I'd like another ciggie. Lead on, Obi Wan.'

'Who?'

'Jedi Brennan, have you succumbed to the Dark Side? The Force, James, feel the Force.'

Billy dragged James up the steps. At the top, he pressed the bell three times.

The lady who opened the door scowled. 'His eminence has no appointments this afternoon, and is not expecting any callers. Please ring tomorrow to arrange one.'

'Angelica,' Billy said, sliding under her outstretched arm, and bustled past her into the hall, 'surely your memory is as long as your divine legs.' Billy raised his hands, palms facing her. 'No dirty talk, please. I've a celibate priest with me. You are far too young for your hair to be tied in a matronly bun. Shake it loose, babe.'

'Who are you, you foul man? My name is Sister Celestine.'

'I am Mister Billy Egan, a master undertaker. I'm here to measure you for a coffin.' Turning to James, he beckoned for him enter. 'See, Father Brennan. This is why I saw corpses in half. Some people are too tall to fit.' Billy pranced to a waiting area by the large double-door leading to the Bishop's study, and sat on a chair. 'We'll wait here while you fetch Malachy and two cups of tea. Milk and sugar in both, sweetheart.'

'Leave this instant. I'll call the Gardaí and have you removed.'

Arguably as extravagant and as pompous as the Drumcreevans, oil paintings of former Bishops of Kildare in gold frames crowded the walls, the irony not lost on James as he stepped over the threshold. 'I'm Father Brennan from Castlebridge. Forgive my friend, Sister, and please accept my apologies on his behalf.' James offered his hand and a wide smile.

Sister Celestine swung the door closed and accepted both. With her incisors hidden behind her blushing cheeks, Celestine proved far prettier and amenable than first impressions suggested. 'Your apology is accepted.'

'Cursed with a dreadful, degenerative brain disease with an unpronounceable Latin name, Billy has delusions of being a funeral director. The Lord is calling him home, Sister. Ours is not to question why. Pray for him.'

'Yes, Father.' All a flutter, she blessed herself. 'Poor man. Is he contagious?'

'Not in the least. I pray Bishop O'Rourke can find a moment to meet with us. It's a matter of utmost urgency. Death does not wait a minute.'

Celestine's knuckle kissed the door with a tap so inaudible the Bishop would need a stethoscope pressed against the far side to hear it. Within a single tick of the grandfather clock, adjacent to the staircase, she'd opened, entered and closed the door behind her. Raised voices drew a smile from Billy. Silence. The door opened.

Celestine slid out and closed it. 'I regret to say his Eminence is unavailable.'

'Is he alive?' Billy leapt of the chair.

Puzzled by the question, she glanced at James, and then fixed Billy with look of disbelief. 'Yes, he is very much alive, but very busy as the Cardinal calls here tomorrow.'

'Excellent. Then he isn't unavailable. His prick-ship is just being himself, a rude jackass. Fetch the Bishop his medication as he'll need a double dose.'

Before James could intervene, Billy flung open the doors.

Exactly what I didn't want to happen.

"Don't worry we'll not hurt his Eminence. Thank you, Sister.' James strode past the nun, flashing a smile.

Bishop O'Rourke's leather chair crashed into the wall behind him. Rocking onto his feet, he leant on the mahogany desk and glared at his unwelcome guests. Behind him, an oil painting of a more jovial Bishop O'Rourke contrasted with the man engulfed by purple rage. His quivering finger pointing at Billy, he roared. 'Who are you?'

'A dying man,' Billy said, lurching to a seat in front of the Bishop. 'None of us know when or where, do we? Anger is such a negative emotion, don't you think?'

Still seething, as he dragged his chair back into position, the Bishop spotted James. 'Wait ... you're Father Brennan from Castlebridge.'

'I am, and I apologise for bursting into your office.' James sat alongside Billy and placed the envelope on the desk in front of O'Rourke. 'After I've explained the content of the enclosed documents, perhaps you will understand the need for urgent action.'

Composure returning to a face accustomed to good wine, fine dining and a touch of makeup, his eminence fixed his gaze on the envelope. 'Very well, you have ten minutes. Twenty copies of these documents exist, is that correct?' His bushy eyebrows coalescing with the deep frown furrowing his brow, he teased out the papers. Hostility, brewing beneath the surface, emanated from him.

'Yes,' James said, noting the judgmental eyes swinging in his direction, 'that's correct.'

'Hmm. Before I read, perhaps you could indicate the nature of these documents.'

Billy jumped to his feet and, leaning over the ornate desk with menace, he whistled as though a shepherd calling a dog to heel. 'I'll cut to the chase. Father Sweeney has been molesting children for donkeys' years. You ignored me once before, you'll not wiggle away this time.' Billy smashed his fist onto the papers, just missing the Bishop's fingers. A gold pen rolled off the desk. 'The proof is here, and nineteen copies are ready for newspaper editors.'

O'Rourke did not flinch.

'Please sit, Billy,' James said, tugging on his friend's tweed jacket. 'The Bishop is not the enemy.'

Easing himself back onto his seat, Billy leaned toward James, and whispered. 'Good Jedi, bad Jedi.'

'Sorry,' James said. 'Your Eminence may recall the name, Conor Heffernan. He accused Father Sweeney of abuse, and was in turn accused of theft. Would you please read the letter we received from the lad?'

O'Rourke stood. 'No need. That matter is closed, so is this meeting. I neither have the time nor the interest to rehash wanton defamation.'

Billy rumbled like a volcano on the cusp of eruption. Fists clenched, he pushed to the edge of his chair, a cobra ready to strike. James reached across and muzzled him with a reassuring nod, noting the smirk from O'Rourke as he did so.

'Your brother retired from the judiciary last week. Cork wasn't it?' James pulled a newspaper cutting from his shirt pocket and offered it to O'Rourke. 'It's the same court that convicted a Kildare boy of theft from a Sacristy. It's ironic and a tad lucky I found the photo yesterday, in a paper purchased by Sweeney.' James scratched his arm, a nervous reaction exacerbating the problems of the flea bite.

O'Rourke reached for his glasses and read Conor's letter. 'I had to prevent a scandal. Conor had been stealing wine. Father Sweeney caught him in the act, and in an ensuing fracas, Conor stabbed him. My brother is a friend to the church. We did what had to be done to protect everyone concerned.'

'You mean, to protect the Catholic Church.' Billy spat on his palm and rubbed his hands together. 'Like Pontius Pilate you washed your murderous mitts and punished the innocent.'

'Sweeney misled you, Your Grace,' James said. 'Leaving Conor to one side, let me enlighten you further. Keith O'Neil was one of Father Sweeney's *special boys*. Ashamed of the acts committed on him, he took his own life. Joe Wall is wheelchair-bound after an attempted overdose. He, too, could not live with the memories.' James paused. The Bishop slumped back onto his chair, the implications draining the blood from his face. 'Eoghan Jacob has not been seen in years, he is presumed dead. All were altar boys, all special, and all sexually abused by Sweeney. There are many others.'

As though the matters being discussed were no more important than the picking of suitable dates for confirmation classes, O'Rourke spoke with unwavering firmness. 'I have received one or two reports of violent behaviour, instances where he lost his temper and struck a child.'

'He does that too.' James leaned forward. 'I witnessed such an event. I've also been attacked by one of the children, an altar boy, who claims he is in love with the paedophile Sweeney.'

'Paedophile?' The Bishop slumped onto his elbows. 'Dear God,' he whispered. 'Are you alleging he ... interferes with children?'

'No.' Billy lowered his voice. 'I'm telling you he rips down their pants and buggers them again and again, and again. I've lived with that disgusting image trampling over my conscience for too long, because you failed to act. Can you see his erect penis? Can you, Bishop? Does it make your stomach churn, your head spin? It should, unless ...'

'Unless ... how dare you? I cannot imagine such horrors. Even the thought of it sends bile racing to my throat.' His voice cracked under the stress, and his hand shook. 'I've never harmed a child, never could'

'We are all guilty of harming children. His sins are my sins, your sins. From the lowest Seminarian, to the Cardinals and the Pontiff, all are guilty. Stopping short of blaming a God he no longer believed in, James sighed, sorry to see a good man suffocate under the weight of responsibility this knowledge brought with it. 'Will you see justice done?'

'As Christ is my witness, I'll bring a halt to his vile actions.'

A look of disbelief on Billy's face, he crossed his arms. 'Before the cock crows is a familiar message. How many times do we wait?'

'That's all we ask of you, Bishop. Stop him.' James pointed to the papers. 'Within those documents, there is a diary from an orphan. Please read it. It's a harrowing account of what Sweeney did to children in the Fifties.'

'I'll need the nineteen copies of these documents. I hope we have sufficient proof.'

'Ha! I bet you do. Do you think you are dealing with eejits?' Billy jumped to his feet. His voice more gravelly than the result of the few cigarettes he smoked, he glared at the Bishop. 'The documents remain somewhere safe. When I die, they will vanish for all time. I trust you less than I trust the paedophile. Prove you are more than another brick in the wall.' Billy heaved himself of the chair, glared at O'Rourke before high-tailing it from the room.

Slumped in his chair, an expression of defeat stippling his face, his eminence thumbed through the papers, his muttering unintelligible.

'Do the right thing.' James shook hands with his superior and followed Billy back to the car.

It's done. The children will be safe, and I'm free to marry Summer.

† † †

Sparks flew from the kettle. 'Bugger,' James said, borrowing a phrase from his friend Drumcreevan. 'That bloody thing is a fire hazard.'

Stripped of personal effects, and despite her earlier efforts at decorating, Summer's kitchen-cum-living room remained a hovel. Callum raced around James' legs, stepping in and out of the mounds of debris. 'Wait until I sweep it all up, then we'll fill your shovel, Callum.' Though exasperated at having his efforts undone, James revelled in being a *real* father. *My son's a bundle of energy. How great is that? My son.* 'Fetch the plastic sack.'

Callum reached under the table and dragged the half-filled bag to James, leaving a trail of spillage. 'Let me do it,' the child said, driving his spade into the dirt. 'Vroom.' Callum tipped some of the load into the bag. Most of it fell back on the floor. James reached for the boy's hand, guided it to the mound of dirt and held it steady on its path back to the bag. 'Vroom.' Callum laughed, but refused further help in doing *his* job.

'Stubborn like his mother,' Jamie said, hearing Summer's footsteps close behind him.

'Like an ex-priest?' Summer slid her arms around James, and poked his belly with her yellow, gloved finger. 'Like a what, Jamie?'

'Hey, I don't know where those gloves have been.' Jamie turned to face her, lifted his hand and flicked back her hair, revealing train tracks of grime running across her forehead. 'Don't you ever wash?'

'I've no one to scrub my back.'

James grinned. 'When we get married ...'

'We'll never leave the bed. Cease your complaining and kiss me.'

About to oblige, Callum slid between them, his blonde curls popping up, followed by his face with so serious, an expression, they stifled a laugh.

Summer ruffled his hair. 'What's wrong, little man?'

'When we get the bus tomorrow, where will I sit? There is only room for two on the seats.'

'Hmm,' Jamie said, making a show of scratching his head. 'I've an idea. If we buy sweets and drinks in the shop, we can sit together at the back and have a party all the way to Roscommon.'

'Jamie.' Callum seemed puzzled. 'Can I have a real suit of armour and a horse, and a sword, and a lance, and Cornflakes at the castle?'

'Of course you can,'

'Will mam be a Queen?'

'Yes, and you'll be Prince Callum, Knight of Drumcreevan, a fearless warrior who eats two bowls of Cornflakes for breakfast.'

'Cool.' Callum ducked under their arms and grabbed the brush. 'I'm Sir Brushalot and this is my lance.' He drove the point of the handle into the soft-backed armchair, toppling it and the bin bag. A Coke tin rolled along the floor into the priest's foot.

James groaned. 'Sorry, Summer. I have to say my final mass in three hours, and I need to prepare. This mess is all yours.' Before she could argue, he planted a kiss on her cheek and raced to the door. 'Billy will collect you tomorrow afternoon at three. I'll be at the bus stop with a sackful of sweets and another filled with Brennan's Bread. Love ye.'

James jumped over Callum's toy car lying between clumps of weeds on the gravel driveway. 'Vroom.'

The smile on his face continued as he cycled back to the presbytery. Sweeney stooped over the open boot of his car. James hopped off the bike, and plodded down the lane. A plethora of curses reaching his ears, he wondered whether O'Rourke had contacted Sweeney. He hoped the bishop wouldn't until after he and Summer had left. *Damn, Sweeney didn't go to Dublin like he said, he must have been summoned to Carlow.*

'Here comes Judas fuckin Brennan, or is it Judas no balls?' Sweeney roared. 'Visited your spymaster, did you? You and Billy no-thumbs are as thick as a pair of scheming sewer rats, gutless liars.'

James ignored Sweeney's ranting and venomous stare. He leaned his bicycle against the garden wall and, avoiding eye contact, strode toward the front door.

Sweeney reached into the boot and grabbed the wheel brace. Raising it above his head, he stalked in front of James. 'I've a mind to split your head in two with this.' He hacked and gobbed onto the path, inches from the young priest's shoes.

James lifted his gaze from the green slime at his feet to Sweeney's manic eyes. A sudden panic gripped the ferret. Too late, he dropped the wheel brace, and, too late, he attempted to bolt. James slammed his shoulder into Sweeney's chest and shoved him into the side of his car, pinning him against the door. His arm wedged beneath the old man's chin, he brought his face close to Sweeney's. Tobacco, bad breath and fear mingled; the stench of his peculiar brand of corruption, indescribable.

'You are a paedophile monster. Touch another child and I will snap your neck in two.' Pressing harder against Sweeney's Adam's apple, he knew he could so easily do it. Sweeney gasped for air, his quivering lips opening and closing like a beached trout. 'Should you think about harming a child, or peek at one from behind closed curtains, I'll break you, no matter the consequences for me.' James held Sweeney at bay with one hand, and kicked the wheel brace under the car. Temper in check, James stepped away from the vile creature, noticing the boxes, coats and other items crammed onto the back seat. 'Bishop O'Rourke will have you jailed. I hope they throw away the key.'

Sweeney wheezed and clutched his throat. Peering out from the greasy tufts of his comb-over, which had fallen over his ruddy jowls, he laughed. 'You're a naïve, little prick.'

'Am I? You're the coward I thought you were. Run away, but you will be found.'

'Run away? Who's running?'

'You are. Bishop O'Rourke contacted the Gardaí.'

'Gobshite.' Sweeney wrenched open the car door and sat inside. His leering face behind the windscreen matched his obnoxious personality.

Sweeney is leaving, Amen. As though lifted into the air by all the angels in Heaven, James floated to the front door. Behind him, the Mercedes' engine spluttered clouds of fumes. He turned as Sweeney wound down the window.

'I've been transferred to Galway. A month in retreat and it's business as usual.'

Shock waves vibrating around his brain, James didn't react in time to the sound of grinding gears and squealing rubber. Disbelief ignited a fury he'd never experienced. He gave chase. Grabbing the wheel brace from the ground, he flung it. It clattered off the boot. Sprinting as fast as he could, he caught up near the end of the lane when the car slowed. Desperate to prevent Sweeney from escaping, he lunged for the open window, but his fingertips could not hold on. Flung to the ground as the car spun round the corner onto the main road, James cried out. 'Bastard.' He pummelled the tarmac with his fist. *What has that traitor O'Rourke done?*

James wept bitter tears as he limped back to the presbytery. *I'm not just naïve, I'm dumb.*

Chapter 34

Like a primordial presence, and more annoying than ever, the odour of stale tobacco infused the presbytery. James threw open all the windows, except for the one in Sweeney's bedroom. Passing the door, he shivered. No breeze could cleanse the evil that festered inside.

What to do? Manifestations of ideas zipping along his neural pathways collided, rendering coherent thought impossible. Despite Billy's reservations, James trusted the Bishop to report Sweeney to the Gardaí. Deceit in everything the old priest did and said, maybe Sweeney had lied his way out of the allegations made against him, and elected for a transfer as he'd said he would. Perhaps the Bishop had acted, and the paedophile had scarpered before the police came for him. Doubt nipped at James' heels as he strode around the dining room. What if O'Rourke had ignored the proven danger posed by this sexual predator and, once again, chosen to protect the church from scandal? James wiped away the perspiration beading on his forehead.

Billy would know what to do. James stomped to the hall. He lifted the phone and dialled his friend's number. No reply. 'Damn.' Frustrated, he slammed down the receiver. Confronting the Bishop being the only option, he thumbed through the phone book until he found the number. After three rings, his call was answered by a female voice, Sister Celestine?

'Good evening. May I help you?'

'Father Brennan from Castlebridge. I need to speak to the Bishop. It's urgent, Sister?'

Silence followed his request. Muffled voices trailed off as she answered firmly. 'Sorry, Father. His eminence is unavailable to take your call.'

'It is imperative I talk to him.'

'I'm sorry, Father James. That is not possible. May I take a message?'

'What?' James thumped the table. 'Tell O'Rourke, if I haven't heard from him before Mass tomorrow morning, I'll assume he has abdicated his responsibility to protect the children.'

'I beg your pardon.'

'Beg away. Give him the message.' James slammed the receiver onto the cradle before she could respond. *He'll not call — I'm an idiot for trusting such a pompous man.*

James sat at the dining room table and penned a letter to Billy. He sealed his instructions in an envelope, which he intended deliver at the bus stop the next day. *Billy can photocopy the documents and send them to the newspapers. That gutless Bishop is an ass. I'm packing.*

When he pulled his suitcase from the top of the wardrobe, he discovered it was smothered in dust. James coughed. With his arms outstretched, he reached inside the wardrobe and squeezed his clothes together as if playing an accordion. Temper wrenched them off the rail, straightening many of the wire hangers. *Feck you, too, God.*

After dropping his garments into the suitcase, he tipped the contents of the dressing table drawers on top, followed by shoes, pyjamas and a toothbrush. About to close the lid, he spied the Bible sitting on the bedside locker, gifted to him by his mother many years earlier. Crooking his arms, he considered leaving it there. Perhaps his replacement could make better use of it. *Leather bound lies.* A smirk forming, he grabbed the good book and flung it out of the window. *Amen.*

From behind the wardrobe, he retrieved his most valued possession, his portrait, painted by Summer. No longer necessary to conceal his love from Sweeney, he placed it alongside his fishing rods. His meagre possessions lying together on the floor, James smiled. He'd leave the church a pauper. *Freedom is more precious than gold.* At Drumcreevan manor he will have both, but first say his final Mass in the morning. What a Mass that should prove to be — the repercussions of his revelations far reaching. A few words on the welfare of children would lay the groundwork to revealing the horrendous nature of Sweeney to the parishioners.

† † †

Reflecting on the many paintings that had played a part in several memorable moments since coming to Castlebridge, James grinned at the image of Padre Pio hanging on the back wall of the church. Unlike the more famous priest, James had no stigmata or physical scars, and intended to be long gone before risking such wounds. Few knew about the tears of anguish he had shed for the *Special* children from this parish. Wheelchair-bound, Joe Wall, and his mother, whose enduring love for her son transcended all else in this world. For those who were yet to be born and abused, and those whose pain and guilt denied them a normal life. Jack, the bus driver, whose mind and body Father Sweeney had abused. People like him and Billy, who continued to be tortured by images no person should see or imagine.

If Billy did as he had bid in the letter, by the end of the week, Agnes Murphy would answer a knock to her door. Surprise would have her step back into her hall, reluctant to sign for the unexpected package held by the postman. Curiosity would tear open the brown paper. Proof of Sweeney's guilt would shatter her faith. Fear would render her immobile, until Agnes' addiction to gossip demanded she shared her knowledge. It would spread like wildfire. For now, she sat on the front pew clutching Rosary beads.

In secrecy, the hierarchy would discuss the rumours she instigated. Bishop O'Rourke would come to Castlebridge and lay blame wherever he deemed appropriate. A week later, Billy would make copies of their documents and send them to the media. In Roscommon, hidden within Drumcreevan Castle, James Brennan and his family would be oblivious to the breaking scandal, and the ensuing repercussions.

Unaware of the evil inflicted by Sweeney, to whom they had confessed their sins, and from whom they had sought and had accepted absolution, Christ's faithful dotted the seats of the church. Baskets, with pennies garnered from pensioners, passed from one wizened hand to another. They listened to his ritualised words and responded by rote. None of them knew he had defrocked his heart.

James glided to the front of the holy table and stood with his arms folded. Allowing his silence demand attention he gazed at the confused faithful.

'Suffer the little children to come unto me. You good people of Castlebridge are familiar with the words of the Christ. Would a loving God let children suffer?'

Taking a step forward James raised his voice. 'Children in this parish have suffered terrible wrongdoings. I tell you now, there is no God. What God would allow a priest abuse children?'

Stunned by his words, parents looked one to another, obviously worried they were being targeted for striking their kids. Whispers rippled across the pews.

'Father Sweeney has sexually abused altar boys.' James paused for effect.

'Operating under our noses, this perverted monster has destroyed many innocent boys. I expected the Bishop would have him arrested. It appears that the Church does not see fit to protect your children.

They have moved Sweeney to Galway. In time, he will bugger the innocent in another parish.'

Agnes jumped to her feet. A rage engulfing her face, she wrung her hands. 'You're lying. Father Sweeney told me you struck Luke. You're saying these things to protect yourself. God forgive you.'

'Sit down. There is no God. By the end of this week you will receive proof of Sweeney's perversions, as will the newspapers. I intend to...'

Disturbed by the back door clanging, he glared down the aisle. Appearing between the pillars, a uniformed Garda removed his hat. A determined look on his young face, he beckoned James. The rhythm of his movements suggested an urgency that James acknowledged with a nod.

What does he want?

James traipsed down the aisle. Nearing the Garda, panic set in. *What if Luke reported me like I suggested he should? Oh God, Sweeney is gone. How can I prove my innocence?*

On reaching the man, conscious of the craned necks of the parishioners, he ushered him behind a column.

'Sorry for interrupting Mass, Father. I'm Garda Sloane. I need you to come with me.'

'Why? Have I broken the law?'

'No. There's been a serious accident two miles this side of Allenwood. My sergeant ordered me to fetch you to give the occupants the last rites.'

'Who's the driver?'

'I've no idea, Father,' said the Garda. He waved his hat. 'We better go. I have a car waiting outside the church.'

James nodded. 'I'll need holy oil and Viaticum. Start your engine. I'll be less than a minute.' Gathering up the hem of his cassock, James raced back to the altar. 'I must attend a bad car accident. Mass has ended. Heed my words.'

Having never faced such a situation, he grabbed the vessel containing the Eucharist. No time to disrobe, James grabbed oil from a shelf, raced outside, and dived onto the front seat of the Garda car.

'Put on your belt.'

James remained silent, letting Sloane concentrate on driving at high speeds. Every car in their way pulled over, reacting to the siren and flashing lights. Within six minutes, they came upon the scene of the accident. On a straight section of road, two squad cars, with their lights flashing, had blocked the route either side of the crash site. Eighty yards ahead, a dark car had ploughed into the only tree adjacent to the left lane. *How unlucky can one get?* A Garda squatted by the door.

Deep ruts in the verge marked where the vehicle had left the tarmac and slid along the ditch for thirty yards, ripping through bushes and other vegetation. Twice it had smashed into the fencing that ran alongside a cornfield, slewed back onto and off the road, before ramming into the sycamore.

'Mercedes 300d,' muttered Sloane. He braked and switched off the engine. 'Are you okay, Father? You look dumbfounded.'

James opened the door. 'I recognise the car.'

'Whooo io it?'

'Father Sweeney's. He's Castlebridge's parish priest, I'm the curate.'

At their approach, the Garda attending the car looked up, rose to his feet and strode to James. I'm Sergeant Cribbin,' he said, taking James by the arm. 'You are?'

'I'm Father Brennan from Castlebridge. Is the Father Sweeney alive?'

'He's not dressed like a priest? Cribbin tightened his grip. 'Yes, but his breathing is so shallow, I expect his chest is crushed. He'll not make it. When I arrived on the scene, he managed a few garbled words. *Priest. Last Rites. Sorry.* Since then, he's drifted in and out of consciousness.'

God, why me, you bastard? 'I best do my duty then.' James gathered his breath. 'I'll need help.'

'Okay. Tell me what to do.'

Locking his eyes on the hunched figure in the front seat of the Mercedes, James stepped through the debris, his emotions braced to deny Sweeney any sympathy. On reaching the car, James stood a few yards away from the open door. He gasped. The impact had driven the steering column into Sweeney's chest, trapping him against the seat. Bone from his right thigh jutted through blood-soaked trousers. A shard of the rear view mirror, an inch wide, protruding from his forehead, reflected congealed blood caking his eyes. Crumpled seats and twisted metal, the dashboard had disintegrated. As though protected from all this devastation, Sweeney's pipe lay trapped beneath a petrol can on the passenger seat. Bile rising in his throat, James swivelled and clutched his stomach.

Cribbin guided him away from the car, and held him while he vomited, again and again.

'I'm okay,' James said, wiping his lips with his sleeve.

'Here.' Cribbin reached into the pocket of his long coat and pulled out a bottle. 'Take a sip of this. It'll take away the foul taste, and help you ignore the smell in the car.'

Not caring what it was, James seized the bottle and took a slug. Whiskey swirled around his mouth, numbing his tongue and the front of his throat. 'Yuck.' He spat it onto the road. 'How can anyone drink that stuff?'

Despite the situation, Cribbin smiled. 'I can.' He took a sip. 'When you do this job, it's as good a way as any to help me deal with scenes like this.'

James handed Cribbin the Eucharist to hold. He returned to the car. Sweeney's breaths were infrequent and laboured. He rasped a throaty wheeze while each movement sent his body into convulsions. His muffled groans were like whispers in a graveyard. Blood, oozing from the corner of his mouth, slid down his chin onto his clerical collar. Imminent death painted Sweeney's face in shades of dried old wood, wizened greys bleached by time.

James knelt with his knee on the sill of the door. 'Father Sweeney. Can you hear me?'

When Sweeney offered no response, he leaned a little closer. Wrinkling his nose against the smell of urine and diesel, he teased Sweeney's sticky hair away from his ear. 'Father Sweeney. It's James, can you hear me?'

The ferret's eyes flickered recognition.

James whispered. 'Have you nothing to say? Soon you will be dead and none will mourn your passing.'

Racked by another spasm, Sweeney's mocking tongue, slimed with blood and spittle, slid between encrusted lips.

'Can you not manage one final act of defiance?'

In a moment of extraordinary determination, the old priest's tortured eyes locked onto his curate. 'Forgive me.'

James thumped the seat. 'Never. Your black heart is incapable of being contrite.'

I guide all you do. You must give him absolution.

'What? Who are you? Why do you torture my thoughts?'

I am. Absolve this repentant sinner. It is my will, your duty.

'How can I forgive such a monster?'

To forgive him is to forgive yourself. Deny him, and your life will be lived in the shadows.

James stepped back.

Cribbin touched James' shoulder. 'Are you okay? You were muttering.'

'Was I?' His emotions in revolt, James forced himself to make the sign of the cross, and held his hands together in prayer. 'Our Father, who art in heaven...'

As though he were a bird sitting on a branch overhead, he watched his hands take the box containing the Eucharist from the Sergeant, open the lid, and extract a single Viaticum.

'This is the Lamb of God who takes away the sins of the world. Happy are those who are called to his supper.'

Pinched between a finger and thumb, he pressed the host to Father Sweeney's lips and shoved it into his mouth.

Finish the sacrament.

That voice again.

'May the Lord Jesus protect you and lead you to eternal life. Amen.'

James anointed his forehead. His obligations as a priest fulfilled, he took one final look at Sweeney, turned and nodded at Sergeant Cribbin. 'He's all yours.'

'Thanks, Father. The ambulance should be here in a few minutes.'

I hope it gets a punctured tyre. James spat on the ground, and sidled back to the Garda car.

Sloane hopped into the driver's side and closed the door. 'Is he dead?'

'No, but unfortunately he will not last much longer. I'd prefer if he suffered for another few hours.'

The Garda blessed himself. 'Jesus, remind me never to make a confession in your church. It's a difficult time for your parish.'

'It was.'

'Between this and the fire, every Garda in the area is out and about, even the lads off duty.'

James pulled on his seat belt. 'What fire?'

'A house in Castlebridge went up in flames a few hours ago. Garda Joyce told me on the radio that the fire brigade have it under control. There may be fatalities.'

Oh, God. My last day is one tragedy after another. 'I better console the unfortunate family. Can you take me there?'

Sloane turned the ignition and revved the engine. 'I'll have you there in a jiffy.'

† † †

Despair froze reality. Clouded images shimmered through the haze of smoke. Every sound magnified, they resonated against the beat of his heart. Gravel crunched beneath his feet. Faster. Faster. James sprinted through the run-off from fire hoses meandering down the boreen. 'Summer,' he wailed. Barging through onlookers, he ducked under the outstretched arms of a fireman. His mind a maelstrom of denial, he refused to absorb the scene he faced or consider the possibility Summer and Callum were hurt.

Faces, so many strangers, where is she? Where are Summer and Callum?

'Father.'

He swivelled, focusing on the soot-smeared face beneath a yellow helmet. Another fireman, his voice authoritative, reached for his arm. 'Come with me, Father.'

James followed him to the front entrance. He'd never entered the cottage this way, as Summer kept it locked. There was no door. Blackened and scorched, remnants of bubbled paint clung to the charred frame. *What is that smell?* More alien sounds confused his thoughts. Scraping echoed from the kitchen. *It's Summer, stripping the wall paper.*

Grunting like a mule, another fireman pulling a hose down the hall passed him.

'Summer?' Lost in the clamour, his voice sounded unfamiliar, as though he had fallen into a pit.

'Come this way, Father.' Stopping outside the scorched bedroom door, the fireman turned to James. 'I've never seen anything so bizarre. Experts from Dublin will have to investigate how flames engulfing the entire cottage left the bedroom unscathed. It's like some supernatural force protected ... never mind, my brain is tired.' He opened the door and stepped aside.

Summer and Callum lay on the bed facing each other, their eyes closed. The glory of her golden hair spread upon the pillow, she clasped her son to her breast.

The're asleep, snuggled up to each other. Callum is holding his mother's hand. He's a good boy.

His feet squelching on the sodden carpet, James trudged to the bed. 'Summer, Callum, wake up.' *They so like to play games. A kiss will get her attention.*

The soft mattress enveloped him as he sat by her side. 'Sssh,' he said, leaning over Summer. 'It's Jamie. Wake up, lazy head.' Beads of perspiration forming on his forehead, trickled down his face, and slid onto his collar. 'C'mon sleeping beauty, Prince Jamie is here.' Desperate her to laugh, he placed a hand on either side of Summer and, leaning forward, kissed her cheek.

So cold.

Nothing made sense. 'Why is my fiancée not giggling?'

From behind James, someone wrapped him in an embrace and, with the gentlest pressure, squeezed his shoulder. He turned his head. 'Billy.'

'I'm so sorry, James.'

'What are you doing here? I cannot wake them. Why is that, have they been drugged? Why are you sobbing?'

'They're gone, Jamie.'

'No, they're not. They're here. Look at the packed suitcases by the window. We're moving to Drumcreevan Castle today.'

Billy slid the engagement ring off Summer's finger. Prising James' hand open, he dropped it onto his palm, and pushed his fingers closed. 'Look at me, James — they're dead.'

Those words, repeated over and over in his head, unlocked a dam of emotion, and released a torrent of anguish. More sorrowful than the cry of the Banshee, he wailed until his voice cracked. James clutched the corner of the crimson bedspread. Rocking to and fro, his head shook in denial, and he howled.

Billy grasped his hand. 'Come, James, there's nothing more you can do.'

'I can't leave them here with strangers.'

'You must come with me.'

'It's my fault. They are dead because I loved them.'

Tears streaming down his face, he ruffled Callum's hair. *My son.* James laid his head on the pillow beside Summer, twisted a lock of her wondrous hair around his finger. 'Sssh, my love.' James reached for her hand. 'Lady Drumcreevan-O'Malley. Will you take this man to be thy husband?'

I do.

Billy smiled through his tears. 'You may kiss the bride.'

James leaned against his friend for support. Standing at the door, he turned and framed Summer and Callum in a memory that provided little solace. 'My Lady Samhradh.'

A crowd had gathered outside. Their whispers were silenced by the sight of the ambulance crew carrying two stretchers up the drive. Most looked away.

'Billy,' James said, lurching to the fire engine. Callum's toy lay crushed on the ground. He reached down, and rolled the broken wheel along the gravel. 'Vroom, vroom.' He fell onto his knees and beat his hands on the ground. 'Oh, Jesus. My family are dead.'

† † †

Slumped on the front seat of the car, James caressed the ring lying in the palm of his hand. He glared at Billy, who stood by the open passenger door. 'I said, drive me back to Summer.'

'You know I can't, nor can we sit here all day. Come into Lavelles. Seanie will lock the door. You'll be safe amongst your friends.'

'Why, Billy? I don't understand what caused the fire.' James swung his legs out of the car. Noticing the ripped hem of his cassock, and the filth clinging to his shoes, his father's voice tripped across his mind. *Son, look after your shoes and they will look after yer feet.* James bent forward, reached down and wiped each foot with his sleeve. *Is that okay, Daddy? I'll shine them later. Why does everyone passing stare at me?*

Billy pushed his way into the pub, and held the door open. James followed. His footsteps as unsteady as a drunk's, he plodded to the back room and flopped onto a stool. Moments later, Seanie appeared at his side.

'Jesus, look at the state of ya. You've left a trail of muck in your wake. Will I put the kettle on?'

Looking up, James spotted his reflection in a small mirror advertising whiskey, and barely recognised the tear-stained face covered in grime. *Kettle. Oh — no.* 'The faulty kettle,' his voice trembled, the words sticking in his throat, he struggled to speak. He gulped. 'The kettle caused the fire, it must have.' Temper overcoming grief, he lifted the ashtray and flung it at the mirror, shattering both. Wishing a flying shard would pierce his heart, he whimpered. 'It's my fault, my fault. I knew the kettle was a fire hazard.'

'Easy, James.' Seanie wrapped his arms around him, and held him tight until he stopped struggling. 'It isn't anyone's fault, it was a tragic accident.'

'Wait a minute.' James shredded a coaster. 'They weren't burnt, so how did they die? Billy, we have to go back? They might be alive.'

Billy climbed onto the stool alongside James and rolled his neck. 'Me feckin' back is killing me.' He pulled a tissue from his pocket and wiped his eyes. 'They're gone, my young friend. Fumes and smoke killed them, I suppose. They felt no pain.'

'Thanks be to God, for that small mercy,' Seanie said, after making his way behind the counter.

The crushing reality sinking in, James lunged over the bar and grabbed Seanie by the collar. 'Thank God? — There is no fuckin God. Give me a whiskey.' He released his grip on the barman and sat, his body shaking.

'I've known that since my wife, Katie, died in a crash.' Seanie grabbed a bottle of Jameson and poured liberal shots into three glasses. 'A day hasn't passed, without me thinking about her.'

'To Lady Samhradh, and our son, Callum. And, to Katie.' James tossed back the whiskey. Grimacing at the burning sensation in his throat and stomach, he slid the empty glass to Seanie. 'Another.'

Seanie refilled the glasses.

'To the dead fuckin priest trapped in his car in a ditch near Allenwood.' James raised his glass. 'May he rot in paedophile Hell.'

Sean swivelled to face James. 'What did you say? Sweeney is a paedophile. Fuck sake. Did he harm my boy?'

'No Sean. But he would have.' James swirled the amber liquid until it slopped over the rim of his tumbler. 'This stuff is fool's gold. I didn't think I'd enjoy the taste.' With one gulp, he emptied the glass. 'Father *ferret* Sweeney is dead. What are ye waiting for, men? Toast that bastard's demise.'

Stunned, Billy and Seanie stared at James. They lifted their glasses and drank.

'That won't bring Summer back.'

'No, Billy, it won't,' James said, his voice quivering, 'but, that one positive morsel helps me fight my urge to jump into the river or the pond, like Keith O'Neill did.'

Seanie filled James' glass to the brim. 'Feck, do nothing stupid. Here, drink this.' '

Christ, Seanie,' Billy said, trying to grab the glass before James did. 'For someone who's never touched a drop, that volume of whiskey would hobble an elephant.'

'I know,' said Sean.

James seized it. 'Ha! Ha! He's dead. Au revoir, Father Pervert, no more... shit. The petrol can.'

In a fit of rage, James flung his glass over Billy's head. It smashed on impact with the wall. The base plummeted to the ground, landed with a clink and rolled under a stool. Slivers, falling like confetti at the wedding that would never happen, covered the flagstones like glistening gems. Drink that hadn't splashed onto the floor, dribbled down the tiled wall. James jumped off his stool, tore his collar from his neck, and flung it into the puddle of whiskey forming beneath the skirting. 'Fuck,' he shouted. Red dots flashing before his eyes, he yanked the skirt of the cassock upwards and, bringing it over his head, howled. 'Sweeney murdered them.' He tossed his vestments on top of the collar and fell to his knees. 'There's a petrol can on the front seat of his car. And, I, listening to that voice in my head, granted the fucker absolution. Summer, forgive me. Jesus, the same words Sweeney used. Forgive me. He didn't mean forgive him for abusing the children. I gave him absolution from murdering Summer and Callum.'

Consumed by utter despair, he held his head in his hands, staring at a crack in the stone floor. 'What does it matter? There is no God, no Heaven and no Hell. Only death. Seanie tried to lift him. 'Leave me alone.' An image forming within the mists before his eyes, he reached out. Summer and Callum smiled and waved. The place seemed familiar, yet, distant, everything indistinct. A woman stood behind them. She opened her arms. Suffused by a sense of calm, James waved back.

They are safe, with me, until you come home. Summer thinks Heaven is cool.

'What? Who are you?' Someone tugged his arm. 'Go away. Come back, Summer, come back.'

'Father Brennan.'

Callum? James turned.

Sean shuffled his feet. 'Is it true? Is Father Sweeney dead?'

'Yes, Sean. He'll not hurt you or anyone again.'

'Good. If you say Mass tomorrow, I'll be your altar boy.'

James opened his fist and eased his little finger into the engagement ring, and slid it up as far as his knuckle. Tears dimming his vision, he brought it to his lips and kissed the diamond. *Suffer little children, and forbid them not, to come unto me: for of such is the kingdom of Heaven.*

'Yes, Sean. I will say Mass tomorrow.'

'And can we go fishing?'

'As often as you like.'

Clambering to his feet with Sean's help, Father Brennan gazed at his friends. 'Seanie, pull me a pint. Leave the bottle of whiskey on the counter.'

'Are you sure, James?'

'I'm a failed priest with a broken heart. Believing I could prevent any further abuse, Billy and I reported Sweeney to the Bishop. For that my life has been destroyed. It seems the world will be a safer place — just not for Summer and Callum.'

'It's a terrible price you must pay,' Billy said, wrapping his arm around James. 'What will you do?'

'What can I do? I can't go to Drumcreevan Castle now, can never be parted from Summer. God has chosen the role of drunken gobshite for me. I best obey. Fill the bloody glass.'

WE MUST NEVER FORGET.

Thank you for reading In the Shadow of the Judas Tree.

Please leave a review on Amazon.

Also by Norman Morrow

Father Mc Gargles

If you liked young Father Brennan, join him thirty years later for some mayhem and adventure.

A stolen trout. An unusual confession. A dead greyhound on a skateboard. Vengeance. A sex scandal. Rumours of a demon and an erotic book

From his seat of power in the back room of Lavelle's pub, Father James Brennan plans revenge. Here, in total secrecy, accomplices are recruited and the scheming begins. But no one can predict the hilarious results that draw the priest into the most unlikely situations and culminate in conflict with the See of Rome.

Rock Pool Echoes (Novelette)

A chance meeting, or was it? The mysteries of The Rock Pool are revealed before the grim reaper has his wicked way. A tale of great trout and a strange old man.

Shimmering Light (Short Fishing Story)

Michael, in the autumn of his life, realises a dream. In doing so, he risks the ultimate sacrifice.

Acknowledgements.

Special thanks to fellow authors for their constant support and assistance.

R G (Mummy's little soldier), C McD (The Noor Trilogy)
A J M (Sideways Eight Series), DJ M (The Renaissance Series)
Sebnem Sanders & Barry Gavin.

No author journeys alone.

Printed in Great Britain
by Amazon